THEATRICAL REALITY

Francis Lis

Order this book online at www.trafford.com
or email orders@trafford.com

Most Trafford titles are also available at major online book retailers.

This fictionalized novel is based upon one man's view as to his world and the nation that he so lives in with some historical background as well as futuristic commentary. Certain names shall seem familiar but as with all novels, it supposes the way that things could or might or even had so been. This is well as verbal conversation with many of his friends and relatives. It shall leave any reader to believe whether one man can ascertain so much information and actually be right if that be the case. It is a most fascinating reading for all who like to read in depth things that the narrator perceives through life's experience which probably is the only way to truly tell a story from the past, present and near future of course in open time for only GOD knows, that is the reason it is called just that, THEATRICAL REALITY.

Printed in the United States of America.

ISBN: 978-1-4269-3750-7 (sc)
ISBN: 978-1-4269-8999-5 (hc)
ISBN: 978-1-4269-3751-4 (e)

Library of Congress Control Number: 2011914127

Trafford rev. 09/26/2011

www.trafford.com

North America & international
toll-free: 1 888 232 4444 (USA & Canada)
phone: 250 383 6864 • fax: 812 355 4082

IN LOVING MEMORY FOR MY WIFE

CELESTE MARIE

AND HER LOVE FOR HER MESSIAH

CONTENTS

LIST OF CHARACTERS

RACHEL'S OLDEST TWIN	ABRAHAM
JOHN'S NIGHT HELPER AT PUB	BOB
BAR DERELICT	CHIP
LAWYER AT BAR	CHARLES
IRISH REPUBLICAN PUBBER	FRED
AMERICAN BIBLICAL NEGRO CHRISTIAN	GEORGE
NARRATOR'S RUSSIAN-JEWISH FRIEND	HENRY
RACHEL'S YOUNGEST TWIN	JACOB
PUB PROPRIETOR	JOHN
NARRATOR'S JEWISH WIFE	MARIE
IRAELIS JEW	MOSHÉ
NARRATOR'S-SON-IN-LAW	MOSHÉ ALEXANDER ROSEMAN
AMERICAN BIBLICAL	NARRATOR
NARRATOR'S DAUGHTER	RACHEL
CUBAN FRIEND OF NARRATOR	SAL
RUSSIAN PEASANT PROPRIETOR	VICTOR

CHAPTER I

POLITICAL CONVERSATIONS

It was a snowy wintry night and the local pub had been open as usual and when I entered I saw a friend of mine at the bar with the proprietor, John, keeping bar. I approached my friend, Henry, and sat down and both of us immediately started talking to each other. Henry was a regular at the pub and knew the goings on of all in our small town. Many times Henry would tell me what occurred, since I was only a once a week visitor to this establishment. This night would be a very different night, because little did I know that Henry was to confide in me, as never before, about things that we had not really talked about. As the early night went by, with John being behind the bar, a few others started to sit closer to us to discuss the things of the past week, as well as many other things. As I listened I ordered a beer and a sandwich to eat and began to be attentive to him, that is Henry. I listened to my Jewish friend of Russian extraction. I began to understand Henry's face with his piercing blue eyes and his ancient look, in the sense that showed many centuries of pain from which it could be fathomed as "anguish", or could it have been "ecstasy". This was the meeting place where we came to discuss our own adventures, or to talk about the world situation with very opinionated commentary by almost all involved. The dialogue was controlled by us who at times might have had too much to drink. Mostly older men met here, except for myself and one other. As a somewhat young middle aged man I found this quite stimulating to converse, but I listened more than speak to what each discussion, or even debate, would involve. I always waited to speak once the topic to discuss, quite at random, was to be spoken about and we would move from one topic to another. Henry was the only American Jewish person who patronized John's pub, but this neither bothered Henry, or us, because we had known each other for quite a few years and knew our talks were open to any subject. As Henry began addressing me directly about the Middle East, I took extreme concern, because he knew how I also felt about our ally Israel.

"Why was Israel giving up more land as they had before, after they won the 1967 War of Independence and the 1973 War?"

I said, "I agree that Israel should not give up an inch more and felt our government wanted to please the oil Arab Moslem sheiks as well as Big Business."

"Why should Israel return all this land?"

Henry again repeated more vehemently.

"This was Abraham's land from GOD to the Jew not to be given away by man."

Whenever Henry mentioned "the Jews" he seemed to de-emphasize it, as if he had no Jewish ancestry, or that "the Jews" was a misnomer.

Chip, one of the other men not a regular, interjected by saying, "Jews ran our entire economy and that the media and Hollywood were part of world Jewry."

Henry with candor said, "There were hardly any billionaires among Jews and that it was not what one had that controlled the stock market. It was wealth that was unequally distributed much more then income."

The uninvited intruder then went back to his table mumbling something about, "That is why I guess GOD gave the Jews Semite ears, because of their inability to listen?"

Our discussion returned to the Middle East and we discussed this new terrorist state called Palestine. This was more theatrical reality and America did not have the resolve to hold out against their allied friends. Anti-Semitism was growing and America's borders could one day close to all Jewish people. Henry understood this because his parents were Russian Jewish. Solzhenitsyn had already given his warning to the West on the BBC. President

Gerald Ford said "I am too busy to welcome such a guest to America."

Malcolm Muggeridge, an English Christian writer said, "This would go down in history for this President, as a sad affair."

Our dialogue became more lively as we discussed the part that FDR and Churchill played in destroying Russian Freedom and eventually the Western World and almost Israel.

The Yalta Conference was a total failure because Churchill and Roosevelt both gave to Stalin, Hungary, Russia, Poland, half of Germany and also allowed through Manchuria the acquisition of Korea by Kim Il Sung.

Our own neighborhood had signs of decadence with no morality and this constant "blackism" of civil rights' socialism. The neighborhood changed from a European Family environment to one of multiculturalism where one's attire started to look like a 3rd World, or Middle or Far Eastern country.

After Scranton and Carter visited the Middle East and Latin America, both regions in the world de-stabilized. I also felt after Clinton, American government had become socialistic, because all three branches of government did what they wanted to do and if a state referendum was passed, or rejected, the courts would always disallow it. I had to admit to myself that John's Pub was his property and he could charge any price he wanted to. Under socialism he could do neither. Only the state had control.

John said, "I have sales ladies that know hardly anything about the product they sell, or who even really owns the company that they work for and whether it is foreign or domestic, and some State Liquor Licenses go for as much as $250,000, but of course, I am not a lawyer or a judge at a country club. The regular amounts are $300."

Henry commented, "The politicians have become like parasites and are in it for pure profit and power and re-election for life, if possible. One doesn't have to be qualified to hold a position of importance in America including the professions. They do, though, have to be POLITICALLY CORRECT which started in the days of LENIN, but today it is in epidemic proportion."

I said, "One woman I know, who has a private business on the side to help her husband, had to go through 9 out of 10 women, all who have managerial positions or own their company and that there are no men. She could not believe that many women were in the American work force and which told her about motherhood in America. A pretty package with nothing in it."

John then comments, "My business is slacking because of a different and rowdy clientele, but I will not serve those gangs and rednecks. Never do I gauge my business by Wall Street, the casino royale, because it has nothing to do with the American economy."

John was a truly patriotic American, because he would not sell Capone style lottery tickets that the government promoted and neither would he serve an over-inebriated person, if he could help it.

After 4 beers I asked John, "Do you think that alcohol is a so called drug?"

John said, "I do not feel it is from the chemical, or even in the legal sense."

I said, "What does that mean?"

He said, "Alcohol is a drug in that it inebriates one for a short duration and no one is killing to get it like they are for drugs. The government wants to collect more revenue by taxing all drugs and so that is why they want politically and legally to call alcohol a drug and legalize all hard core drugs."

John included, "Even Mr. William F. Buckley, Jr. is for drug legalization, a staunch Republican conservative, but his close friend Chuck Colson totally disagrees with him."

Fred asked, "Is that the same Chuck Colson that signed the ECT DOCUMENT along with Pat Robertson which stated that Roman Catholicism and Evangelicals were the same in preaching the Gospel of grace and grace alone?"

John, Henry and I all said, "Yes."

I added, "J. C. Sproul and Dr. D. James Kennedy wanted a retraction for politicking with the Bible's true interpretation, but neither Mr. Colson nor Mr. Robertson would do either."

After about eleven o'clock that night Bob came in, who was John's night helper, to clean up. Bob had come to better success through unionism and was a diehard proletarian. Bob had risen through the union and now felt he was the worker's defender and saw things in a different light. His success had certainly blessed him, at least he thought so. Henry and I were in total agreement along with John that unions now were poison in America because of their demand for more benefits along with usurious high wages but no mention of quality workmanship, reliability, et cetera, not like Toyota and Honda and not because the Japanese were smarter, but that they were more conscientious about their work habits.

Henry and Bob started to attack each other because one was for management and the other was for labor. It was to me American foreign-owned Big business vs party unionism. Both had their downfall, but not once did I interject into this heated discussion, because Henry would have thought I felt that unions were okay, being I had a union run business, even though I would not have, and Bob really would have felt I was too much of Henry's friend to be objective. I nonetheless entertained myself by listening to both. Not until later in my life did I discern that capitalism was avarice and nothing more and that unions were group minded like socialists in the proletarian virtue. Both sides had contributed to the pollution of morality in America, but yet came to subscribe to the same ideology in the end.

Theatrical reality was heating up and by the late 70's and the early 80's Carterism and Reaganomics were both at work. One in the "social" gospel and the other in the Bitburg with the name "Dutch", as is "Dutch" Kennedy had. Reagan though did reverse his stand on abortion and apologized for it to a pro-life side. The Democratic Party at that time had become a party of socialists and eventually would create the Democratic Socialist Party, or the Progressive Party, with the Congressional Black Caucus, a major part of it.

The always entertaining FDR and his New Deal to Kennedyism's Irish Catholicism and anti-Semitism and the underdog mentality was in along with Big Brother. The "races" were blending, but by infidelity and separating more and more and the American Negro was Demanding and descending to racism by being the American "black", then later on the African-American. This multiculturalism starting out in the 60's at most all major colleges and universities and civil rights' organizations, or superior rights had become full blown civil rights's socialism with "race" and class warfare and quotas, set asides, sexual orientation and affirmation action which already had appeared in Nazi Germany's by-laws. Equality came to mean "all the slaves would be equal in the cogs of the machinery", a Stalin quote.

As long as government remained big and foreign owned, Big Business became bigger, because there were no longer any anti-trust laws (such as Mobil/Exxon) and if there was, nobody seemed to care, or most Americans were too ignorant, ingratiated, or to apathetic, to care in the least.

Bob continued filibustering on his right as a shop steward and his own wisdom now was much clearer.

I thought to myself that, "Materialism kept growing and morality kept falling and the mishap, or dysfunctional family, grew epidemically with matriarchy in charge, especially in Germanic and minority areas. The similarities were so much alike, without the authority of the father, as head of the household. Genders were starting to become "farsighted" that made sexual orientation possible. Males could marry males in the state of Vermont, as well as females marrying females. Along with that came pedophilia a major runoff of homosexuality."

I am getting a little ahead of myself in this story.

Fred said, "One billionaire who lived in New York State had promoted pro-Latin ugly Americanism and his name appeared on buildings in Puerto Rico and now Spanish was appearing as an equal language to English everywhere government was. This appeared to be another Quebec with it's insistence on French. Was not the "Yugoslavian" example enough with their multiculturalism of the Bosnian Moslems, Croatian Roman Catholics and the Serbian Russian Orthodox with each their own religion, history and language? A people without language are soon to perish."

Chip again, a derelict of the bar said, "Maybe this billionaire is in love with their women?"

We all paid no attention and continued our own conversation.

John often played a variety of good music softly which many times annoyed only a very few young customers, because they wanted "garbage stew" and John would flippantly say, "What do you think this is a bar?"

The whole group just began to laugh until our sides hurt.

George, an elderly Negro Christian man, intervened by saying that, "Negro spirituals were turned into what is now called the Blues which is sensual and depressing and took my folk from their GOD. Years ago Paul Robeson was a devout Hollywood Communist, but was rejected by Moscow. Now all that filled the ex-Soviet airwaves were jazz and a broken down version of the Russian language served up by Radio Free Europe and The Voice of America. Lenin had always kept his eye on the American Negro for his own benefit."

Henry inquired, "Whatever happened to the 18,000,000 members of the Moscow Communist Party, when the Soviet Union broke up?"

George replied, "England and the West had welcomed Gorbachov, and Khruschev's son was made an official legalized citizen in the state of Rhode Island. Once when Gorbachov ahead of the KGB, a young American girl wrote Gorbachov a letter in regards to freedom and about a year later she died under suspicious circumstances."

I thought to myself about Adlai Stevenson a brilliant man had also died under suspicious circumstances while he was in London, England some years ago and the fact that America had done a 360 and then I ordered another round for our group.

I commented, "It is good to know that John's price of beer did not go up and that inflation was in America, but not John's establishment."

Henry said, "It has nothing to do with inflation, but everything to do with good vs evil. The avarice of capitalism has no honor and that it appeals to human nature only and does more to promote socialism than anything else."

I facetiously inquired, "Could I then say that you are not a socialist, but a non-conformist to utopian avarice?"

Henry said "Capitalism is an economic system and socialism a totalitarian ideology. One needs an ideology with capitalism and the other already has one and that usually after capitalism comes socialism."

Fred added, "With socialism there is no private life, but only a state public one, hence the state is one's home religion and workplace and that atheism, as Lenin had done in Russia, did replace Russian Orthodoxy with the religion of Marxism. This iconoclastic religion travelled to Mao in Red China, as well as to Nazi Germany and continues to this very day in the former."

George said, "Lenin wanted Trotsky, or Mr. Bronstein, to follow him, but Stalin got in the first pick."

I then asked George, "Was it not Stalin who would not go to his own mother's funeral, because a priest would be there and also Stalin's father on his own death bed shook his fist at GOD?"

George said, "Yes", to both of my questions.

We had come full circle, so to speak, in our conversation.

Fred said, "Immigrants, true immigrants, of Russian Jewish background and their children are the best at teaching their children the English language."

I responded by saying, "That should come as no surprise, since Russian Jews are one of the most brightest people in the entire world, barring none."

I sipped my beer again and said, "This unique combination of Russian and Jewish is far superior to the version of American and German Jewish who concern themselves only with homosexuality and it's legalization, finances and of course their extravagance and look down upon Polish and Russian Jewry."

Henry only looked at me directly in the eye and smiled gently, as if to say, "thank you".

Henry had much foresight and where with it all and many times we would listen, because Henry was somewhat older, than the rest of us.

Speaking directly to Henry I said, "The Eastern mindset is much more family oriented and that without their foreign heathen religions, such as Islam, Hinduism, Buddhism, etc. that the Eastern church is going forward and the Western church is dying. Our society is upside down with group mentality and individualism, barbarism and tribal mentalities."

The next beer was ice cold, or at least I thought much colder, than the previous ones.

Henry did not protect his own, when he knew they were ungodly, immoral and corrupt. He did not like Henry Kissinger, ex-Senator Jacob Javitz, the Hollywood crowd, Mo Annenberg the government made billionaire(like Ross Perot) and other secular Jews. Henry had one time met many important people in his lifetime, but when questioned about who was the most unique person that he had ever met his answer was Al Anastasia, the head of Brooklyn's Murder Inc., because Henry had said, nobody would have guessed what kind of business that Al was in and that he was very articulate and also dressed as a businessman would and tonight when he conveyed this to us, again out loud Fred made a comment as such.

"Was that good or bad for businessmen?"

We all then just laughed hardily.

As night got later more patrons were coming in and in fact one Israelis' Jew, named Moshe', came along side us and then we all proceeded without decorum to sit at a large table. Moshe' was quick tempered and very on edge and always seemed to be in a hurry and did not care for most American Jewry, he being mostly Sephardim. A part of his features showed him Sephardim background. Many times Moshe' would use the phrase, "no problem".

Henry started with Moshe' by saying, "American married Jewish males are good providers for their families."

Moshe' replied, "One has to become more than just a good provider. One has to be a "priest" and good father to one's family."

Under the dim light, one could see that Moshe' and Henry were patriarchal family men. They were loyal husbands and good fathers and were not the run of the mill American Jewish male.

Moshe' continued with, "I have looked all day again for a job, but when I mention my name and where I was from, I could see that there was a problem."

Also Moshe's accent was a dead giveaway.

Henry said to Moshe', "this area is predominately Germanic, or as I say, Anglo-Saxon with a sparse touch of Roman Catholicism and that this area is always afraid to hire a Jew for fear that they might take over their business and that is the reason why so many have become professionals."

Moshe' just stared at Henry and said in his hard Sabra accent, "I only want to work full time and am not interested in politicks, or welfare, when it comes to my work."

Henry torted, "Moshe' you should be more interested in local politics, if you ever want to get a good job with decent benefits. Only Masons get good jobs and good promotions."

Moshe' exploded and grabbed Henry's arm and said, "Do I need to a degree to work in a factory, or an assembly line? What good is an education with no morals and a hard heart and soft body and soft mind? It takes both a healthy mind and a healthy body to become whole."

Henry acquiesced quickly and realized that Moshe' would not listen, until probably after a few more beers. Philosophy was not one of Moshe's strongest assets, but that was indeed a plus.

Henry, whenever he spoke, was usually very cognizant of his surroundings. Henry by his very own nature was a natural born salesman, but yet his philosophy was almost always first. Diplomacy was Henry's strong point and with Moshe' it was not. In all fairness to Moshe' many others were getting hired who did not meet the qualifications and because government had federalized the work force to promote their own agenda, whether it was local, state, or federal. This grandfathering trickled down through all 3 levels of oversized government, so that "the wheel that squeaked always got the oil." Henry's Eastern mindset was not concerned with food and unnecessary cleanliness to the point of it being an obsession like it was with most, for example, Italian families. Even the well-to-do Italians never hired maids.

Henry many times spoke about how homosexual fashion designers with their long hair came up with most political rhetoric, or POLITICALLY CORRECT answers. Henry was not an ostentatious person, but many times was very expressive with his hands and would gesticulate in what he was talking about. Henry by no means played upon the Jewish issue, only when he felt that someone was being anti-Semitic and was not over-sensitive like most German-Jews were, otherwise he firmly admonished, or corrected them. Henry had once had his own business, but after 5 muggings by the so called disadvantaged in a slum area, he retired from that and continued to spend more time with his family. Henry was a versatile man and most of it was self taught and not of an educated breed. He had this talent, or ability, that was innate. He also was a quick learner, even at his older age in life.

Just when we were about to leave or the night, Moshe' quite inebriated got up first and said, "The Germanic people are strange and that they are cold and arrogant with a total lack of inner affection and are miserly to outsiders and are sentimental in that they only see their own family in need, because of their large ego."

As Moshe' said this I thought to myself in my foggy head, "I wonder if Moshe' knew about the 3rd Reich's Butches in their entire hierarchy and in Hitler's Youth Corps and that most of them all were homosexual pedophiles?"

I chose not to now dare mention this, being in the state that Moshe' was in and for that matter myself. Our own United States Supreme Court just about legalized homosexuality and pedophilia in full along with infanticide and atheism…

CHAPTER II

CHAMELEON LIKE - PARASITICAL

Another week had come and gone and as I entered John's Pub I saw Henry with his back to the door, so he could not see me coming in.

As I approached the bar, Henry turned around almost instinctively and said, "Hi good friend."

Just by that invitation I knew Henry had something important on his mind. I did not ask the proverbial, "How are you Henry?"

I just said, "Hi".

I was waiting to let Henry tell me what was on his mind.

About a minute later Henry said, "Do you remember what Moshe' said in his drunken stupor before he left here last week?"

I said, "I vaguely remember some of it."

Moshe's remarks had bothered him and he wanted to know what I thought of the Teutonic people, being that I was not one.

I hesitated and then my memory came back to me.

I carefully mentioned about Nazi Germany's pink swastika today in which America was promoting more of the very same thing. I also mentioned about the one and one half million Jewish children that were murdered in Nazi Germany and as to the why which I felt was their homosexual pedophilia state and culture. I included the fact Martin Luther was an austere anti-Semite later in his life who hated all Jews with a passion.

Henry said, "This is the 21st Century and not the 16th, 17th, 18th, or even the 19th Century."

I said, "The Truth does not change."

Henry retorted, "How come there are no Gentile religions that America could claim as it's own?"

I said, "In a way America had laid claim to that in part, when the First Pilgrams in the 17th Century founded Plymouth Rock and the document called the Mayflower Compact to avoid England's Anglican English Church and England's GOD along with England's monarch and the Europeanism that was in Holland."

What I was saying was not at all new to Henry, but I first had to establish a basis for his questions, or I would get no where and because sincerity had been to Henry and myself at the utmost. I had to start where history had been written correctly, since I agreed with some novelists who believed one had to write in the present and with the future as "open time".

I said, "WAR AND PEACE was written daily, as it was occurring in a public periodical and was serialized monthly by Tolstoy."

This seemed to grab Henry's attention.

Changing subjects Henry asked, "Why did America take in the Jews not before the Holocaust?"

I responded by saying, "To my knowledge America did take in the Jews before the Holocaust, plus other nations, but it was not the large original amount that they had promised to, hence 6 million murders."

Henry said, "I know that 7 million Gentiles were also eliminated and amongst them were the Poles, the Spanish, gypsies and homosexuals and that the only ghetto my father had known was in Poland, but not ever in America."

I commented to Henry, "In one instance you are wrong. Homosexuals were not targeted for extermination. Only about 5,000 died in all the camps and many who were alledgedly suppose to be homosexuals, were really priests and Christians, as well as Jews and that is why Menachem Begin later fought for the state of Israel to protect Jews and as a member of the Irgun. During the British Mandate he warned the English to stop hanging the soldiers in the public squares, but they still refused and the British just ignored him. Menachem Begin pleaded with them to stop, but they still refused, so he made a phone call to the King David Hotel saying that in 45 minutes it would blow up. The English in their sly and arrogant way disbelieved the phone call and hence many died in the explosion, because of the British."

John had got caught up in his work and was listening to our conservation with interest and then asked, "Was it not Eisenhower that later refused the entrance of Jews to the shores of America? Saying that, "The Jews to the shores of America would bring diseases to America."

Henry quickly said, "Yes", and said also that, "Ex-Senator Everett Dirksen, even has a building named after him called the Dirksen Building, had allowed many ex-Nazis into America, the same as Clinton had done with the Communists later on."

I looked directly into Henry's red and glazed blue eyes. This discussion had indeed become deep and told me more about how the rich and the well educated dealt with their own, even though the media plays on the poor and the disadvantaged, or the middle class, constantly to subterfuge the real truth. In fact the glorious FDR and Churchill were prime examples of that and one book called MEDIA, THE CULTURE OF LYING…

After too many beers Fred said, "The only reason FDR got into WWII was because Pearl Harbor was attacked. Did not Joseph Kennedy Sr. side with Nazi Germany and tell America to stay out of the war and then was appointed by FDR as Ambassador to England? The curse on this family is still there, because of anti-Semitism."

Later that night I had to help Fred out of the bar and drive him home safely.

As our discussion continued, Sal entered and was listening to our conversation. Sal was of Cuban descent and knew a lot about his homeland. I had always remembered what Sal had said about Fidel Castro and his anti-American sentiment which he felt later drove Castro to the Soviets and the Red Chinese Communists that supplied him with much. Back in the 60's Communist China was giving Castro $1,000,000.00 a day. He believed Red China wanted in first. Then along came President Gerald Ford who eliminated the Monroe Doctrine which made the Western world, or hemisphere, an open target for world Communism. Years earlier William Randolph Hearst of Knight-Ridder publishing and a billionaire media magnate precipitated the Spanish-American War by insisting that the Spaniards were brutalizing the Cubans which they were not and even an American President told Mr. Hearst to refrain from printing lies. Sal knew his people were the businessmen of Latin America and believed that is why the Communists wanted the small island of Cuba. World Bank would ravage and rape the land for Big Business. No loans, if one was not a nation no matter what for! He also understood the mistaken identity that most Hispanics had against Americans, but that they failed to realize through ignorance and deceit that it was Big Business and the rich and well educated who raped their lands and that repatriation to America through government was a wrong vendetta, or approach, to the problem. ("Who is it that takes you to court? Is it not the rich?"). In Peru Sal knew that 70% of their fish went to American dog food, while the children in Peru starved. Even one time a man from a famous family in upper state New York and ex-governor went to Latin America for a visit and almost caused a small revolution, even amongst the Indian tribes. There was no love loss for American Big Business, or it's avarice in capitalism.

As Sal chugged down some strong liquor, with a beer as a chaser Henry, John and I were waiting for him to speak up, since Sal was well educated.

The same governor that Sal told me about before was the very same one who put down a terrible riot at the Attica State Prison as governor and was condemned for this in the media, but if only the public knew what some of these felons had done, they too would have done the same thing! Sal then spoke up and said, "The ex-Notre Dame University President in South Bend, Indiana, Mr. Theodore Hesburgh, is a good friend of, none other than the Marxist leader, Daniel Ortega and the Sandinistas and Nicaragua's Liberation Theology which is spread by none other than the Roman Catholic's own clergy."

John abruptly told Sal, "You will have to speak much more softly, because many Irish Catholics are here, such as Fred and that he was counting Sal's drinks."

We all laughed, including Sal and Fred, till our stomachs hurt.

In addition to this I said, "I had seen this Pope admonish one in the Order while in Latin America by shaking his finger at him, but at that time knew not as to the why."

Much had happened, but little was being truthfully told by our media, or our own government.

I commented to the group, "I remember when a Chicago Police Officer gave a compliment to the Chicago Seven by saying, "That they all acted like gentlemen in the courtroom. Did he not know what crime they had commited, or that to act otherwise while on trial would be horrendous?"

One does not get a special reward, or a trophy for paying their bills, or for doing what any good citizen should normally do, but then again these were not normal citizens.

I had changed outer politics to inner politics.

I went on to say, "One time, when I was young, I was visiting a local Masonic Lodge for the entertainment and the arts and there on a shelf, was this small statue that said, "THE ARAB PATROL". How wonderful to know that the Shriners supported Islam and anti-Semitism to the fullest. America's founders, or at least some of them, had been Masons. Did not the Masons know that Luis de Torres a Sephardim Jew, was the first "white" man to claim property for the new world under the guidance of Christopher Columbus who also might have been a Jew?"

Henry reverted back to our earlier conversation about Germany and said, "There was a town, or small city, of about 100,000 where the German woman went wild over the "black male GI's" and is not Little Richard, the American founder of rock and roll, a homosexual? The first couple of stories were not too well known in America for some reason. John F. Kennedy was married twice in his life."

Yes, though inebriated, theatrical reality tonight was growing but I thought to myself, "Was not Lenin a stage name for his real name Ulyanov and that Lenin's Comissar of Education was the first to coin the term POLITICAL CORRECTNESS and America thought they phrased this term, as well as the word, freedom.

Henry understood Israelis' history and about the Menachem Begins, Moshe Dayans and, David Ben-Gurions, (David's brother a hot dog concessionaire, by the name of Green), the Ezer Weismans, Jabotinskys, etc. Henry also understood America's political parties, such as republicanism which usually meant Anglophilian government by parliamentarian free elections and it's Germanic roots of Protestantism's anti-Semitism, such as the Reagan Administration's employees, George Schultz and Casper Weinberger even though Caspar was part Jewish.

George interjected, " The Entebbe Rescue in Uganda complimented Israel taking in the Falasha Jew out of Marxist lead Ethiopia and by destroying Saddam Hussein's nuclear reactor quickly."

Oscillating back to American political parties. I said, " The Clinton Administration appointed 24 homosexuals, knowingly, in their Democratic Cabinet and in the White House staff. Everyday Mr. Clinton served in the WHITE HOUSE destroying America's moral fiber, as well as American sovereignty."

John again going back to Middle East said, "The war in 1967 and 1973 on Israel were from Egypt and Syria. Shimon Peres was an errand boy for Dayan and Begin, because Peres was a Harvard business graduate whose poison Ivy League education was a detriment to the average Israelis, but not to the Knesset, or our United States Department of State. Golda Meir, born in Milwaukee, was too fascinated with Henry Kissinger which made for poor politics. With the West conceding more and more countries, the Soviets at that time were usurping one after another and when they took Angola, a wonderful place to wage nuclear war by sending in Soviet Cuban troops to create a civil war the entire West just looked on. Whether it was sexual deviancy in Nazi Germany World War I and II vs. Jewish Orthodoxy, or

Lenin and Stalin's Soviets vs the Russian Orthodox Church and the peasants and the monarch both socialisms had a deathwish for mankind. This same ideology came to America by disallowing first the Bible in 1962 and school prayer in 1963 along with Roe Vs Wade in 1973 and as far back as in 1857, the Dred Scott case. All these judicial fiats had done away with GOD first and then humanity. Along with it came the Boy's Scouts of America Case 5-4 just in favor of normalcy and not Nazism with also another case, Internet child pornography made legal by illustrious Extreme Court with only 3 dissenting votes consisting of Scalia, Rehnquist and Thomas."

As John spoke I watched Henry's expressions which were strongly Sephardim, dark and rugged, but his diplomatic Ashkenazim background. I could articulate from his demeanor that American Jewry especially New York City style was sickenly too liberal and secular and that this Russian Jew wanted no part of this cancerous tumor called secular New York City.

As the night was ending down Henry said, "There is a negative connotation, whenever even with a Jewish Person, they use the word " Jew " when there is an alternate word, or words such as Jewish, Jewry, Hebrew (to cross over), Israelite, Israelis which are all more properly apropos'. It is not like the nationality Greek which has no real alternative. It is intended through ignorance, or prejudice in a true context and not a POLITICALLY CORRECT one to denote either anti-Semitism for the Barney Franks."

John asked Henry, "Is it true Henry Ford was an anti-Semite?"

Henry replied, "He was more than that and in fact had many Ford plants in Nazi Germany which the Allied Forces along with Sunoco Oil were never bombed. Mr. Ford did apologize for his remarks only after a United Supreme Court Jewish Justice emphatically made him do so, As to the why, one can only wonder. Up until a few years ago there were no American Jewish owned Ford Dealerships anywhere in America. Sexual deviancy vs the Jewish people, the underlying reason the Nazis exterminated the German-Orthodox Jews first. Now today Islamic Jihad, innately socialistic might too be hiding behind some kind of sexual perversion."

Fred, our Irishman, mentioned, "With a Jewish mayor in Dublin, there was relative peace and calm, because Roman Catholicism and Protestantism were kept at bay which did not incite the bright, but argumentative and over indulgent Irish. Many other nations from a historical perspective have had a negative relationship with the Jewish people. For instance, in Sweden they remained neutral to the Holocaust while millions perished and had their Quislings. Yet pornography did not bother them. Country after country tried their hand, but failed to eliminate the so called Jew. They do not respond by sharing the true Gospel and only see finances as a positive, or a negative, when a Jewish population is around. The Gentiles do not even know to distinguish between Sephardim and Ashkenazim, or even what tribe they are from, let alone which type of Judaism they come under, or even if they are believers, such as Messianic Jewry. In America a new-Nazi homosexual pedophile in Skokie, Illinois got permission to march through a neighborhood with HOLOCAUST survivors and guess who sponsored it? The atheistic and anti-Semitic and socialistic ACLU founded by none other than a Communist by the name of Baldwin. Mr. Glasser loves his misery. Mr. Collins, a neo-Nazi homosexual pedophile organized this entire event with the ACLU's full knowledge. "Blood is not always thicker than water."

Henry stated that, "Israel is about 55 miles wide and only about the size of New Jersey and that the West Bank comes deep into Israel and that the Gaza Strip on the West Side is populated with about one and one half million Arab-Moslems, but has a wall, a restricted zone, something the West Bank is working on. The American and English governments want to formulate this Palestine Terrorist State along with Europeanism. There would be no Jews in this state and this state would try to liquidate Israel, as a state, by Islamic Jihad."

I said, "Israel is the only non-dictatorial state in the Middle East, since it is a Jewish state and not a Moslem state. People are not murdered, as in all Moslem countries, if they are Christians, or Jews. Messianic Jewry though is the exception, as far as proselytizing in Israel itself. It is a secular state, even though it has rabbinical courts. Messiah is missing. One sin from Abram and Sarai and now this fight between Semite brothers. Ishmael was a warrior and Isaac was a sort of priest and shepherd. These two Semite people from Shem, one of Noah's sons. The same father, Abraham, for Isaac and Ishmael, but a different mother. One's mother was Hagar which was Ishmael's and Isaac was the son of Sarah, Isaac got GOD'S Blessing."

John commented, "Lucifer had invented all the sin from the beginning and sickness also came into the world. After Lucifer sinned, pride, GOD threw Satan out of his orderly position along with one third of the angelic host who had moved from their original positions set by GOD. GOD created Hell originally for all of these fallen beings. There are different levels of heaven, as well as Hell."

The night had ended for me early and I left with Moshe' for home. After we walked a little while down the street with it's uneven and broken lights, I asked Moshe', "Would you like a cup of coffee at my place, since we were only a block away from my house?"

Moshe' said, "I would like that a lot."

As we turned the corner, my house stood in plain view with about less than 50 yards to go.

We entered and I asked Moshe', "Sit down and relax, Do you want anything to eat?"

He politely said, "No."

After our coffee I asked Moshe', "Do you like it in America?"

He said, "It is quite different, than Israel where church, or rabbinical courts and state criminal courts are separate."

I said, "At one time America was the same in regards to church and state, but socialism usurped the church's Christian authority with little, or no effort. Israel too was and is a secular non-Messianic state and in America there is no longer any public opinion and the ones that speak out have an axe to grind, or are ready to make a killing financially. The West glorifies youth and the inexperienced in life which goes against the laws of nature. The older in life are to lead."

Moshe' replied, "Israel is where East and West meet, but that Israel is an Eastern State."

I asked Moshe', "Why Israelis upheld 50,000 abortions a year, since there are only about 17,000,000 Jewish people in the world?"

He said, "I really did not give it much thought, but now that you asked the question I would seriously think about it. My grandmother said that the Jews were the hardest people to love and that one must always choose one's friends carefully and always check another's background before getting married."

I asked, "Is it true that the Jewish scribes of past always used another pen when they wrote the word of GOD, YHWH?"

Moshe' said, "Yes."

I then commented, "I believe the Jews are special, because they were chosen and not chosen because they are special."

Moshe' just smiled kindly.

Theatrical reality really had done a number on the world and especially the Jewish people. Here is a most misunderstood man, because of Israel's right by GOD to exist and to eventually be a "light unto all the nations." It is important to know one's history.

Moshe' motioned for one last cup of coffee and then said, "Rabbis are not allowed to read the BOOK OF DANIEL" and asked, why?

I said, "Since Daniel correlates with end time prophecy and the BOOK OF REVELATION the enemy has blinded the religious rabbinical leaders of today and of past centuries amongst the Jewish people. Today in seminary schools what is not taught is that Daniel was bilingual and very bright and scholarly. At one time all Ivy League schools were seminaries but now are poison Ivy socialist schools. These think tanks deal in atheism and POLITICAL CORRECTNESS."

After this Moshe' said, "Good night", and went home.

The next day I decided after work to make a trip to the pub.

I thought to myself, "Was I addicted after my first drink to alcohol and did I have an addictive personality, or was it the stimulating conversation that I found so challenging?"

As I entered the pub, nobody I really knew was there, except John the proprietor. So I went up to the bar and had a draft beer. John was surprised to see me, but perplexed in the sense that something appeared to be on his mind. John's wife had died some years ago and he was still raising 3 children alone. The undue burden of being a father and a so called mother must háve played heavily on John, but he never mentioned it. Since John was not busy, I struck up a discussion about parenthood with him, being that I myself was not married and never had been and had no children and was celibant all my life.

I spontaneously asked John, "Do you think motherhood is dead in America?"

I could tell John was struck by my observation about his inner thoughts and the fullness of the question.

John directly said, "Being a bartender I hear a lot of gruesome and unnatural stories, especially when a drinker has sometimes one too many and no one always knows when that is, until they open their mouth usually. Motherhood is important, because with a wife and a mother at home there is no missing part to any family, because a mother brings compassion and nurtures more, than the male usually does. A man cannot really fulfill a mother's total role and to remarry many times, or another time, invites a dysfunctional family. Motherhood in America is near death and fatherhood has dissipated to an extremity beyond hope. Many times patrons will give braggadocio claims about how macho they are and how they feel, when they go home to their old lady. Usually it is the alcohol that brings out this ugliness in them that is underlying. These hung over dads are guys who work all right, but have no sense of maturity, or responsibility, when it comes to family and do not care to listen to any sound advice, except, if their own government is giving them something, or their own ego needs feeding. The opposite sex is being brutalized, because these men only are just that, men and not fathers, husbands, uncles, or even grandfathers. They refuse to see life in marriage as a commitment for life and that fatherhood is not just biological, but much more spiritual than that. The largest pro-abortion group in America is the "white" American male. This bothers me very much. Our adolescents are actually not guided and are left to themselves to self-destruct. This all is a spin off from FDR and the rebellious 60's generation. Both had failed to see the importance of family values, such as hard work, honesty, winning and losing responsibly, compassion, dignity, honor and BEAUTY. This failure has not occurred overnight. It is by osmosis, or a gradual process of family disintegration along with the government's need for parasitical existence and of course their own individualism of power. Instead of encouraging the young, we are doing exactly the opposite by living out our lives, as if on an immoral Hollywood screen. I never had much respect for Hollywood, because of what it stood for and that is absolutely nothing. As a father and once before a husband my responsibility has greatly increased. Life has no easy answer. Many men who are married do not even pay honor to their wife, when she attends church, or synagogue, while they usually have other important things to do. This self-esteem was and is nothing more than egotistical pride and self-pity, that nurtures on self and self alone. OBE, or Outcome Based Education, as well as situation ethics are destroying our children, because it stresses materialism and everything also is based on feelings and survival of the fittest. John Dewey and Thomas Mann's idea of socialistic public schools was always a failure, because it is anti-family and anti GOD, but group thought. Our athletes are nothing more than illiterate iconoclasts and prima donnas that are poor examples for all our children and youth. Government has no bright leadership and neither do sports, the arts, business, education, et cetera. The government loves the high salaries of professional athletes because it means more taxes to collect. Even alcohol itself is not the knave, if one drinks in moderation, or rarely and has an inner sense of responsibility for others and oneself. The male image in America has become so depraved that males are now marrying males and public opinion does not exist. People are worse than lost sheep who when they fall down must be literally picked up and often wander and wonder, while they go astray lacking the proper shepherd, but yet rely always on self-preservation first and foremost. While still others are searching for this death wish to fulfill their urge, as well as a major anxiety in adolescents and as well guidance by either a physician, or an uncle. I have seen most men and women drink, until there was nothing else to stew about and they continued to become more depraved. The more the flesh is promoted, for whatever reason, the more barbaric man has become. Yes, John Locke is probably where most of this materialism, without GOD got started. Eve's usurpation of authority by being the first to be deceived, or the only one to be deceived, by Satan, but with Adam it was quite different. He knew what he was doing, but blamed it on Eve to GOD. Eve was not created out of dust like Adam was, but was created from Adam. Some men want their wives to rule the roost and take authority. There is some kind of twisted psychology behind this bizarre conduct. Even the roles are being switched, where the female supports the family and also where the wife no longer even needs the male for procreation in marriage because there is cloning, embryonic research, lesbianism, feminism, artificial insemination, et cetera which are all part of this New Age pseudo-science. The idea of quality time is nothing more than proverbial escapism from the reality of family life and plays into the hands of the rich and well educated who do not want to raise their own children. Self discipline and obedience is never stressed as to the wholesomeness of life and liberty. All the ism's and "social" words have infested our society at even the subconscious state of mind."

John's dissertation was quite indeed much more, than I asked for. It was just why I came to John's Pub.

I thought to myself, "What if John had opted to give up his children for foster care, or make money and where abuse emotionally and physically was in epidemic proportions? The transfer, or transition of human resources from one environment to the other, time and again."

Right now I look at my glass of beer and ask myself, "If it is half empty, or half full?"

In our own society it was half empty, because what GOD had blessed us with we either wasted, corrupted, or destroyed on immorality, debauchery, fornication and abomination. What else was there that we failed to do what was not pernicious and pusillanimous to our own and to others? Could the glass have been half full? Yes, but what have we added to the glass in life to make it so? GOD had done most all of it and we were just the instruments without a melody. Now that GOD was leaving us to ourselves, as some Deists earlier had thought, we were drowning in an abyss of reprobation. We have forgotten our YOM KIPPUR, our DAY OF ATONEMENT, as well as our PASSOVER from evil and have not celebrated most of all THE FEAST OF TABERNACLES which all believers and Messianic Jews should now observe, but where was that ever preached? Was this too much beer, or was it something else that made self-reflection and not self-esteem make me look at myself from the outside looking in? How did I as a human being, serve humanity and not humanism? Where did this leave Henry and Moshe' who I knew were moralists, but not Messianic Jews? Was it to be the JUDGMENT SEAT OF MESSIAH, as to the GREAT WHITE THRONE OF JUDGMENT? Listen, keep and most of all do is what I felt was what Deuteronomy 7:12 was saying. Were our private lives becoming a public spectacle and had sacredness been replaced by quality in the family? The family institution set up by GOD was meant for this love to shine through, also to the family of men, as well as nations. How long would it take for America to realize that only future OPEN TIME was possible and not socialistic CLOSED TIME, man's prognostication? Had not Tolstoy and Dostoyevsky both written in the present and as artists viewed the future in OPEN TIME and was not WAR AND PEACE serialized and written, as it was occurring then? What was I to say in regards to the Russian pogroms, to Moshe' and to Henry, even though I felt the combination of Russian and Jewishness made for a most unique blend of foresight and brilliance? Maybe it was the 1,000 year old Christianity and the Old Testament people that made for this unique blend? They too share our view, motherhood and fatherhood, with fatherhood being the most important as to the authority and provider in society. Since most Jewry in America was extravagant and misguided, I did have to approach this with much contemplation and proper discretion. How would they feel, as well as my Gentile friends, about America making deals with Communists in Moscow and Peking along with Havana? No sooner had I thought this, then along came in Henry. I kept wondering about how to approach Henry, or should I wait for Moshe' too, that is if he was coming today?

"Henry is Moshe' coming today?"

Henry said, "Yes and Moshe' will be here in another 5 minutes or so."

Henry looked ready for his first conversational beer to swallow and also eager for a stimulating conversation, but before I could say anything, Henry threw a direct question at me.

Henry asked me, "Are you Roman Catholic, a Protestant, a non-believer, or an atheist?"

I hesitated before answering, knowing what this probably was leading up to.

I said, "I am not any of them that you've mentioned and that the Bible and the Holy Spirit along with Messiah (remembering always to use Messiah with Jewish folk) and of course GOD the Father, are what I follow. Roman Catholicism is ECSTASY IN CHAINS and Protestantism is rationalism, or ANGUISH IN INDEPENDENCE."

Henry then asked me, "Would you please explain to me more in full what you mean?"

I said, "In the first instance, Catholicism means materialism over the Truth and Protestantism is a protest of Catholicism and uses rationalism to make decisions. At the heart of the matter I feel religion is stressed by culture, foreign at that, and not by faith in universal freedom which is wrong. One has to be <u>listening,</u> <u>keeping,</u> and <u>doing</u> according to GOD, which requires man's free-will obedience under GOD'S strength and not our own. It is by grace, unmerited favor that carries me. Religiosity into denominations, or religion, is a trap American has fallen for.

We as Americans, are not the light unto the nations and our own arrogance and false pride has somehow gotten us into trouble with GOD. The Bible is GOD'S Will and the RUACH HAKODESH interprets through constant prayer for me as to what GOD'S will in my life should be and that Y'eshua is the long awaited Messiah who has willingly died for all and then resurrected for all and so defeated the enemy, death and sin, as GOD in the flesh."

Henry's next question was, "What about the Inquisition of 1492?"

I responded quickly, "I do not subscribe to Roman Catholicism. It is to GOD alone and that all believers, true believers, feel that way."

Henry stared at me and I could see there was much to absorb for now.

I thought to myself, "This had nothing to do with Norman Vincent Peale's nothingness on positive pure reasoning," but I did not say so.

Henry continued in questioning, "What do you think of America's Founding?"

Before I could answer, Fred, my Irish friend, said "Some of our Founding Forefathers were masons and deists and I do not understand why they wore powdered wigs and silk stockings and other effeminate attire and why only John Adams had owned no slaves and was for a monarch and not a democratic/republic which is right by might, or majority rule?"

I could see Fred had had a little too much to drink and I could not let what he said go unanswered, since Henry directed the question to me.

I interjected, "America was set up, as a type, not a form of democracy and that republican government is a sort of fail safe mechanism to restrict man's ego, if possible and to provide for equal, free and balanced elections. Capitalism was picked up from John Locke's Engligtment with an absence of morality, but with materialism which stresses less physical and more mental work, but without GOD which will eventually do the opposite with coercion in the extreme and that science and logic precede

GOD. Now with Islamic Jihad in America, spiritually from John Locke proved disastrous. This English GOD of GOD SAVE THE KING, or Caesar, is what America entertained, without the real King Messiah. The United Nations here on American soil prove to the world, that would religion by man, not GOD would have our approval for such things as NAMBLA, the occult, world globalism, UNICEF and other euphemistic, but deceptive terms. Even Allan Ginsburg is a member of NAMBLA which means NORTH AMERICAN MAN/BOY LOVE ASSOCIATION."

I quickly guzzled down my beer and started drinking another that was in waiting. Moshe' had already been here, but I had not even noticed him come in.

I said, "Now that we have become a second "Yugoslavia", or Quebec with our own multiculturalism, America has decimated itself with heathenism through this new socialism. Even our own local corrupt government officials, with some homosexuals, promote the cause. Everything turns from worship of GOD, Messiah, to worship of ourselves. How much in one second worldwide is perverse and sinful and does GOD see?"

Almost everybody appeared shocked and thought I had taken leave of my senses. Maybe I had? After all I did have quite a few beers by now and my inner anger, or hostility was at the boiling point.

Soon we moved ourselves to a more private area to a table in the corner. A few others joined in our debacle' of debate. Fred had also not finished what he had to say and this Irishman was raring to go.

Fred said, "The Federal Reserve has private stockholders and the United States Post Office is privately owned, but publicly run just like Benito Mussolini had done in Italy with his Fascist Party."

Moshe' said, "That sounds like economic fascism, as well as political fascism and seems to be on the verge of someone's own paranoia, since fascism interrelates with Sodomy."

My response was, "Paranoia, or not, theatrical reality was in play and that you need to see the light of day before night struck.

Even Maxim Gorky referred to Nazi Germany as a fascism of deviancy."

With that Henry intervened as usual with clear and concise composure being the so called elder statement of the group, besides George, who was already pulling up a chair at our table. "What is theatrical reality?"

I remained silent to his question as if I did not hear it.

I asked George, "What do you feel about the alcohol and drug situation in America?"

George said, "The Federal Government in trying to call alcohol a drug in order to legalize all hard core drugs sold illegally for some government tax revenue."

I also then satirically said, "This must be John's drugstore and not John's Pub."

Everybody laughed.

Henry switched gears and asked Fred, his political nemesis, "Since you are a staunch Republican, or GOP'er, GRAND OLD PARTY man why is it that Reagan-Bush, Irish-Anglophile, sold the AWACS airplane to Saudia Arabia, when Israel is suppose to be America's ally and why was George Schultz and Casper Weinberger both ex-employees of the Bechtel Corporation that had contracted for much Saudi Oil, or at least contracts and at a time Saudi Arabia had no standing army just like Japan, but needed a spy plane to spy on Israel?"

Fred retorted, "The Republican Party is Lincoln's Party and is for the average working man."

Henry quipped, "You don't mean the Abraham Lincoln Brigade?"

This was intended to ridicule Fred's answer and it did, because we all laughed and roared.

Henry continued, "I fail to see the correlation, since Republicans always bombast about Big Business."

Fred fired back, " If that is so, then is it not true that the Democratic Socialistic Party is for the state and not only Big Government with a capital G, but also Big Brother? Henry again responded, "I do not question the Democratic Party's ideology and their sincerity, but am asking, does not the Republican Party in essence speak the same language?"

Fred said, " All foreign languages are alike, when one does not understand any of them and that is the way it is with foreign ideologies."

Henry questioned, " How comes, capitalism, which is not foreign, treat the poor in America like a Foreignor in his own native birthplace and socialism which is foreign, is treated like homemade apple pie?"

Fred said, " All I know is that after capitalism does come socialism and I would in no way subscribe to the latter."

"Does not your Bible say, " And the love of money is the root of all evil?"

"Well is it better to be red than dead?

"No," Henry replied, "Never is just anything better then something."

In summation I felt what Henry was driving at was," What had Republicanism, or any party, done for the universal freedom of man that the Democratic Party also could not claim credit for and do not say, "Take down that wall Mr. Gorbachev?"

"Do either you know who one of our own 4 star generals in the State Department is pro-infanticide: involved as a Colonel in My Lai Masaacre and that our own State Department wanted the conflict in Southeast Asia to be lost, this better red then dead phrase? Did not also World Bank's President at the time, Mr. Robert McNamara, as Secretary of Defense too, ingratiate the rich and well educated on both sides of the fence? Is this McNamara anything like John Robert McNamara," I said?

"What about the Khmer Rouge and Ground Zero in Cambodia and that Thailand kept all Western Big Business at bay by making them sign leases and then showing them the door, whenever they chose?" This was Henry's question.

Finally George intervened, "It was a poor folk conflict. Never even a declaration of war and Lyndon Johnson had construction firms in Vietnam and used to sign all his own billboards in his original signature one by one down south whenever he saw them, because of egotism. Who was it who wanted John F. Kennedy out of the White House? Did not Jacqueline Kennedy say to him on the plane, "This is what you wanted?"

Henry got in quickly, "President Kennedy was made a target for assassination, but the lethal bullet was not from Lee Harvey Oswald. This first bullet, or shot, was fired by Oswald, but hit the curb and, being a military bullet, ricocheted onto the President's face, or the fragments did. That is when you hear the President say, "I have been shot", and he immediately covers his face and then the first secret service car, being the President's speeds up almost instantly, while a Secret Service Agent in the second car which is a convertible, is sitting on top of the canvass cover with his safety off on his AK-47 rifle which is rare indeed and as the first car speeds up, the second car does the same, knocking this Secret Service Agent back and with his finger on the trigger area releasing a shot from his AK-47 into the back of the head of the President, by accident, careless nonetheless. This second shot is what killed the President. Truth can be stranger, then fiction."

Fred then passed a question to Henry, "How do you feel about INORDINATE AFFECTION?"

"What does that mean," Henry asked?

Fred explained, "It is when anyone took care, or more care, and more concern for animals than for human beings. It is misplaced affection, and speaking of animals did not Karl Marx loathe mankind and consider man an animal, and did not the mule restrain the prophet's madness? What about Lenin, Stalin, and Trotsky? Did they not use fictitious names because they too were vicious liars and thugs and gangsters and were like the actors in Hollywood and also the animal world?"

Moshe then answered, "Marxism should not be equated with world Jewry. Was not Stalin's real name Dzhugashvili, A GEORGIAN, and was not Lenin's real name Ulyanov who was only one quarter Russian, and of course Mr. Trotsky, whose real name was Bronstein, but who was a German-Jew, like Marx?"

I asked Henry and Moshe, "What do you think of German and American Jewry?"

Both said "As of now not too much or at least their ancestry here."

Moshe said, "Most of times Jews are only interested in either financial banking, or in being trial lawyers, and that they German-Jews have inherited the German culture. Russian and Polish Jews have much more respect for family and life and that American and German Jews feel somehow superior, but as to why I can not figure that one out? What have they truly done to pioneer the State of Israel, but give philanthropic with strings attached, such as self-preservation and their own Western extravagance? The Russian and Polish Jews are a more sturdy lot of both the physical and mental labor as well as the spiritual!"

As the night went on we continued into other nationalities but that mostly of European descent.

Moshe' said, "The Polish worker is a hard worker, but that through Catholicism wastes all their energy on seeking more in materialism, except perhaps for Pulaski who was not like a regular Polish national who can only do one thing especially well, but was versatile that is Pulaski was. They have this insatiable appetite to save like misers and hoard money like the German. Otherwise they are okay."

I said, "Being Polish myself, or at least half, I conclude that is right. They are also very obstinate people and penny pinching. Now for my other half, the Italians, they are fashion nuts and cleaning freaks to the point of obsession, but it is not a sin to be poor, but a sin to be dirty. Food is also an obsession. It must be the right color, taste and temperature, or it is bad. They are ignorant about most politics and politicians, and Catholicism with them always means money and success, success, success. They are usually bad military people, but excellent in law enforcement and usually as judges. They tend to be womanizers like other Latin cultures, as well as the American "Blacks".

"They are not Sicilians, or mixed with Turkish blood, that is the Italians are not. Most Sicilians are mobsters, pimps, barbers, or run businesses in America as fronts for the La Costra Nostra, or the Mafia. They are liberal as the Democratic Party. They made it bad for most Italian immigrants into this country. They launder drug money and are involved in many nefarious business doings.

The Italians are a versatile people like the Jewish people are as well as the Irish. They are usually good husbands and fathers and are the authority figure in the home as compared to the German mindset of let the wife rule the roost. Italian mothers are probably the best in raising children. They have assimilated too much to capitalism and Catholicism. They are close knitted by family, not by groups, like the Jewish and "black" peoples are. They did overthrow Mussolini once they found out what he was. The Germans did not with Hitler, the Austrian. The Sicilians are very dark complexioned, but allow no American "Blacks" on the island of Sicily."

Fred chimed in on his ancestry, "The Irish are notorious drinkers, who love to just argue. They are very bright and versatile and a well-spirited people. They will argue for the sake of arguing and if around an Irish drunkard you have probably encountered the worst kind of person, barring none. Either Catholicism or Protestantism, or the arrogant British are to blame for their conflict in Ireland or the fact that the Irish love to just fight or argue.

They are very obstinate people. And by the way the next round is on me."

The round robin filibuster continued into the realm of the infamous Nuremburg Trials and some of their own judges who should have been on trial.

Now I finally opened up Pandora's Box and said, "Did anyone know that Nazi Germany's hierarchy were homosexual pedophiles and deviant thugs that ran the 3rd Reich and took drugs and dabbled in the occult? Hess, Himmler, Hitler, Rohm, Goerring, List, et cetera and Hitler's Youth Corps leaders were all Butches, or homosexual pedophiles. They were a vicious lot and very brutal just like today in America with the radical homosexuals who live the same lifestyle. The German people need a leader to follow and are also miserly like the "blacks ". They love uniforms as do the homosexuals. The wife is the head of the household. They are an austere people. Just listen to the language itself. They are also persistent at getting something right such as hammering a nail one hundred times until they get it straight. Over and over in constant repetition to perfect something. They are not congenial or very friendly. They like a winner, not a loser at all costs. Their innocent expressions reveal nothing. They are cousins to the Austrians and the English, hence Anglo-Saxon. In our own HOLLYWOOD there are even Communists, such as Paul Robeson was as well as Burt Lancaster, Richard Burton and now Ed Asner. The Greeks are very envious and the Greek and English democracies do not work in a majority of cases. There were 4 democracies in the 20th Century that went immediately to totalitarianism.

They were Russia, Chek's democratic China, the homosexual Weimar Republic and of course Italy who since 1946 has had a different government every year. A monarch is the only form of BIBLICAL government."

Charles, a lawyer said, "Barry Goldwater made a comment about a famous news broadcaster who lied up the Hudson River and was in the business for 25 years at that time, is an iconoclast and a true blue Communist. By the way Barry Goldwater was Jewish and Polish and not Polish-Jewish. Joseph Kennedy was a pro-Nazi and was made ambassador to England by FDR. The Pulitzer Prize was named after a man who believed not in consumer oriented news and reporting the facts as they are, but in commercialization by Big Business and the media and party politics. A good journalist only need be a good citizen with good writing skills, but does not need a degree in journalism. College journalism teaches POLITCAL CORRECTNESS and the media controls the political parties. All owners of newspapers control the content of their newspaper and no one else."

"What about abortion and the death penalty? Do they equate to the same conclusion?" This was John's next question.

I said, "Murder and killing must be separated. I can never murder an animal, but I can kill an animal. The death penalty is not murder under jurisprudence and now with DNA. Abortion or infanticide is always murder unless the mother's life is in danger.

I shall not KILL in Hebrew means not to MURDER. Even though a Court decreed murder and not killing legal, it must be absolved, or ignored. There is no legitimate reason to ever murder, but to kill has to do with war, or the animal world, or in cases of accidental death. Whether by judicial fiat, or Congress, Constitution or not, murder is always murder and if done on a huge scale can be called a HOLOCAUST, or infanticide. Serial Killers, no serial murderers. A government relinquishes all its authority when it promotes, upholds, or allows even one murder to be called legal, or to occur. Never has GOD said that murder be called a "right." The death penalty is Biblical, infanticide is not. A soldier even learns to kill, not murder, because he and his enemy are taught to kill according to war and as soldiers. Law enforcement in a civil government, or civil environment, is first taught to apprehend, them if no alternative to kill in self-defense and not as the trial lawyers and our judges have decreed to all our law enforcement officers. They are not on the firing line and they live in well secured and plush neighborhoods and can go home at night not being afraid that they may get murdered. Companies such as Prudential, Burger King, AT and T, American Express, Microsoft, Tom and jerry's Ice Cream, Green Giant, Johnson and Johnson, Levi-Strauss, Chase-Manhattan, Scott Paper, Archer Daniels and all others uphold murder in the first degree, no ands, no ifs and no buts. As for Fuji Films and Wal Mart they, both promote the liquidation of Israel by printing maps that have no Israel on them. Who are these so called monsters, or how could we call them as such? How could any of us exclude ourselves or others from the human race by claiming monsterhood no matter the evil? Animals have no accountability and neither do monsters for after all what is a monster, but a legendary figure. Image that, almost a hero type... How dangerous it would be for us to give credit to a legendary hero for murder, or to an organization or other institution when it is man's own belief system that indicts him always. His false belief in a party ideology which always appeals to group thought, or special interest while an individual has a view, all be it sometimes a wrong view, but nonetheless it is one person and if more than one that two persons, and so forth and so on and who are not in collaboration with an ideology. Organizations per se do harm because they do not breathe as an individual, but suffocate as an ideology. It is the ideology that holds them together no matter what still the end which is what usually occurs. Human beings become less human and just more like being. Non-existent as to a purpose in life and never to have been known to God, as if that person had never existed. Did Darwinism or Darwin himself discover a new revelation, or was it this old age deviancy that man is less than what GOD has said that he is? It was not Creation vs Evolution, but good vs evil. It was a lie, as opposed to the Truth. "Let us make man in our image." Creation is faith based not an invention by sin, sight and sense with only reason and no heart. Yet one does not visibly see and yet it is Truth and one does see and it is invisibly a lie. Insanity? To all believers, this is a fallen world. Was not the earth about only 10,000 years old with a 30-mile crust? If man was here millions of years he would have long ago destroyed himself, because now in only less than "7 days" man had already done immense evil. Man would be an extinct species by now."

Moshe said, "What about these 4 evil Gentile empires in the BOOK OF DANIEL?"

I said, " King Nebuchadnezzar was the first Gentile king, then came Media-Persia with of course GREECE with Alexander The Great who failed, because most Greeks by nature are very envious, even of their own brothers, but are very bright. Greece is now a Communist country mostly because of this trait. The last and most brutal Gentile empire was Rome, the 4th empire. In our own country we have Hispanics who refuse to speak the mother tongue, English, and our own government says, 'Go ahead and be bilingual.' Vietcong live in our small town thanks to the State Department; 'blacks' have become more arrogant, or why else call oneself 'black' instead of just another American? Black anti-Semitic racists, intimidate many American Jewish businessmen so that they sponsor anything that they want or need, and what about the non-assimilating and almost arrogant Oriental mindset in America? Maybe their homes would have done well to have their house windows on the side only, as they do in the Orient, and not in the front where the street lies and as we do in America?"

How far would this inebriated insanity continue, none of us knew, but on we marched?

George asked, "What about Martin Luther King, Jr. and his Moslem and Communist associates? Is this to be in defense of the terrorists? Why was Bobby Kennedy murdered by the Moslem Sirhan Sirhan? Was the surveillance on Martin Luther King, Jr. a valid reason? John F. Kennedy ordered it. Mr. O'Dell, a well known Communist, was a close friend to Mr. King and organized for him while in New York City after Mr. King promised to have no more dealing with him. Guilt by association? What about the debacle in the Bay of Pigs and John Roselli and Meyer Lansky?"

No one could say George had ever sold out his faith for anything and could not an American "black" be a Communist, or in fact a Nazi?

Moshe chimed in, "What about the murderer, Yassir Arafat and his PLO was founded by Ahmed Shakain and the Arab countries hid Nazis and gave them aliases, such as Erich Atlen later known as "Ali Bella", or Willy Berner alia "Ben Kusher", or Colonel Baumann alia "Ali ben Khadier". Wasn't Mein Kempf read by all the terrorist organizations and terrorist countries, such as Kuwait in the Persian Gulf, as well as Algeria and even Northern Sudan in Africa? Mufti Haj Amin al Hussein was the father of terrorism.

India, Mali and Nigeria were all pro-Arab and did not Ghandi's daughter, or supposed daughter, when alive sell out her own people to the Moscow Soviets? Was not Ghandi at one time a war time revolutionary? Did not the Mufti go to Nazi Berlin? What about Charles Lindburgh and Charlie Chaplin and there Nazi affiliations? What was it that Lenin said, "Use the cinema to promote the cause. "

I finally intervened as a judge would between childish lawyers and said, "There is a "social" Christian who are more dangerous, then any atheist, or socialist, "a wolf in sheep's clothing". How has America, or SAMSON come to lose his strength morally and how physically and in such a short historical period of time? Built on sand, democracy which can never withstand the measure of time. Our 3 ring circus of government only now needs one party to take control."

We had gone much further, then any of us wanted to go, but could we not be free to speak our minds and come to agree, or disagree? Theatrical reality has not been predisposed, but has been talked about by the so called literate, so to speak. It was the rich writing about the rich, that we had to watch. We should question everything and I mean everything. Were our opinions just opinions, or were they something much more then that? Was not socialism strangling us? Was this alcohol to make us stronger survivors to endure what? Self–preservation and convenience? We were not shedding any blood, but our infants were. Did we really care that is the church?

Henry's conclusion was, " Does anyone conclude that the American Negro ever mad the transition from agriculture and crafts and hunting as a whole from European slavery, when their ancestry was from Africa and would they be able to be Westernized by capitalism, slavery by consumerism as a people and with democracy as right by Might and more " rights "? Tribes usually rule by age in a more socialistic way, but will assimilation by the Negro be impossible? After the EMANCIPATION PROCLAMATION, The American Negro still is lacking this self confidence, because again it was coerced upon him, or his ancestry and from 1865-1964 where was the achievement that was to be seen? What appeared was anything but. All one could see was another form of slavery much worse than before and that was more ruthless and brutal then one could ever imagine.

It's "race" warfare with the help of government and the rich and well educated. It has nothing to do with the family institution, or race by human kind. Over 90% of Negro girls and women are having children out of wedlock, or choosing infanticide in all the major cities just as Margaret Sanger, the Naziphile, would have wanted. It is not poverty that is the issue, but morality. Government is trusted more then GOD, because many know what GOD'S answer is already. The rich, the famous, the well educated have more mundane talent in the sense that they have what the world wants, or needs, but most of the time is poison to one's heart, as well as the soul.

Socialism usurped the very consciousness and the innately American family institution amongst the Negroes and the "village" is not the enclave any normal person needs. Now today the American Negro is worse off than ever before, because now it is not plantations, but soviet "villages" that always ends in death and self-destruction for most all involved. Once accepted, it shall reach its own level and then eliminate, since it has no bonds or healthy relationships, but only party ideology with a death wish. Paul Robeson who was devout, still could not convince them to be accepted, no matter what, or how hard he tried. To relinquish and then now to promote from this coercion of a foreign ideology, not for freedom, but for the elimination of oneself. Total annihilation would come first spiritually and physically and then the pharaoh of forced labor with no end in sight. The "collective" workshop would certainly do the trick and the Communists and the New Agers shall then do away with all the socialists, because they did not go far enough and that the American Negro is the last of his kind to oppose, in part, this spiritual oppression in the entire Western world. Again the socialists shall not go all the way, so they shall be the first to go. Do not call in the wolves, if you are in trouble, for once the wolves get rid of the dogs then they shall get rid of you."

My conclusion is as such, "Christians that do not worship the true GOD, but an simulation of the only opposing power in the universe and that is Satan and his cohorts and his one world religion of government shall bring with them this "social" gospel for "social" Christians. No separation of church, or better yet, this church is the state. This church being the occult. Many elderly have died off into oblivion, never knowing why they were here, others not wanting to know, but a few obligated to know GOD'S purpose for their life and where only senility comes to rule for the elderly and relatives are absent for these elderly who have become orphans of the state. FDR's Keynesian Economics of "social" and secure death. Our senior citizens and senor citizens are group categorized for in the future disposability of one for the other would be made easier, if the state is the padre and the providers, instead of GOD and all fathers. Caesar has taken GOD's share. The state wants to be worshipped and probably it's officials think, " Everybody must think like us and bow down to us as an iconoclast of royalty." This was the end of my short dissertation.

CHAPTER III

MESSIAH vs THE WORLD – IS IT SPRING?

Finally spring had arrived and the seasonal colors were starting to bloom. As I was walking through our park, I thought to myself looking at a statue of Abraham Lincoln, "When was it when we did not have an Anglophile, Germanic, or Irish President? And why was this so? Was our conversation about the Masons, a few months ago true while I was at John's Pub I guess something inspired in me this thought about liberty and justice for all and not so much about physical freedom, because what did I know of being without it? Spring was blossoming and so were my thoughts on this beautiful sunny Saturday morning. Yes, even our park had changed since I was a child. Very few people used it to just stroll and relax.

They were too busy with mundaneness and superficiality. I then thought about Henry and Moshe and thought to myself how even the Jews had not obtained the position of president, even though 2500 Jews were here during the War of Independence, but then again it was just as well, or they too would be blamed for every evil under the sun. Why was it that wealth is not taxed on the super rich, but salaries and wages are on all others? Those involved with the super rich must be hired executives? Lord Keynes, a homosexual socialist, taught FDR at Harvard and who FDR adored, hence Keynesian political economics. (Also college presidents and administrators, generals, corporate lawyers, foundational executives, a few wealthy Jewish, Arabs, Indians and not Native Americans, a few Hispanics and Negroes and of course Europeans, such as the English.) Why was ownership and control of America's Big Business the most secret aspect of American society, barring none? Now it appeared it was ARAB ISLAMIC controlled through London bank accounts. With the media controlling all political parties, one could see why capitalism was important and why Saudia Arabia was kept well, even though no American " blacks " or American woman, or any Jewish, were allowed and also in Chile there was to be no American " blacks " at all!'I proceeded with home on my mind and thought about my placement of a book called HOW HARVARD HATES AMERICA and was it true? If so, why? While on my way home from my morning stroll something caught my eye at a distance that was beyond belief. As I drew closer, two elderly gentlemen were having words with each other and arguing terribly. There was almost something comical about someone else's tragedy. In this case these two septuagenarians were in battle with their canes, as if ready to strike one another physically and with intimidating words, if there could ever have been such a thing. I could hear one say, "Just you try and make me "and the other responded with "Oh yeh." After a few minutes the cartoon characters left and peaceably went their own way. Yes, even the elderly were upset or up in arms and stress and anxiety which are different had begun to turn on the elderly. With anxiety there is always stress, but with stress there is not always anxiety. The elderly could not correlate with peace of mind and were also too busy to worship and serve GOD. The elderly did not want to get old with grace. Many were relics of a past life and were off center as to GODLY wisdom and use of their life's experience. What had frightened them into a life of abuse and sheltered ways? Where had patriarchy and leadership gone? Even Benito Mussolini's wife cooked in the kitchen and did her household chores. Changing my mind to go home, I soon found myself in town and near a restaurant that was somewhat shabby in appearance, but clean and the food was all home cooked, I entered and saw Victor the proprietor making a sandwich for himself, as he usually did at this time of the day. He then sat at the end of the counter and ate his lunch. I sat down besides him and began to converse.

"Victor what is on the menu for today?"

"Anything and everything."

"Heaven forbid, there is that awful statement I had heard before. "This is what I thought to myself.

"Could I please have a chicken salad sandwich on rye?"

"Okay."

As Victor went back to make my sandwich, I thought about Victor's background, being all Russian and a little Ukrainian. A huge man with big bones and a beard, so full that it must have always been there. Victor's face was congenial and he himself was lighthearted, but with a deep booming voice with a slight Russian accent that almost fit to a tee. This old Russian image of a peasant, so kind hearted and full of life and down to earth. Victor was originally from a small Northeastern village in Siberia where the natural beauty of the Russian scenery could be seen. Many years ago he came to America during WWII, or thereafter, managing to escape the West's betrayal at the Yalta Conference toward the Russian peasants. He fled Europe wisely and settled in America at that time always wanting to go back home, but had not been able to, because of the Soviets. Now he had found a home in our town with friends and neighbors who loved him and who he loved. Yes there were some who were suspicious of Victor's Russian background who always confused him with the Soviets, or did they? What ignorance can do, but the educated too? Yet did not the colleges and universities preach that it was the Russians and not the Soviets that one could not trust? Did they not also refer to " Russian tanks " and " Soviet Ballets "

I asked Victor, "How do you feel about detente's, the lessening of the rope? "

Victor said, "The Communists are up to their old tricks again by lying in order to build up there constant war machine and try to supersede the United States and have first attack, if possible. There is not an ounce of truth from those scoundrels. "

How true had Victor spoken, but yet the American government, Big Business and Hollywood, along with the media, now wanted relationships with Peking and Moscow, still. Victor had lost relatives when FDR and Churchill sent back over one and one half million Russian peasants to Stalin's Soviet death camps. As time progressed Nixon visited the Soviet Union and as a lawyer for Pepsi Cola in the Soviet Union was respected by both Moscow and Peking. Armand Hammer, American born, the "Henry Kissinger" to Moscow opened up capitalism with socialism, or was it vice versa? Pandora's Box was opened and Peking through Kissinger and Haig also wanted in while both regimes of thugs starved their own people and destroyed the soil forever, as well as the people, especially the peasants. Socialism in anything was death and destruction. Victor was Russian Orthodox an Old Believer, though with not many left, so he had a clear view of his historical background and was devout in his Russian GOD. It was a faith that had been kept to by the Russian peasants and did not seek world recognition. The peasant in Russia was the soul of the nation before the Revolution and Russia only endured 8 months of democracy in 1917 from February to October and actually went not from a Christian monarch to a totalitarian regime. The Bolsheviks destroyed the Monarch, the Duma and Russia all together. The upper elite and the Monarch's relatives went along with first the Mensheviks and the bureaucrats. They had separated from the peasants, the people and tore them too from the Russian soil. The rope was made by the West to hang itself! The Soviets had no rope, nor why should they? Serfdom and Russia's freedom had been done with many years ago. Russia at one time was free just like America, before the Revolution. After this inhumane socialism, came brutality and death for almost 66,000,000 people, or more. Would America repeat? England would again certainly try this time in America like they had done to Russia. A 1,000 year history of Christianity with only about some seventy years of Communism. Yes, Victor had known what most Westerners did not know, but was thankful for what little he now had. Victor would have no overseer, or boss here or self-age, or own one financially, or be in financial debt. This was an albatross to the one who owed money and if your boss, or employer found out about it, he could rattle your chains for fear of you losing your job. You would have to comply. One time I had visited Victor's home and his wife was most gracious and treated me as if I was a close relative and brought out a food tray, as if I were also a king. Such Russian peasantry was quite different than Anglo-Germanic rudeness I had too many times been invited to. The Irish and the Italian were also usually hospitable hosts. Victor was a proprietor who used the freshest butchered meats and fresh caught fish, but yet somehow managed not to over price, or reduce quality, or make his produce an issue, or avarice, or politics and not follow the government's lead, or that of Big Business. This was not warehouse food which had many carcinogenic preservatives in it. Many of Victor's customers were either Polish, Jewish, Italian, or of course Russian of which there were very few. Illegals though were accepted and others who would not speak English nor why should they, if they wanted government support from the taxpayers rolls?

Eastern hospitality from humble Russian peasants, so wonderfully honest, pleasant, benevolent, extroverted, sincere and hardworking and assimilating without government coercion and nothing, but goodwill as any good neighbor would. They did not force themselves upon others to accept their politics, or lifestyles of heathenism, if they would have had any. They were too intelligent to be lead by the nose and did not commit that immoral misdemeanor. There was always this feeling of honor, not arrogance, when one was around them. No connivery, or chicanery here, just loyal patriotic Americans, so humane and normal and willing to serve, not being coercive to their fellow man. Yes Lenin, a Westerner, had replaced the Russian Orthodox church with Marxism and it's atheistic religion of there is no GOD. One could see the very same thing now here in America occurring, what had happened in Russia before the Bolshevik Revolution and especially after, when there was no reason to hide, or subterfuge, the evil about to come. The elderly were yielding to the young academically and would not debate, or challenge their younger counterparts. Fashion designers were creating so called POLITICALLY CORRECT news and the civil righters, like the neo-Nazi AFFIRMATIVE ACTION, especially in the colleges was in 3rd Reich style. Agriculture was dying, because of farmers selling out the farm and had been given welfare subsidies. Environmentalism, confiscators of private property came out of Hollywood, the UN and the federal government. The lie was repeated time and again with hardly no one to dispute, or refute it. Matriarchy also by the civil righters oversaw patriarchal way of life that America had for many years, or at least some of it did. (ISAIAH 2 "And ye shall be ruled by women"). Foreign immigration consisted of force feeding the American people into accepting the government role of "Love America, or leave it", but strange how none of these officials felt the same, nor why should they, the gravy train was sweet and long lived. Then there was this amnesia to have all in America forget GOD, the American GOD and substitute it, not even for Europe's GOD, but heathen religions sold either on deathwished, or the arrogance of "we are here to take over the fort" and with government approval, as well as the controlled media, Hollywood, the rich and well educated for financial and moral support. Yes, America was taking this same totalitarian path Russia had taken some years ago. No one would listen to Solzhenitsyn's interview in 1973 from the BBC, or Sakharov's warnings, or the book called "FROM UNDER THE RUBBLE".

Victor's sandwich was delicious and soon afterwards I left and headed for home. Soon I was in my small library where I had critiqued all my books, as to the author and the publisher. Did I know enough about America's history and not revised editions in multiculturalism? Did my books encompass any theatrical reality or were they truthful? It was important to try and know the truth and to reveal it publicly with the right timing such as the present. For America the truth did not matter only money and more of it. The utopians could only see green. One only can go forward never back as to the way it has to be. Why no comment by the Evangelical church, Judaism, German-Jewry, New York City Jewry, the Polish in Catholicism? Who do they suppose could commit such barbaric acts, just the Bolsheviks? Were not the same elements here now in America, such as NAMBLA, PLANNED PARENTHOOD, THE

HEMLOCK SOCIETY, PEOPLE FOR THE AMERICAN WAY, THE ACLU, ET CETERA? Yes, but more than that the sins to the 3rd and 4th generation, as well as emulators of HIMMLER, HESS, GOERRING, BLAVATSKY, HITLER, ROHM, LIST, ET CETERA. But the one and only, can you believe this, the Simon Wiesenthal Organization upholds Nazism for the Butches B'nai B'rith as well as the HOLOCAUST MEMORIAL in Washington, D.C.? They must uphold their own such as Barney Frank, Alan Ginsburg and Joseph Lieberman, as well as the honorable US Supreme Court, except for only 3 Justices and only 1 of the 3 is an Anglo-Saxon. I thought daily about our own precious and innocent children, babies, and young youth being tortured, raped and murdered as Jeffrey Dahmer and John Wayne Gacy had done as homosexual pedophiles. The media would certainly speak out? One only heard about the Catholic Church and most of them were about 70% proof. Our government and our society, as well as business and sports were sick as hell. Our government, meaning the courts also, were accomplices before, during and after the fact and the ACLU, the UN both said, "SO WHAT AND WHO REALLY CARES?" They encouraged this sensual perversion of the lowest kind and they said, or at least it was implied, that they would defend and protect, no not the children, but the criminal by their statute of "HATE CRIMES" and Sodomy and to leave well enough alone, so that they could roam and rape and of course not coerce according to their version, but the "ONES WHO HAD ASKED FOR IT"? What insanity and the church says, "We must love the sinner and hate the sin", WITH NOTHING OF COURSE ABOUT THE CHILDREN. It was a rendition again of the NAZIS, but other nationalities they shall oppose it, such as the Italians, or will they? The highest court in the land voted a 5-4 to keep the BOY SCOUTS clean, but 6-3 to allow child pornography on the INTERNET. The GIRL SCOUTS already had one third of their leaders as homosexual lesbian pedophiles and BIG BROTHERS were a hit with their criminals and a reincarnation of HITLER'S YOUTH CORPS came to be.

Suddenly I heard a hard knock on the door!

I thought to myself, "Why not use the doorbell?"

I went to answer the door and it was none other than Moshe' and Henry come pay me a visit, but why unannounced and why the hard and urgent knocking on the door? I had both them sit down in the kitchen and could tell from their eyes a sort of fear with almost an expressionless face. I gave each one of them a cup of coffee, but they hardly noticed it.

With some reservation and apprehension I asked them, "What brings you to my neck of the woods?"

Henry was first, "I have urgent and important news to tell you in regards to immigration and Israel."

I thought to myself, "What does that have to do with me? I am a legal citizen by birth?"

Henry continued, "No Jewish folks are allowed to leave America and travel to Israel for any reason according to the news."

I asked, "Did the government, or the State Department confirm this themselves?"

Moshe said, "The New York Times had a column written by a well known journalist who had reliable sources."

I repeated again, "Did the federal government confirm, or deny this?"

Henry said, "It was confirmed by the Jerusalem Post where I saw it in."

Henry spoke again, "Israel refuses to obey the US State Department in regards to dealing with the Islamic-Arabs and their so called peace accords."

"What else was said?"

Moshe', "Israel because of this is no longer an ally of America. It jeopardized their interest in the region."

"What interest?"

Henry said, "Most likely the rich Arab oil sheiks and their investments in England which had more money invested in America, than Japan did, because this oil money went through England's hands."

"All this for crude oil?"

Henry, "What is the saying in the Bible?" The love of money is the root of all kinds of evil."

"We have enough oil, but the Congress will not allow us to drill for it claiming their socialistic environmentalism especially in the US Senate."

Henry, "We cannot argue with you. We are losing valuable time. We need to take our families, as asoon as possible, to Israel for good. We cannot afford to become possible HOLOCAUST victims."

"With an Anglophile President you have a good point. What is it that you exactly want me to do for you?"

Henry, "Since you are in the export and import business, we thought you could help us, because of your international connections and access to visas and passports."

I thought to myself, "Does he realize what he is asking me to do and what if the government finds out? What will happen to my own relatives?"

"Who used the word obey in regards to Israel?"

Moshe' said, "It was the President."

I said to myself, "This sounds again like Taiwan, or the Taiwan issue, when one US Senator said, "We need Red China over Taiwan, because it is much larger. A sort of better red than dead Bertrand Russell statement."

"Okay", I said, "But on one absolute condition. You cannot tell even your loved ones, until we are ready to leave that very moment. You did not already share the fact that you came to see me for this very purpose to anyone including loved ones?"

Moshe' and Henry both said, "We did not, because we knew if you did help that you would do it under this absolute for sure and that even our families could accidentally let slip this good news."

To me it was like a lawyer who knows his client is guilty, but does not want to know, or even tells his client not to confide in him too much for fear that he, the lawyer, would too be prosecuted, if questioned, for perjury and lying to the court. But I realized why Moshe' and Henry had come to me. They trusted me as an American Biblical and my protection for the State of Israel, as well as the Jewish people, who made up about 2% of the American population, but oh what brain power, when used for GOD!

Henry then said, "The Guardian Angels are already storm trooping in certain Jewish neighborhoods."

"Germanic Brown shirting with anti-Semitism and socialistic style Islam", I thought to myself.

Henry had tried always to stay informed and must have somehow before this announcement publicly seen something coming. Whether it was Nazism, or racial warfare Henry would indeed know first. His would not be paranoia.

My next question was, "What caused Moshe' and you to have such concern? This visa and passport restriction could be lifted at any time, if Israel cooperated."

Henry said, "Moshe' had applied for a visa to visit Israel and was told they were not being given out any longer to Jews going to Israel, or in fact anywhere else."

I asked, "Are you sure that is exactly what the custom's official said?"

Moshe' said, "Yes, yes. I was shocked, because I am a native Sabra and told him that. My fear was if I cannot just visit Israel what would that mean also to my family, or even Henry's family? They also wanted to know, if I had other relatives besides immediate family here and I said no."

Henry asked, "Should we report to police headquarters?"

The First and Second Amendments had been abolished so Aliyah to Israel was not practical, but not impossible. We later found out Israel was experiencing a decline in immigration like never before, plus there were no Jewish tourists going to Israel. I thought it was due to the constant terrorist attacks, but now this explained it in full detail. There were about 6 million Jews in America and about 4 million still in Russia and Israel mainly had the rest. The world Jewish population was at about 17 million, so one could expect persecution and elimination, wherever the numbers hit that "high" plus the fact Israel had little oil and was receiving $10 million dollars a day from America. Once ex-President Carter said, "All funds should stop to Israel."

It began to look bleak for both Israel and worldwide Jewry, as now America was also closing it's borders to all foreign Jews, a fact I also later learned about. Jewish ghettoing by national standards. The world systems were ready to form an alliance to possibly attack Israel first through people restriction to Israel, financially and then physically through attrition in Israel. The boarding of food worldwide was a great concern even for America. Gold and other commodities were in plenty, but proper food and safe drinking water were in short supply. Induced famines were inflicted by man and then real natural famines started to occur. Socialism destroyed most of the world's agricultural base. My immediate concern was to now advise Moshe' and Henry and at least help them seek a trip to Israel for good, along with all their relatives. My own business dealt in the import and export business, as mentioned before, so I had some reliable connections with the Israelis' State. The Israelis' State would not refuse any foreign Jew, except when it had done so to mobster, Meyer Lansky. It was for sure that they would be received. Israel would need more help, than ever, since anti-Semitism was growing worldwide and the end of the age appeared to be approaching, when spiritual ramifications could not keep up with political ramifications which is always the way it works, but not on such a cataclysmic proportion. The spiritual renewal always takes much longer to come to fruition, or completion, than does the political manifestations.

I quickly took Moshe' and Henry to my shop and at once they knew police headquarters would not be needed. I proceeded to fill out forms stating that "So and so were Israelis' citizens and were returning from a brief stay here in the states on their passports." With most of their paperwork done within a short few hours, I had them and their families with little luggage ready to leave for Israel along with their aliases. Every remaining hour was valuable and had to be used wisely.

I thought, "How many Americans, or American Jews, refuse to believe and not make it out later, within the next 24, 48, or 72 hours?"

As we approached the dock early at dawn everything appeared okay and Moshe' and Henry plus their families with the exact head count, entered upon the cargo ship which allowed a few passengers that would exodus them out of America hopefully for good. We said our good-byes, because never again would I see them face to face, if everything went as well as now, or if something unexpected would happen out at sea. Hating to see them leave yet knowing there was no other choice available, I prayed as never before for their safe journey to Israel. At the other end Israel would not refuse their own, because of their Jewish background and this is why Israel had become a state for all world Jewry no matter if one was an Iranian-Jew, Polish-Jew, Italian-Jew, English-Jew, South African-Jew, Syrian-Jew, Egyptian-Jew, Russian-Jew, Moroccan-Jew, German-Jew, American-Jew, French-Jew, Irish-Jew, Ethiopian-Jew, et cetera, because of religious persecution and anti-Semitism.

I returned back to my office tying up any loose ends I might have overlooked and then stayed up all night wondering what would be next to occur.

The next morning was a Sunday and I missed house worship, because other things involving Moshe' and Henry had to be taken care of at their places of residence, such as mail, making it look occupied, keeping things as usual, etc. As long as I could keep their absence silent, it would work out better for them, until they had reached Israel itself, or at least Israelis' waters.

Everything in society was normal, as if it could be, so really the government's action was still not being made fully enforceable. If that remained so, Moshe' and Henry would have a better chance of making it home.

"Were they to be part of the remnant in glorified, or unglorified bodies? Had I done Messiah's will, both as to what and in how to do it?"

All these question entered my mind, as I returned home to rest.

GOD'S chosen were returning home after being away for over 2,000 years of wandering and roaming as Moses had done and

America would be that much weaker and poorer for it in regards to academics and genius. How many Jewish Nobel Peace Prizes were won by American Jews and also what was insane, those strange Norwegians had given it to none other than the terrorist Yassir Arafat who murdered men, women, children, soldiers and babies in Israel and ambassadors and his own people, such as using their own children as shields to defend his terrorist's attacks. The Nobel Peace Prize lost all honor, since then.

"Was the beast raising his head again from Nazism, or from Rome?"

We had with this new persecution of Jews, a second Naziphilia probably happening worldwide. As to the days, they had become like years in time, waiting still to know if Moshe' and Henry made it.

Whenever Scripture spoke in exact numbers, it always referred to the Jewish people. This I did know about GOD'S special way for them. The roots were being firmly planted by GOD, but in America and the rest of the world they were being ripped out.

As I finished work on Monday and as a matter of fact, I stayed away fron John's Pub, so no one would become too suspicious as to why Moshe' and Henry were not there and I did not want to have to answer any questions, until they had arrived in Israel safely.

CHAPTER IV

ALIYAH GENTILES?

After about 2 weeks I finally made a stop at John's Pub for a beer. Fred was already there drinking down another beer with Sal aside of him. I approached the bar and both seemed a little surprised, since they had not seen me, or for that matter Moshe', or Henry, in a little over two weeks.

Their first question was, "where have you been and where are Moshe' and Henry?"

I did not know if that question implied more than just what appeared on the surface. My answer had to conform to normal consistency and could in no way reveal what I had done, because of future repercussions to my own relatives, who also would be affected. My answer was firm and to the point without any sign of overplaying.

I said, "I have not seen them in two weeks," which was not a lie.

I made them almost like most physicians do, ask question after question on their own initiative and would not volunteer any extra needed explanation. If, as to their whereabouts, I should subterfuge ever so slightly onto another item, or issue. Quite surprisingly their questions were short and not too many which also could mean that they already knew and did not want to know anything extra like most defense lawyers do so they can say, "They never knew," when in reality they did.

Fred said, "Work at my job is slowing down."

Sal said, "It is the same at my job."

This already was part of this implosion as to Aliyah and soon we, like Russia, would feel it's affect.

They asked me, "How is your business doing?"

I said, "It is the same as usual, except now that I am importing much more, than ever before and most of it is mostly foodstuffs and that the prices are starting to soar incredibly. Our exports consist mostly of technology. I believe, if this continues some kind of famine and pestilence in America will soon be prevalent, either because of hoarding, or because our entire agricultural base is dissipating rapidly in America. Our farms are becoming collective warehouses for government storage, but are not producing much, because of subsidized money and control which means more welfare and the number is growing. I always try to stay clear of government contracts and their red tape, plus their new policy of world distribution of wealth. America today is socialistic in many forms and individual personhood has become group thought from senior citizens to abortions. America long ago accepted it's worldwide role to help this New Age Movement."

I guess by saying all this out loud I was revealing my anger as to what was occurring now in our own country in an indirect, but non-divulgent way.

I continued, "The rich and the well educated mostly from BOSTON," the Harvard of the East" along with the "New York Yalers", "the St. Louis and Baltimore Princeton paper Tigers", "the San Francisco elite in the New Age Stanford University the Harvard of the West", plus the city of brotherly love and the Philadelphia Penn quakers" are all promoting socialism. It is the rich telling, or writing about the rich, not the poor and not the middle class writing about their own, or about another. It is here with a touch of "mucho gracios" and the Padre' mentality of Mexico with "get in line, Achtung."

Sal looked at me, but being Cuban understood what I was saying since the Communists wanted Cuba, the businessmen of Latin America and with Mexico being a socialist state and with the state owning all oil wells and Big Business there.

Fred kept looking and drinking and listening which was unusual but could be ready to roll onto some kind of conversation that would tickle his fancy.

Fred asked me, "What do the Irish have to fear if anything?

I said, "Nothing in particular, as long as they too go along with this worldwide system that is this Internet idiocy, where through computers they can alter infant food formulas, or change hospital records and promote mesmorization in New Age Occultism which is silent, but real with a death wish and the ultimate" mark".

Fred asked, "What mark?"

I responded by saying, "You will know in due time. Since we are killing, or murdering our own daily by the thousands, we have multiculturalized America by bringing New Age Aryans along with the swastika and all with Islamic Jihad from the Moslems, as well as other heathenistic cultures. (" Do not be unequally yoked.") Israel is blocking the other heathenistic cultures, plus the world's path, but peace has to reign from within Israel itself to the rest of the foolish Gentile world. Europeanism must certainly propose, "Friends, Romans, countrymen lend me your ears." Caesar now wants what belongs to GOD alone, worship and our lives to live for Him. This Caesar also shall have reign where the sun never sets and for most where it never rises again."

Fred and Sal seem dumbfounded by my filibuster, or was it their drinks that made their minds spin, but thought much slower.

George said, "Would you folks all come at a table in the far dark corner with me? I have something to say."

We all obliged him to the table. This was not George's regular table, or approach at all. Usually George, when he had something important to say would politely ask us to his regular table, not that George had done other wise this time. What is it that George had to say that was so important and did it have anything to do with the Jewish question, I thought to myself?

George began as such, "Did any of you know there is a government decree on all Jewish folks?"

I remained silent and unmoved, as if I did not know anything about it.

George continues, "ANYONE who is not Jewish folk and assists the Jewish folk will be prosecuted to the fullest extent of the law."

I asked George, “What degree this measure serves and why the Jews only?”

All George could reply was, “They have been barred, that is the Jewish folks from leaving America and holding any government positions.”

I thought, “Affirmative action Nazi style.”

The first was not new to me, but the second was and spoke to me of a more serious nature of what we were heading for. Israel was now not just an enemy, but “the enemy.” The “roots” had been severed from us “branches” probably here for good. This “tree” though would still remain whole.

George’s summation was, “I wonder what shall happen to Moshe’ and Henry. And their loved ones?”

I only stared and said nothing. George was an American Biblical who tilled the soil with his hands and could repair just about any type of machinery. George had many grandchildren and great grandchildren and kept track of all of them, as they did of him. His wife had died a few years ago of cancer and since then he would come into John’s Pub mainly for good food and a beer, or two.

As we all had already lowered our voices, so that we could barely hear each other, we decided a few of us to go to my home for some black coffee and more conversation. We left John’s Pub and walked by a few small shops owned by some local Jewish merchants. We could see nothing that would indicate a disturbance, or movement of any merchandise, or anything unusual.

I thought to myself, “The Jews probably knew about the first decree a while ago, but left everything as is in order not to arouse any suspicions. It was after hours and these shops normally would have been closed anyway.”

We walked some more and noticed more than usual that squad cars and a few Guardian Angels were on patrol, but were not ostentatious in the sense that anything was about to happen. We finally reached my single home and I invited George, Sal and Fred in. I got all of us coffee, plus a sandwich to eat, while we played cards just in case the authorities would show up unexpectedly. From now on we all knew America had changed and there would be no revival without the Jewish people. Every tree has "roots". We no longer would have any Messianic Jewry, something I was almost sure had been taken care of by government authority and many unbelievers. I believed they had been incarcerated by preaching the Gospel and were all saints in the Lord. What could the 4 of us do to protect our families, or friends and ourselves?

George suggested in correlation to my silent thought that, "Since I am a Negro man, no one will mistake me for a Jewish folk and that you are all invited at any time to my house, whenever the need arrives or whenever any of you needs friendship."

Would Sal go back to Cuba and if he did, what was there to go back home to and how would he exit from America, but possibly through Canada? No, our stay would be here to see things through, wherever and whatever that meant we had to do. Now that D.C. was being taken over by world dominion in ROME Jerusalem, Berlin, London and New York, we knew we were here for the long haul. If we went along with what this treaty said, we knew that the rest of our natural lives would have to be more of this theatrical reality. We knew also that apologies would be in order for all the known "terrorists", such as ourselves, because we did not hate the Jews, nor did we hate our own country. Yes, one President had made the ultimate change for America and for the worse. Fame is always hard to deal with almost for all, but as for infamy this individual loved it.

It was near midnight and until 12:15 AM, a time when the occult was most active. We continued to discuss our futures, as well as that of our families.

My suggestion was, "Why not work together to form a kibbutz, if private property is going to be confiscated by these environmentalists and in that way our families can be together and supply and meet each other's needs, as well as watch out for each other?"

Sal and I had no immediate family, but Fred did and George's children were all grown up.

I continued, "Never has anyone ever owned land in America, ever since real estate taxes were started. If one became delinquent with 3 years, or less, they can take everything even if one has no mortgage and the mortgage that one does pay is so usurious, yet our government lent to the Soviets billions of dollars for less than 1%, plus gave wheat for livestock which they sold to other countries for military technology. The banks could repossess a home within 3 months if delinquent. Why not also home school any children that need it which would protect them from either lack of law enforcement due to the socialist courts and the daily increase in crime whether it was reported, or not, and more not, than likely. Does not the unemployment rate also include people who enroll in our military, so that the unemployment rate will always appear low. This our government has never told us about. Alas there are too many gangs that run wild and still do and the criminals harass all GOD fearing people for the government, to keep all the believers and moralists in line. Law abiding citizens, GOD'S laws, such as us, have much to fear, because all things have become legal. Our Congress now serves for a lifetime, even though we hold so called elections. We have become like England use to be, when in both the House of Commons and the House of Lords one had to be a relative of an incumbent in order to serve in government. Democracy has certainly become right by might, or majority rules and totalitarianism over anarchy will soon reign. We keep hearing, "peace, peace, let there be peace" and yet there is now no real peace. This peace that is coming is Satan's peace in order to promote one world religion and government. Accolades of praise are coming for this new world leader."

We all finally agreed that a kibbutz would work for us, as a backup in case seizure would occur by the world environmentalists. For months afterward we drew up plans for our survival and kept it secret, even to our own families and relatives. We no longer could rely on outsider, or this new government least of all. For us it was now here, not to protect us, but had become in fact another enemy. The world had gotten smaller, because centralized world order kept control of everything by networking which means each cell,or network, could fall, but would have no affect on the other networks. We had been warned years ago of this world of totalitarianism and refused to listen. Maybe we could have delayed it from spreading like cancer so fast. Now America had real ghettoes and numbers were being counted block by block. Survival of the fittest came to mean, we were in an animal world totally, since man's debauchery went beyond all hope. Each day, hour and minute would be a challenge to survive, because somehow we all knew that what was coming was now inevitable. We could only continue and wait to see where we would be and freewill would become a burden, but nonetheless one, we had to use. There began to appear diseases, plagues, famines to such an extent that even our relatives were dying off one by one. In fact Fred was ill and getting worse and George was already elderly, but because of age he would certainly be looked at differently, or would he? Sal and I were doing okay, because time had been good to us, but for how long we did not know. We had heard that nuclear armaments had been used in some parts of the world, but all radio and television, as well as media, was state of the art world controlled. Were we being told everything supposedly, or was most of it a façade as before? Our movement was limited to a certain radius, as if one was on probation, or parole, and check points were set up and repeated stops had to be made and proper identification shown. This had started with 9/11 and the administration for 8 years that encouraged in defense of the terrorists. My import and export business was really no longer run by me, even though I was doing most of the paper work. Other businesses like mine were doing well, because they dealt in all kinds of contraband, I had only one alternative and that was to go to Israel and possibly learn more about this one world government.

The United Governments of Nations had become what it always was. The United Governments for world businessmen for the promotion of world socialism which meant at first atheism and then the occult. The "social" Gospel had set up this to appear sacred in order to replace GOD with Satan in the people's mind and heart. If Satan could physically appear he almost would.

The unholy trinity was making it's mark and by emulation, not creation, controlling all of our very lives and what was this all about. But nothing more than theatrical reality. Man would not be free anywhere upon this earth anymore for now.

If man would not be stopped, he would eliminate his species with a little help from his friends. God was somehow, even though it became hard to see, faithfully in control. Eventually Fred passed away and Sal and I had no relatives left after a few years and decided on the one previous thing I had thought of before. We had to leave America which would not be to much of a problem, since none of us were Jewish.

Our trip would be two way tickets, but only really going one way and not coming back. We did not really know what age we were in because we did not communicate with too many people and none of us know who was, or were really Christians, since most self-proclaimed Christians either acted not like, or thought like Christians, since they did not read, or understand GOD'S holy WORD. Christian businessmen were always higher priced and Christian bookstores carried New Age books on their shelves. The good life in America was too good. Christians would drive the best cars and wear 4 buttoned suits and eat in the finest restaurants constantly, or these so called "Christians". Christian sports' athletes were multimillionaires and lived high off of the hog. They forgot about what Y'ESHUA said to the rich young man, or did they, or did they even know that part of HOLY SCRIPTURE?

Our society had one way streets; merchandise in stores that was displayed as hodge podge; abbrevations; billboards that would display young women in swim suits but were made up of different women from head to toe; our military especially the Special Forces would be taught to be like an animal one week and then act like a gentleman to a formal affair, such as a dinner and psychiatry had become like Sigmund Freud with his cocaine addiction who stole his psychoanalysis from Dostoyevsky and then the fact that we had 25% of all the world's prisoners and 5% the world's people.

If we arrived in Israel, we could expect a number of different things. We had to seek the real Holy Land and not Rome and it's

7 hills, if that indeed is what it still was? News was slanted and always limited. Hear a lie enough and you will believe it. Pravda was not reporting truthfully as it's name implied. America had become a two fold socialist state. Nazi homosexual Germany and Soviet class warfare, but most of all this love of the uniform and gun mentality that Sal, or I never really took an interest in.

Would the NRA have a revolution? I rather think not. Civil wars are messy, one must use spiritual inner strength and not force to change, if possible, but inform others about a corrupt government. What would Americans do, if anything, if they already let 42,000,000 babies be murdered which meant that 420 rose bowls filled to capacity at 100,000 each would be the number of murders, since 1973. All were without arms and defenseless. Where was this NRA then? The church too was scared straight. We also could not relate to the hoarding of anything, for we had learned that in a kibbutz, not a "village" all was shared and none belonged to one and there was no Germanic sentimentality, or English colonialism, or Anglophilia.

Both of us were dark complexed and could easily pass off for Sabras visiting on business.

The morning we left we flew to none other than London on the SST CONCORDE in about 3 hours time. This SST CONCORDE was an invention of Howard Hughes who also owned at one time TWA and had a fling with Ms. Hepburn. Then we boarded an EL-AL airline jet to Tel Aviv which use to be the capital, but should have always been Jerusalem. Yet the Islamic Arabs wanted it for their false worship. We entered Israel and checked in at a Tel Aviv hotel and started right away to track down Henry and Moshe'.

As I went down to the lobby I met a beautiful young lady whose face lit up the room and whose eyes smiled with much joy. Her compassion could be felt readily as we discussed the situation in the world.

This beautiful woman named Marie, had told me that parts of America had been destroyed physically by nuclear attack and by a rogue state. The curse on America had already begun in America for not staying allied to Isreal. There could be no going back to an enemy that refused to repent for not helping Isreal, instead of Germanic Islam and socialism. I wondered where had all the Hollywooders, Wall Streeters, and the media hid themselves as well as the socialists in government and in positions of authority? I knew Congress had a real underground railroad under the Capital going out of the city.

"Yes, Marie you are all that this man has ever looked for." She was very inquisitive and sometimes over concerned about certain things and was extroverted in a non-abrasive way, but all in all she would make a wonderful wife. If we would marry, then I could remain in Israel forever, as an Israelis' citizen, because of Marie's Jewish background.

Marie said to me, "America chose the wrong cause. I hope you are not offended by what I just said?"

I said, "I am not, because it is so true. Self-preservation never works. America, or Samson, my metaphor, has left Anglophilia, cut his hair and is gone spiritually, but Israel who is so small is still existing, even though one at times can hear fighting in the distant background, such as we can now hear. To not only have something to fight for, but someone. Marie you are that someone."

I would marry according to her religion , Judaism, but would in time try to let her know about Messiah, if she already did not know. This was a time I felt was biblical prophecy. I was truly in the Promised Land. GOD'S promise to Abraham and his heirs from the Egyptian River to the Euphrates River. This would be Israel in the OLAM HABA.

After about half a year, we were married on the day of YOM KIPPUR in a house. Later our pastoral minister rabbi was shot and killed. We remain respectful to it and in our hearts we knew GOD had blessed our marriage and Sal was best man and he too was engaged. We would all have to serve 2 years in the Israelis' military, since we were not ultra-Orthodox, Hasidim, or Naredi. David Ben-Gurion had made it optional for the religious whether, or not to serve in the military. If we survive this we still would have to be ready to defend our homeland. Marie's people were from Krakow, Poland and in fact had helped set up the state of

Israel back in 1948 like Menachem Begin. One of the asinine Hollywooder Jews made a ridiculous statement to the affect that, "One should not begin with Begin," but what did secular Hollywood know about pioneering, except in the field of socialism and immoral perversion? Also Jerry Lewis was nothing more than a spoiled brat who only wore his clothes once and then disposed of them. How could Hollywooders ever live the life of a real Eastern Jew?

"Most of Israel was founded by hardy Russian and Polish Jewry who sought freedom and their own homeland. Central European Jewry and American Jewry were not instrumental in Israel's founding, nor their maintaining the state, but did make good tourists and gave millions in philanthropic causes, but felt they should know what was good for Israel from across the ocean like a television quarterback. The Sabras would have no part of it, at least since Ariel (the Lion of GOD) was prime minister. This nemesis of money, always had strings attached, one's own self-preservation must always come first. Europeanism had affected this part of Jewry and so they could not and did not understand Russian and Polish Jewry. Eastern, not Western family tradition had grown, so the West could not understand the normal natural family. American Jewry never understood church and state, because mate and mate had become one in the same to them, especially American-Germanic-Reformed Judaism, " Marie said.

"Materialism, capitalism, to pure materialism, socialism, developed extravagance for American-Jewry. Even Spielberg supported the Naziphiles of homosexuality. Intermarriage broke down family tradition and even the Consevatives were pro abortion and pro homosexual. In Israel here the Interior Minister would not recognize the Reformed or the Conservative sects of Judaism. He disregarded the Israelis' High Court ruling, something America long ago should have done. The ultra Orthodox and Orthodox both though did hold true to the Old Testament without the key to the heart, a Resurrected Messiah and that Daniel not be read. Messiah had with Abraham and in Daniel appeared as a Theophany and had also appeared again in Israel as King, without the kingdom, because of their unbelief as a nation, a people, so Messiah had come and gone and would again come for the Second Advent for then the "70th Week" could begin," I said.

"Yes, Messiah was always here through the RUACH HAKODESH still in the world, but world Jewry, the veil of Moses had been lied to, not by GOD, many times in the Catholic Church centuries ago laid claim to Peter, a Jew, as first pope. Catholicism did not encourage Scripture. How could it? It did not know it. After all it was not the Jews, but the Romans and it's 7 hills that did say, "do as the Romans do." Antioch believers must have later mishandled the Messianic faith? After all was not this New Age really the reincarnation of the old Roman Empire, or at least it's new leader which was made of bronze and clay?" I questioned.

"One can see that even today in the Gentile world, or church, that other darker foreign Christians do not matter, but yet Israel took in the Ethiopian Falasha, before "black", yes "black" Marxsists' leaders killed no murdered them all. Sudanese Christians would not fare so well. They too would be crucified by another form of socialism, called Islam, "I said.

Now with the right mixture, ECT and others, this new Christianity was actually, "not what does good have to do with evil", but one big happy financial family. Heathenism and demon worship did not matter.

I thought to myself, "now Israel would probably take the bait and soon face annihilation by the Gentile powers, except for Petra, Edom and the remnant."

"To me time is of the very essence every day. Where is this historical prophetic clock at exactly and how long is it to the end of this age and not the end of the world, by the way which does or shall not exist?" I asked.

Marie kept staring at me because my mind had been everywhere, but I knew I needed to share this with her. The Gentile nations would include Arabs too vs Israel, as probably a first strike.

"Why has America followed Masonry and multiculturalism down the tubes? America has a catch 22 so to speak. What could George Washington possibly do? Become King? Was it that he did not trust himself, or was it the fact of what the king of England had done with the law? John Adams would have supported him, but Greek democracy, heaven forbid, with republicanism, English style, were all Western mindsets and could only lasts for a few centuries in peace, if that, or until? Even the Reichstag voted 497-92 for Hitler and the Nazis on March 24, 1933. Did two German candidates run too close an election campaign, so they chose an Austrian, a cousin? When has democracy, or socialism, really ever worked and for how long? Human nature as such, will not allow it, "I said.

"This terrorist Palestinian State can never come to be. It is too late. It is nothing more than the enemy again and it's chance to move in on Jerusalem surrounded by the Gentiles and has the stench of multiculturalism. Where is socialism in the Old Testament in regards to the Israelites? Foreign heathen nations are there, but that is it. The languages are different, the money is different, but most of all their gods or god is different. After the Jordanian Arabs, then what? The radical Syrian Arabs, the sneak attack Egyptian Arabs, the lying Kuwaiti Arabs, the without a leader "Gamaliel" Lebanese Arabs and of course their godless Islamic Jihad and worship of demons, "Marie questioned?

Did America want Israel to be like us, multicultural? Marie's female relatives had to endure coerced infanticide by the homosexual Nazis because procreation of religious moral Jews had to be forbidden. Her relatives committed suicide rather than go to their homosexual harems and their houses of ill repute, as well as fornication and abomination. How many children were molested and murdered? About one and one half million children and Elie Wiesel's book called NIGHT confirms a lot about this pedophilia and also the movie EXODUS when Sal Mineo is asked, "what did they do to you in the concentration camp?" How many times the Old Testament pointed to Messiah? Jeremiah, Abraham, Isaiah, Daniel, Isaac, et cetera. "You shall smite my heel, while I crush your head." Was not Isaac as Abraham's only son? How about in Daniel and the furnace with One and His three friends? Or Jonah and the whale? For how long? Three days and three nights? The Passover and the shedding of blood analogous to Y'ESHUA... Isaiah 53 and His crucifixion and not just any crucifixion. Why would a Major Prophet write about an uncommon crucifixion? Psalm 22 and the list goes on and on does it not? GOD, the FATHER, could not be plainer than this, I thought to myself.

The complete Hebrew Old Testament with no pick and choose deletions, or revised twice editions if one chooses to do so and would believe the truth. Either one has faith and that sin and heaven were both taken care of , or they are deceiving themselves into believing, oh no, not a tradition, what tradition, but a bold face lie of Satan the father of all lies.

Arguments don't explain the mystery. As Rocky Marciano once said. "When one is angry they cannot think." "Come let us reason together."

To be obstinate is ignorance, but ignorance in the sense that they choose not to believe. Deafness of the heart now that shall make one Pharisaic. There is also malice, contentiousness, pride or whatever else excuse one can conjure up, but shall never do, or undo the RESURRECTION. In the end there is eternal light, or eternal darkness and the conscious state does not die. All these things are so true. What would our children, or child come to believe about Messiah? Oh, not that there was just GOD, but as to whom His Son, Messiah is personally now and of course RUACH HAKODESH making up the Trinity. If Messiah had not come would the world be here now? Man would have reduced himself by now to oblivion. If billions of people were dead already, why would it stop after that and since the process of life continued on, it must mean that Messiah was continuing on, or how else would the world be in existence? In the Old Testament never is the term Christianity used. Why? Who was Messiah coming for? Was it not His own, as a nation, if they would only believe? This would have fulfilled the "70th WEEK" of Daniel, but yet GOD knew the future, so hence this "LAST WEEK" is unfulfilled. Did

GOD interfere with man's freewill? In JUDGES, THE BOOK OF DANIEL and other BOOKS, Gentiles were involved. What about RUTH and Naomi? Or Jacob crossing his hands or arms with his 2 sons? Messianic saints, such as Moses, David, Jeremiah, Isaiah, Joseph, Isaac, Jacob, Abraham, Daniel, Hezekiah, et cetera all those believers, plus many more, when Messiah had not yet appeared and now, when He had already appeared there is a lack of Messianic faith. The Promise that He was coming. Read carefully, not to set up His Kingdom alone, but what else? The Gentiles now had to be included for "even the dogs eat the crumbs that fall off of the table." And why again? Because of lack of faith by Jews only who were no longer Jews in the faith even up until now and shall be for most. Messiah would return not one time for choice for that has already been made possible, one is truly saved, but twice. So Messiah would appear 3 times. In 1 A.D.: the TRANSLATION of the church; and to set up the OLAM HABA. The first appearance was in conclusion, for all Old Testament, New Testament, saints up till the TRANSLATION time, or the Second Advent. The second appearance for some and the third for ruling over the earth with the remnant and the Gentiles with glorified and unglorified bodies from both. The Biblical 3 speaks to all this GOD/man. Three times same GOD/man before ascending, after He descended, returning fully to an earthly kingdom. Born to us mortals, like us mortals, not in eternity then. "Always was, always is, always will be." The Body being partial, the Body then and the Body coming back to rule in the OLAM HABA. So one time or two is the basic question? How shall He appear, if it be the first time? As a baby, but yet already before appearing in a Theophany in Abraham and in Daniel? We can say for sure what already has been. It need not be repeated to the religionists, or ACLU atheists.

Marie and I were expecting our first child and my wife was fulfilled, even though the world was in turmoil all around us. It started to seam like the world was looking to Israel for peace negotiations worldwide. Many promises were being made that the world situation for peace was well in hand. As days and months went by, America had become part of the European community no matter the geography, but now "the kings of the East" were forming their own pact, or peace pipe, even though they did appear bent on this peace too. The dragon and Gog and Magog were quiet for no long lasting peace, after all Communism meant most of all, anti-humanity.

Sal and I started our own business and both had small families and knew more now about the world situation, than we had in America's illusion of grandeur. Would the West ever meet East and if it did would it be good, or bad? Instant telecommunications, plus lasar scans and astral projections were in use. Privacy was almost null and acquisition of life's essentials became harder and harder to get. How many millions, had died before the first day that Moshe' and Henry had to leave America? No, not love America, or leave it at least for real patriots. The others could go, even though we left our hearts with America, we nonetheless left only physically. Many others had left both and some kept themselves physically there, but were spiritually foreign to America. As more months went by, we finally had a lead on Moshe' and Henry in Israel. We knew that Israel could never extradite their own back to America like Churchill, or FDR had done to the Russian peasants. America had sold out it's own liberty for this New World Order. We noticed that both in America and in Israel, there were all kinds of surveillance cameras that were first used for traffic violations, but continued on to become Big Brother. One's private life had become public and world socialism was in vogue. Red China, we had heard might be making a conventional military move within so many years across the dried up Euphrates River.

It was winter here and Israel snow was falling in Jerusalem that gave Messiah's birth a special meaning for me, even though His birth did not occur in winter. Marie was gradually starting to see what Messiah had to do with the Jewish holidays and feasts. She was seeing all she had missed that fulfilled her heritage by Messiah. Finally Marie accepted Y'ESHUA. She would be raised Judeo-Christian, Old and New Testament which meant Messianic Jewry, as Y'ESHUA and the disciples had worshipped.

Our daughter, Rachel was a beautiful child with green eyes like her mother and light hair, and with a temperament like mom. She was a joy to our lives.

Getting back on track about Henry and Moshe', we found out they had stayed in a flat and were now living somewhere in Tel Aviv the ex-capital of Israel. Our search continued and finally we located them in their flat complex where both families were in tact and healthy. Their trip to Israel had been quite smooth and they had much catching up to do with us and vice versa. We shared our stories with each other and came to a full knowledge that Americanism from England had indeed been part of the European-Americanism, which meant the old nation had lost us, but we nonetheless loved her for what we knew she had once stood for. Our allegiance was to an old glory that once meant not just physical freedom, but religious life and liberty and justice, yes justice, even for the poor and downtroddened, something Americans had departed from GOD, to a New Age god.

In Israel was where things too were changing quickly and the electricity in the world situation was coming it seemed to a cataclysmic occurrence. We were now again feeling what we once felt in America, even though we were in Israel. Our movement became confined even more and at times small tremors of the hot earth would occur. Israel too was feeling birthpangs, to say the least and we could almost tell something was about to occur and as to what it was, we just could not be sure.

Marie, Rachel and I relied upon our faith as time went dangerously on. Was this near the end of the age, or an age, where political ramifications were too fast for a spiritual rejuvenation that nonetheless always moves slower? Now this New Age Movement was moving fast, because it was not spiritual rejuvenation, but spiritual heresy, or debauchery. It was from the very pits of Hell itself, if possible and was growing as a monstrosity, or as a cancerous tumor does on a healthy body. We had in fact heard that this beast itself was soon to stay right here in Israel and we were shocked with fear inside, knowing that now we were locked into this ungodly being and could understand why all the nations were meeting for one reason or another in the Middle East. This age had started in the century of John Locke and now Shirley McClaine, John Denver, Churchill, ex-Senator Hatfield and many more were part of the dabbling occult. The iconoclasts in America had become, or were either socialists, atheists, New Agers, et cetera. The world all around us continued to be decadent and hectic. All nations we knew were going to come against Israel in the near future. Nations that could have been allies seen the opportunity to promote this one world government. Even though so called allied nations supported Israel, they were not for it to be a light unto the nations, but as a darkness in a dark evil world. This was drawing all nations to Israel, the heathen Gentile nations. That did everything, but encourage the Judeo-Christian faith which Messianic Jewry was.

Marie, Rachel and I had planned to make a trip to America, but felt even though Marie was Jewish and Rachel half Jewish and a Sabra, the risk was too great and for me it would be out of the question. We stayed within the smaller and smaller confines of Israel that now looked like a lot less, than Abraham's Covenant. Terrorists' groups were recognized as freedom fighters and legal organizations. Nationalities had disintegrated which made getting the Gospel out more difficult, but one religion started to stand out worldwide. It seemed to us that this peace was superfluous and superficial, but most even in Israel, followed it because of the promised peace that seemed to be occurring worldwide which gave us a false sense of security.

One day we received an Internet letter from George in America who we thought was no longer alive. He did not say as to the why but we felt that something major must have occurred. George had stayed to his own faith and was continuing as he always had, close to the soil and became stronger for it. George had never played follow the leader in civil rights, or to him, reversed racism, but was one individual who tilled his small property, as his father had, and who kept his real faith and did not trade it in for political expediency.

He had once said, "He saw his own people fall by the way side by materialism and false illusions and it hurt him deeply inside."

Similar to what Rev Shaul had said to his people, or about his people, "If they only would believe."

We knew Sal and me, that George would stay the way he was no matter what happened even to him. George was always a true blooded American Biblical who was a veteran, a farmer, a Biblical scholar and would never give in to expediency, or leisure, or the lie. George was a man who represented the Truth first and foremost.

We wrote back to George and had asked George, "Is there anything he needed?"

Of course George wrote by Internet back that, "Everything is as he had expected it to be."

George was quite literate and self-educated as a peasant, almost a Rasputin as such. We always felt George's GODLY wisdom was upon us, whenever we met, even though George was of few words. A, if you will "George Washington Carver" who was told, "You take care of the peanut and I'll take care of the world." George did just that, and our George's "peanut" was the Word of GOD also George was now in Arizona. I told all this to my wife.

Marie then said, "The Arabs wanted all the Jews, years ago, to be sent to Arizona and New Mexico in America to live and stay and to make it their homeland."

I could not believe my ears. This then could expain the truth about Islamic Arabs and the Palestinian State back then, with no room for the Jews, or the state of Israel. This was as bad as Nazi Germany's liquidation of all Jews in the world, if they could have done so and not for economic reasons, far be it so, but because of the German-Jews moral stand done against Nazi Germany's sexual deviancy. These world wide evil powers of anti-Semitism were growing and The Red Horse was out, Communism and then some.

George had said, "The climate there was good for his health, since it was dry where he was at," even though George was about 4 scores and 7 years old.

He was like Caleb in the Bible, when he had asked for his land at 80 years of age, so he could work it. There was no “social” security then.

George was truly a GOD fearing man. Israel was being broken down into North, South, East and West and some how fewer and fewer Jews were surviving and had become like multicultural America. America’s younger days in the South had always seen a rebellious area and never learned what true liberty and justice for all meant.

I thought, “Was not Judas Iscariot the only Disciple from the South?”

George also said, “America seemed like a foreign nation with many languages and foreign cultures.”

I had called to recollection, while I was back in the States, what foreigners were doing to homeland Americans by government decree and how arrogant they had become, or how arrogant they already were when they entered America. They came to America for a ready made life of luxury and leisure and wealth, a sort of Casa Blanca and play it again Sam and this time it was Uncle Sam. Neo-Nazism had controlled and murdered 51,000,000 babies and yet promoted these foreigners into America with the rich and well educated’s approval. We had 300,000,000 and after 51,000,000 murders, we still had some 300,000,000 years later. There was no attrition, because rich foreigners came to America to get their share and to do harm to America. Their’s was not to flee aggression, but to flee jurisprudence like Khruschev’s son did in Rhode Island. They had long ago heard of our most perfect union. What union? No one ever said or did they? There was the corrupt Teamsters, the Screen Actors’, The Union of …… What union had this been, since it was never made clear as to what sort of Masonry this involved? America had always appeared Anglo-Saxon in every sense of the word. No other culture or nationalities ruled at the top, even though tokens were thrown in during Presidential elections to make it appear democratic. The hidden facade about America was that England and Saxony, or the Teutonics always had control, or wanted to control at the helm. At America's founding it had been all right, but as years passed, even non-Christians started to take full control and much prejudice ensued against real Christians. Even German-Jews began to act and look like their previous nemesis. Anglophilia would not release it's colonial role over America. Everything was inherited including the color red as in Redcoats and England's liberalism. Would England ever let go? "The British are coming, the British are coming." I could see that if England fell, which it had, except for Arab oil, America too would tumble. There was no relinquishing their hold onto their last and biggest colony, America, of course, with Islam's money and wealth.

Why the war with their cousin Germany? Self-preservation had to be preserved and nothing else would do until Germany was ready to eliminate England's rule over America and wanted to rule it first hand, or destroy it and not through England, but through Islam. Catholicism would not do, no matter what and no matter how much America wanted them to.

Going back in history Japan though would spoil their mindset, for it would attack Pearl Harbor causing FDR's blueblood to concede to England's side with no reservation when the Yalta Conference took place. Nonetheless the English blueblood, FDR, kept England in control by appointing Joseph Kennedy as Ambassador to England and could not allow uncontrolled Nazi Germany with Hitler to do what even some of the Krupps, Fricks and Chamberlains could not restrain, or could they and was it just the Austrian? He had gone too far, or had he? FDR and Churchill would find another way to once again ingratiate themselves by selling out the Eastern store of millions upon millions and to this very day they continue, or at least their kind continue to promote Communism and socialism in Red China and in Islam. More Capitalism to help our enemies. The honor of capitalism to promote socialism to full fruition into more Communism. MOST FAVORED NATION STATUS along with Moscow and North Korea and Havana for the time being. Who really had won out? It already began to look like Communism had. Albert Pike and his Italian friend in the Illuminati had devised 3 World Wars and there was one more to go and did not America tell England to release Trotsky? When Russia was striving many times to align itself with other Christian nations, England only responded by claiming Russia was their enemy and much too barbaric. Then Stalin arose and Communism with it and the Anglophiles could see nothing, but love and compassion not for Russia itself but this foreign ideology called the Soviets and its butcher with the moustache. Remember the Franco-Germanic political philosophy came home grown in Europe. America was prospering well and that was all that mattered to most of the well educated and the elite. It had forgotten about universal brotherhood, not kissing cousins and freedom for all in Europe or at least half of Europe. One and one half million peasants would be sent to their sure death, because Churchill and FDR had never given up, that is had never given up on self-preservation, but had given up the spoils of the victors in war, including Hungary, Poland, one half of Germany, Korea and many others so called freedom which was not to last even one century (1945-2045) and allowed in-roads into America right after World War II. Expediency by way of dealing with Satan himself and knowing full well. It did not matter about Catholicism's Poland, or Hungary, or Kim Il Sung's Korea, as well as Southeast Asia and Angola and other African nations, but one would say how could they know the future? If they were not European colonies, then the hell with them all and Russia of course. Let the Soviets and the Chinese Communists murder millions upon millions and take whatever they wanted, but only that dear old Londontown be forever preserved and who knows the "beast" just could come out of there.

Italy was socialistic and since 1946 had a different government every year.

France went the same way by the Jesuits and Catholicism and earlier was in opposition to Germany in the 19th Century and were a socialistic nation.

Poland was Catholicized through the Roman Papacy and the Vatican and thought themselves to be always of nobility.

Germany was reunited to become once again a nemesis to Israel.

Greece was a Communist country and held onto their envy and so called democracy, or at least they thought.

Spain was socialistic and had Pablo Picasso, another diehard socialist. And the list grew, because expediency by the rich and well educated was used over and over again. The Communists felt otherwise and also felt that only men would hold despotic positions of power and could always take over the weaker sex and so far they had time and again. It had happened in India with Indira Ghandi and in the Philippines, Argentina and almost in Israel and also in England.

The West and parts of the East had fumbled the ball and made matriarchal rule over patriarchal, while the Communists were steadfast on their male dominance. The wild wild West according to Washington D.C. indeed did become wild and was inflicting it's weakness to other countries and continents world wide. Feminism was the way socialism would be swallowed up by Communism. Equality came full circle to include even the animal world for animals had evolved to equal rights, even though this reasoning was no better than ours, such as women in the infantry, women in, or on police forces, women driving trucks, et cetera. This hodge podge of insecurity had come to ruin America more than one could ever imagine. Men were afraid to speak out against feminism, or infanticide and the young took control over the elderly with the elderly wanting only to be left alone to live their lives, or was it the younger generation who cared not for them, but only what they could acquire materialistically? Also family was exchanged for tribalism and gangs and gangsterism, so that no accountability would be made to a Father figure through the biological father.

Every thing became legal and doing your own thing was just this almost anarchy. Even the Negro citizen had been corrupted by the rich and well educated for they were told they had the most perfect solution, and little or no effort would have to be made in order for 2+2=4.

There would be this enlightened people, free in slavery never to mention a worse kind of slavery to come where all the slaves would be equal, after all why should one make more than anyone else with more talent?

The only thing that wasn't told was that wealth would still be unequally distributed, but of course that had nothing to do with equality since the rich and well educated had been involved. This was their exclusionary rule. Higher wages, higher taxes, but not real wealth, spiritual, or otherwise.

I had to remain firm for love of my country, while I saw its spiritual heart being ripped out by avarice and power. Always this #1 mentality, but as to what only the elite knew and just that America was the greatest show on earth. The entertainers of Hollywood were magnifico. Constant ego phrases by the rich, such as to size and wealth, but not of heart, or spirituality. With grabbers and whippersnappers getting anything they could. They sold out their own nation, as well as people, for this near future utopia where nobody would, or wanted to work and blossoms would bloom year round. This boredom with honor, duty, honesty and hard work was not important. America had found a new way to unleash this most perfect union, or world order, or course, with Europe's atheism. There had to be more to life, than just envy, jealously, self-righteousness, self-esteem and the 5 sensuous senses? The quintessential happening was on its way, and now Israel had this quintessential being ready to partake, or would appear to the entire world, to have all the answers. Of course, their own disgruntledness was of their own seeking, but someone had to be inconvenienced. It was the morbid fear of loosing it all and at any time that worked on America's materialistic mind.

Yes, America became indistinguishable between socialist states and almost looked like the Eurodollar. One individual in America, more than anybody else one could think of, if they so chose to do so, had totally destroyed America's spiritual lifeline because of the position he held and for how long and for his foreign ideology and immorality. This person had set in motion, or had injected America with lethal cancer. Agencies, companies, corporations, government officials elected and non-elected, so called business partners, too, were placed with exact care, to do their most possible worse for us, for as long and as far and as fast as one could do. What made it more incredulous was the fame that this individual was received with everywhere with accolades showered upon him. Never going back, or looking back, just straight ahead mowing everything down to the demise of America. It was like a novel where the victim would become the criminal and the criminal the hero in the story. Hollywood could write no better script and in fact wrote most all of it. This was in defense of the terrorists. Pure Marxist/Leninism, America by apathy chose it's own kind of cancer. An entire decade day by day immorality, treason, corruption, murder, et cetera. What one cannot see doesn't hurt them. The nation had become, or this individual became like the nation, there was nothing to compare from, or if compared from the lowest scale. Let us not give this individual this much credit for all his shortsightedness.

America would survive, but for how long no one knew and what would be the Masonic outcome? It would not be absolved this time. The land would spit us out. A few voices objected, but the court of public opinion through it out. There was to be no objections raised against the terrorists in the court of public opinion, if there was one at all. Fine dining and fine dressed and always selling out to the highest bidder, because hatred of one's own country was greater while other men could and would lay down their life for another. Never oppose the so called "underdog" mentality. "Honor not the mighty and respect not the poor" was forgotten.

Coming to America now to escape prosecution and not persecution and justice, plus to embark on a government sponsorship of a totality of freedom. They could now do what they wanted and would be handsomely rewarded for it. The criminal element came not to hide in America but to seek recognition for their malevolent conduct and knew all would be well. This was not the attitude of immigration with appreciation, but to escapism where now in America all things had become legal. It was an iconoclast culture something like Mao, or Stalin had been but was candy coated red to appear even moral, but whose mentality and morality could one be talking about? "White" was the presence of all colors "black" was the absence of all colors, so which choice had America decided on, right, or wrong?

All these thoughts continued to go through my mind and even the fact that the swastika had become to mean something good and collectible, but as to what nobody said. Even India's original swastika where rat temples are worshipped came again into play. Was I concerned about the rodents? (It was Hinduism, Islam, Buddhism, Marxism, Nazism, et cetera!) What had American Nazi homosexual NAMBLA imported from their cousins? America was ready for this occultic symbol and ideology. Why were the Masons involved with the Arabs and the Nazis? Some related to symbolism called anti-American. This New Age of Barbarism was reminiscent of Auschwitz and it's crude Germanic ovens from the Krupps.

Communism grew into New Age philosophy. It had to through attrition. The Germanic-Franco Philosophy was born and raised in Europe and no where else. Why "race" and class warfare I thought? The rich and elite knew to keep everyone at each other's back. Also first Nazi-Germany had endorsed homosexuality from the top down which the Soviets did not, and second the Soviets knew what the West would do to supply them with all that they needed, home grown class warfare. Red China was included, but would be much worse.

Hitler and Stalin were good friends, so the socialists had to die for the ultimate, the Communists, or Communism. This is what all socialists, or socialisms directly pointed towards this Europeanism stayed till the end in Berlin and Europe did not want a "Stalin" in proper Europe, but Russia would be okay. As for FDR and Churchill one proceeded onto infamy and the other dabbled. Both were already deceived by the enemy.

Never a World War with all the nations involved, but on the horizon was just that, a real World War with the "beast".

Ours had been a war within Europe mainly and ended in the Orient somewhat. If we could not defeat tiny Nazism, plus Japan and Italy, how could we defeat the ever presence of an all encompassing ideology of Communism let alone the entire New Age? Red China's Peking and Russia's Moscow, Cuba's Havana, North Korea, India, et cetera all now were very major in this world wide ideology.

Since there appeared to be no real nation that upheld GODLY jurisprudence, the world community had taken hold of socialism in many different forms, innate, or not, and Communism was coming to form, but now had to deal with a real personality who here was some one not an organization, government, or ideology. There still was this clash of ideology vs the occult itself. Yet both were quite evil. The worse of two evils? The enemy was drowning his own and was coming for his own at the top levels of evil.

How had America lived such a short life?

One group had an underdog mentality which proved disastrous, while another group went along with the winner no matter what. Both had been in error, because there had been no moderation and both followed group philosophy, or even individualism, of do your own thing. Many cultures that were here did just that, but more in the latter days that these "saints" were stressing and coercing this "diversity", or this pulling apart with such non-friction. This squeaky wheel always got government and the rich and well educated's oil.

Stressing always the facial differences and antagonisms from which the rich prospered as usual. This nothingness, or emptiness meant to harm, or destoy the American spiritual body. Non-assimilation by racism, religions, nationalities, rich vs poor, elderly vs young, male vs female, black vs white vs red vs yellow vs brown, male vs male, female vs female, but not occult vs atheism. This was their "diversity".

This trend, downfall, continued for quite sometime with one's own neighbors not caring, or knowing about each other. This ungodliness of alienation with more than one time too many criminals becoming the poster boy for the jurists, especially the defense and trial lawyers and the judges as well as the pragmatic politicians. Forever getting their wheels greased by governments' POLITICAL CORRECTNESS, Lenin style.

A mental issue such as more schizophrenia, or demonic possession coming in epidemic proportions and these mentally ill held positions of authority in power. The normality of society had become reprobation and the called abnormal were the few remaining who took abuses from a majority. Seeing the end of the age not because it was so, but because American Christians did not want to be inconvenienced. They did not want to suffer through lack of convenience. Being the fact that it might be so, that is the end, the world continues and America is barely perceivable anymore, since depravity had gotten here first. This depravity was honored both in action and in silence by trophies or money, and not honor, such as " Honor your Father and your Mother", if one had one around, or one had any at all.

This exploitation of being great, or at least saying, we are great, when it was not what America needed, but goodness from above and humbleness from us. This dress rehearsal of World War II that now was on the world stage with it's degradations continued. GOD'S name could only be heard in profanity. Again this Samson had cut his hair and lack of self-discipline and GODLY faith came to bring about America's spiritual demise. This "Delilah this Woman" had infected Samson.

All along man in America thought it was through his own achievements alone. He achieved his own vanity and eventual downfall. This greatest was just a façade for ego, fear, and loss of mundaneness. Even the churches were flowing along the river with state sanctioning, while the state held the mind and the heart and not the hand of GOD. The Roman handshake was not followed where GOD cannot let go, but we always do. The regular handshake which in vogue always let's go. Unpatriotic? The warrior like Germanic-Franco political philosophy carried it's virtue also to America and America's biggest war was not fought on a physical battlefield, but a spiritual one and had always been.

The weapons were unbelief, materialism, ego, vanity that attacked the American body and left it sick.

Again the church was silent and did not respond to the cry and rationalized in the mind to reform, or even prophesized, when it should have eulogized. " Speaking in tongues " that were foreign that nobody even knew what language was official. Everybody was seeking their rights, or right, that were not unalienable, but their right to be wrong, no matter what. This too was tolerance, diversity, and ego. Egocentricity, or machismo had become the American mindset and faith was in what one could only see. We knew what Roman Catholicism was, at least some, or few of us, but also Protestantism was too scared and ad to rationalize about good vs evil. Think out every issue before anything could occur. The heart of the issue had become anything but from the heart. Jewish backaches continued and most of American Jewry had hierniated discs. Y'ESHUA'S cross? They too had lost their roots. The left behind had no sense of direction, but would try to make the best of it in America through extravagance.

The entertainment had become debauchery, as the rich and well educated nonetheless endeavored it in real life. America had died and in the spring of it's life, there would be no plowing and at harvest there would be no reaping, but only weeping and gnashing of teeth, or reaping the whirlwind.

This individual turning technical revolution was sinking humanity further from humaneness. The status quo kept their hierarchy and promoted more of the same, this world's insanity. Why was the world insane and was America becoming spiritually retarded as a collective body? America has supposed that the moment was more important, than the literal and eternal future. After all, right now the status quo was not giving up this luxury and heaven on earth for them was forever in the here and now. The other was for a later time and for some no time at all. This could wait, or not to be believed in. Faith usually meant to us to wait in time, but whose time? GOD, or ours? The exchange for ego to accrue? Why even the poor in America had become so affluent that homelessness became an occupation and a profession, as well as panhandling and prostitution too. This was feminism's careerism along with lesbianism.

As more of these visions made up a historical perspective, as such for me, I started to realize the present was most important for that is where history stood. In other words we as individuals were making and would make history as a people and not the rich and well educated, because with this collective body it would occur. The people followed like blinded sheep, or a herd of cattle be it good, or be it evil.

Now that Europeanism had grown more and was poisoning the rest of the world with debauchery and atheism, after all who educated Ho Chi Minh? This new government had instilled the draft even in America, or course, with sovereignty and not national at that. America was for that. As to the why, no normal person, if one could find one, could explain.

NAFTA, GATT, NATO, the UNITED NATIONS, et cetera all were correlated and orchestrated for this one world government. Had I entered the fire itself coming from the frying pan? I was not like chicken little saying, "the sky is falling", but after all a world leader was right here, or would be here in Israel. Sometimes when no one has nothing or at least only a little, they have more courage and are not afraid, because when one who had never had anything, there is nothing for them to miss, or to fear, in regards to mundaneness. Fear that any day one may take all away and by force and government, alone has a vested interest in acquiring from others that which is not theirs and usually do it through unsurious taxes in capitalism and in socialism by blood. "There is nothing to fear, but fear itself." Yet he did not practice what he preached, but caved into socialism for he too feared all might be lost and much was and so obliged by signing the store away and at that to a well trained butcher. America I thought always had this morbid fear of self-defeat that is why they continually make one hear the ingratiating terms, such as we are the greatest but at what? We are the biggest? We are the best, quality of life only, or bigger is better, et cetera. All to convince oneself that this morbid fear had to be suppressed and as long as we had materialism the rest could go fend for themselves. What one does not, or shall never see, or know, nor wants to see, or know, need not concern one. This was part of America's demise, Big business was always CIA-KGB types. This phobia of being without. Without all these necessitates and at that this pinnacle of civilization, we cannot speak out too loudly against our enemies, or so called friends. We must have self-preservation and remain pusillanimous in the face of the enemy. Give in, just give in a little more and all shall be well, but all would not be well and hence now I find myself in a foreign land and homesick for America, the soil of my birth, but yet I cling to yet this self-preservation, Roman style, even though I am in the real Promised Land, not yet completed by GOD. America had learned to accept this fear from the media which of course had innately gotten it from Pulitzer and Pulitzer from possibly Masonry to remain furtive, or covert, about one's so called success. This time though this one world leader does appear to want to reveal to all and to be subservient to him with the power invested in him and nothing short shall do. Now it would appear that this mutation on life had turned out to be the only natural, normal one amongst all the billions and yet criticisms were found not against him personally, since his morals were inherited and beyond this world, but against GOD.

Attack the individual, at least, since he might be different, or because he must not be different there is nothing original in evil and this New Age is actually ancient vileness, evil just as before the flood people got married and went along their merry way. It is only new, because we at this time shall experience what has already been prophesized and it is new to us personally, but also this is the " 6th day ". The future is " open " only to believers as this so called New Age makes all others doomed and unsaved and cannot see. Even parents treat their children, as possessions (day care) or objects that belong only to them or the state as such believe anything they do had to be for their good that is for themselves. Objective-evil that is a part of our very nature and " subjective evil " only subscribes to the notion that man is good, but it is his environment that has made him bad. If this would be true, then what happened to Adam who was placed in a perfect environment or paradise where there was no evil only the allowed intrusion of Satan by man into his world in a stand up angelic form, but unable to control man, because of man's freewill? Freewill can mean to do good, or to do evil, with the latter never of GOD. That is why GOD chooses. What environment made man, or Adam sin, or fall, if one does believe in good vs evil, or GOD vs Satan?

How would have Adam sinned without no sin and in a perfect environment? Oh yes, I thought it was Eve, but what if Eve would not have been there to be deceived would Adam knowingly still have sinned?

In obedience: listening, or reading, not just hearing and keeping in one's heart and mint, but also doing, or not doing, are the hardest. A total of 3 step process and without all 3 there is no obedience, hence rebellion, or sin. Did Adam listen to what GOD said? He had to and not optional as Adam knew. Otherwise why would GOD band him from the Garden? Did he keep? In other words did he retain what GOD had said. GOD had certainly approached him. Not come as you will, because of yet, he did not sin and knew in his mind of no sin. Adam kept, but for a short time and that was when religion was brought in. Satan said, " GOD did not say? "Satan's do's and don't's. Here is where religions fail, because they do not get to real listening, but just hearing. Listening is the first part of the process and must be included in obedience, and keeping and in doing, or in this case not doing, then is GOD's will served. If Adam obeys there is no sin, or fall and Adam and Eve live in the Garden in perfection forever. Adam's body brought sin in, Messiah took it all out with Him. Y'ESHUA struggled in his soul at Gethsemane, but an angel came to inspire Him. Could Y'ESHUA have sinned?

Theological in the sense that Adam was created, " YESHUA was Begotten, one in being with the Father. " There was again no sin in Adam, but freewill was there to choose, but in GODLY obedience, not in disobedience. If Adam does not sin, then there would be no Bible. The Chosen People would been all, because all still could, or would, have been innocent, or without sin wouldn't they? The time of the first sin was early in time itself and became transcendent, because it was committed by them, Adam and Eve, both created beings. Eternity was gone, along with innocence and a perfect environment and Hell became opened to man, because of man's will and because man did not listen to GOD's audible voice. Without this sin of Adam and Eve, the Tree of Life would have been… and death physically and spiritually would not have occurred?

Would time have started for eternity? Only after Adam sinned does Gensis speak of "the heel and the head". Being able to sin in innocence in the perfect Garden and then banished from the Garden so that Adam's eternity would be not continual from the Tree of Life's fruit. Did the tree die, or was it removed by GOD and how long after sin? A similarity could be made in the sense that Messiah who knew no sin and Adam who also had not sin did the opposite, but one in GOD'S will and the other against GOD'S will. As I endeavored to contemplate now the Protestantism of America's Founding, I became disillusioned by the fact, not so much of slavery, but the denial of miracles and isolationism of individual relationships, because GOD is all about relationships. Worship of the Father, or to glorify GOD, through the SON. This "anguish in independence" Adam maybe? To add to this, the problem of Roman Catholicism coming in an "ecstasy in chains". Adam after sin maybe? In other words, materialism for the truth having nothing to do with Christianity in the American Biblical sense.

America had slaves and hunger, yet the church refuses to help spiritually our own here. The tenses are correct. We travel worldwide to promote our religions, or Europeanism's religion and yet foster care, infanticide both grow and grow. Let us help our own American family first each and everyone. Stop avoiding our first immediate family by travelling world wide. The American family needs to know America's GOD first. It is as if a mother and a father with their own children serve in many civic organizations, or church organizations, but forgot their own children. Rev Shaul called this "worse than an unbeliever

", yes this family too. Delegating for dead beat dad shall not do, only biological fathers and adoption works for different reasons. When serving others through GOD, we serve GOD Himself. This though is not worship, but serving. Adoption is difficult, because pimpism in court exists and preys on our children by these parasites in the judicial system. This " blind leading the blind " by so called jurists is absurd. Let nothing become an idol before a holy GOD. Not serving Him, not giving, not sacrificing, but only and through Him shall His eternal will be done. We are all foreign missionaries. All saints are missionaries of some sort. Some have even made their worship an idol.

A Jewish grandmother once said," If you are a believer in Y'ESHUA not only must one proselytize, but all must be actively in someway opposing infanticide. "

In 1898 Webster's Dictionary the meaning for any abortion is infanticide. It is this lessening of good vs evil. The murdering of all infants in and out of the womb.

I knew of one couple that had to picket one at a time so that their property would not be confiscated. While one picketed the other at home prayed, but also had to remain apart by law because if husband and wife would picket together, the government could literally have taken their home.

CHAPTER V

THE REMNANT AND THE GENTILE WORLD

As months went by, we met more Messianic Jews in Israel and others from all over the world. They were coming back home to their Promised Land which for generations they had not seen. They could only dream of it, but now that dream had become a reality. Israel seemed to be getting shorter, or smaller and not to mention Jews were surviving the revived anti-Semitism in the world. I was glad I had met my Jewish wife. We were as one in Messiah Y'eshua and were carrying on a Biblical tradition of staying within the only faith. " Do not be unequally yoked. " We were hoping our daughter would too marry a man in the future who knew messiah, but we would encourage and teach, but never coerce her into such an important decision for life, even if one could, and when and if she made it. " Do not be unequally yoked." We did allow her only to date believers.

Henry and Moshe' were near to Messiah and their long lost faith that was so rich in heritage, richer than any in the world, since this was the very roots of Christianity. "Salvation is of the Jews." So much Jewishness in the entire Bible, how could one deny whom GOD had chosen through Abraham's faith, as His special seed? Y'eshua was a Jewish man, as GOD in the flesh and "the Word became flesh." What a wondrous joy I could feel as I knew that I was in GOD'S will. I could not support the physical Israel, because as of yet, prophecy had not been completed, but the spiritual Israel was approaching and in Y'eshua. I had much joy for this Promised Land. This New Jerusalem that was to come down from heaven and the expectation of seeing all the Brit

Hadasha and the Old Testament Saints in the future as GOD 'S Word had so lovingly said.

When was the seed in me really planted, and if planted, what would make it grow? Theatrical reality was all around, even now in Israel and especially in Israel, but in the atmosphere there was this yearning to see this Messiah even though the physical realm was becoming more dangerous, as well as the spiritual. I could feel the Spirit and my convictions and conscience, no matter what, could not be changed, no matter also the physical condition, or state. It was this constant joy and not state of mind, happiness, that filled my heart and soul. It was not a physical type of freedom even though our freedom was still not totally restricted.

I found out that freedom of one's conscience is what mattered most and could only be through Messiah and only in mortal human time. We grew in the Lord as one, because He was fulfilling our life to help and do for others before ourselves. My rights did not matter, but my fellow man's rights and as well as my own responsibilities and hopingly he would reciprocate with the same kind of Christian love and if he did not I would through Y'eshua continue to give up myself and it is in this that I was reborn.

There were no isms involved in the faith, the faith of our fathers of Abraham, Isaac and Jacob. A worldwide religion could never be especially when it gave credit to itself and the flesh and not to Messiah.

Spreading the Gospel meant not catechism, or the Synod. To American Biblicals was first to share with others who were unbelievers and not to entertain, or beg, or argue, maybe plea, but to come into contact with different ones each day who had never heard.

There are always people we never really have met, or took the opportunity to share his command for us to do. There are many that never really hear it in person, personal via one on one and when it is done, or not done in churches, it is usually legalisms. They only hear about salvation for themselves and not about their responsibility to their fellow man, yet GOD shall do most all the work? How would one hear it, but yet people have been saved with just a Bible. The Bible though can translate through Ruach Hakodesh into salvation. Even to one's own family talking salvation could become a death sentence, because it was forbidden. This is not a delegated television responsibility, or calling, but a command in the army of the Lord. Delegating is for elections and the idiot box does not suffice through finances. There are more Christians in Red China, than America and they live in a totalitarian state. GOD works through Ruach Hakodesh. Everything was delegated, even man's thinking to computer, unto government, sovereign, or otherwise and world religion said, "We shall take care of everything." The "saints" were then, in Western style Europeanism, controlling what they had heard, or interpreted, or felt they heard. This is the herd and not heard of mentality. In essence millions were not missed, because the Ruach Haodesh moves in mysterious ways and not by man's will, but by GOD'S. Group salvation is what one sees and not individual, personal take the love and the time in love to love through Messiah for not only one's salvation, but to glorify the Father.

Self-incentive is important in spreading the Gospel, if it is ever that. "Two by two Y'eshua sent them out." How does mass media emulate Ruach Hakodesh, when it comes to not just salvation, but love? Each individual must truly partake. This is not wholesale marketing, but individual choice like Adam, or Eve and not Adam and Eve. Two sins not one. Two souls not one. Individualism is not a loving individual.

One also should be willing to say to one's fellow man, "Here take it all, it is yours. I give up my so called rights for you. It all belongs to GOD."

We are only the instruments, the stewards, the caretakers, not the owners, or the centerpiece and does not think that if GOD wants one saved that they shall not be? Y'eshua had bought us with a PRICE. Every thing, as a believer, is His. It is not our's to sell usuriously, or just for a donation of, or contribution of, or to entertain, or even to be paid for, but to and in a GODLY form, love and love means sharing about Calvary and sharing in charity to others freely and having Messiah's love in us by allowing Him to do His will. Charity to give lovingly to others, that is the believing poor and the unbelieving poor. "Hope, faith and charity, or love. " Otherwise why did Y'eshya stress money, or finance when He dealt with man so many times?

It would have mattered in America, if every true believer would have had a personal one on one witness and not just that, but to see in action the love that same person has for all others. Not presenting archaic documents, or laws, only the Bible and to help feed, clothe and provide shelter to the poor, the destitute, the lonely, the unwanted, et cetera.

Court ruling would not have mattered, since freedom of conscience could and would have prevailed, if not seared, by repeated ventures in refusing the Gospel. No one else shall do what GOD wants you to do, yet GOD can use another person, church, or nation, because all three not collective bodies and not organizations, or at least they should not be. This let someone else do it, or it is not the right time, whenever then would it be, washes out not GOD'S will, but GOD'S will at that time for one's own personal life.

Once the truth is known in the heart, that good vs evil can be almost always discerned of course with proper prayer, proper worship first, praise, reading of Scripture, or knowing Scripture heartfully not just to recite, or memorize. Truth in this way sets one free. "To pray without ceasing."And of course the battle within all against this good vs evil constantly.

There is no barring freedom of conscience, unless it is seared which means repeated refusal of the Gospel. In this age of grace it is still opened and sometimes with access and excess one can turn the other way. Does not Messiah say that, "We each one of us are accountable to GOD first and then to others? " There is no delegating what disciples should and would do. Not by coercion, but willingly to admonish, correct and discipline those fellow believers. The word discipline is in disciple. To be obedient to GOD'S authority only not as Judas Iscariot, a demon. A metaphor? Hardly. (John 6:64, Job 17:12, Acts 1:25, John 6:70).

Our only form of eternal government, Messiah as Monarch. One cannot agree with an oligarchy, or a democracy, but a Christian monarch they can. There is no authority in the first two according to GOD"S institution of Biblical government.

Did not man make the cross, a tree, the only symbol of His eternal love. Never lost, though through history, no matter how old. Yes we miss the simplicity with which GOD shows us, even though many times Christianity is complex. Life was never meant to be easy and convenient after Adam's fall. Things that are difficult now and most are, especially ones we have a deep interest in are to be worked at which requires a challenge and even stupidity is easy and clear. I had seen the handwriting on the wall for America. America, as early as the 19th Century, into the 20th Century showed an unbiblical nonsense by separating politics from morality or vice versa and that is GODLY morality what other kind could there possibly be?

America's founding was sincere, phileo love, but not in agape' love. No one can make another a piece of property and coming to America the natives would be hostile and unbiblical, because of this unknown civilization that was upon them. They looked and acted differently as well as spoke differently. Their fear lay in the fact that as in the animal world they had to survive at all costs and protect their domain and could not reach to higher aspirations. Who were these predators that they must have felt through fear were invading the North American continent? Not until two individuals one from each side made a spiritual bonding, could there be brotherhood. " We are all one race." The Lord's words meaning human and humane race with ability to think, but at what level?

I was glad Marie and I had made out a pro-life will and not a pro-euthanasia living will which had no regard for human life. The medical profession had lost it's humane being and even the Hippocratic Oath was not required and death was now part of the learning, if one could call it that. In Israel there were more doctors per person, then any other nation in the world, yet infanticide was prevalent.

With about 17,000,000 Jews worldwide and diminishing why would anyone deplete their own population even more and in fact do it Nazi Infanticide style?

People were crying about doctors and the death penalty, heaven forbid, and found that atrocious, but did not find infanticide as much? They did not want doctors injecting death needles into convicted hard core criminals, murderers, but yet thought, or did not think, that even partial birth infanticide normal? Was this equality for all, or not? Now even the poor emulate the rich and kill by infanticide and drug their very own. Honor not the mighty and respect not the poor. Yes, the poor became sicker than others, because of their ingrained closeness to GOD. An ignorance about education, dissolving quickly into nothingness. In Colombia, South America they found in the ground of convents aborted remains of babies from nuns in Catholicism.

The State knew that a majority of the population laid below themselves in education and the thirst for power made them want to rule it over others religiously. The rich committed spiritual and physical suicide and isolationism and the poor murdered and did envy to themselves.

Moderation is indeed needed, but how can wealth, not salary, be evenly distributed and would the rich want to do that? The rich prefer to squeeze water out of a stone, the poor and the poor see what they do not have what another has, no matter what. Jealously is not having, but wanting, or in want all the time.

The State's best interest is for itself and herein lies the danger in a democratic/republic. Spreading atheism's spiritual poverty for most officials who do not have, or know the light of truth.

The ABOMINATION OF DESOLATION, the GREAT TRIBULATION, when the GOSPEL OF THE KINGDOM shall be preached, not the GOSPEL OF GRACE. This shall last full 7 years, Daniel's 70TH WEEK for the Hebrews. Ones in the TRBULATION will have to die for GOD, or be persecuted severely in order not to lose their soul and refuse THE MARK OF THE BEAST.

King Nebuchadnezzar, Babylon, the first Gentile king had a dream which was GOD'S plan for the Gentiles. The 4 evil Gentile empires, were Babylon, captivating power; Media-Persia, power that held all in subjection and awe; the Grecian formula and then the Roman legal acumen and martial perfection and then the OLAM HABA.

The Antichrist was to renew the Old Roman Empire and its 10 kingdoms. Babylon was a monarch, Media-Persia was a monarch, Greece a democracy, and Rome an oligarchy like an imperialistic military. Eight generations pure was Nazi Germany. The recessive blue eyes needed to have both parents as blue eyed and blonde haired.

Daniel's first 6 chapters are history and chapters 7-12 are prophecy. The FIRST BEAST is represented as a lion and in the metal of gold. The SECOND BEAST is in the metal of silver and is the arms and the breast and 3 ribs; Libya, Babylon and Egypt. The THIRD BEAST with 4 heads and is in the metal of brass in the belly and as a leopard. The FOURTH BEAST with 10 horns with the metal of iron which has 10 kingdoms and 10 toes is Rome. The "little horn" is the Antichrist. Being in Israel near the end of the age meant more Jews came home, who could, plus more danger for believers.

Theatrical reality was not for believers and for unbelievers…

The FIRST PLAYER is the West of the 10 nation confederacy. The Antichrist most likely was a European Jew, as well as the FALSE PROPHET and was procreated from the sons of gods, angelic demons that is the Antichrist with the daughters of man, a Jewish woman. The same as before at the time of Noah's flood and the arc.

Probably a German, English, or Russian Jew in the Nazi New Age style from infanticide to homosexuality and euthanasia. The BEAST raises his head again

The SECOND PLAYER is the North with Syria, Turkey and Russia. The THIRD PLAYER would be the Kings of the East: China, Japan, Korea and other Asians. The FOURTH PLAYER is the Lord and His Army and the 5th PLAYER is Israel who is non-active.

After the TRANSLATION most of mankind shall become devious.

There will be a few believers until the end. Churches will promote heresy heathenism shall reign. More demons along with Satan shall be upon the entire earth, since Messiah and church had been translated into heaven. Messiah and Satan cannot be in the same heavenlies, hence Satan and all his cohorts shall be thrown upon the earth and for 3 and ½ years he shall fool the world and the second 3-1/2 years he shall create wars that would have lasted years, but shall be made to last into only days. The destruction shall be as never before.

Israel and Europe and America shall be one alliance. Russia and then the South; Egypt, Libya, and Ethiopia will go after the Antichrist. North and South then lose. Then the Antichrist moves into Jerusalem. Again the North and East will alarm the Antichrist. The East, North, South and the Antichrist merge along with West to eventually oppose the Lord at Armageddon in Megiddo, Israel, the Valley of Jehosophat, from Bozrah on the southeast to Megiddo on the north-west. There shall be 1600 stadia, Revelation 14:16. The march of GOD's indignation from Sinai through Idumen past Jerusalem to the mighty field of Eshraelon's plain. The battle is outside the city, Isaiah 29:6. Then a great earthquake with Jerusalem in parts, Revealation 16:18. A worldwide earthquake. The whole earth's configuration shall change. Satan shall be bound for 1,000 years. The living nations shall be judged as to their acceptance of the GOSPEL OF THE KINGDOM.

After the TRIBULATION those days shall be darkened and the moon shall not give light and not a star and the stars will fall from heaven and the powers of the heavens shall be shaken. (Matthew 24:29; Isaiah 13: 9-13; Joel 2:30-31 and Joel 3:15; Revelation12:14) Then He shall appear (Matthew 24:30) and then the OLAM HABA shall come.

This was right where the heart of the world civilizations were. Where the East meets the West and where GOD chose to set up his earthly kingdom. Would I be involved in the AGE OF GRACE, or AGE OF THE KINGDOM?

"In the twinkling of an eye" to be TRANSLATED. The beginning would appear to be soon. Marie, Rachel and I could soon rejoice in our Messiah, Y'eshua. His Second Advent would soon come and it would be joyful for all saints, as opposed to those who refused and were not chosen by GOD'S grace through Calvary for their rebirth.

I had remembered in America, how we went away from Y'eshua's birth to Christmas and not Hanukah or even Passover. The West's Christmas was commercialized with trees, Santa Claus (whoever that was), wrapped gifts, frosty the snowman, Rudolph, the Grinch, et cetera. Everything, but Messiah's birth and resurrection in where the love lies?

At Biblical Passover other secular events had taken over, instead of Calvary. The church had acquiesced on GODLY moral issues for fear of what? Could it possibly be of this "social" gospel, that was nothing more than "eat, drink and be merry" in the house of GOD?

Everyday started to become a holiday, from birthdays to Halloween and religious holidays became just another good time to have a party and become inebriated and overstuffed. The West worshipped food as did Europe and Israel and it could be readily seen in the obesity of all, plus fine dining was increasing in this darkened area, as well as malnutrition.

Who would keep the faith in America? Even the elderly knew of socialism's "social" security for life and this constant bombardment of retirement. Retirement from leading society to almost an instant death of isolationism and convenience even in death? This was what I was also remembering of Balshazzar's America. The handwriting was on the wall from eating-gluttony to "garbage stew" music. Nothing in America was normal. The family had become gangs and groups and even procreation was not by natural process. The Anglophiles were in all of this. How instrumental the Germans were with their systems of legalisms and rigidity and anti-Semitism, plus homo-eroticism. Europeanism and Americanism and now it appeared Israel too, had made a covenant not for good, but for another purpose with the future in mind. Could America ever have freed itself from Europeanism in homosexual Nazism and it's rhetoric of nothingness and useless affirmation of "what is there to live for"?

It seemed that Israel too would take on a Western mind, because of German Jewry and American bankism. Freedom came to mean why make any GODLY law, since all things were legal, though not necessarily moral? Morality had nothing to do with it. It was in the interest of this all freewill freedom, because to most man had created god, or atheism in the sense of egoism. Worship was a lost art and praying too much meant demanding things from GOD, or as gods demanding for ourselves always.

Was America doomed from the beginning, because Protestantism did not believe in the miracle and had made "reason in anguish" it's main intent? A cultural religion without much compassion and without a sense of GODLY humor and only idiosyncratic inefficiencies integrated from a one country perspective and being Western religious Europeanism. One of our documents mentioned Messiah by name, but only indirectly, such as some distant Deist GOD. I know many may say that is sacrilegious for me to say about America's founding and it must be multiculturalism, at least in part now?

It is one unit of Europeanism with John Locke's socialism in the Renaissance where physical labor outgrew to industrial and technical and scientific mindsets. Where was the heart in all of this? Yes a few had their hearts transformed, not reformed in mind, but yet the nemesis of history was carried in the thoughts from Europeanism. Our serfdom was materialistic slavery and had nothing spiritual in it. It introduced to us all that no matter what, the West would always find a new idea to solve the problem of the mind, but not the heart, but when this new idea was a lack of compassion it failed to realize, for the most pat, that the future was in "open time" and that history would be distorted, by historians and only the immediate present is what we would really know, or would be able to write about, for it's truth and accuracy, as long as it was truth and at the right time and that we were seeking nothing momentary, or to please our own whim at the moment.

From not hearing, or learning, from an older Christian nation we chose to cling to Europeanism, no matter what. One nationality would coerce and show their poor, England and the other would rationalize everything France and hide their poor. Usually the world thought of England as safety and liberty in where it lie geographically.

As we know, history is an inexact science and only in the contemporary can art perform truly with BEAUTY, or harmony with GOD. It is in truth that man through art has beauty in it. We must not rely on the historic alone and forget about today. A true artist must write immediately and of the present and tell of happenings just as one would themselves picture it for real. There can be no deviations, but if deviations supposedly appear in the true art, they shall dissipate quickly, because sometimes a people, or nation, do not always see what an artist sees and did not Messiah so prove that? Hyperboles, or exaggerations, or as one would call it stretching the truth does not and cannot exist in art, because BEAUTY shall shed the light of truth on it.

Most of America's written history then was written then, but now also is being written now, hence multiculturalism and shown publicly which is the lie. Multiculturalism has its roots in Marxist/ Leninism. It would appear that since no real Negro artist has of yet been able to describe in contemporary terms their rich culture, hence they may never assimilate...

This bearing down of rigidity in Europeanism. One cannot understand the American Negro unless one as such is one, or unless a PUSHKIN from the higher ups can translate in actuality like a Negro would, but it is indeed rare. The assimilation of Negroes has not occurred amongst themselves, because of this "race" issue. One only sees "race" and not Messiah's race. The people of the land must catch up because of the way this post PUSHKIN would express himself ahead of time in the sense that the common person was not yet literate, or up in education to understand his writings, not because it was false, but because it was written at a higher level. In due time though it would be discerned by the people themselves. So the Negro cannot ever assimilate into America for lack of a GODLY education does not allow it and national loyalties come into play? Is this American, since their new soil is not their own, but government's and bilingualism only emphasized that point even more with so called diversity?

By government mandate everything was officially brought to them which made them suspicious of the government, as well as the rich and well educated who became their wealth. There was nothing that was not hardly brought to them also without major profit by the promoter. One must first speak on equal terms and not give away but allow the Negro to buy and at a fair price material that can be read that entertains them and keeps their interest. Having the state mandate everything means more suspicion by this people and others more. It is important to stimulate one's interest, so they would want to read, rather then reminding them of their own miseries and the do's and don't's of society. You shall not embarrass them in regards to things they should not read. Make reading enjoyment not an official sanction of government. Also promote, or encourage reading in English to make it all inclusive and not exclusive meaning only for the rich and the well educated to learn. Exclusivity makes all concerned suspicious about why one wants another to read and in a foreign language different then most Americans?

Thoughts upon thoughts kept floating in my not too clear memory. Past days about America's failure, because theatrical reality never works in truth. An all consuming avarice in capitalism itself and then socialism, capitalism's next phase. Most would say that if one did not subscribe to capitalism then surely surely one had to be a socialist? Far from the truth. One is an economic system and one an ideology. Negative theories do not work in GOD'S plan, never have and never will.

America probably was dead sometime after the initial start with this Masonry, Quakerism, Mormonism, slavery, wigs, silk stockings from the British and of course Europeanism. Who could not discern this take-it-with-you attitude? It would last even 200 years after Washington. Inheriting eventually all the foreign religions that anyone could thing of. Everything was okay, as long as the belly remained full. America's epitaph would have to read something to the affect that the Germanic-Franco deluge had reigned over the pentagram stars to uphold materialism as always. The land would spew us out. Would Europe keep it's tail, America? Right now England had to because of Arab oil. Would Israel continue close ties with Europe in the end time scenario? Would these 3 be one part in the end time scenario?

Yes a great multitude shall come out of the GREAT TRIBULATION in glorified and unglorified bodies. The GOSPEL OF THE KINGDOM Messiah preached the first time on earth. Was not the last 9 chapters of Ezekiel referring to the OLAM HABA TEMPLE? The TEMPLE shall not be in the city, but on the mountain. Who were these two witnesses during the TRIBULATION? Enoch and Elijah?

Did not they lay out in the open for 3 whole days and on the 4th day stood up and came to life and were called up to heaven by GOD? Did they not witness to the Jew and the Gentile? Did not Peter witness to the racially mixed in Samaria and then to the Ethiopian, a eunuch, by Philip and was not Philip then translated? Peter had the power only with John along to baptize in the power of the Holy Spirit which did not occur until Peter came. The GREAT TRIBULATION in a 1/2 Week would have changes that would normally have taken a whole 19th Century. Would Palestine be full of the world's Jewry, when the Antichrist in the GREAT TRIBULATION is partitioned by him?

If Jews were held hostage in America that would, or could mean that eventually only Messianic Jews in Israel fleeing safely to Petra, 144,000 would be saved, or would it? America has had some 100,000 Messianic Jews too. More reason to keep them in America. A large amount in percentage as to how many Jews were on earth, 100,000 of maybe say 8,000,000?

Marie, Rachel and I decided to move to Jerusalem. This was Israel's capital and with much movement about it. For us it would be cheaper, since my job was now located here and farming was not a viable option for now and tourism was out. Here my job consisted of government immigration which meant I would probably experience foreign travel. Of course America was definitely on my mind. My trip there I felt was a must. What would the tail of Europeanism be like? I was soon to find out. On my journey were many foreigners and some Americans. It was obvious to me that America was still a "closed state".

Before Sal and me had left for Israel, Washington was crumbling from within. It did not have a wall like the Kremlin that was 13-16 feet thick, 26-55 feet high and 1 and 1/4 miles around. We felt that everything we tried to do was being blocked, not personally, but in a societal way. There was really no Mosaic Law and "golddiggers" were all over. There was an SS police state disguised as legal protection, but was in affect another Sodom and Gomorrah prelude for the one world government. Home was still home in the sense that I still was an American at heart.

My responsibility was to obtain the release of Jews for Israel. As in Vietnam the Communists made each wealthy Vietnamese give $10,000 in gold in order to get out of Communist Vietnam and the same thing was true in this scenario. One knew who got out of the Vietnam... My direction would be mainly Polish and Russian Jews, but without the money. American Jewry had assimilated so much into Germanic Reformed Judaism which approved of homosexuality, infanticide, euthanasia, et cetera and correlated with Europeanism and avarice and vile vice and knew nothing about their heritage and could care less that they more than their tradition, let the lie transfix them.

New York City was a cancerous tumor of Sodomy, the occult, drugs, criminality, avarice and was in it's last stages of malignancy. I was suppose to acquire through diplomacy Reformed Jews, what else, or secular Jews who willingly wanted to return. I, though, took it upon myself to seek out Messianic Jews first, since they knew what their stay in America meant and their desire for the Promised Land. This was the only faith group in all the world that could GODLY leave any nation to seek Israel and not be considered unpatriotic to their native born land, or homeland.

Wherever one went there were cameras and militia people all around, all in uniforms, another Sodomite fancy. Many would look at us with suspicion because of our background. Paranoia was prevalent and conversations were vile and obscene and usually dealt with environmental global warming, or New Age health care systems, or stores and products. POLITICAL CORRECTNESS was just as Lenin would have wanted it. The poor were educated by the dumbing down of John Dewey's government fiat, as well as Thomas Mann's. There was no concern for truth or real academics. Churches had "social" hour gatherings like entertainment halls. New Age occultism, mysticism in astrology, hypnotism, animal rights, multiculturalism, emotionalism, OBE, health care, or school based health clinics for infanticide (but not earring approval or aspirin), Soviet day care with pedophiles, Sodomy lessons, Wotan occultism and so much more. Constant rigidity was imposed and privacy was a misdemeanor, punishable by law. Hand in hand one could see Butches of all kinds and in all different "races" and motorcycle gangs with Nazi ornamentation from head to foot. Youths of homosexuals could also be seen in groups.

Marriage pictures could be seen in the Internet with 2 males or females in so called matrimony which all started in the occult state of Vermont.

The United States Supreme Court grew larger as FDR had wanted and had it's own Commissars to enforce their own rulings. The Justices were all POLITICALLY CORRECT and could be heard using obscenities in the court room. Congress was the English Royalty and one hardly heard from them and one had to be related to get in. The Head of State was a committee of higher Commissars, including feminists mostly foreign. Washington D.C. was now known as Diversity City, the DC in Washington. Yes America had changed for the worse.

I decided to visit John's Pub and found out it was a Sodomy, or Stonewall Riot, Gay Pride Day type of dirty bar. The neighborhood was in fragments as to people and there were endless blocks of vacant strip malls and broken concrete and asphalt with hardly any pedestrians at times. This ran continuously into the suburbs. There were rodents and insects of all kinds from blood disorders. These pests were running to and fro like squirrels would. Farther into the countryside was soil erosion and lack of farming and clean well water. All was collective and subsidized farming. Housing developments appeared right alongside with rolls of corn, wheat, alfalfa, et cetera. Most grains were not edible for humans though. Edible food was like gold. A day's wages for a loaf of bread.

There were few healthy and normal children, but mostly handicapped, or children with deformities. Graffitti which was called "Ebonic Writing" embellished most walls and nefarious gangs could be seen. We nonetheless kept moving backward depending on how one looked at things. The stench of dead carcasses and bodies one could smell. Disease and filth, because of famine with pestilence that followed.

As I got ready to leave for Israel, I could not help, but think that there were no longer any such thing, as an American, or a nation called America. There was much diversity now with pink swastikas all over. They could now show their true colors, because the Jews were not as powerful as once before in finances in America. The architecture was symmetrical, even the churches looked like pagan monstrosities in New Age form. It was cold and depressing looking, Soviet style. Rust could be seen on most metal parts, as on cars, or on buildings and signs.

The currency was the Eurodollar and the Smart Card. Measurements were in the metric form. Legal tender was considered confederate money. The card had an image of 666 the unholy trinity and 2 lightning bolts. Cars were very rare and movement of vehicles was limited. There was an incarceration of areas and there appeared to be a mark of some sort on almost all of the inhabitants' hands or foreheads.

The BEAST, once dead, had again come to life and again raised it's head from the European Gentile empires. Women were clones as they appeared with little, or no hair on their heads. One could not differentiate, especially at a distance, men from women because of unisex clothes too. It was Mao's look alike attire. There was a feeling of death and doom to one's soul.

As I began to return some 48 Jews back to Israel, I suddenly realized, as they all were together that there was no 2 Jews from the same immediate family. This journey had been most horrendous for me. It was a shot to my solar plexis. Mankind was going to self-destruct himself quite soon, or become extinct, if something, or someone did not intervene soon.

After other trips to jolly old Londontown, I soon discovered many Taj Mahals and other kinds of architecture that resembled Islam and India. Rainbow signs were everywhere. My travels around the world took me to so many odd places, or was it this New Age? In India it was filled with destruction, famine and pestilence with rat temples for worship and all New Age hieroglyphics and the origins of the swastika, plus even Northern New Delhi was in ruins. Cows were no longer sacred. The old time Internet developed through consumer participation voluntarily to now the digital capsule worldwide which could be implanted. No nation was exempt. The more East I travelled famine and pestilence and death I could see with totalitarian royalty ruling. In China the Shih Zu dog was gone as well as the real masters. No one blinked an eye. All roads lead back to Israel which scared me, because of Messianic Jewry. Outer space meant more intrusion on one's inner space. There were no affections, or heart felt feelings. Consciences were a vacuum and completely seared. Nuclear holocaust was quite evident in certain areas in the world. This was to always be privileged information. That is why Angola was taken. The Soviets sent Cuban communists to start a civil war. People lived in caves in Spain and elsewhere.

Governments induced famines to help reduce their populations. The Antichrist's domain had most all the world's food. Anti-Semitism was increasing and had to be dealt with, that is the Jew. "WORLD WAR I", a real World War was soon coming. The common universal language was computer devised. Procreation was less and less by natural means. In Monterey, Mexico, good old Mexico again, U.G.O.'s and Big Business set to try to collect, or initiate a global tax, or taxes in the trillions of dollars, 13 trillion and to do it through the United Nations. Procreation yes was only for the chosen ones. Charitable children non-profit organizations were eliminating people, hoarding food donations, molesting children, et cetera. Self implosion amongst man's own kind in where profit and avarice now lie and self-preservation. One by one children were being murdered and reported missing from their homes and no one took the knowledge, homosexual pedophiles, like John Wayne Gacy and Jeffrey Dahmer had done years ago. Whenever I was writing, or talking, I had to be careful like other believers had too, because of such an increase in demonic activity that could interpret our writing.

The lowest point at sea level in the world was in the same land where the highest "king" on this earth would rule. Jobs were becoming government controlled. Even Rome's 7 hills were sinking. Most things were commonly, or collectively owned. Every item had a number. Parties and religions were all the same, EXCEPT ONE. Food wasn't accessible worldwide. Fish was exorbant. Preservative were in all foods and carcinogenic in nature. Common necessities were by planned obsolescence. Military colors were red, black and white. Uniforms lasted longer, than regular clothing.

Did all the Gentile nations come in, even from the 1040 Window?

The test tube procreation had grown and was producing something not quite human, or humane. This was the spirit of the age.

My travels to Africa were limited, thank goodness, because Africa was a no man's land. Crucifixes from the air could be seen as well as piles of human debris. Yes Rhodesia, a diamond capital at one time and named after Mr. Rhodes from the auspicious Rhodes Scholar program at Oxford and Cambridge all this was decimated but that had been for the good, since slaves were kept to work in the mines under lock and key. South Africa was stripped too. Somalia, Egypt and Ethiopia were all gone as wastelands. Nothing was worth anything, for lack of food and clean water.

Ham was needed to the New Age. In Ethiopia I managed to find more Falasha Mura. South Africa was in tribal warfare where it had started and apartheid was not the only issue, as one had always wanted all to think and believe. It was tribalism, or tribal warfare. In England the poor were openly sold as slaves. Human resources I thought only referred to business personnel, but the Anglophiles meant natural resources the same as rocks, hills, land, animals, water, et cetera.

All big corporation executives were into New Age ESP, transcendental meditation, yoga, CRT screen imagery and hypnotism.

"On earth as it is in heaven", was no longer so.

The Ishmaelites were falling fast due to Islam but to New Age mostly. At one time there had been 750,000,000 Moslems in Africa and they were not attacking others because of oil, but now they were decimated.

Children's names such as Satan, Lucifer, Jezebel, Wotan, Baal, Beezelbub, Sagittarius, Scorpio, et cetera were being used. Stealing was everywhere. People had to eat, drink and have shelter. To be caught stealing was a capital offense. Either one starved, got shot, or beheaded. There were so called religious pentagram courts which emulated rabbinical courts at first. Being a believer could mean loss of job first, then no family and death eventually by separation, starvation, or execution in masses, plus death by relatives. Self-Preservation was a must now. Many relatives cashed in on believers' fees in their own family and friends, by so called blood money. One's worse enemy could be one's own family. All BIBLES were being burned and made illegal. Revised Wotan editions were occultic worship books. The word GOD could only be used in blasphemy out loud. Dogs, as well as cats, were eaten as regular food in some places as well as human fetuses. Man had Neanderthaled. The search for GOD innately put there was being sought in Hellish places. "The father of all lies"' would soon be thrown out of heaven and onto the earth, if he hadn't been already. His major tool was discouragement in the past.

The Trinity always eternal, not created, would soon be removed from earth. Months went by and how could tribes and nations get along when individuals did not? American Biblicals were not, nor could they be anti-Semites. The "roots" were always Jewish. What would Protestantism do without Catholicism to protest about? This was not Original. American Biblicals were born Americans founded by GOD in America. There were no ism's in our faith. We were to help the poor and defend the helpless, the weak and the innocent. We also had to present ourselves to GOD first and then to others before ourselves. Love GOD first and glorify the Father through His Son Y'eshua.

Utopian sermons do not work and not spreading the whole Gospel meant incomplete. This pursuit of happiness does not exist. Deism is dead religion. Joy is from Messiah alone and always is with an American Biblical, or at least should be. Circumstances account for nothing that we can conjure up, such as happiness, or the pursuit of.

In Israel I did not want to proselytize American Biblical Christianity, but Messianic Jewishness. Marie and I worshipped as Messianic Jews like Messiah and His Disciples. He is the Father of Abraham, Isaac and Jacob and Ishmael, but Ishmael chose Islam later on and never did he get GOD'S spiritual blessing, only a physical one. Europeanism had no part in Messianic Jewry. Israel was totally secular in Zionism, nationality and not faith for most Jews now. Israelis were not Hebrews by faith. Only Messianic Jews were Hebrews, to cross over, by faith.

Americanism was in America, because of Europeanism and not because of the American Biblical. We imported everything from Europe into America. America now had to depend on Europe and Israel. American men had tattoos and bold heads that were shaved with effeminate earrings in their ears as Old Testament slaves. There were too many skinheads and Moslems, both socialistic in ideology all around us. Israel was worse but yet 144,000 Messianic Jewry and some others had to go through the entire TRIBULATION along with some Gentiles without "the mark of the Beast". The 144,000 would be hidden, the others would not. There was the Judaizers, or unbelievers the Pharisaical, or Sadducces, or Zealots.

GOD is always exact in accordance with His Word, when he counts the Jewish people. And all of the Israel shall be saved means all after the GREAT TRIBULATION. The secular by hereditary birth, Jews like Marx, Freud, Trotsky and yes even Einstein and Jonas Salk were not Messianic Jews.

Not being closer to GOD, but fellowship with Him moment by moment. GOD was not worshipped, but now Wotan was. The Jewish veil from Moses was still on most Jews and blinded them, so Satan had them as well as all unbelieving Gentiles. What can any Jew do, but believe?

We all committed parricide, because of Adam's fall and because of our own sin. One sin is all it took. Who would want to save any of us, besides GOD in three persons with the Son taking on human form and into His body all sin for all of time? Undying love and quintessential from GOD for no sin can touch GOD the Father.

Insanity of the cerebral cortex, not to believe. To realize that GOD says who He is and what He has done and shall do for all who just believe. The disease of not believing from the spiritually dead and from the old man Adam's heart. It is the spiritual heart that accepts Messiah first, not the mind, or brain. This in itself, requires faith, because we do not see it taking place, but it does take place, because He is the giver of this invisible faith. The senses do not perceive it, but the spiritual heart does. Some say insanity is incoherent and in a way so is faith for you do not alone choose, or see for it is GOD who does the choosing and who provides the faith. "Many are called, but few are chosen". Does GOD pick and choose with freewill? They hear his voice and they respond for whatever moment in time and it is sealed by GOD'S faith and chosen and not ours. He says, "You are mine".

Mr. Thomas Jefferson believed in an idea and not in GOD and that is where he came short. He did not trust GOD in the present. Faith is in not seeing GOD, but believing in Him in one's spiritual heart. Not to believe in GOD is insanity and not to believe in

Messiah, is pure insanity and Satan knows it and thrives on this. How does one suppose, such as Jefferson that he missed GOD'S calling yet believed a Mason's worldly lie that now is the time for all things when in actuality eternity is. Benjamin Franklin too was deceived probably also by ego. Abraham and Sarah were different they accepted GOD by faith, but refused to believe in what GOD had said what He would do through procreation.

Now Semites killing Semites both sides mostly secular at that. Judaism vs Islam both that propose one GOD but no Trinity. So Trinity, no Messiah, the atonement for all sin hence the lie they die for and believe in.

"The Word became flesh." Impossible? GOD spoke Adam into being and was not even procreated. Y'enshua grew from an infant into a child to an adult and could have stayed on earth.

The ready made easy to see Western world in the flesh, yet even demons and Satan know who GOD IS. They also know who Messiah is. Man evolved, but as to spirituality probably 3 or 4 generations. Where did the animals get their names? Do animals become homo-erotic, or murder their own species most of the time? Reasoning allows us to determine to do evil, to kill one another, no murder one another, but is it the transformed spiritual heart that discerns love? Man murders GOD then wants to praise Satan? Why else would man disbelieve faith, by not choosing GOD?

My wife Marie struggled with many of her close family relatives who also chose to serve the flesh and have Satan control them. Even some of her relatives who were ultra-Orthodox Hasidim did not now believe in the State of Israel, until Messiah finally came, who were of course unbelievers. Their wait would be eternal. Judaism also had no complete answer for the Jew. Only more religion to worship over, excluding GOD. Israel was in deep trouble and with alliances in different parts of the world who were sharpening their swords.

America's Armageddon had occurred already. Democratic/republicanism could only uphold, if GOD was holding it up. It changes and Messianic Jews could lift America up to Messiah, because their faith stayed the same and was American.

Western values meant the Renaissance and lack of spirituality. The most important part was to worship Messiah to give glory to the Father and nothing else. As the Russian peasant's spirit was ignored so were the believers in America. What protection would America need for unbelieving?

The West in 1789 and before with the French Jesuits instituted materialism for the truth. Then was Reformed by the Germans to institute racial and homo-eroticism. Racial, because Orthodox Jewry refused sexual deviancy which the elites in Germany indulged in. This Franco-Germanic political philosophy did not start socialism, but brought wholesale anti-Semitism, anti-Old Testament, plus "social" justice to full fruition with help from FDR, Churchill, Stalin, Hitler, et cetera. Now Moscow and Peking had it too. Lenin to Brezhnev, plus two more, as compared to 11 Presidents in the United States in the same time span. Oligarchy vs democracy which helps crush the human spirit. A monarch had 1, or 2 kings at most for that duration and the stability would have most assuredly endured.

Roman Catholicism's Liberation Theology and homosexuality and without grace, inundated especially the West to believe a lie. The Jews were always refusing royalty even Messiah. It had to be all, or nothing and by their time, or else.

Was there enough to buy a loaf of bread? Oh, and the glorious adolescents getting worse nonetheless and glorified for it. Nothing to encourage goodness. The rich and well educated love it. The elderly did not want to get old gracefully. Life had been good to them. Youth was quintessential no matter how misguided with no experience in life, they were made to lead blindly.

The world was moving at a fast pace that even nations could not keep up with the political ramifications and the spiritual suffered. Yes only a future nation following this monarch could be as one, including the rich and this monarch in Israel would already be performing miracles and the world would say, "Long live Caesar; long live the king." Sound familiar?

I remember in America that being in a denominational setting was more important, than with a Holy GOD. Gog and Magog or anti-Russian sentiment, was only heard every time Israel was in trouble or England needed an escape goat. And it was not the Soviets, these Russians, mind you. Did Stalin, a Georgian, know something about FDR and Churchill as the Supreme Court Justice that made Henry Ford apologize?

Can an entire nation of people be evil, or is it party organization as well as government and ideology? The system and not a nation, for there were none other from the North, Japheth, or Moscow that would come down upon Israel? Would Japheth be the future system of world dominance from the North? One must always be correct to know of Japheth's origins and where they then migrated to. I asked myself from where did this system become inherited from that Russia had? Such questions do arise frequently when one does use common sense to answer them carefully. It is government most of all one must fear, masses are always blinded by another form of light whether by a mass, or large mass.

The majority in a democracy are never right and in a monarch, a Christian one, the light of truth is shed upon him. An individual is easier to convert than an entire nation. One remains to the soil, the other to egoism and self preservation. America had a Vietnam, a poor man's conflict of don't shoot, unless shot at and self preservation here that was constantly being raised from afar and also don't apprehend criminals here at home, since they were in the inner cities and not yet in the palaces. What shall we do? Was not the entire Southeast Asia under attack from Communism and yet we cried, "But not us please." "We must defeat the East," "but as to whom in the East..."

For quite sure, nor did they care. Then Red China played it's fiddle like Nero who also set fire to Rome and still we gave Most Favored Nation Status to the Communists and not the peasants in China, or Taiwan itself. It gave us a sense of self preservation.

I remember when England's king said, "I am law and slavery shall stay" and so it did in America too.

Why did we as Americans then bring slavery to America?

The brothers of Shem had two different nations...

Different mothers? Ham by the way did not invoke any racial curse for those who have a mistaken agenda. It was a homosexual one!

Then too the Western media said, "All Arabs were bad", but never distinguished between Islam and Christianity and also which countries were non-Arabic, or non-Semite people.

What about Judaism which was secular and the fact Messiah was missed, GOD in the flesh?

Again prejudice arose, or did it against the Jews? Who were the real Jews never came up never this but why was anti-Semitism growing which did include Messianic Jewry from most Jews themselves? And why Messianic Jewry from all sides of Jewry, especially since the Jews were secular and a much larger group? No way would Messianic Jewry want the status quo religion of Judaism. Even secular Jews agreed with the "religious" Gentiles for the most part. Anything but Messiah, GOD in the flesh. So who are the contemporary Pharisees today and who are Messiah's disciples? Remember the Majority do not enjoy the truth or joy of GOD. It is the small remnant that acknowledges Y'eshua Messiah at Calvary and that He rose, or had risen and He is the only true GOD who had to die and resurrect and not just come for their kingdom. The Pharisees would have it otherwise. America's own Sadduccees amongst America, the ACLU, had long ago already gotten into the graces of the government and the separation of state and the people showed. The Pharisees sounded better, but their hearts were not in it, or were they? It was show and tell.

We had seen the Judaizers with Mr. Bronstein and company but with their own demise. America's south of the border padre' was in socialist land where prejudice simmered and the hammer and sickle was enforced by an Alpinist axe. This know how reflected negatively on the axe, but not the hammer and the sickle. Our St. Petersburg, New York City and our Moscow, Washington D.C. became spiritual oppressions. In Peking and it's oriental mindset one should be seen all the time, but not heard from ever.

CHAPTER VI

TO BABYLON

Months passed and Marie, Rachel and me took a trip to New York City to visit some friends and relatives of Marie that she had not seen in years. They too were all Jewish. When we arrived at the airport we were escorted by a couple and immediately went to their home outside of New York City, northwest. We noticed there were none of the usual Jewish ornaments outside their door, or inside their home. Nothing in fact in America had any religious symbol to it. There were churches and synagogues, but they were entertainment centers serving as houses of worship. The bibles were revised totally and there was the Torah, or Holy of Holies so to speak. There were no libraries. All music "garbage stew" in church services and synagogues.

Loud speakers were at all major street corners and cameras at all traffic lights. All cars had a governor on them to keep all speeds to 35 miles an hour, except all government, or police cars. It appeared an armed militia was everywhere and certain roads, streets and highways were restricted, or out of bounds, almost like the 38th parallel, or the DMZ. All cars had to have an official New Age rainbow tag on them in small print.

Greepeace and the Sierra Club had taken over all environmental issues. Also what was apparently clear was that there were no real Bibles, absolutely none and number two, absolutely no private firearms at all. Both were capital offenses according to the United Governments. Foreign police officers and foreign military personnel were mixed in the English speaking troops with foreigners in command. Foreigners of many different languages saturated America and fear was quite evident, since most common people could not understand what was said and were basically "illiterate." Newscasts were in all foreign languages and the old BBC sufficed for the English version as Radio Free America and the English accents one could not make out from their verbosity. Local news was only reported, but of course untruthfully.

The Arabs had bought out London, as well as England itself, and England more than Japan had invested in America, but now all were going toward Israel. Even bilingual people had a difficult time understanding on their computers the foreign print in newspapers that was printed in America and elsewhere. Water could not be used for bathing daily, without special permission. Meter locks were attached to them that blocked off. Land was absolutely scarce in the sense none could be bought in a free market and what could be bought was worthless for farming, or living. Ninety-five percent of all land was owned by them. Taxes were collected by the individual commissars, or from the individual appointees. Real estate was the wealth of the world and why not it held all the human resources, or "human resources". Red China's land attrition moving towards Siberia with Western help was also getting hostile with lack of bread and water.

Would the occult replace Roman Catholicism or swallow it up? Many famous contributed to socialism, such as FDR, Churchill, Stalin, Freud, Trotsky, Einstein, Chamberlain, Krupp, Rockefellers, Dewey, Baldwin, O'Dell, Dellums, Hall, Glasser, Blackmun, Daschle, Harkin, Hatfield, Streisand, Edison, Mao, Lenin, Kinsey, Sangers, Hammer, Kissinger (Kissingers) Haig, McNamara, Dirksen, Clintons, Fords, Denver, MacLaine, Eisner, Spielberg, Kings (Stephen and Martin), Ginsburg, Thuns, Kruschevs, Castro, Minh, Keynes, Turner, Fonda, Carter, Scranton, Hayden, Mandela, Tutu, Hitler, Mussolini, Ghandis, Gorbachev, Eatons, Mellons, DuPonts, Stoshberries and the list goes on and on. All these of the rich and famous and well educated for the most part along with the powerful contributed to the world's spiritual downfall. Some idiocy though was involved and much short sightedness. Rarely can one find an intelligent and well educated person. The reason for this is because when one is educated it means that they are very knowledgeable and worldly, but not necessarily intelligent. Intelligence has to do with GODLY morality so hence the above had little, or any of this second virtue.

One major financial institution I remember quite well in America had the following incredible scenario.

It was a corporation that controlled a particular area, or community, or communities and was spreading like cancer and was being run directly by New Age mentality. Most the employees were either homosexuals, bisexuals, pedophiles, cross dressers, transvestites, Moslems, Hindus, American and foreign businessmen and many women or should I say young ladies inexperienced in life's endeavors. It also had some ex-officials or relatives thereof that were pro-Nazis and anti-Semites. One official of foreign descent was in the almost exact image, or facial image of Hitler except he was much taller in stature. The board room was filled with pro-Nazi dignitaries. Many employees in World War II and who were affiliated with the Nazis hired many Nazis into their other business endeavors. Many times FBI agents during World War II would pull those individuals out of their plants. One could readily see this strange people, as one Russian Jew called them speaking of the Germanics in which sexual deviancy was normal. This corporation supported all POLITICALLY CORRECT organizations that were non-profit and how many businesses claimed that stature with the IRS SUCH AS HOSPITALS? Infanticide, homosexuality and euthanasia were just a part of their New Age agenda. It was an anti-Judeo-Christian corporation. One extra benefit was to make propositions to other young girls and youth by senior officials of higher stature. One needed to get ahead, but at this price? Very few intelligent and aware heterosexual Christians were hired and they were too scared to speak out. For a front some bisexuals were married and heaven forbid had children under their care. This sexual deviancy is what had occurred, or crested WWI and WWII. German-Jewish Orthodoxy who in Germany were highly moral and controlled the media would not tolerate this sexual deviancy. Nazis, such as Hitler, Himmler, Hess, Rohm, Goerring, Brandt. List and also

Frederick Krupp himself were all homosexual pedophiles. These men were vicious brutes and set up the Nazi Party and not Hitler, as well as the concentration camps. It was this deviancy first, then the Nazis and not vice versa. The elites had to silence this scandal by creating the first World War. Hard to believe? Not really. One and one half million Jewish Children were murdered brutally. Why children and so many of them? Hitler's Youth Corps was made up of all homosexual pedophiles as was America's Girl Scouts were, or at least one third of the Scout leaders were lesbians. The Jews had to go for exposing Nazi Germany's national vice. The Kaiser and others had to cover their deviance from the German public during, or before the First World War.

Anything now related to AIDS in this same corporation was funded and mind you not for AIDS' patients, but to promote homosexuality always. Here is AIDS' origins that is from the male plus male sexuality, or deviant sensuality. There were married couples of the same sex getting benefits the same as a married couple. Even these married couples were getting county government benefits for their homosexual buddy in and through the county government. The sin had travelled to the 3rd and 4th generation in the Germanic clan and the curse was still there due to their vile anti-Semitism. Out in the open one could see the sexual deviancy in this corporation, but let one man propose to a woman and all hell would break loose. Most of their men showed no interest in the opposite sex; it was the same sex that was very popular. Again the hiring of young college brainwashed females and males would be approached by older lesbian Butches and males who would, if possible, violate these youths so that they too would become addicted or be too scared to speak out for fear of loss of job, family, or family shame in some cases, or even denigrating gossip and hardships made harder at work. To even most straight Germans, it was if it did not exist. Incredible, but true. The human resources department was also run by mostly homosexuals, what else? Even out of town stays for the opportunity to coerce or persuade to join this Nazi group of sexual deviants. Most homosexuals held high positions of course. The board had some on its group and also knew of the nefarious and abnormal conduct, or behavior, but chose to ignore it or collaborate after all money and power and prestige was involved.

Our children and youth were becoming demented and destroyed as well as molested by the most vicious and ruthless homosexual pedophiles. One can easily see why Nazi Germans were so vicious and brutal, because this is a severe mental and violent disorder, especially the Butches, male and female who wantonly rape, torture, or murder children everyday in this country. And most thought it was only in the Catholic priesthood, how naive'. It is in all walks of life and especially around children and the innocent and unknowing. Some homosexuals hide their sexual deviancy well and some effeminate males were not homosexuals of which were few. I remember a young Jewish mulatto man that had a "black" father and a Jewish mother. After some time they divorced and the son stayed with his biological father. While in school, many of his own "race" abused this sensitive and caring young man because of his Jewishness. After some years, this young man turned to a transvestite and such an outgoing and caring young man became a cross dresser, which deeply saddened my heart. Of course his father was a pimp who got prostitutes for city hall employees. How just one life was destroyed by "black" anti-Semitism and homosexuality of which both were prevalent in Nazi Germany. Oh yes, there appeared to be an interesting correlation between the Germans and the "blacks" and that too was this sexual deviancy. In fact in Nazi Germany in Naziphilia or Naziville there were none other than "black" male prostitutes, the same as Hitler was when he was young.

This Naziville mentality, or mental illness, in such a small town made gangs, crime, drugs, prostitution, dead beat dads, child abuse all spread again like malignant cancer, plus the fact illegals were brought here to work for the mostly GERMANIC and CATHOLIC firms. This area was about 60-70% Germanic and the incidence of AIDS per 1,000 was only second to Washington DC. Also what appeared and of which this town was known for, was a huge foreign pagan shrine of which the inhabitants most of which were too ignorant to know what it stood for. This perverse sickness was shunned publicly, but also overlooked by the "black" civil righters who started to see trend of the mental illness in their dead beat dads' communities. What could one expect, when civil righters themselves legitimized this sexual deviancy amongst their own movement to be more POLITICALLY CORRECT and to serve this physical people with a most base desire. Civil rights are always superior rights, but in these instances they were in all ways inferior.

Back to this corporation I was speaking about. Turnover was tremendous and nobody knew hardly anybody and qualifications were by ancestry, wealth, political persuasion, to the 8th generation, or being POLITICALLY CORRECT. Loners also were hired as well as the deaf and dumb. Arrogance at the top was their trademark and the status quo wanted it that way. Just so more profits came in legal, or illegal. It did not matter, even if the stock holders had to make up for this asinine leadership at the top. This again was Germanic sexual deviancy founded on monkey business. Illusions of grandeur was at the top holding down a few important but conflicting interests. As usual, the Germans remained quiet and played follow the leader, or foreign leader, to the tune of billions of dollars and more money in their pockets. The sewer had a stench so bad, even the dead would have to roll over. "The love of money is the root of all evil." England's House of Uncommons, or unusuals had legalized homosexuality in the late 1990's and America shortly thereafter followed. Like father like son. The Aryans were up to it again for thus a third time, this time in America. The Anglos and Saxons were now not only cousins, but kissing cousins.

Back to our present day trip to America. Our stay in America continued and other thoughts on the past and present emerged from my memory. Americans had not grown over night. It was started back in the gay 90's of the 19th Century. Then came FDR's New Deal of socialism "social" security and Keynesian Economics.

The world appeared as it must have appeared to Noah before the great flood by GOD. Debauchery, Nephilism, heathenism, infanticide, suicide, homicides, Sodomy, sensuality, bestiality, perniciousness, pusillanimous acts, the occult and perversion of every sort. Cataclysmic events and abnormal weather disasters had taken affect like in the Old Testament. Farming had died in a once plentiful agricultural nation. The American upside down pentagram had always puzzled me as I look at it. Why were there only 5 points, not 6 or even 7 points on each one, after all there are and were many Old Testament writings on many of America's buildings? What did Masonry have to do with this, if anything? Quakerism's ridiculing of religious freedom was something they were suppose to have left behind? This was so similar to the British Mandate against the Irgun, when they hung at, random in public squares Jewish soldiers and were told to refrain from such barbaric acts. Where was their parliamentary government then? And all from a Christian nation? England's arrogance once again showed. "A wolf sheds its fur but not its habits."

As we travelled around Babylon I found it to be as New Age as Israel was, but even worse. One had to keep their faith almost to themselves, because proselytizing was illegal and demonic activity was ambient. There was no official national language to converse in or do business in. Identification by computer was the language of the land. Checkpoints were numerous and mass transit was reduced, as well as the population and was used only in a need basis. Air flights were few and the population had diminished considerably. Medical technology provided for this.

Our journey would take us to the Canadian border, or at least near it and we did not know really why at first. We later found out that the metric system was in affect and so there were no miles to measure one's distance, but kilometers. Yet the Canadian border is not, or was not fifty miles North of New York City. We found out that Canada was part of the original 50 states with 11 or 12 more nations and that there were no boundaries actually in the South either. So, the distance from Canada was actually nil because the border had been moved southward to include Quebec and all provinces and called them territorial nations. So now we had French in the North with Spanish and Portuguese in the South. Why did America need these languages, when especially Latin America did not need English, but did need our wealth and independence? Who was the real UNDERDOG now? There were at times a commonality of one language who once in a while could speak any one of many languages. They kept their conversations to the weather and other non-important things. We had already heard about the public loudspeakers with its obscene New Age world anthem that played so early in the morning.

Voice recordings, never real voices, so no one knew where any official of importance was and an emulation of Tokyo Rose. All voice recordings also were like finger prints. Each person had different markings. A micro chip was already embedded in some people, either in the forehead, or right hand. Only certain children to the 8th generation were conceived by artificial insemination or invitro fertilization, as well as embryonic stem cell research and cloning. It was not a right to own, or to do anything and privileges did not exist. One had to obey what was laid down by the local New Age network format. A crime against the community was a crime against the world. Tribunals were quickly set up every where just for this.

One was not exonerated as before when an Irish youth would appear in front of an Irish judge and the judge would say, "You're a fine handsome l-a-d" and then only would slap him with a small fine. One now cold be exiled but few knew where in the world. Gulags did exist, but few even knew about them let alone where they were. America's crime accelerated, because defense lawyers had convinced the Negro and others that it was all right to release hard core criminals and it was their turn to get even now that they sat in the jury box. The judges and lawyers themselves released felons on purpose to destroy the moral fabric. Some also believed in wealth, fame and this utopia, but most were scoundrels who had committed the same kind of crimes from the bench itself. Outer space stations were Big Brother's eye with astral projections for the future movement. Mortality rates must have been in the millions in America alone since I had left, not including infanticide.

If one got sick heaven forbid... One may not come out as before or come out at all once they entered the hospital. Cremations had grown 500 % and dead bodies tell no tales and if cremated quickly their remains do not either. Forensic medicine became the sociopath's pathology. The MD did not stand for medical doctor, but monetary diagnosis. Death was now called a part of medicine and big business. I called it murder... to relieve overpopulation less people to watch they then could use less water and food so forensic medicine, or their pathology was dearly needed. There were all kinds of conflicts, but none about human life, or the sanctity of human life. There were pre-nuptials that were arranged by elderly businessmen who married young "trophies" that stipulated, "if for any reason she became pregnant that is the wife that was legal grounds for divorce. He wanted his cake and eat it too."

Was the TRIBULATION here? Marie, Rachel and I were still here or could it be that TRANSLATION would occur in the 70th WEEK?

On our return home, I mentioned to Marie, "How glad I am to have you for my wife and such a beautiful daughter, such as Rachel."

Marie kissed me and cried with much joy and said, "I love you too!"

Life was worth living to the fullest that GOD had to offer. GOD was still in control and always would be, even though cataclysmic things were happening.

Politics and religion were now occultic not as they should have been with GODLY morals. Back in Israel we could see more fear amongst the believers. Demonic activity was much greater in such a short time. Something was transpiring in our very midst, but was now visible. Jerusalem, or Old Jerusalem had it's 8 Gates. First was the DAMASCUS GATE the most beautiful of all. The second one was the FLOWERS GATE, or HEROD'S GATE. This was the gate the Crusaders breached the wall and took the city of Jerusalem on July 15th, 1099 and proclaimed it for the Latin kingdom. The LION'S GATE opened towards the Mt. of Olives. The DUNG GATE is where the Western Wall is today. The ZION GATE had bullet holes from 1948. The JAFFA GATE lead to Jaffa. The NEW GATE opened in 1899 linked the Old city with the Now. The GOLDEN GATE is the oldest and most famous gate in which Y'eshua passed through on His way to the Temple. This was sealed by the Muslims in 1541 in order to prevent Messiah's entrance, but concrete and stone shall not stop Him.

CHAPTER VII

A VISIT WITH SAL

I went to see Sal my Cuban born friend and we discussed with much concern about the leviathan that appeared to be growing right under our very noses. Sal was an aeronautical engineer with also a degree in Business Administration.

Sal explained to me the insidious technological advances in the world of space stations, missles, briefcases, computers making computers, lasers, infrared, ultraviolet rays, head and light sensors, et cetera.

Now he talked about microchip cards and veri chips that were already in use and would have all in bites which could from conception to death give an entire person's life history almost moment by moment and which was stored in a memory bank. It was a great informer against all believers, or if they were not a New Ager.

He said, "Legal tender is becoming extinct in order to control buying and selling and a smart card is already here to do any and all business financial transactions with any company, or anyone."

Sal's scenario was indeed Big Big Brother. We both believed the Antichrist was in the world, but could not venture to say his age and if this individual was just Jewish, probably, or Gentile, male, yes, or female; known, yes, or uknown; half human and half demonic like the Nephilim with all of Satan's power and the FALSE PROPHET who was also probably Jewish. No, this was not the so called "Protoccols of the Elders of Zion" here, but something much more real, than a legend.

All we did know was that the earth, or the entire globe was changing for the worse. They were all crying for peace. More demonic activity with manmade created famines followed by pestilences and plagues. We remembered well Ground Zero in Cambodia where millions were forced by the Khmer Rouge into the jungle where they died and yet these same Khmer Rouge had been exonerated by at least the business world, as well as politicians in the West too.

Amnesty International, Greenpeace, the Sierra Club, the Club or Rome, the Vatican, World Bank, Masonry, the Templars and the Teutonics yes even the Knesset in Israel, were all a part of this New Age agenda.

I started to go back in history which is always dangerous, if one wants to be accurate. It was to the time of the Vietnam conflict and our own treasonous State Department who put our sons in the line of fire and were told as policemen are told, "Don't shoot unless fired at." Easy for them to say their sons were in colleges and universities, or conscientious objectors, or even traitors. How the North Vietnamese flushed out South Vietnamese and had the American troops believing that they were fighting the Viet Cong when in actuality they were fighting the South Vietnamese peasants on their own land. What was Southeast Asia really all about, if not to defeat the spread of anti-humane Communism in that part of the world? Yet Robert McNamara and David Rockefeller both of World Bank along with entertainment from Hollywood's Jane Fonda, her husband Tom Hayden and later a US Congressman, imagine that, and also the Chicago Seven, Herbert Marcuse a Nazi-homosexual from World War II and other illustrious Hollywood socialists and Communists such as Richard "the Anglophile" Burton, Burt Lancaster, Barbara "the recluse" Streisand, along with LBJ's homo-erotic narcissism, Richard "the Quaker" Nixon, Henry "the twin" Kissinger, Walter "by the Hudson" Cronkite and others of the rich and well educated iconoclasts of the 60's rebellion and anti-American entourage who were allowed by our own government to tour Hanoi, as well as other Communist countries, as average American citizens and not as US diplomats and to speak for all Americans... I wonder why? Some saw it as a way to ingratiate their pockets and obtain, or usurp power by force called subversion. The Secretary of Defense, Mr. McNamara was a big part of this debacle' that occurred in Southeast Asia for the sake of capitalism. This is how far capitalism extends to 58,000 + American lives plus 2,000 American civilians who the Soviets never returned of which Big Business and government just forgot including our real POW's and MIA's.

Roaring Thunder is a disgrace to honor our dead by the sound of Pagan, or Hell's Angels' motorcycle gangs. Was not the leader of Hell's Angels from Holly wood and was he not an anti-Semite derelict? Our dead soldiers need man in proper attire for military decorum not rebel rousing rednecks who cannot articulate why our dead died in vain and why we should not have won the war and why America's moral fiber was almost split in two from this tiny Southeastern Asian war. Twenty one gun salutes would be apropos' and not Hell's Angels on wheels with longhair and hippie clothes unshaven and totally out of decorum and the infamous State Department, but for the families who lost their sons in this conflict that should have and could have been won. These globetrotters still travel the globe making more wars to the highest bidder. So socialism does follow all capitalisms.

The media controlled the parties and the billionaires controlled the media and socialists, pure materialists, controlled the billionaires' wealth and power. Of course the billionaires in wealth wanted to appear to be controlled. Where else could easy money, wealth and power be made, but on the backs of the world's poor as usual. Not enough even their young men would give their lives, not for them, but for a just cause, but that would not be enough. They would have to sacrifice their lives for the wealth and power of the iconoclasts, these globetrotters. The super rich needed more than just blood money, they needed what Lenin was after, absolute power which corrupts absolutely.

Our soldiers were like security guards with a US emblem on their uniforms. They would be downsized and defeated by Communists and New Agers in our own government. Where else would such absurd orders come from for our military? Yes, these young men, or at least most of them would give their lives thinking noble causes, but the rich and well educated did not care. They would in fact rather see slave labor and illegals at work, that is the rich and well educated. Whatever they articulated, it meant the sacrifice of more lives such as the Beijing Conference. Only the retired generals without qualifications would attain lifetime pensions and luxuries just as had occurred before the Russian Revolution.

It was these young poor noble men and not the infamous rich and self seeking lot that would give their lives. There was also another general who earned his honors in the My Lai Massacre in Vietnam. Only Captain Medina and Lieutenant William Calley, a simpleton were court martialed for murdering an entire village of South Vietnamese civilians. The Colonel could not be found to answer any questions, the same as... Now for more honors he would be made Secretary of State, but with no qualifications whatsoever, except his shiny stars.

Sal said, "Thanks to the homo-erotic Lyndon Johnson and his construction firms in Vietnam", as Sal swallowed down his glass of port wine, "No more Westmorelands for more lives. America has no moral fiber and forget that universal freedom is all about, but yet we told tiny Vietnam to fight it's own war when big and great America could not? America already has a 38th parallel and the DMZ. Then Quakerism came and said there shall be peace after we sacrificed 58,000 lives, mostly poor and farm boys, and did the rich say, "Come home safely and with honor and make us all proud"? The real heroes never came back. The Soviets had to kill them for they would not talk. Where are their names in a memorial? We have many memorials for the socialists in our nation as it already is."

Sal had told about Africa and said, "Why were Ethiopia and Angola taken over by the Soviets? They used Cuban troops to create an Angolan civil war. The butcher Castro was in power. Then Carter and Scranton made their debut in the Middle East and in Latin America and all hell broke loose... Carter left his peasants on his own plantations and spoke about human rights and Habitat For

Humanity. Whatever habitat could that possibly be, for humans, or animals? They also indulged in disturbances with Carter and Scranton creating more enemies, than friends. Jimmy Carter's own Zhigniew Brzezinski help install a Polish Pope with the Vatican. Did not also Roman Catholicism's Polish sect lean toward Soviet Communism? After all Poland was only used as a cover from the West, the Soviets own paranoia. The West was too scared to do anything. Also did not the Moslems encourage their young in the Soviet Union to join the Komsomol, Young Pioneers in all Soviet Republics? That is why Islam likes communism and Nazism. They both are innately the same as Islam in ideology. So much for tranquil Islam, or say Afro-Communism in Angola and Mozambique."

Sal continued, "Who inspired the Sandinistas, but Catholicism's Liberation Theology. As capitalism grew, socialism ate it. Anyway "eat, drink and be merry for now your time has not yet come, but through complacency and apathy and self preservation the praying mantis shall devour the male. Universal freedom was never important. England proved that time and again. Soon iconoclasts, or in defense of the terrorists" and Sal drank his 3rd glass of wine "like Martin Luther King, Jr., Jane Fonda, Tom Hayden, the Black Panthers' Marxists, Angela Davis, Mohammed Ali, Ron Dellums, Reverends Jesse Jackson and Sullivan, the ACLU, People for The American Way, the United States Supreme Court, Congress and our half witted generals all would be held up as heroes. This again is in defense of the terrorists. Where else could the rich and the infamous use their 'race', celebrity, or money to promote our enemy's cause of tribal socialism? Why was Cuba and not Haiti, Puerto Rico, the Dominion Republic, et cetera taken by the Soviets, or the Sinos and they would have? Was it because the Cubans were the businessmen of Latin America?"

Sal was really steaming and hot. I had never seen him like this before. Who could blame him? He probably would never get to see his relatives again ever alive. Again Communism was saying "better red, than dead".

I thought, "But what about our soldiers? Were they too better dead with red, since they too had their hands tied behind their backs to defend themselves? The United Governments were not united nations, or peoples. They were to be a Mao type of organization that is to incite the masses against each other. A nation was a country that involved a people, not a government of thugs. A people have a collective spiritual form some less, some more then others. "Government is absolute power, raw power," as Washington had once said.

"How is one to defeat something that is prophesized by GOD and should we," was Sal's question?

I said, "We must never collaborate with the enemy, or our enemy even in America. For it is his last stand before being vanquished. We may not and shall not defeat this evil in the world, Messiah has destroyed the works of the devil, but we do not have to succumb to it's perniciousness. As once occurred in the Nazi Germany, a few did not sell out their soul to the devil whether they were, or were not believers. It was not Hitler alone, but his thugs of sexual deviants and a nation that allowed it to all happen, not once, but twice starting in the early 1900's. The entire nation was at first deceived, but after that they were not as to World War II. It was not as we are told, because of an economic depression, but spiritual and moral depression. But again to cover up this sexual perversion with the higher elites and Hitler's gangsters. In today's world, world Jewry, as never before takes on evil ways as a collective body of pure evil such as in Reformed Judaism."

Sal was listening, but had more to say.

"Does that mean that anti-Semitism shall be used as a façade now by this new royalty? And will it be used to promote sexual deviancy as before? Who can defeat the Rothschilds, Chase Manhattens, the Lourdes of London, et cetera?"

All of these questions at once made my head spin along with the few beers and wines that I had.

My response to Sal was hesitant, but nonetheless I proceeded to reply with much care and apprehension for I myself had always wondered about this one question and therefore could only answer, "That most Jews will refuse to be saved and shall also be part of this Antichrist and according to GOD'S will only a remnant shall be saved. The Antichrist might be Jewish, because some Jewish women still believe they shall have Messiah, hence the Antichrist through the paranormal. Satan would emulate, as close as possible, to the Holy Trinity. The number 666 probably represented Satan in the middle, with the FALSE PROPHET and the Antichrist on the ends of the Greek alphabet. All 6's because 7 is complete, as GOD is complete. A totally possessed individual with all of Satan's powers. Remember Satan is a spirit and cannot procreate and must use a human being and demonic being to consummate this totally evil being. This one can't have freewill that is why I believe it will be a Nephilim. A fallen being with human appearance. The elect shall be almost deceived that is the Jews. The world would be destroyed unless the days be shortened. We have to choose now not later or after TRIBULATION, or we shall go through the TRIBULATION unsaved Satan knows his time is short. With Lucifer's fall came this name Satan and one third the angelic host. All had freewill, none can say otherwise, but GOD shall choose. Alone in deep hell for all unbelievers. Who could say that they truly did not know good vs evil, or that GOD never put a search for Him in them? Adam had a tree and it's fruit. Satan did not have any physical temptation, because he is a spiritual being. His own pride that he invented was to be equal with GOD. All men have this search for GOD put there by GOD whether a Gospel is preached, or not, but it must be preached nonetheless. It does not confirm not to preach, but said man himself had freewill and was accountable to GOD for his choice. To know Messiah is to have Him in your spiritual heart. It is not head knowledge. A real saint has a transformed spiritual heart by grace and Biblically this is a saint. No one can canonize a saint only GOD can know and give this gift from His Son Messiah. This Body is the saints in the entire world and not by any sect, denomination, religion, et cetera. This Body was parts some lesser some great, but all equal in this Body. Messiah is the head of this spiritual Body. The other church is the Crusader from ages past. France even more, than Italy, accepted Roman Catholicism's image and hence the Jesuits' French Revolution. The French always know everything there is to know, hence pride blinds again this time in a collective people. This BEAST from Nazism is raising his head again with a mortal wound, or was it the Old Roman Empire?"

The Dialogue continued with Sal knowing that maybe in part he would come to understand more, as to the why I felt the way that I did and believed in what I did.

Sal said, "What about this 'Rapture'?"

I said, "There is no such word by name mentioned in the Bible but it does speak of "in the twinkling of an eye". In Daniel's 70th WEEK with 69 of them in and one more to go, being the TRIBULATION, or 7 years. The first 3 and one half years is to set-up and deceive Israel and the world and the second half, THE GREAT TRIBULATION, to cause havoc, war, chaos and evil of all kinds, all to turn against Israel itself. Afterwards ARMAGEDDON would come with Messiah and the translated saints at Megiddo, Israel which would then bring in the OLAM HABA. Satan would be put away for these 1,000 years."

As our conversation continued on, I felt the sense of an ominous presence in the room. Was someone, or something peering in our conversation? The facts Biblically were all there, but as to whom we probably soon would know.

I told Sal, "The Father we will never really see ever, even in heaven. Chapter 4 in the Book of Revealation somewhat describes GOD the Father and about carnelian, jasper and emerald. Daniel correlates with the Book of Revealation. Each WEEK represents 7 years for a total of 70x7, or 490 Hebrew years with 69 WEEKS already fulfilled and 1 week left to go. The 69th WEEK ended with Messiah riding into Jerusalem in 32 AD. This is where the Hebrew Time stopped and the Gentile time began. This can be calculated to the very day since the Jewish calendar, or one of them had 360 days in a year from 1BC to 1 AD with no 0 in time. One AD started the first millennium in AD. Not until Messiah resurrected did even the Disciples resurrect. Calvary had to occur first. This Death was for all sins. Messiah defeated death by dying to sin and being GOD in the flesh before and after. Y'eshua this GOD/man, "The Word became flesh and dwelt amongst us." Even in the Old Testament, whenever a Theophany occurred it did not provide resurrection power for the Old Testament saints, when they died. They all went to Abraham's bosom. They were waiting for Messiah. Y'eshua on earth was here, not in heaven, so there was only one Saviour. He grew into a man and started His ministry at age 30 and was crucified about the age of 33 and one half years. Abraham's near sacrifice was a forthcoming of Messiah, the sacrificial Lamb, an only son that Abraham had of the chosen people, the Jews. The church age of grace would move into the age of GOD'S KINGDOM, during the TRIBULATION. TRANSLATION on the saints, first the dead in Messiah and then those alive in Y'eshua. Days later all hell would break loose. Three and a half years for the Antichrist to deceive and 3 and one half years to rule ruthlessly the world over. ARMAGEDDON would follow, then the OLAM HABA. All unbelievers would resurrect at the end of the OLAM HABA and appear each one individually before the GREAT WHITE THRONE JUDGMENT and then be thrown into the burning lake of fire forever. Hell would no longer be. All believers in the FIRST RESURRECTION is two part, would appear before the JUDGMENT SEAT OF MESSIAH for their rewards, or crowns and then to be with Messiah forever to reign. This too would occur one by one. Yes, life is a series of choices. We must each decide about GOD personally, not by group religion, or even denomination, or mental reasoning. The time would be unknown. Death had not occurred for Elijah and Enoch for GOD took them. Only the Father knows of this "TRANSLATION."

Sal had always heard that good works were the only way, or how much one gave, or how famous one was and even if one was baptized or took communion is how one got saved. I knew Sal had been taught the do's and don't's of religious salvation and or moralism and not by grace alone. "My grace is sufficient for you." He did not know GOD like he knew me personally. "If you have seen Me you have seen the Father, I and the Father are One." He knew about GOD only and not Him personally.

Sal asked, "How would this twinkling of an eye occur?"

I said, "As far as I know this spiritual resurrection will occur first with people who had died but whose spirit is alive in Messiah by His grace and then ones alive on earth with the same spirit will also rise to meet Messiah in the air. There will be a worldwide disappearance of millions which will shock the world as to what happens. Some will finally realize that they have missed the boat and this will include many churchgoers and others who feel their religion, or denomination, or works will save them or anything else, except the one true GOD and Messiah's crucifixion, death and resurrection which is known as PASSOVER. Only resurrected ones can resurrect with Messiah. The RUACH HAKODESH will be gone from the earth and all hell will break loose on this earth. Then the GOSPEL OF THE KINGDOM will be preached by believers not the GOSPEL OF GRACE any longer. All believers will have glorified bodies, just as Messiah who had been TRANSLATED. We will, or they will be able to touch, if one could and yet material matter will not affect them, plus they can eat just like Messiah did when He returned to doubting Thomas. Our thoughts then will transport us from one place physically to another in the blink of an eye. So much for E=mc(2). This will be the quintessential body. If one dies before salvation, after the TRANSLATION they will be eternally lost. In TRIBULATION, ones who have not heard the true GOSPEL can be with GOD, if they do not take the mark of the beast and will probably die for their faith. Some believe once they have heard the Gospel before TRANSLATION and then entered TRIBULATION still could be with GOD by death on earth and without a glorified body and would help rule in the OLAM HABA immediately... Sal please read Romans 10:9-10. Also all children with no age of accountability and all babies, born and unborn, but conceived would immediately go to Paradise upon death in this church age of grace in a mature state. "And the 24 Elders would bow down to worship GOD continuously." In the OLAM HABA babies live to be 100 years old."

Sal was still puzzled at what he had just heard and was wondering what he had heard and if it was true. His facial expression was frozen and said, "Could all this really be true?"

I continued, "GOD, the Father, is a spirit who is omnipotent, all powerful; omnipresent, everywhere and omniscient, all knowing. He knows all our hearts and our thoughts. His love is everywhere at every time knowing everything. His love for us is never conditional and we separate ourselves from Him. He never separates His love for us.

Our next discussion was held at a small café on the outside because the authorities started to look in churches and some homes, temples, mosques and synagogues. The Word needed to get out, but one had to be careful about oneself, or their family could even be telling on them intentionally, or unintentionally. One can remember in America what the Children's Defense Fund by the UN and Hillary did to the American families.

I said to Sal, "When the Jews as a nation rejected Messiah, as a nation, as a people, Israel, the Hebrew nation, it occurred on April 16, 32 AD. Messiah coming into Jerusalem is when the time period for the Hebrews stopped as a nation. From march 14, 445 BC to April 6, 32 AD was a time span of 483 years to the day, calculated in days. The math was 69x7=483 years, or 69 WEEKS with 360 days which would equal 173,880 days with 1 more WEEK, or 7 years to be fulfilled. TRIBULATION time is 7 years times 360 days which equals 2520 days, or 84 months. One half of the TRIBULATION is 1260 days (Luke 41-44 and John 1). What is to occur will be the following according to GOD'S Word the Bible. The FIRST PLAYER will be Europe, the 10 nation confederacy; the SECOND PLAYER will be the North with Syria, Turkey and Russia; the THIRD PLAYER will be the "kings of the East" with China, Japan, India, Pakistan, et cetera; the FOURTH PLAYER will be the Lord and His army of angelic hosts and the saints; the FIFTH PLAYER will be Israel, a non-active participant, trampled over for the last time. Israel and the Antichrist make a covenant which deceives Israel and

Europe, then the North attacks with the South. The North African powers, such as Egypt, Libya and Ethiopia will come after the Antichrist with the North and the South being then decimated. The Antichrist moves into Israel and into Jerusalem itself in the first half of the TRIBULATION. The North and the East will alarm the Antichrist. The East will have millions of conventional soldiers and the North and the South and Europe move against each other. Then comes this ARMAGEDDON. They will all forget to be at war with the Antichrist, as well as each other and will get together to fight the Lord, but will lose and hence the OLAM HABA. Messiah's rule from Jerusalem shall continue for 1,000 years. As this is occurring this ARMAGEDDON on earth, in heaven the archangel Michael battles Satan and his cohorts with Michael as the prince of Israel. The rescued people, the Jews out of the TRIBULATION and some Gentiles will establish with Messiah the OLAM HABA, plus the resurrected people, the ones who evangelized during the TRIBULATION. About one third of the Jews shall be spared, or saved. The FIRST RESURRECTION was Y'eshua Himself. The SECOND RESURRECTION, the TRANSLATED Body of Messiah in the age of grace before the TRIBULATION, AND THE THIRD RESURRECTION at the end of the TRIBULATION with the Old Testament Saints such as Moses, David, Isaiah, etc., plus the TRIBULATION SAINTS who had died. The FOURTH RESURRECTION is the unbelievers at the end of the OLAM HABA. The two main resurrections are one for the saints and one for the unbelievers and approximately a little over 1,000 years in between them. One in the TRANSLATION and one at the end of the OLAM HABA. The saints appear at the JUDGMENT SEAT OF MESSIAH and the unsaved must appear at the GREAT WHITE THRONE OF JUDGMENT to be judged for their sins one at a time. The second half of the TRIBULATION shall be called THE TIME OF JACOB'S TROUBLE. The only thing that does not work out in my mind is the 1290 days, instead of the 1260 days, or 42 months, or the 3 and one half years which would equal 30 days more, or 1290 days not 1260, then there is an additional 45 days from 1290-1335?"

After about my 3rd cup of black coffee and Sal's 4th one I said to Sal, "Only GOD has the right exact count down to the very day and time. There is also no mention of Christmas, or an Easter in Scripture anywhere to be found. All these holidays are more of Europeanism's religiosity in religion and not in Biblical faith and exactness. The PASSOVER is the real resurrection, death and crucifixion represented by Messiah's Calvary. This is when the angel of death passed over the Hebrews while they were slaves in Egypt under Pharaoh for about 400 years, and then Moses lead them into the wilderness. The Hebrews' first born sons and livestock were spared and the Egyptians' first born sons were not, including Pharaoh's. The Hebrews had spread the blood of lambs on their doorposts so the angel of death would pass them by unharmed. This emulation was of Messiah's shed blood at Calvary. Hanukah in John 10:22 is the FEAST OF DEDICATION which celebrates the opposition to Antiochus Epiphanes who brought a pig into the Temple. This is a sort of first antichrist to the real Antichrist in the TRIBULATION period known as the ABOMINATION OF DESOLATION, Daniel 8:13, the Antichrist. Seminaries now teach that Daniel was 2 people, which is not true. Daniel spoke and wrote both Aramaic and Hebrew, and so in Daniel 8 it changes from Aramaic to Hebrew by Daniel himself and not another person. Also all rabbis are forbidden to read the Book of Daniel which by the way is in the Old Testament, because I believe of it's correlation to the Book of Revelation or John's vision at the end of the Bible and deals almost entirely with Biblical Prophecy which I believe is upon us now."

Sal only looked more bewildered and maybe I shared too much at one time, or had unintentionally missed something, or even made a mistake, but nonetheless it was a stimulating dialogue with Sal my friend. After this discussion I was ready to leave and think about what we had just heard.

Sal said, "Glad to have had you over."

I said, "Yes, I can say the same for this conversation," and then said, "Good night."

CHAPTER VIII

DIALOGUE WITH MARIE AND THEN SOME

Later that night I shared with Marie my discussion with Sal and said, "America fell because it compromised GOD'S Word which is His will and took itself to be a god, instead of worshipping GOD, Adam compromised and lost paradise; Abraham compromised and almost lost Sarah; Sarah compromised and still there is no Middle East peace; Esau compromised and lost his birthright, although his progeny, Bela, an Edomite, became the first Semite king; Aaron compromised and missed the Promised Land; Samson compromised and lost his eyes and his life; David compromised and lost his son Nathan; Solomon compromised and lost his throne; Ananias and Sapphira compromised and lost their lives. America compromised and lost GOD'S protection, His blessing, and possibly it's collective national soul. America had welcomed another god, money. We allowed foreign gods to be worshipped. We ignored the 10 Commandments and the Mosaic Law that Y'eshua never abolished, but fulfilled. We thought of egoism and self-preservation. Our music became "garbage stew". Even the beats in this "garbage stew" was summoning the demons. America had not cared at all about the innocent. American churches had been Europeanized. Only American Biblicals and Messianic Jewry follow GOD'S Word, plus when GOD will use unbelievers in some cases for His good."

Marie asked, "Why had America followed a Gentile religion?"

"My best guess would be that one, the Vatican and the Anglican and Protestant Churches all sought expansionism, not always of the Gospel, but of their particular denomination, culture, or even language as the German language missed by one vote to becoming the official language of the United States. Bickering was endless as it was in Europe for centuries. Not so much of laying down one's life literally, but a world religion of theological politics, or schisms. The second reason I believe is that the TIMES OF THE GENTILES failed in part to proselytize to the Jewish people generation after generation, no matter how stiff necked they are. Who did Peter witness to, when GOD told him to? Was it not the Gentiles and one could almost say that was in THE TIME OF THE HEBREWS? The third reason is another god, or gods, replaced the Father of Abraham, Isaac and Jacob with maybe too much of our Founding Forefathers, as well as worshipping by consent the religions of Islam, Hinduism, socialism, Marxism, Buddhism and of course money and the love of it. "You shall have no other gods before ME." American democracy also turned to Greek Democracy where "might is right" and changed from only a type, to a form of democracy. Our brave new world in America became pusillanimous and pernicious and our youth became promiscuous. If one was a child, or infant they had to hope they would not be infanticized or raped, or tortured or lead astray by all the evil in America. For youths and adolescents it is not so much peer pressure, as it is the older generations that emulate all the wrong things with a few exceptions. The Baby Boomers rebelled against GOD and were acquiescent about moral or immoral issues and did not guide or oppose or speak out against evil, even in their own homes, churches, neighborhoods, schools, communities, governments, and we had plenty of those... As middle aged adults we allowed ourselves to be desensitized by Hollywood and government, plus capitalism. We also were too preoccupied with our own little self centered world and with what government threw at us from all sides to keep us so busy we forgot our own. The elderly became the senior, or as I called it, the senor' citizen where the Padre' mentality took over for their lives, as far as income, health and even family. They acquiesced to the young and the inexperienced in life and thought constantly about how to retire from life, itself. Martin Luther King, Jr's mother was killed by a "black" man. Timothy McVeigh worked with 2 Moslems to blow up the building in Oklahoma City. The so called "right to work" discriminated against handicapped individuals starting in the states of Florida and Connecticut. Churches almost all were 501 C status government churches and the underground church grew. Masons of the 33rd and 34th degree knew what was going on in America. The University of North Carolina had required all freshmen to read portions of the Koran, and the NEA proposed "Blame America" programs to remember 9/11, and 7th graders in California were forced to simulate Muslim worship in order to graduate. Also they were by then that is all Americans brainwashed with euthanasia by socialists and unstable people of all kinds in prominent positions. One no longer needed to be qualified to hold a position in America just to be Lenin's original phrasing POLITICALLY CORRECT, or to uphold evil by calling it diversity, tolerance, et cetera, anything but what it really was animosity and rebellion. Who was this rebellion really against? GOD Himself... The church, Marie, was obsessed with me, myself and I and taught self-esteem, instead of self initiative, or self discipline. On center stage of theatrical reality is this coming ruler, or dictator. Who would solve the world's peace Problem? I remember when mandatory seat belts and non-smoking laws seemed viable and harmless, but were only an opening up of Pandora's Box for an invasion into one's private life. If seat belts save lives and they do why are motorcycles not either outlawed, or given speed governors on all of them? Here is an inconsistency in government regulations, because their concern is not safety but control as well as taxes on cigarettes so that they can break up family-run companies who will not sell out. Another example is in the state of Maine. There is no smoking allowed except in one's car, one's home, or the designated room in a hotel, or motel and guess where the Bushes reside? Do environmentalists not know that one volcanic eruption itself does much more destruction such as a century's worth to the ozone layer, but yet there is no hole in it? What is their real agenda? Confiscation of all private property and not ecology?"

Marie asked me, "How does this affect Israel now?"

I said, "One of our Presidents is definitely a New Ager. His name is not important. This man started in motion something that cannot be reversed. With this more wars, strife and terrorism worldwide has started. We again in America are preoccupied, this time with self such as jewelry, car -- America's status symbol - drugs, pornography, pleasure and leisure in excess "garbage stew" Hollywood's insanity and iconoclasts with their face lifts, cosmetics and divorces. We can never do without and that includes our cars, or transportation. We need fuel for the rich and well educated's ideology. Convenience with no self-discipline to restrain ourselves from our wild West impulses, such as not to do without. This debacle of our own making continued on till 9/11 and from there it was all down hill. We involve ourselves willingly with Islamic Jihad which in turn pressures Israel to make only one kind of decision and that is self-preservation, but with a totalitarian outlook. Never can we do without, or abstain from. Our over indulgence takes us even into carcinogenic foods to the point of obesity by malnutrition. Our GNP became our Greatest National Pollution and not of our air only, but of our very souls. America is noted for two things all around the world, and they are stealing and taking drugs. Now stealing becomes ever involved in Big Business, such as someone else's eminent domain and our fait accompli is to give Islam what it wants, America. Even in our department stores there are signs in dressing rooms where one tries on new clothing that says, "Not responsible for items left unattended." This is not because of other customers but because many times the store's employees will steal, and so the store has to in some way legally protect themselves because they do not really screen job applicants, plus the government has inserted federal guidelines or restrictions to let private enterprise be non-private to hire the unqualified."

Marie then asked, "How is Israel as an ally to America?"

I said, "The question should not be how much Israel is an ally to America, but how much America and for how long will America remain a loyal ally to Israel? America has multiculturalism and wants to share it with Israel like homosexuals who like to snare AIDS. Plus 30% of all American "blacks" are Moslems and that number is growing and so is their Israelis' anti-Semitism. Something else America wants Israel to share, since America neither has the courage, or moral fiber as a nation to do what Israel has to do and that is oppose violence by not lying. America though will be guided not by Japan's interests, but by England's investments in America. Guess who owns England? Arab Islamic oil money. Most of America is also foreign owned and not by our friends. The rich and well educated continue to globetrot all around the world looking for this globalization. Not for ecology, but for world control and power. Now it appears that America, Europe and yes Israel might form an unexpected alliance. So now we see what has happened in regards to Israel and America, as well as Europe. Let us not forget also that American Biblicals, Messianic Jewry, Russian Orthodoxy and some Evangelicals will be outcasts. More Judaizers will persecute even their own flesh and blood, hence blood is not thicker than water, whenever Messiah's blood is involved. Israel shall accept this ruler by being deceived, but by then it shall be too late to turn back. Satan again emulates not only geographically, but in numbers. The unholy trinity of Satan, the Antichrist and the FALSE PROPHET. America and Europe will need Israel in the pre-TRIBULATION and TRIBULATION. Israel will be the center of all things, but for evil. All roads will lead to Jerusalem."

Marie looked so frightened at what I had said. She then asked me. "What do you think will happen to Israel as a nation and a people?"

I said, "Eventually when all is said and done Messiah will rule from Jerusalem in the OLAM HABA. Satan will be locked away for 1,000 years and the lion and the lamb will lie down beside... Before all this will take place freewill will become much harder in obedience to GOD'S authority. GOD'S love shows most, when we do what we do not want to do even though it is GOD'S WILL.

When we do not believe GOD is around, is when really GOD'S will is marvelously at work and His love is even more wonderful, if we remain silent enough to hear it in our spiritual heart."

As I finished saying all of this to my wife, I hugged her passionately and told her "I love you as Messiah loves the church." She just cried.

We both knew that Messiah had to be first in our marriage and not our mate who was for this life. Messiah was eternal.

I went on with other stories to uplift Marie this time.

I said, "I have heard of people now who have been TRANSLATED from one place to another physically. One occurred in Siberia where a Christian traded places with an unbeliever who was to be shot in a line formation with each 10th prisoner to be shot. When the Christian awoke or opened his eyes, he had been TRANSLATED to another place where all believers in a circle were in prayer and with him in the middle. Or when a group of saints were praying in the woods again in Russia and silently to themselves as to where they should meet again, knowing full well a KGB agent was amongst them, but not as to whom it was in their mist. When they all met again to pray the location to all of them was exactly where to meet, except for the KGB agent. They were once again saved from this intruder for evil. Or the time when African Christians, now these were true Africans, could not cross a raging river, but were lead to walk on water to get to the other side. America was not formed, as a colonized country for England. America was set up for only one faith, Judeo-Christianity. It was not set up for any other religion, or religions. If one is to believe old, but original archives with no revisions, then our historians today are wrong and after all history is an inexact science. Novelists and not historians can write history much more accurately and precisely. America had one GOD as Americans with no hyphens, or foreign religions. Who said anything about Mohammed, Buddha, Confuscius, Martin Luther, the Vatican, et cetera? It was faith then the state and not vice versa. Freedom to worship out loud and not by the ACLU'S Communist Manifesto of Marxism. Why would anyone risk their families' lives and property for an ideology, especially since most did know the Good Book and slavery was mentioned in it. Either one tells the whole...

Why one lies? The revisionists in America chose to lie. No not about slavery, but about how America was founded and by what faith and who were the individuals involved. They had a devious agenda but with no brights for brains. From the Scottish Enlightment the English believers left England, the Anglican Church and the king. All three were English. They went to Holland first, but believers were marrying unbelievers and also one could not proselytize there and maybe for the best of it. They set sail for Cape Cod in America for the Christian faith. There were later about 135 Rhode Scholars in one place. Never before in the world had so many scholars come together in one place. What were the majority of these men? Christians and not Moslems, or even Messianic Jews. There were some Deists. The Enlightenment brought in the Industrial Revolution, or the subsequence thereof."

I thought to myself, "When Elul the last month on the traditional Jewish calendar is, it will probably be preceding the TRANSLATION of the church whenever that does occur."

"No, there was no Roman Catholicism at all as in Constantine's time. This plebiscite of men, even in a majority, by far were Christians and some Deists. Who else set up America's government, or at least it's founding in the 17th Century? One nation, or nationality, or so came to be. American Biblicals never left this premise. Many Europeans brought a Christianity, but from their own country and did not assimilate ever, as American Biblicals who knew their new founding of America's GOD and not Germany's Protestantism, Italy's Catholicism, England's Anglicanism, Greece's Greek Orthodox, et cetera. Only a few Messianic Jews stayed to America's worship of GOD, and herein lies the real truth. American Biblicals and Messianic Jewry are the only two who had America's GOD. This was Messiah's way for America. The "roots" with the "branches" hence revival. In Israel there had been 12 individual tribes, but then one nation. One worshipped the true GOD by Messianic faith in Israel. The other worshipped a god, but all were in different nations today, such as Syria, Egypt, Lebanon, Saudi Arabia, Jordan, Iraq, et cetera. Each nation had a different god or did they? Israel was a holy nation, not a holy tribe. GOD chose Jews, because of Abraham's faith but who supplied the faith? The Hebrews to cross over have to do just that. Russian Orthodoxy was not any other nation's way to worship their GOD founded by St. Cyril and St. Methodius. What luggage did they bring? The commonality is this Russian Orthodoxy is Russian, American Biblicals is American and Messianic Jewry is Israelis. The real church started at Pentecost in Acts with all Jews. Out of these three examples only can Messianic Jewry transport faith, because who else are the roots and what is the Bible mostly about? And if universal faith it must begin with a Jewish GOD. Russian Orthodoxy and American Biblicals must attach themselves to Messianic Jewry for that is where salvation lies, in the Jews. Y'eshua came to earth as a Jewish man, so Israel is more than national like the other two, but universal. "A light unto all nations." Who might that be? The nation of Messianic Jewry? All men created equal in GOD'S image as human beings with free will. "Let Us make man in Our Image." Slaves brought to America had inherited their master's faith, or better yet the Master's faith. Most American Negroes were not a nation but a "race" as in color. Through man's evil GOD brought to fruition the American Negro, or American Biblical in most cases. This then became not a nation within a nation but a faith of people known too, as Americans hence American Biblicals by the Negroes. "We are all one race, the human race," but with one national way to worship GOD. Was there any such thing as an African, or "black" Christian? There were, though, American Biblicals. "Race" does not determine the heart, but does race determine if one is a human being? Again we are all one race the human race made in the image of GOD. The people in Russia were the peasants, especially in the 17th, 18th, 19th, and 20th Century. They stayed to their land and to their GOD. The people in America were American Biblicals and Messianic Jews and most were poor as in Russia and they too stayed to their GOD. Both "peoples" founding their own GOD, yet worshipping the One the Jews call Messiah. As the peasant in Russia was almost entirely destroyed by socialism, “the people” in America were too almost destroyed by capitalism. In America the American Negro was assimilating into America not because of civil rights which lead into another form or forms of slavery. Let us take in Zimbabwe’s white farmers who were told they should leave their homeland, because of civil rights by way of President Mugabe. It was the American Negro’s closeness to the soil in America, just as was with the Russian Peasants in Russia. What was meant to set them free only enslaved them once again and not by visible chains, but by invisible chains to the soul. What can please GOD, but faith and is it not unseen? Again pure materialism, socialism usurped the Negro’s plight from slavery into another age of one much more destructive. The destruction of the heart and soul. The spiritual always works slower than the political and expediency can only do harm for a people who again must now all catch up. These People are Americans. Now the state and not the individual would enslave not only the Negro but all Americans for when a part of the body dies all of it may surely die with it. Once called property the Negroes by the United States Supreme Court in 1857 of the Dred Scott Case who was at the helm? Was it not again the rich and well educated? To be told one is free is not freedom, but only a play on words. With freedom comes first responsibility, or responsibilities and the rights of GOD alone. If one does not know the method, one cannot obtain the principle behind it and shall fail to comprehend. In America, Marie, up to 80% of the American people got some form of welfare, or socialism from the state. Group mentality was applied here always. Individual views did not matter only party’s special interest, or ideology. Was slavery ever an individual view, or was it ever honorable? One must state the truth with compassion and we must first be Americans with faith in an American GOD, as American Biblicals, hence a nation not a tribe or village shall spiritually do. Who has put us in our own birthplace with no choice of our own? Some of us have not even seen the light of day out of the womb and where is their defense attorney in government?

Do any of us have a choice as to where we are born? As with you, Marie, a Polish Jew, a Jewish person first by ancestry, but a Polish citizen by birth. A unique combination of being a Jew also and a non-Orthodox Russian blends naturally well because of the mixture of a society. They do not know Messiah, but the Jew is Christian by nature. These Hebrews must cross over to Messiah and to Israel. They seek Aliyah, because GOD is calling the Jews back now. A Jew now who is Russian-Jewish and wants Aliyah can do it for two reasons. Whether to be a national alone or to be with Messiah in Israel which is home. A sort of American Biblical, or Russian Orthodox, but not so with Messianic Israelis' Jews. When GOD calls them back out of whatever country, are they unpatriotic to that old country? Israel and Jerusalem is being willed by GOD to come back home. Only Messianic Jewry get to know and understand what GOD truly wants. Since in America a nation was founded upon faith in the only GOD and not another's GOD, it was not at it's inception a religion. A new nation found their own GOD. Jefferson and Franklin never found the American GOD, as Messiah, but King Nebuchadnezzar and even the infamous Jeffrey Dahmer did! Yes, Mr. Dahmer. Since they, Jefferson and Franklin, chose no other religion, they chose the Bible by mental ascent, but not Messiah in the heart. Roman Catholicism would have not impressed these scholarly men, since the Spanish Inquisition, the Crusades, Constantine, et cetera were not what they sought and Judaism only served history without Messiah. There were 2500 Jews during the Revolutionary War, so America was not anti-Semitic either. America's War of Independence, though was not a Bolshevik Revolution, or a civil war. It was a war fought as a spiritual revival with a foreign aggressor. Marie, there were different kinds of wars, conflicts, et cetera. It is important to differentiate between them. For example Vietnam was a conflict where our soldiers could not shoot unless shot at a sort of vaudevillian rendition of the Keystone Cops. This is what civil law enforcement is taught. Apprehend first then shoot, if necessary after all else fails. The Korean War also was similar to Vietnam, because it had a 38th parallel. Both World

Wars were not real World Wars, but this one shall certainly be. In the second part of the TRIBULATION the Antichrist shall have wars that would normally take decades, but only last days, once he is in for his second term of 3 and one half years. This end time scenario is not the end of time, but shall be first of the first WORLD WAR ever. The Antichrist shall supply many civil wars. Democracies do not last long, only a Christian monarchy can. Monarchial Government is the only Biblical form of government. Whenever LORD in the Old Testament is used, it refers to the Father. Whenever Lord is used it refers to Messiah. The enemy has been judged, but not yet sentenced. He has been defeated at Calvary for all believers and unbelievers."

I said to Marie, "I almost forgot to check my mail on the Internet."

Government's Postal workers' jobs were all eliminated by this. I searched through the mail, until I found what I was looking for. There it was my application to Greenpeace. I had time to respond but there was a yearly fee. I would wait, until the last minute to decide, if I would join. I had requested this application by mail to appear democratic and voluntary. I could see the number 666 in small print at the upper left hand corner. I brought this all to Marie's attention.

I said to Marie, "They want an immediate commitment now, but I do not intend ever to join a New Age organization."

Marie as well as Rachel who had come into the room both said, "We also will not sign up."

I said, "This not signing up could limit our income coming in over the Internet in the way of higher international taxes. It could also affect our assets, my job, Rachel's schooling."

I said to Rachel and Marie, "There were two colleges in America - I believe they were in Florida and in Arizona - who implanted a mark of some kind which the authorities said it was to determine which students were students and which were not in order for them to be admitted to all sporting events and extracurricular activities." I said, "How clever all this was," at that time to a friend of mine who did not understand in the slightest what I meant. They were getting their New Age foot into America's door again via the college route. This was what brought us to where we are now in the world, an awareness as good citizens to always be vigilant. The Jewish people had failed as a nation last time to Know Messiah. This time He would not let them. Religious holidays are nil. Bethlehem has no sign of Messiah's birth and Nazareth to me was only a speedway. The Dome of the Mosque, or Rock has been moved for our New Age Temple. Jerusalem is being occultic in all ways. Islam is taking a back seat to this New Age religion. To me I believe the Antichrist is in the world and shall soon be here in Israel. The talk of this king is in the wind."

Marie and especially Rachel were listening even more intently than before.

"There shall be no more Knesset, or parliamentarian type of government. We are close to Daniel's 70th WEEK. I believe most of the Gentiles are in. Indoctrination is in vogue by the rich and the elite, or else... With many executives in closed rooms is this New Age hypnotism and out of the body far Eastern experiences. Nature now is very abnormal. Harvests in America are none. Europe is running low. Astrology is growing, not astronomy. Already I believe nuclear holocaust has occurred in the world. Even my job is being downsized, because only 100% New Agers are... and also this monarch is reducing everything to one source. I also believe man is going backwards. Our spirit in our own nation is falling. We three do have Messiah's joy in our heart and not happiness which is a state of mind. When one is poor not rich does not one depend on GOD? It is true that no one is striving for poverty except government so that the people are always in want. The poor need GOD, the rich have their god here on earth. They search and search for this ever elusive thing called happiness. Faith is not seeing, but believing and how else can we please GOD but through faith in Messiah's strength and not our own? As believers we know not just about a god, but know Him Personally as we know each other. Were not the Jewish people looking for the physical kingdom and not the spiritual one and a king to take over and because of this were blinded by Satan not to see Messiah Himself? They too did not see the forest for the trees. That is why the contemporary must be written as is now and publicly and the future is all "open time" because only GOD knows the future and to presuppose and not prophesize is to play the role of a creator and to work in "closed time". Let us truly pray to see today and write about it all truth never distorted, because history is an inexact science and the future has "open time" meaning again only GOD knows. Man must be concerned about the present. It is common man that makes history. Without this man's history would not occur as such. In Russia the common peasant made the history and like perhaps no other nation showed always their trust and loyalty to the land not part of Europeanism like Americanism. To be un-Russian or unknown, or un-American is a hate crime, or to hate one's country of native birth. This separation of nations into tribes, villages, plebiscites, or YUGOSLAVIANS per se, does not make for peace, but for hostile diversity. See how different and obnoxious we can be. This was European bickering for centuries amongst themselves. Theirs was self-serving, egotistical and a materialistic mind set with no heart for GOD, but for this world only. "Get away from Me I never knew you." The Russian peasants showed freedom of heart was more important, then free in the physical. Freedom of action was their belief in GOD. Not wishing to be slaves, but only to be left alone by socialism's bureaucrats. They served their monarch well. Freedom of conscience meant GOD fearing and not freedom to do anything. What had Messiah stressed? In America it was said after civil rights, "Let us just educate the poor, but without GOD." Even Benjamin Franklin understood education without GOD was nothing, but empty knowledge and he was a Diest. Revival from the poor and the Messianic Jews, because "salvation is of the Jews" and the poor look unto GOD, if not destroyed by socialism and atheism. In America it is the American Biblicals and Messianic Jewry that give up their rights and always are for others and wish them well and if more talented, then more to wish them well with. Also in America there have been too many sects to oppose infanticide and brutality in the Negro family that their children have to unwind by destroying public property. The women in society have lost their way and sold out motherhood. They still are more compassionate than most men. Nazi Germany and before women had been dehumanized by being used as procreation objects alone, as well as from Roman Catholicism. A woman is not just a female, but a mother and a wife and later a grandmother with much intuition about her children and nurtures to her children, especially at a very young age. To desensitize women and to encourage them to be like Eve's socialism as to the role in authority is to usurp Adam's role, even if the man acquiesces to it, is wrong. Life has to do with normal healthy relationships, such as the immediate family, or else GOD would not have given His Son through Mary, the Jewish maiden of Virginity, or created Adam, then from Adam, Eve as wife. This is a nation's strongest institution, the family. It is sexuality, not sensuality, in a lifetime of marriage. There are two innate sexes, not more, or less with different reasons for being, but yet working as one in matrimony through Y'eshua for life as a family. "Be fruitful and multiply." What could we have done without you Marie, my wife, or you Rachel, my daughter and our aunts, grandmothers and nieces? Why is it also that the very poor Jewish person sees GOD in Messiah, as personal and most Jews do not? Most Jewish people have been westernized, since Israel is an Eastern State. Both Ashkenazim and Sephardim Jewish people have been affected by this materialism. Why not evangelization of the Jews? Now Aliyah by GOD to Israel is occurring quickly and still Israel is mostly secular. They are returning, but not really knowing why, because they do not really know who Messiah is. Even the Russian and Polish Jews are Europeanized and not evangelized and hence Judaism occurs and not Messianic Jewry."

Marie was such a beautiful wife and mother. She came to Israel from Russia's Poland with Menachem Begin with good and bad memories and not much Westernized materialism.

I went on to explain, "The 12 tribes have to be all in Israel maybe not yet complete in regards to Messianic Jewry and their virginity, plus 12,000 from each tribe exactly, GOD shall know when these are the ones, the remnant, that shall be saved and hidden by GOD until TRIBULATION is over completely. They shall have GOD'S mark on them. There also shall be Jew and Gentile that will not take "the mark of the beast" and not die in the TRIBULATION. Marie your tribe you told me about was the sacramental Levite tribe who are allotted land by GOD, in the Old Testament, but could not own it the same as the Catholic Church later had done to their own priests so they would or could not get married. Your family was one of the three in the Levite tribe and was called Kohath. I believe Moses and Aaron his older brother were from that particular family and not tribe. Jacob had 12 sons, hence the 12 tribes of Israel, although Joseph was Jacob's favorite son and was almost killed by his own brothers, but Judah stopped them, but they nonetheless sold him to relatives of Ishmael who in turn sold him to Potiphar in Egypt. Joseph was his youngest son. The other sons ahead of him missed out on this blessing because of their sin, such as Judah the oldest who committed incest. Joseph made a tribe of people, or a family into a nation. What was meant for evil, GOD made for good. Here is this collective spiritual body."

As another month flew by, or was it my age in years that made time seem to fly by? Nonetheless another trip by government was taking me to another part of the world in Africa. It was to Ethiopia and the Mosaic tribe of the Falasha under "black" Marxist government persecution, because of their faith and not their "race". Nothing was mentioned in the world media about these "blacks" persecuting Ethiopian Jewish Negroes. Why was that? Did it have anything to do with POLITICAL CORRECTNESS? One was lead to believe all Negroes were "blacks" or even Moslems, even though 30% of American "blacks" were Moslems in America, but why? Most borders were having wars. Most countries would not accept Jews, but retained their own by coercion.

Yes Jacob had 12 sons from 4 different wives, plus one daughter. Polygamy? No. God was procreating the Jewish people knowing that they would be persecuted. Jacob's servants were not slaves. Two of Jacob's wives were maidservants who gave birth to some of the 12 tribes.

Looking back on America and it's taking on of Islam, Hinduism, et cetera, because capitalism only knew economics yet avarice too. Socialism encompassed more like Islam did. It was an ideology and not a faith. America was doomed. It was now no longer a Judeo-Christian nation and much before that had lost it's GODLY spirituality. If Abraham, Isaac, or Jacob would have done what America did, they too would have disrupted, or interrupted GOD'S plan. They did sin, but always loved GOD and chose no other kind of GOD over YHWH. The moral idea of GOD preceded the nationality which precedes civic duty which today is improperly called "social" justice always, or Communism, totalitarianism. Any culture beside the Christian one and there is such a thing as a Christian culture.

The "simpletons of success" want not only wealth, but absolute power just as oligarchy dictators do, but want the world to call them capitalists, or businessmen to sound legitimate and sophisticated. These ones in capitalism have contributed more to promote socialism, then anything else has, such as Ruppert Murdoch who controls the Fox networks and one can see by what violence he lives by behind closed doors, even though he says he upholds free enterprise, but what is free enterprise with no holds barred? After capitalism always comes socialism, pure materialism, no GOD just ingratiating the senses in their physical world. After all world government and world bank, proper noun, or not is the same? Could the length of America been extended? GOD'S plan shall always continue for His good no matter what man may deviate to oppose it. GOD does not interfere with freewill, but He has foreknowledge and more than that shall not lose any of those that are His and He knew of us even before the world was formed and in all of eternity.

Agriculture in the world was dying rapidly each day and so were millions of people. Agriculture keeps a people in touch with their own nation and the unity of belonging to a national origin and not a group. It is not based on "race", but on a culture with civic and moral duties and a language and a history. Agriculture is in hard honest work plus it requires a keen mind of nature's being which transcends a mental acuity and brings vitality to the spiritual health and wealth of a nation. Shepherding of course is more docile, but agriculture is essential, since Adam's fall. What kept Cain from getting GOD'S blessing? Agriculture attaches man closer to his land more than machinery, or technology ever could. There is a vacuum without agriculture in a nation no matter how educated and advanced it may seem. It helps bond the family as opposed to tribes hunting constantly even though to them it is their way or life. Not all need to be Westernized, or Europeanized. Heaven forbid... The process of elimination must begin with man, because of his ability to reason which animals cannot and since they cannot man must protect within normal reason and not use inordinate affection. Man is dangerous to himself, but to others mostly, but more importantly is his survival just because of this same kind of insane reasoning. This is why GOD must be in man's heart, or cannibalism and narcissism shall occur. Did not Messiah say He knew what was in all Men's hearts? That is why Messiah addressed money most of the time, not because it was important, but because man would always fall in "love" with it.

The Industrial Revolution was just that a revolution upon man's inner spirit and mind. With this progress came a progressive mind. Industry says, "Do this, or that" and only robotic gestures are performed and for what? Mass production? Nothing creative in the true sense of the word. Nothing to inspire. Who shall be the first to go first, on one's job, then in one's time, all of course happening over a period of decades? Who is not carrying their weight? Who is not POLITICALLY CORRECT? These dead beats must surely... Could the devout to GOD be the first, or among the first?

Grace has been given by GOD. It is for GOD to choose that gift of salvation, but us to carry the faith on in daily living until our last breath. To help the orphaned and widowed and the poor. To reach out to one's enemy and to pray for them. Messiah's perfect sinless body took all the sin and evil ever by man and carried it inside of Him on the CROSS. The blood shedded had been sinned stained, but nonetheless Y'eshua as a man shed it profusely and willingly.

The Father cannot be directly worshipped, or there is no Trinity, no Calvary, no GOD, no world, so to speak. One can try to pray, but with Messiah can pray. Messiah is the path and only path to get to the Father. Yes, Begotten not made one in being with the Father. Religion says worship me. GOD says I AM... Never did Messiah ever stop anyone from worshipping Him while on earth in human form, or in heaven.

Cultural religion, first in Christian nations is different from each other, or it should be. Each nation must find their GOD as a collective body. In heathen cultures though it be heathen, they have their own gods, or god, or culture. Examples such as Mesopotamia, the Aztecs, the Incas and our own Americanism based on socialism.

Charles Spurgeon believed that most people would... Sounds good, but not really. He believed so because of the immense infant mortality rate which says little for most of man's religion and his religiosity and Europeanism, but a lot about GOD'S mercy and love.

Pulling out the "roots" and trying to transplant, or supplant does not work. Nomenclature fetishes with importation and not cared for exportation created in America a multicultural socialist state. Americans left home spiritually while entertaining the world wide slavery of the New Age. Yet was it not the poor who carried all of the world's luggage on it's back? Now it appears that there are too many to feed, that is of the poor and now some must surely go and do not believe for one minute with all the non-profit organizations to collect for world hunger that it is going to them. The rich and well educated must too become slaves, or else extragance, greed, gluttony, corruption, theft, luxury, convenience and lust must all be given up. Anything but that, but this other master is a rigid one and even too wants your very soul...

As I started to have a conversation with Marie, I continued somewhat where I had left off before hours ago.

"From the North of Israel shall come this red leviathan who by the way Europe created known as "social" Justice, or Communism. In France itself came this socialism and was exported revolution. This idea of state as god through religion. Then Germany picked up this political philosophy, hence the Franco-Germanic Political Philosophy. Why did not Christianity grow after suffering under this tyranny? "The Antichrist is now in the world." Transformation not reformation was needed. Anti-Semitism too was in place which severed the "roots". In Russia too the same occurred in part and what GOD planned for good, man's religions planned for Evil. The 4 evil Gentile powers showed the decadence as each part of the statue from the top down showed a lesser valued metal, until at the feet which is where clay and iron came to be. The TRIBULATION appears to be here. Angels, such as the 4 HORSEMEN would be released and some already are. Each nation has an angel, but Israel has GOD the Father. Marie, man is becoming more un-GODLY and women are usurping roles that are for men, for that most men have abandoned which goes against the laws of nature. Our age is just about up. This earth is only 10,000 years old with about a 30 mile crust on top. Subterranean waters had once helped flood the earth not just atmospheric rains. In my home country Dawinism was taught along with evolution. The West had too much vaudevillian antics from Hollywood and it's sick imagination. They would even reveal how to commit heinous crimes and how to get away with it. Either they were possessed, or were high on something, or were into one of the isms. Vaudeville then came to main street America and guess what even so called Christians supported this filth by buying their music, watching their movies, hooking up on the cable, as well as going to the amusement parks of filth too. This slap stick comedy became a realistic tragedy. Redundancy over and over again until it would sink into one's mind and heart and they too could play the part of the evil hero. These "robbing-hoods" were in full attire mostly from Anglophilia. Romanticism the same as Keats and

Kipling gave to piracy and Stalin's banditry was their story to tell. The Turkish Sicilians with their village vendettas were dying out quickly. Murder tends to eliminate one's own. The Mafioso, or La Cosa Nostra is still dealing in evil deeds, but too has grown small. All this does is make it bad for the Italians in America who are just honest and hardworking, but America rarely separated the two peoples and why should they, they had become just like the Sicilians. Even a Moslem over a Christian is shown as an icon in America in the art of pugilism. Anything, but GOD is allowed to surface. Each century grew worse, or should I say decade and worse for America until American Biblicals are far, few and in between. To our south was Liberation Theology which now appears in our Israel. The conquistadors of Spain and Portugal kept their idea alive with chance, luck and golddigging. Affirmative action Nazi style was also imported by one particular President. The Monroe Doctrine was driven out by a Ford. Freedom of the press meant freedom from the truth and also meant to be immorally legal. The spoken word of slander had become the written word for "libel". The written Word of GOD and slander was the Lord's name in vain with no offense in society, but in fact blasphemy was upheld. Constitutional government meant the world of man not the Word of GOD. A democratic/republic that became more democratic and less of a republic, hence right by might. Russia was told try democracy and for only, yes only 8 months did it last and that was from a Biblical Monarchy. America's republic turned to an oligarchy of thugs, as Russia had. Russia had 1,000 years of Christianity, America about 100 years. Both used capitalism but one from a Christian monarch and the other got it's origins from a Christian democratic/republic. Judicial fiat was installed and jurisprudence was always a hung trial of jurists. There was not rule of law, but just the first. One party size could fit all."

"Monarchy for Washington was an option and a good one. He chose the lesser one. Oligarchy was not a choice, hence now anything would do over chaos, such as democracy. One can only go forward never backwards. Private property always meant someone else's right to take advantage, or to take even more. Now

Marie, we have worldly demonic powers vying for evil, including Israel. The church given to Shimon HaShaliach was the Body of Messiah, the saints. Even the synagogue was foreign formed in Babylon. There was no Jerusalem, or Temple then. Only in Israel was the temple built and 46 years at that, but Y'eshua would teardown and build it up in 3 days. GOD had taken His Sabbaths back with 70 years of exile for Israel in Babylon during Daniel's time. Sabbaths and the debate of blue laws had America in deep trouble with GOD."

I said to Marie, "I think I'll lie in bed and read Scriptures."

Realizing that only through the translation of Hebrew to direct English and Greek to English was I reading GOD'S Holy Word. Translation nonetheless not from the King James Version which was also too "pronounced" for me, but the International Version, because it closely related to the original languages the scribes wrote from. England's English I felt had not a format to be exact in grammar, or the exactness of words and as to application in life, it was too sophisticated that is the King's English. Was this part of the English people who were highly educated? A cultural way of presenting oneself? A rewritten text could be strict in a linear form, but as to metaphoric sounds it was quite self serving and redundant. Too many ego influences as to the thee's and the thou's except when GOD is always a proper noun. The message also falls short as to what the meaning means. Maybe my education is not enough, or I do not have an English mindset. After all, I do speak, write and read English, but not with hyperbole. To an Englishman it would all appear normal at least for the well educated. Mr. Webster re-wrote America's English, not England's English with hyperbole', but for clarity, consistency, conformity and to establish an American English language. English is not universal in the sense that it conveys clearly to all, or as if an Englishman could write a story as if a Russian wrote it. For example in Russian the language is universal. Pushkin, the poet, is the evidence. Pushkin could write in Russian about other cultures and languages, but when read by say a Frenchman and directed to be about a Frenchman the Frenchman would think another Frenchman wrote it and not a Russian. Pushkin could write in Russian a poem about an Englishman and when an Englishman read it, he would have believed another Englishman had wrote it. No author in any language could do this. Why? Russian is a universal language and English is not. Pushkin was also a genius. If an Englishman wrote say about a Russian it would sound, as if an Englishman had written it. European languages have limitations for the most part, except Latin, but then Latin for the most part is written not spoken and transcends only a Western European mindset. It has 3 genders and is used in all medicine and botany. It is emotionalism that runs in all the Latin languages, such as French, Italian, Spanish, et cetera which have a flair and harmonic style, but lack a substance as in Jerome's Vulgate for ones not of that culture and as to an in depth analysis and hence is limited in the expression to other languages. Sometimes when a language has flair it has little similarity in content. It may even sound melodious, or refined, but the universal form is not there to translate to another language. Almost like a musician who plays a piano and can go into to other instruments, because the piano is a universal instrument. The Soviets chose Russian for this very reason. Also the Soviets wanted to make it appear that Communism would and could be equated with Russian which is a lie. The second reason is because Russian is a universal language and what no better way to spread their propaganda, but then by way of universal language and also to lay all blame at the Russian and not the Soviets' feet and there is a difference. Russian can cross boundaries and borders and bring across the message to the entire world. The goal of Communism! Exportation of violence through a Christian universal language called the "social" gospel. Their propaganda worked because Churchill and Roosevelt both Englishmen believed or wanted to believe the lie. It made it appear that all Russians were communists, or that the word Russian and the word Soviet were interchangeable which they are not! Many times intentionally one could hear one talk about a Soviet ballet, but never a Russian ballet, or a

Russian tank and not a Soviet tank. What was a Soviet ballet, or a Russian tank? Communism is an inhuman ideology and Russian is an entire people made up of different nationalities, like America is, but now multicultural in either case.

The Vietnamese people, I was told, cannot continue to speak fluent English or they lose their native Vietnamese tongue. Oriental languages such as Chinese are "look say" and not phonetic like English is. The German language is rigid, bold and direct, but German classical music is the best in the world. Repetition to perfection is a Germanic trait and works well in the art of music, but not in political philosophy. Beethoven, who was deaf when he wrote his symphonies and concertos, proves the genius and this striving for perfection, even though he could not hear his own music. He was to be an infanticized baby. Classical music had no match except for the Jewish folk songs, Russian folk songs, Italian folk songs, and of course religious hymns of old. American music had become "garbage stew" mostly. The European nations have strong traits that follow each of their cultures. The French think Paris is France and the language is over pronounced. There are no doors on their restrooms and etiquette becomes an absurdity. The Poles feel, as all nobility should self-righteous and superior and have these illusions of grandeur working, but are too monetary in their mindset to the point of being skin flints, in plain language. They are married to Catholicism, and therein and of itself lies the problem. The Italian is obsessed with food, clothing, cars, women. They romanticize just about everything, but are very poor politicians because of money and power and their Latin passion and ignorance. They are usually good judges and law enforcement officers. Italian mothers are excellent. They are a versatile people like the Jewish people and the Irish. If Roman Catholicism stayed in Italy, then probably it would have disappeared. Europeans have much diversity, so they constantly bicker and fight, but not because of multiculturalism but because of prejudice. Europe mainly consisted of two religions, Roman Catholicism and Protestantism, but now Islam was growing as well as atheism and the New Age. The Byzantine Empire split and Russia survived for 1,000 years all together as a humble people, even through they too make up a part of Europe. Both Russia and Europe eventually failed and all civilizations do come to an end, some much quicker than others.

The next day at breakfast I said to Marie, "Today we hear so much about "social" responsibility and yet preclude that this must be good. Totalitarianism is all rights for the wrong reasons and absolutely no responsibility to one's fellow man or even for one's own, or themselves. Samson, or America had grown strong and had a proper upbringing, but chose later in its life, like Sodom and Gomorrah, to oppose GOD. This was Lot's better land over Abraham's land. This braggadocio went too far and Narcissism set in and soon the lady of the world took over. America's moral strength was gone. Man's wish to be god did not turn out to be all that man thought it would be. Who would admonish, correct, guide, discipline and love as only a Father can do? The mishap family was so entangled that nobody knew whose own relatives were whose. It was a foster care society. The national image was gone and multiculturalism was in. Not one nation under GOD, but many heathen nations under many gods. GOD had confused man in Babel so as not to do evil, but man did the opposite which was first to impose many languages and cultures to do evil. First no cohesion then totalitarianism over anarchy. No cohesion, but coercion there was plenty of. One to force oneself onto another and call it brotherhood and civil rights like the bussing in the Boston area. Non-profit organizations and how many of them were they who pilfered the poor to promote more socialism and hooliganism in the inner cities and elsewhere it needed to be? Body builder homosexuals, plus "black" muggers from our own local YMCA and United Way. Now how non-profit can one get? Collect food to hoard from the poor for the New World Order. And the hospital's compassionate appeal as a non-profit organization, but just so the patient got out quickly to make room for more profit 'clients'. And who were on the boards of the financial institutions but yet again the rich and well educated. If one wanted to get sick just visit a patient, or be one and that would do the trick in most all unclean hospitals."

"PBS joined the bandwagon and said also that by need donations to pay for their state run media television and radio stations a lot like Pravda. With these donations it would pay down the rich's taxes."

Marie was very attentive to all this new information that I had just told her.

After some time Marie, Rachel and me took a trip out of Israel proper, and went to the city of Petra to see where possibly all Messianic Jewry, 144,000, would be protected from Satan until the end of the TRIBULATION that would encompass all of Jerusalem and Israel. Jacob's 12 sons were these 12 tribes who would help Messiah rule in the OLAM HABA. We were amazed by our journey to this hidden city, as we travelled by horseback through a narrow path that was surrounded on both sides with high mountainous walls for a few miles. Marie was becoming very interested in the future of her people, the Messianic Jews. She now understood that only a remnant would be saved during the TRIBULATION period and that these Jews would meet all of the Old Testament Saints. These were, or would be, GOD'S real chosen people through Abraham. This is what real anti-Semitism was because it hated Messiah and His flock of Messianic Jewry. Secular world Jewry by birth only would not suffice and neither would Judaism. "The road is wide and the path is long that leads to destruction." There were some nice Israelis' nationals, or Sabras, I had met who would not see the kingdom of heaven. Individual not even family, or group "freewill". Adam and Eve who were innocent were capable of sinning so were not perfect, but who had a perfect environment? Oh yes, the socialists and the New Agers! Right? So much for the environment and poverty alone. Who should change, or what should change if the latter at all be true? Man, or his environment? After all what was a few billion lives? And how perfect shall it be? Shall it be more perfect than GOD who is already perfect? More perfect than GOD made it for Adam and Eve? The Word was given to the Jewish idea that came from GOD and which Abraham, the first Hebrew, chose by faith alone to give up land and country, Ishmael and his only true son,

Isaac. Faith supplied by GOD but accepted by Abraham in faith, and so GOD chose ones for salvation.

After our trip to Petra I believe prophecy for Marie and Rachel and myself became even more important because it dealt with her faith personally and not some foreign unknown god. "The roots of salvation." Our private life was becoming one with our public life, hence totalitarianism. All religions became one, except the Judeo-Christian faith which was not part of this New Age Movement.

My mind went back again in years. The American "black", I thought, had been free to leave, but never chose to, but why? Would not one want to leave the land where they were coerced to be by ancestry? Could it be they were more American than they chose to believe? Amongst themselves were different factions and schisms. Usually under suffering people unite and do not divide, but was there real suffering? The American "black" was somehow coming apart without faith. The schism was even amongst their own male and female and the animosity the women had for their own men, but just so they said it and nobody else! Islam was usurping their own inner freedom and peace of mind. The rich and well educated introduced heathen education by unionism's NEA via multiculturalism. Marxist/Leninism was directed at the American Negro because they had been made the "iconoclasts" of equality and civil unrest, and everything would spring off of this because "race" could always show itself or prove itself in the most logical way couldn't it? Their forced bondage which always would be played upon would be America's nemesis forever. Self-pity is hard to dissipate in oneself especially when one had not gone through it. Who would or could be let to forget? The rich had too much to lose and everything to gain off of this persistent dissension and reverse racism would remain silent until... The media kept everyone well informed daily so that they always had an audience, a passive one at that, to appeal to. Their concern was next to philanthropic government, or state socialism. Let government have gambling and slaves, but not individuals? Government always knows best like in Dred Scott and Roe vs Wade? Human nature enjoys itself more often than not because the jurists themselves had done worse behind closed doors, so how could they prosecute their own or themselves? The same thing happened in Nuremburg. Some of the Jurists there should have been on trial themselves. "Let bygones be bygones." American Biblicals would have no part in this. (This charade by the rich and well educated.) Utopia would be right around the corner, at least for the living now. It is always easier to live off of another's death. Sort of like short term life insurance not universal life, or how about one's whole and only life? Cain's inner cities were decadent but give the lottery a chance to work, the numbers would come up. Reparations would certainly do the trick since the New Deal and the Great Society failed. It was owed, but by whom and to whom? Certainly the dead could not collect and resurrect off of the living, or could they? Or maybe the living had the power invested in them to collect? But who would pay? Not the rich, heaven forbid... But then again who owned slaves? Oh yes, the poor! More was to come, such as do your thing and have all the sex and disease you want, but heaven forbid, if you procreate, or even get married, or even allow the child to be born, or to remain in the womb after conception, or become a none deadbeat dad. Have all the pernicious fun like the rich without the wealth or prison time, of course who do not also like to raise their own children either. So why should you want to? In fact don't raise any at all, especially since government shall supply all your needs and your wants. It is called the process of elimination, and since they cannot flee or fight like you can and shall silence them quickly like in Silent Scream before they cry, then tell the young how savage they are and incite their inner passions even more and guess what? We all get what we want and need? You get sex and fun and we make a "killing". What one does not know does not hurt them unless you happened to be the victim. Human resources you remember them are always expendable whenever it involves somebody else. Other elements, criminal and otherwise, were working in high places and principalities. Desensitize man over and over again and guess what? The zoo shall be opened for everyone. We are having too much fun right now. This was the obituary column to the American family. Real slavery is the only way to be truly free, especially since you get to choose your evil. Live, you live, but let die that is others until it is your turn. This Pied Piper was playing his New Age occultic tune of "come follow me". Americans had grown out of, not into, grown-ups. The Internet, computers, cellular phones, hand held computers, telephone systems, receivers and transmitters (if it can transmit it can receive), and astral projection imaging was soon coming. How exciting. Twas the night before darkness and all through the (his) land not a thing could be bought or sold without the mark of this man. All senses were pervertedly experienced and meant we did just exist. Whoever gets the most toys wins. This pickup truck mentality. The elderly's, "I lived my life, you live yours", would come sooner than they thought, that is the "social" security generation. Retirement would indeed be early, much too early than thought.

Another discussion, this time late at night with Marie alone, had to be spoken.

I said to Marie, "This Hercules, or homosexual superman, a euphemism is in vogue. Stay busy, be noisy, but please GODLY silence. All is reasoning which makes schizophrenia appear as reality and illusions as true. The Charles Schwabs are volunteering that is voluntary death their far gone conclusions. Everything appears in secure "closed time". The world certainly will know it's future but will not care about it for our children and grand children. Again with history being an inexact science and ourselves barely remembering last week how not can one more than assume the future? The present is ours to make as individuals as a collective body called a nation. In between thought and action there is sometimes only a blink of an eye. This limbo can not always be discerned maybe, except through habit. We are creatures of habit. Theatrical reality plays a big part in man's human nature. An uncertain future in time for believers but not us to eternity. For unbelievers it will too be a certain future in eternity, but a different location whether one chooses to believe it or not."

Marie asked, "Who writes history better, an historian or a novelist?"

I responded with, "Marie history written by novelists are far more accurate, as long as the novelist writes as an artist. Historians usually do not write as such. Historians are much less accurate because they write in the past and not the present and hence cannot link the two. An artist must also include themselves with that society and beauty; harmony with GOD must always be included. Historians claim infallibility. In "fore shadowing" one says this did or did not happen, as if they were there and would remember correctly and write it as it actually occurred and also they would contend it did not have to occur. (it could have been prevented for sure, oh yes), since the historian is relegated in the past only. The possibilities history could have taken with the reader understanding of course the future, or knowing for sure the future. Too many possibilities, except in the present with one's true perception of the real truth that most do not see. There is also this present guided from the past, if possible to the future in this clairvoyant "foreshadowing" with not ever knowing for sure either one, the past or the future. How can one explain this ever? 'Sideshadowing' offers what is happening and what could have happened and what might happen, or might not happen. The novelist does not write in non-fiction, hence makes nor has to make an exact assertion as the historian always does, or his presumption. To be historically accurate the artist shall try and the historian shall miss most likely because of all the above. That is why all Biblical history is accurate, convicted by the Holy Spirit. It was GOD written. The Bible is not a history book but a living present Word through a living Messiah. "The Word that became flesh." 'Side-shadowing' had become a reality for me and now I hope for you, Marie? Can you now see why I chose to share His true Word with you?"

Marie looked at me and cried with such loving joy, it made my heart feel overwhelmed with Messiah's love.

Marie then asked me, "Please continue with the artist."

I said, "The truth about the future is unknown as to the time and as to its unfolding. Marie, I must make public what I am telling you. Theatrical reality is a false illusion of this world and only Messiah, or the Father can make it the Truth and not actors on a stage of life. I cannot serialize it in the present, or a periodical which is vital, but sharing the present with you I now know gives validity, as you Marie are my public. Artists write to include themselves with their nation good, or bad, as a part of the people like we the people in the present and never as them, but again always as us. History did not have to be the way I described it, or as it actually was. It could have had other possibilities, unless I write it in the artistic present and again I must write it publicly and most truthfully. Only socialists pretend to know the future their utopia, or better known as "closed time" and distort and change true history and destroy the present. They "foreshadow" the future as to what it shall surely be and accepting the present as only the inevitable outcome which means that between the past and the future are theirs' to interpret only, so man is predestined by their calculations with no control of the present that they live in and man is only protoplasm. It means that the present moment which now is history and combine that with the past, so there is no difference between past and present and the lie is believed. GOD shall tell us what to do, but Satan will tell us how to do it when we allow him to. Satan will try to dialogue to convince us that thinking about something sinful is the same as doing that sinful thing; hence he says go ahead and do it. When we refuse to have a dialogue or refuse to continue in this evil action,he shall accuse us to our face of being not a saint but an unbeliever. The dialogue must be cut off or it shall be you are still guilty indeed by reason alone. Even if that action was done, did that person say as in an assault, have a preconceived idea to murder? Satan cannot read our minds. New Age occultic philosophy always has the preconceived notion or lie that good is evil and evil is good; hence you thought about it, you might as well do it. Thought by guilt association, or that thinking and doing are always the same or that one's intentions are always known when they carry out an action. Yes it is sin, both the thought and the action, but they are two separate sins and sin is contagious, but also the fact the one does not always know oneself even though habits can lead to intentions, or one's actions can lead intentions over a period of time. A seared conscience, when one refuses to believe the Truth time and again. Satan's court question of "Do you still lie?"

Marie then asked about prophecy in regards to the entire Bible.

I said, "Environmental concerns are external and do not suffice to change man or his nature. Beings have this void which must be filled by a loving Messiah in one's spirit. Without Messiah, this void is filled with something else ungodly. The kings of Judah and Israel were all mostly evil, but of course Israel asked for a king, when GOD told them He was all that they needed. Only Daniel and Joseph, Jacob's son, have no negatives told about them, and Elijah and Enoch did not see death. They all 4 did sin for only Messiah had no sin. King David was a man after GOD'S own heart, but Saul repeatedly tried to kill David; David refused to retaliate against the king. Most of the inspirational psalms were written by David. From the lineage of David comes the Messiah (Ruth, Gentile). The Israelites were told never to mingle with heathen people as a nation. Jews were not to marry unbelievers. "What does good have to do with evil?" "Do not be unequally yoked." Both these scriptures are still for today as they were for the Israelites in the Old Testament. King Solomon too abandoned GOD for foreign women in his later years. Solomon was David's son who built the Temple. "Vanity of all vanities."

"The Jewish person, Marie, can be the hardest person to love, as one Jewish grandmother once said, but Catholicism is worse to witness to. For Gentiles to perceive Jesus and Christ instead of as Y'eshua and Messiah is quite difficult. Never has any church replaced Israel the 'roots'. The mindset is old through religion that forgot who the Jew really was and who Messiah is. This is almost to the subconscious thought of "How can Christianity, so Gentile, be replaced by Jewry? Who are these outsiders that were usurping this Christian church by not only denying it, but also persecuting it?" Here is where religion, Satan's tool, played its part, because the very idea of Christianity was not taught as a Jewish faith but was letting Jewishness be ostracized because of

Europeanism which usually meant religiosity and not Messianic Jewry. The mindset had long ago been set, and the enemy knew that to keep Jews and Gentiles apart like he did some of the fallen angels would be to do what Messiah said not to do in regards to man, or why was Shimon HaShaliach too sent to the Jews and then the Gentiles?"

Marie was listening intently as I spoke sometimes in question form.

I continued, "Messiah's admonishment of the Pharisees was for the educated and rich Jewish hierarchy again who needed to feel important and proud and not to separate Messianic Jewry and real Biblical Christians. Many seminaries taught more anti-Semitism within the Gentile camp; thence Jewish and Gentile against not the religious, but against each other. Also, because of the Gentiles' religiosity in Europe preached that "the Jews killed Christ" (Gentile verbiage). Remember Pontius Pilate's reference of Calvary to Y'eshua being "King of the Jews" -- an utterance by Pilate, a Roman to escape goat all blame to Jewry alone, yet Rome was the real legal authority, and also GOD wanted all generations later to know who Messiah really was. Yet Messiah was not opposing His own death. He gave it up willingly. Y'eshua knew the price He would pay for us for He loved men for all times and all places whether they accepted or rejected Him, for His love is unconditional. It is ours to choose Messiah after Messiah has said you shall be mine.

"His way into our lives, you cannot refuse. No sin can eliminate one. GOD cannot sin, yet if He would have not gone to the Cross we all would be going to hell. Only Messiah, not Confuscius, Mohammed, Buddha, or anybody else claimed to be GOD in the flesh. Many false messiahs have appeared and have tried to deceive the Jewish people, but the Antichrist shall deceive all. The complexity of theology lies in the fact that man does not take the time to really know GOD in the flesh only, just about a god or gods, or in nothing. It is many times by hearsay or by such religiosity which only can reform the mind, not transform the heart in most all cases. The possibilities to believe are always there provided they do not repeatedly refuse the Salvation Gospel. GOD provides one faith. Some believe GOD has a two-faith religion. 'Many are called, but few are chosen.' To the elect in Y'eshua who accept Him. Chosen are those who hear His voice and respond as His sheep with the foreknowledge that GOD already knew who they would be since He would lose not a one. Could one call that chosen? Man does not know who shall or shall not be saved. GOD does the saving and the calling and not man, nor his religion or church, et cetera. When we as believers pray for others we must pray without ceasing for them as Rev Shaul said, and the Holy Spirit shall convict. Many so called believers say the time is not right to share GOD'S grace. We are commanded not asked to share the Gospel in love to all. The Ruach Hakodesh is there to do the convicting. We are there to preach the Word one on one or to many at a time. GOD shall provide many opportunities for us to share His love, not our ego or religion or opinion, or only care about just our own so called salvation, if we are saved at all. For us as believers we never know when enough or when who, where, or even why salvation would occur. Again, faith, but faith for others in the sense and according to GOD'S will and that to do GOD'S will is to do it faithfully meaning under the power of the Ruach Hakodesh. The Ruach Hakodesh too can interpret for us to GOD in words too deep for us to understand or even pray in audible or inaudible words. The only prayer that GOD promises to hear from an unbeliever is the one of salvation. GOD is not limited though to hear other prayers if it is in His good will and serves for His purpose alone. Marie, now I shall try to explain to you the OLAM HABA as best I can and as the Ruach Hakodesh leads."

"This 1,000-year reign shall have even the beasts of the field at peace with one another. Animals do not reason, hence no souls. They rely on instinct alone so many times attributed to man also. After this 7th day, or the OLAM HABA shall come this 'New Heaven and a New Earth'. The New Jerusalem from heaven shall have passed since Adam. The church was for made at Pentecost in Acts. Shimon HaShaliach was head of the saints, the church the Body of Messiah and was not in any papal sense locked into the Gentile religion for at this time it did not exist. The Head of this Body is Y'eshua. Messiah's church is not organized religion, but saints saved by grace alone and hidden from man in totality, individual by individual. 'Go two by two.' There is not denomination with GOD, only the spiritual heart. Only GOD knows who is truly saved, but we can accept Messiah's love in our hearts and have the assurance that we are saved. (Romans 10:9-10). Once in GOD'S family there is no repudiation by God. This is known as ETERNAL SECURITY. We are to be 'the salt of the earth'. Will we sin? Yes, but not a license to sin, but to confess our sins to Him immediately and we are quickened by the Ruach Hakodesh."

Marie then asked, "What about the poor and the outcasts?"

I said, "Marie, an example I shall give you is about the American Negro. Since they were brought to America involuntarily, their choice was taken from them in regards to physical freedom, but GOD provided a way to know Him through all His misery. Some slave owners were believers who shared their faith no matter how weak their faith was in regards to slavery itself. The method was wrong; the message was right. America has a personality that is spiritual. Like an individual, it too shall be judged. The point is this. What man used as a negative or an evil, GOD used for good. Many slaves came to know Messiah, not so much because of man but because of GOD'S good will. The early rich and well educated refused to work their bodies also, hence slavery provided that physical labor which in part was carried from John Locke's material and European Enlightenment outlook without the spiritual. Even though all rights would be returned, or in this case never had been, they would always remain a people, American Negroes, as long as they remained close to their GOD and the soil. This no one could remove, that is their obedience and faith in and to GOD. Many believers may appear uneducated and backwards, but their hearts are right with GOD. Usually one can see an educated person who lacks intelligence or GODLY morals, but it is rare indeed to see one who is both educated and is intelligent, or has GODLY morals. This is not a class of people, because they were considered property, nor is it race. In relation to the Israelis in the physical sense they are a nationality, not a faith yet. Not all of Israel's Jews are saved or shall respond to Messiah, nor shall most in the world. Only Messianic Jewry again people of faith shall be in GOD'S holy family from the Jewish side, or 'the roots of salvation". One group, for instance, had been from the country of Ethiopia called the Falashas being brought to Israel that you already know about and who, by the way, still worshipped as Moses did and were more of a sign for the world to see that GOD was calling His people back to the Promised Land. Even though not Messianic, they were called back home. Now here is where Messianic Jewry can share Y'eshua's love with them. GOD needs no prompting from man; GOD has brought them back for His purpose as Hebrews to cross over, and not their purpose."

Marie said, "Why are certain things occurring in the world?"

"Marie, the clocks in the world will probably have by computer synchronization that is in actual physical time, be as one clock for the entire world, and night and day shall not matter. Only by nature shall man know the old time schedule and time zones. This uniformity will be to give more centralization and control to the New Age system. How that would affect insurance policies and other things, no one would know for sure. Remote control flights with no human element, or terror in the sky from within and mach speeds to exceed the SST Concorde. Ishmael's nations could be depleted by the Antichrist and severely weakened. The oil rich Arab land would play only a minor role possibly. All religions would have to bow down and worship the Antichrist like in Daniel's time. Now invisible elements would be in control. This totalitarianism would reign supreme for a while. Demons would be constantly watching believers, the unbelievers Satan already had. Now ghettoes, real ghettoes like Auschwitz but worse, would appear worldwide against all believers. People, whole peoples, shall be eliminated by nuclear, biological, demonic, or transition as Stalin had done, who, by the way was an instrument of Satan's on a smaller scale than this Antichrist shall be. American Jewry had used for years their pretentiousness for anti-Semitism which was nothing more than the Ira Glassers and their atheistic world view. Real anti-Semitism, though, came to America and world Jewry or shall come in the GREAT TRIBULATION. The 'root' problem had to go, as well as the brother Ishmael and all other believers Messianic and Gentile. The 'branch would not be spared' either. American Biblicals and Russian orthodoxy, the Old Believers would be at the top of the list because their faith is true and the national faith was not exported like some kind of socialism or 'social' gospel. The forerunner or emulator of the Ruach Hakodesh would be the FALSE PROPHET. All of the Bible had to be removed. All false religions would first be used to persecute worldwide believers and then they too would have to go. Only the occult would do. Remove Christianity and the Bible from the minds and hearts of all peoples. The world would get spiritually smaller, when the Ruach Hakodesh would be taken out of the world Only evil would prevail and a few believers, Jewish and Gentile, would be spared. Mainline denominations would not be recognizable. Satan loves to work in religions within Christianity or outside of Christianity, such as Judaism, or the Mormons. Believers such as you and me and our daughter Rachel should not fear for we shall be TRANSLATED in a "twinkling of an eye" to be with Messiah forever. 'Come now Lord Y'eshua.'"

In Marie's eyes I could see hope and peace because of Messiah and her faith in this Holy GOD, the Father of Abraham, Isaac and Jacob. "The Word that became flesh, now in a glorified body, such as we shall be."

CHAPTER IX

THE PARRICIDE OF GOD BY MAN

Human man, not so humane, drew GOD'S blood which emptied for all of time onto the ground of Calvary with nails against the flesh, human flesh, to support the entire body of Y'eshua. Tearing at the very flesh fibers themselves, little by little with Y'eshua pushing up trying to be able to breathe with His heart becoming like wax and a crown of sharp nails like thorns piercing his tender skull and shedding blood profusely from His capillaries and a huge spear plunged viciously and with force into His side puncturing His body with His GODLY blood now draining out of His body with hardly any left from His lean frail carpenter-like body. He was hardly clothed for ridicule and embarrassment. His face was grotesque and became distorted, and He could not be recognized as being human by His face. This disfigurement was horrifying yet He endured the excruciating, searing numbing deadly pain through His entire body and being as a man, and no cessation, Satan would make sure. This was man's parricide…of GOD through His only Son Messiah. "And the vineyard owner would now send his son, certainly they would listen to him?" Arms outstretched as if doing an iron cross except for hours with every nerve ending tightening and tearing and ripping and every muscle aching. Spasms occurring involuntarily. Gravity was doing what GOD had created it to do; pull down steadily and with equal force with no regard even at this time, for GOD'S only Son on the tree. Adam's tree was so much different. Flesh attached to the wood splintering and tearing and shredding His flesh with metal spikes nailed in as one would nail a board upon another board. The friction of the metal hitting His flesh first, the outer epidermis, to puncture through and pierce and penetrate into skin and blood vessels. First the capillaries, then the veins and arteries and, like an awl into a piece of wood, the blood exploding and bursting and hemorrhaging inside and then outside from the spear plunged into His side. His hands would have to help support His entire body and the spike would have to pierce both hands tight against a large beam until these spike nails themselves could go in no farther or else the hands would tear too much while hanging, except the skeletal system could always hold the entire body nonetheless along with the feet to push Himself up in order to breathe. This would not be suicide. Maybe they feared the hand would tear more apart while hanging from gravity's pull, except for the skeletal system? No, these were professionals at this sort of thing, but always to their fellow man, but never before to GOD. Hour after hour with each second now becoming like minutes, 60 long counts to each minute and then 60 minutes to each hour and then each and every hour. This lean frail body of a carpenter, wood of course, was not made for this way of Roman Carpentry called crucifixion the bottom of the statue in Daniel. It was not nails being hammered into wood like carpenters do, but Roman soldiers pounding centimeter by minute centimeter with dull spikes, but hard as steel to pierce more efficiently into His human flesh to make sure death would come but slowly. No bones were broken. It was easier that way of course for the Roman soldiers to attach His body like a sign on a wooden post. He had to be punished before His death and one man had to suffer for the nation. This was a criminal, but not Barabbas he was POLITICALLY CORRECT. With the smallest amount of fibers, cells, tissues, muscles, nerves, as well as larger blood vessels such as the arteries and the veins would eventually be ruptured as well as suffocation and heart failure, a broken heart, Hematomas or huge circular protrusions and contusions could be seen especially in the facial area. Could this really be GOD, this emaciated body of a man? As He pushed up from His feet and nailed hands for leverage the crown pushed down even more into the holes already there enlarging them. The neo-Cerebral-Cortex was still working, "Father forgive them they know not what they do." His hair was mangled and somewhat long, because of His levitical priesthood, but was ripping and tearing at the very roots in the skull and with each voluntary and involuntary movement something somewhere on the body was being destroyed in the physical. Spasms of the muscular system were locking in. The joints had no fluid and were like stone against stone. The brain was starting to close down. The brutalized body was also closing down as to organs and the regular blood flow. The body's circadian rhythm was destroyed. The pain center to the brain, or in the brain was still working. The cognition of things bursting and rupturing inside could be felt. All the senses were starting to go and soon it would be finished this murder of GOD in the flesh. All men and all generations have done this to GOD through unbelief, sin and Adam's fall. Before the crucifixion Y'eshua would drag this tree for some time stumbling and falling. The Stations of the Cross were harsh and He was hardly able to get back up when he stumbled and while being whipped to continue on. Finally He could not lift no longer and another soul would do the carrying His beard was grabbed and He was spit upon in His face and was physically brutalized unmercifully. It is the innate character of us and our human nature to respond to this good vs evil and is in all men, but we must choose, yes choose one. "All have sinned and fallen short of the glory of GOD." "He who is without sin cast the first stone." Why this crucifixion then? For all Our sins, yet we crucified Him and continue to do so when we do not believe who He said He was and is and forever shall be. "If you have seen Me, you have seen the Father, I and the Father are One. One GOD? The mystery of GOD. Parricide, yes to GOD in the flesh by created man sin laden and ready for Hell instantly. No not I, I am innocent and I would never do that to GOD... No one is innocent only Adam and Eve were before they sinned. This is our race that is the so called human race.

Many came in His name, but did they endure the cross and then resurrect for sure? Was the body stolen? After all only a huge boulder was put at the entrance with guards. What man in the flesh can resurrect with all the torture and blood loss? By man's unjust law, by an oligarchy of Rome and democracy by Israel and yet a Monarch to be, but GOD'S law for justice for GOD had required it or did the Jews? "I do what my Father tells Me." "I came to fulfill the Law and not abolish it." Now infanticide, man's evil law said, "Kill, or murder again and again." And man did this to fulfill his own evil intent, but GOD resurrects the unaccountable. "A wolf sheds it's fur but not it's habits." Resurrection of life to all believers.

Holidays in America took on a carnival or circus atmosphere. Satan's Halloween Party was in vogue for many years. This was inherited from the Druids. Offering our children to Satan for something we thought was free and harmless. These handouts all had demonic influence. Christmas, or Christ's Mass was another emulation in religion. Santa Claus was giving gifts, except one. Easter with bunny rabbits and eggs and all other insidious insanity. Even the name was wrong. Passover the word itself expresses that GOD passed over the Hebrews and their first born sons, but GOD DID NOT HIS OWN SON. All other legends and folk lore meant absolutely nothing to GOD. Biblical Scriptures require no celebration of Y'eshua's birth and where is this Christmas, or Easter by name in Hebrew, or Greek mentioned? Thanksgiving is what the Pilgrims celebrated to GOD for a thankful harvest like the Hebrews did. Our Thanksgiving had become anything but in later years with gluttony and sports. The 4th of July was the time to explode violent devices and have carousing and guess what, Christians participated. If one had to be in a war, they would not want to be. Other unsubstantiated holidays, such as Martin Luther King, Jr's birthday was in defense of the terrorists. Phrases such as "happy holidays", "spring recess" and other secular phrases meant absolutely nothing.

The rich telling about the rich always must be followed very closely. Not the rich writing about the poor, or the middle class writing about the poor, or any other combination. Words such as the Industrial Revolution, mass production, piece work which became nonsense, because they were nonsense to the whole nation's spiritual soul. The agricultural base was destroyed and the constant noises of brutality included chain saws, motorcycles, machines, planes, gears, power mowers, trucks, trains, cars, rockets, missiles, et cetera and America forgot what the word work meant. All of this told of the cold brutality and aimlessness of the American society.

Few artists, if any, appeared at first in the field of literature. They glorified no Truth, but themselves. The rich continued to run to America. Technology became America's so called savior. Simple spiritual sense functions could not be done properly. Conversations could not be held that were intelligent.

Our own children for the most part were being destroyed by Hollywood's horrors and filth. Lenin always said, "Use the cinema for the cause." Government contributed to PBS and to Roman sports' fiascos with prima donnas as the main players and usually the most gullible.

Evolution, as ludicrous as it was, was believed and taught as a serious religion and as history. Again Lenin can be quoted, "Attack all the brains of society."

But where could they find the contemporary brains? The rich and well educated were just that and no more and lacked intelligence, or originality which meant GOD, or GODLY. Where could or would these brains come from? Certainly not higher education which taught socialism, egoism, avarice, ignorance to GOD'S Word and His Will, plus being shortsighted and live for today only and the ultimate, convenience.

As to democracies, they were cooked up to be more than they were ever to be. The Russian Revolution, the homosexuality of the Weimar Republic, Chek's China and Italy were all democracies that came to nothing representing true freedom. Where were all these freedoms with land that democracy promised, or was it man? Voting in America came down to 10-20% for all eligible voters and that too became a joke in apathy? And the ones who voted were mostly voting for socialism, or self-preservation. A President had to be voted in fairly, if that was at all possible. Jurisprudence was non-existent. Many anti-Americans made Americanism their home such as Gorbachov, Kruschev's son,

Stalins daughter, Angela Davis, David drug lord Dinkins, Nelson Mendela's "apartheid", Dr Theodore Hesburgh and invitations were given to Jerry Adams, Yassir Arafat, Fidel Castro, Aristide, Vladimir Putin, et cetera.

As the new year, or Rosh Hashanah, began I could feel this sudden urge of society to accelerate, even more so without care, or regard for one's fellow man after all there was not immortality? Now even fathers' and brothers' were selling their own sisters and daughters as bait to business and why not, they too had to make a living and a profit from good old capitalism. Prostitution was a business women's job too like careerism from the feminists. Soviet day care would take care of the procreated, or kids and not children. What was different from Hollywood's own?

Legal tender was known as illegal tough assets, because it had become illegal and tough to get a hold of. Anything over $10,000 was illegal to carry, yet it was one's own money, except possibly for drug dealers, but then again their "profession" was legal and they needed to carry that much of tax free "income". Anything and everything again we hear it is America was legal except GOD.

Europe's "beast" was soon to come to Israel's stage. Wanted by popular demand this effervescent iconoclast. For three and one half years there would be demonic festivals, until he got down to the real business at hand. Already Turkey could block the flow of water and Euphrates River cold be crossed by "the kings of the East". Islam too would yield, or else. Misdiagnosed schizophrenia was nothing, but old fashioned demon possession.

My job was becoming harder to do, since our boundaries were getting small. Nobody could come, even as government employees, so easily in, or out. Entire countries were remapped for reconfiguration and rivers, streams, dams, lakes, seas, and oceans were all given principality names. Demonic surveillance seemed almost constant. The TRANSLATION had almost to occur immediately, unless we were not saved, or we would enter into as believers the first half of the TRIBULATION and be not oblivious to missing persons who were believers? Being in Israel

Messianic Jewry for now would be spared for there were not really many Gentile believers that I knew. Secularized Israel was harder on Messianic believers. This "twinkling of an eye" was not just a metaphor as to how fast the time, or the duration would be.

Old friendships had to be watched carefully. Families could be included in this too. The good old upside down star, the pentagram, the 2 lightning bolts, and karate symbols were prevalent, plus the rainbow along with reincarnation and India's swastika. One's own children were suing parents for mental and physical cruelty, such as discipline, curfews and of course corporal punishment. "Do not spare the rod to spoil the child." Only believers had whole intact families. The youth were worshipped and glorified and childhood did not exist. Medical death schools taught trial and error and more error when operations were being performed.

Millionaires were falling one after another and being one was not hard since lottery and gambling was legal. Even billionaires were eliminating each other, or were being eliminated. Corporate buyouts were world wide and with more convenience came less and less freedom.

I later had a discussion in depth with Marie again. It was about moving somewhere else.

I said to Marie, "Why should we not consider moving out of the Middle East? The alliance between Europe, America and Israel is growing."

We felt we had only one realistic choice. We both spoke English fluently and read and wrote it. French was out and so was their socialism and Catholicism. "Canada" we thought about, but again French posed a problem as the official language. Australia was a sitting duck logistically. Africa in Angola, or Ethiopia, or Morroco had their own problems and were attacking other smaller rogue states with nuclear attacks.

Marie and I would soon have to decide, since more land was confiscated by this one world utopian government. Jerusalem was becoming like London, where the royal family owned one third of the city. Israel was a multicultural state. The Israelis' constitution meant little, because there was none. The Zionist state became ever more secular. Even the Hasidim had to move near Megiddo, Israel. A lot of Ashenazim were coming in, because Europe was getting hostile. Israel had become secularized except for Messianic Jewry. The Hasidim did not believe Israel should exist, until Messiah came so they would wait no matter what. When I had come to Israel, there were about 17,000,000 Jews worldwide. Now I had been told there were about 10,000,000. Intermarriage stay in the state you are, infanticide, staying single and much persecution reduced the numbers, plus Reformed Judaism had endorsed homosexuality so there was no procreation coming from there. Conservative Judaism soon followed suit and Orthodoxy was split. Constant use of GOD'S name only in profanity was all that one could hear, but yet some unbelieving Jews felt they were doing what GOD had wanted them to do. The Jewish people had no roots. No Old Testament holidays, except for Hasidim and Messianic Jewry.

Now Rome was getting into this picture more so. It represented Europeanism along with Islam. Rome with it's feet of iron and clay.

A statue in Daniel that showed this 4th Kingdom was to resurrect again. Children were never told they had more beauty then any Shakespeare, Schiller, or Dicken's novels combined. The enemy had attacked children viciously. "Be fruitful and multiply." The family institution meant our children were our Precious ones. Now without family our children would be at peril and be part of the generational state.

CHAPTER X

END OF THE AGE?

Near TRIBULATION, ever so near, I started thinking about Adam who was created in about 4004 BC and died from sin in about 3074 BC. He lived to be 930 years old, with Seth born in 3874 BC and dying in 2962 BC at the age of 912 years. Skipping to the 7th generation from Adam to Enoch who was translated to heaven at the age of 365 years, the number of our own Western calendar year. Then comes his son Methuselah who was born in 3317 BC and died in 2348 BC and lived to be the oldest human being at 969 years old. The flood occurred near this time. Jumping some more in generations, we come to Noah who was born in 2948 BC and died in 1998 BC and lived for 950 years. He had 3 sons named Shem, father of the Semite people; Ham, father of the Canaanites (Sodom and Gomorrah) and Japhreth, the father of all others. After Noah's flood, the subterranean and atmospheric waters which created it dissipated the water firmament around the earth and with it the longevity of man's lifespan considerably because of harmful ultraviolet rays and other harmful affects which entered earth's atmosphere from the sun. Nephilim, the sons of gods, demons, mingled with the daughters of men (human women), which was part of the reason for the flood. Angels were not to procreate. Man's total perniciousness upon the earth was horrible. Many years later came Abram in the same family line from Shem and who was born in 2056 AD and died in 1881 BC, living only 175 years. His son Isaac follows in 1956 BC and died in 1776 BC (Declaration of Independence number) and lived for 180 years. His son Jacob was born 1916 BC and died in 1769 BC and lived for 147 years. There are the 3 that GOD richly blessed with Abraham being the first Hebrew, with Isaac a forerunner of Y'eshua and Jacob the father of the 12 tribes. Abraham also fathered the birth of Ishmael, the father of the Arabs of Hagar his second wife, hence came the Semite people or the two Semite people the Arabs and the Jews. One would receive GOD'S blessing the other would not in regards to faith. Isaac was almost used as a sacrifice to show the forthcoming of Messiah and also to test Abraham's faith in GOD. Jacob was a twin, the younger of the two who received the blessing while the older Esau did not. Jacob's son Joseph by Rachel, his one wife the one he truly loved. This Joseph changed Israel from a family into a nation. Joseph was born in 1746 BC and died in 1635 BC and lived 110 years. The children of Israel were slaves in Egypt for about 430 years from 1706 BC to 1276 BC. Then Moses who was chosen by GOD lead the Israelites out of Egypt and out of slavery. When Pharaoh refused time and again to release the Israelites on his word, GOD finally told Moses to tell His people to sprinkle lamb's blood on their home doorposts, so that when the angel of death came through all of Egypt all first born sons and first born male animals would be spared for all the Hebrews, but not for Pharaoh, or the Egyptians. Moses was born in 1356 BC and died 1236 BC and lived for 120 years, but did not get to see the Promised Land, because he struck the rock and did not speak to it as GOD had told him to do. Moses also wrote the first 5 books of the Bible called Pentetauch. (Islam too.)

Judah's hatred for his brother Joseph, the younger brother brought about the Kingdom of Judah and the Kingdom of Israel, Joseph-Manasseh. These two sons from Jacob. The kings of Judah started with King Saul who started out good, but did evil later and also called up Samuel, the prophet, after Samuel's death which was blasphemy. Then came David son of Jesse then King Solomon son of David, et cetera. During this time only one interruption to the Davidic line occurred and that was ATHALIAH, a wicked queen, who ruled 6 years. The last king was Jehoachin. Israel was taken captive for 70 years in the Babylon under King Nebuchadnezzar. King Nebuchadnezzar in 586 BC became the first Gentile king. Daniel at this time was exiled too. The Book of Daniel and the

Book of Revelation go hand in hand. The time of the Gentiles started in 605 BC when King Jehoiakim, Eliakim goes to Babylon. Jeremiah the crying prophet who also said to GOD, "I am only a teen-ager" was Daniel's contemporary. The prophet Isaiah a major Prophet wrote the most profound prophecy about Messiah's crucifixion some 800 years before it occurred at Calvary which is found in Isaiah Chapter 53 in the Old testament.

Isaiah lived between the time of the King Uzziah and King Hezekiah with a few kings in between. The Israelites were exiled by GOD, because they did not honor GOD'S SABBATHS. Israel, the other kingdom was totally eliminated by GOD, but not Judah, the kingdom and not the tribe. When King Hoshea was king he was taken captive to Assyria in 721BC. The Book of Revealation is a vision given to the Apostle John, the one that Y'eshua loved. It speaks about the 7 churches and the 7 church ages with the churches at that time in Asia and the 7 letters that Y'eshua wrote to each of these 7 churches. Rev Shaul had gone to Macedonia not to Asia.

The FIRST CHURCH is EPHESUS, losing your first love. The SECOND CHURCH is SMYRNA illegal religion by the Romans. The THIRD CHURCH is PERGAMOS, the church settled into the mundane world. The FOURTH CHURCH is THYATIRA, rich and accepted by the world with the devil, Jezabel. The FIFTH CHURCH is SARDIS, in 1521 A.D. the Augustinian monk, Martin Luther, the Reformation in Germany which ran on money. The SIXTH CHURH is PHILADELPHIA which exists the same time as LAODICEA which is the SEVENTH CHURCH and represents democracy and is consumer driven and not authoritarian and a liberal church at the end of times. PHILADELPHIA is the church of brotherly love and which is the TRANSLATION of the saints.

Another Biblical seven is the 7 Dispensations. The FIRST ONE is innocence, Adam and Even in the Garden before sin. The SECOND ONE is the world, the conscience after sin. The THIRD ONE is the human government and Noah. The FOURTH ONE is the law and Moses. The FIFTH ONE is grace my Messiah. The

SIXTH ONE is the TRIBULATION of 7 years and the SEVENTH ONE is the OLAM HABA of 1,000 years.

Individual personalities played a most important part in all of this and were chosen by GOD, and so I continued to think of the 4 major personalities starting with the SANGUINE personality, which is a person who is popular and fun filled. The second one is CHOLERIC which is so powerful, but cold and calculating and usually leads or rules, are not good people persons, and make up 6% of the entire world's population. The third one is MELANCHOLY which is a personality that is melancholy, or depressed and is a perfectionist. The fourth one is PHLEGMATIC which are ones who are usually peaceful. No one person is just exclusively one of the four.

The most accurate history is Jewish history according to GOD's Word, but yet the Bible is not a history book but about a living Messiah today. Yes I thought all His history with yet the present and much much more in the future.

For years animals, over children and other people got better care and attention. This was what is known as inordinate affection. Misplaced and out of priority affection. Better and more concern for the animal world while babies, believers and children are dying. The world had really believed that man was an animal and that animal rights which meant animals could reason, as well as man and that animals and man were the same stupid specie. Darwin's evolution and Marxism's ideology. The insanity of environmental globalization was to eliminate people where and whenever and to keep the animal world alive, or so they said. It was more to confiscate private property, destroy marriage and the family and equate equality with the no reasoning animal world for man's own self-preservation and ego and power. Who most benefited from man's total annihilation? Since some of the angelic hosts did not obey GOD and left their positions, maybe GOD chose man, then in innocence, to do what angelic beings could not do, "be fruitful and multiply", or GOD was just continuing in His plan for man no matter about the angelic host?

Satan has a stand up brilliant countenance to deceive Adam and Eve before they sinned, bringing sin into the entire world. Continuing to spread sin, Satan was not content with one third of the angelic host, but now homo-sapiens. In fact just this one, Adam. The third mission was to destroy man completely and eventually have him too thrown in Hell, each and every progeny. GOD'S only Son Messiah was not spared and in fact over and over again in the Old Testament GOD announces plainly His Son's visit to earth to save originally the Jews and set up a kingdom, or then a race of human beings. Satan had thought when Y'eshua was crucified that he had won, but in fact Satan had been condemned and judged for Hell first, in GOD'S time, then into the burning lake of fire. This was this pride of Satan, to be equal with GOD and be like Messiah which he could never have been. Maybe before man, Satan saw Messiah as equal to GOD and as His Son and felt envy in his mind even though he was the highest angel? Do angels have spiritual hearts? Of course Messiah was Begotten not made or not created like Lucifer was before he got thrown out of his position in heaven and was called Satan (Isaiah 12). Demons are angelic fallen beings who have no gender and cannot procreate and cannot receive forgiveness for sin. Hell was made for Satan and his cohorts originally. In Latin, too, there is a no gender grammar.

Are UFO's, lights of Satan's power in demonic forms, normal to man's sight? This military force could be Nephilim, but with limitations. GOD is always in control no matter what we as human beings may do, or believe, or do not believe. GOD, though, only does good according to His will which is in His Word. Diseases, death, famines, crime, et cetera all came in through Adam's fall, or free-will fall. With Job GOD let Satan do everything to torture Job, but GOD said he could not take Job's life.

GOD always has the final say as to His will. Sin and death, not separable since Adam, go hand and hand. Angels do not die even once, but then they cannot obtain salvation if they have fallen away.

GOD has two wills. He has an absolute and permissive will sometimes we find hard to discern. GOD can allow a tragedy to occur permissively because in GOD'S overall plan it is already a future that He knows, or is the past to Him. Sin and desire must go, then GOD's grace, or GOD's grace then repentance at Messiah's Calvary. It is also to have patience with importance. Pressures internal and external are defeated and one is to pray without ceasing. GOD's promises to claim as truth for us and then GOD's total peace. To know GOD's will and the habit of holiness has taken hold on earth as it is in heaven.

The European Holocaust was a religion of sexual deviancy mainly. It could not address its own religion. If Protestantism stayed in Germany, then possibly the Holocaust would have been prevented. What did man in the democratic world, or in Judaism do to protect or know about their own people? Why the blind eye? GOD's permissive will came in, as far as man's chosen evil, or freewill. GOD's absolute will cannot look on any sin, hence Calvary. Man's freewill allowed sin, His permissive will, plus Satan's occultic power to overtake an entire people almost like he did Adam and Eve in Garden. The same occurred in Russia. Man chose to blatantly ignore GOD's absolute will. GOD does not murder and GOD is a GOD of love, and power. The resurrection was a demonstration in love, perfect love even above agape' love. A Sodom and Gomorrah episode in Nazi Germany who had the better land. Messiah shall always answer yes, no, or wait to all believers. His response nonetheless does not go according to our will. If we are silent, apathetic, uncaring how can we as the human race want free-will according to GOD's will? Our will to be taken from us? Would we not then say and with logical reason that there is then no freewill? Which is it, freewill, or no freewill of course along with Messiah's choosing among the brethen? Freewill to do what is GOD's will, or our own will? We would all hope the former for the good of mankind. "We are our brother's keeper."

Joseph Kennedy told America to "leave the Holocaust as is." Why? Why have the Kennedys experienced such tragedies? Coincidence? "GOD shall bless those who bless His people and curse those who curse His people" The sins travel to the 3rd and 4th generation. When the German-Jews opposed evil, who responded to help them in the rich and elite besides other German-Jews? Remember sin is contagious. One cannot turn a blind eye to one's own sin, or even someone else's sin. One can pray, admonish, correct, help, but never turn a blind eye. Who shall the believers judge? The West chose to sit that is the elites in government and in business. It did not condemn them. Capitalism and self-centered democracy as long as self-preservation was maintained. FDR was aware for quite sometime. Even after the war the Western elite again chose to even help socialism spread at the Yalta Conference. If one does not follow history, real history, as it is being written then and with the light of truth one can see how we have come to the debacle' we now face. Self-preservation and ego are terrible things. Many so called leaders in democratic states want to appear as popular iconoclasts with something original to tell us, no matter the price others must pay with their lives. Democracies are popularity contests and rule by parties with an ideology, not a special view, as an individual would have. Miracles, not rationalization, should occur, but man blocks GOD's will to do what He does through mankind. Man allows Satan to do his evil. Messiah defeated Satan and his works on the Cross. Adam allowed Satan's evil in and also escape goated to blame Eve who was deceived which Adam was not. We repeatedly hear where was GOD? Where was and is man? GOD is omnipotent, omnipresent, omniscient. Where was man and his freewill to do good? Who held him back? Yes loudest about this all was man's self-preservation. Then again in America a Holocaust worse then slavery occurred and where were these men as well as secular Jews? Were they not in fact all for the very same things that Nazi Germany was for? Who could not possibly know that homosexuality, infanticide, euthanasia, et cetera was not all part of evil and Nazi Germany? Yet they cry Holocaust, but to whom and for whom are they crying? They have become what they never physically opposed, but only verbally for most and that is to blow off steam for their own egoism. Anti-Semitism? No, anti-GOD. National faith is important such as Russian Orthodoxy, the American Biblical, the Sudanese Christians and Israel's Messianic

Jewry. If Messianic Jewry cries out about any holocaust, one can rest assured that they speak the truth and do not glamorize evil. This real national sovereignty and not political parties, or any political philosophy, for none are good. In Europe there are 3 religions; Islam, Roman Catholicism, and Protestantism. If we contain two, Roman Catholicism and Protestantism, then Islam would grow more rapidly, or would it? If each European nation worshipped GOD, or founded their own GOD, there would be less bickering and feuding and less chance for Islam to have grown in Europe or America like it has. Religions should "export", nor import. When immigrants come to their countries, they should with love greet their country, if possible, about their national faith and not encourage heathenism from other nations. To assimilate into a society means Judeo-Christians melt into, not bring diversity or animosity which is the true word and diversity which is by all means a euphemism. Europe was congested by actually one religion, hence European nations became hostile to each other and Christianity disseminated from Rome, or Berlin no matter what the German Reformation brought because there was nothing Original in it, but only a protestation of one size fits all and which power source would rule first and this is not what faith should be all about. It is almost like bringing a foreign language to a native people who do not understand it. Maybe the Orthodox Jews would have assimilated better with the Germans if the Reformation would have stayed in Germany alone and would have removed the innate anti-Semitism that even Martin Luther had... Culture to the Judeo-Christian faith would have meant... Judeo-Messianic Jewry and national Christians from each country? German Christians could have assimilated better in one national faith; hence the real Judeo-Christian faith for there was no Judeo or Christian faith in Nazi Germany for the most part. Why would the "branches" not be witness to the "roots" no matter what, since the Jews are Christian in nature? Was it the idea of Catholicism and its Protestantism, or protestation, as such that kept Protestantism anti-Semitic? Grace, but not for Jews? Individual freewill must extend out, not group mentality.

Homosexuality is group mentality and started WW I because the elites in Germany needed to cover up their scandal by proposing a war. They duped the German people. This reprobate sin is highly contagious as well as infectious, both literally and figuratively in regards to AIDS too. It was sacredness, not quality of life that should have been addressed. Deviance downed the entire nation into a falsified war by the rich and well educated. With "quality" in human beings come this Nazi mentality of superiority of the master "race" which in essence in the demented "race". It is sin with an abomination and was left as a malignant tumor to fester and rot an entire national body, or the collectiveness of a national soul. Now America was rotting and festering from this "bubonic" plague.

When we as a people say Israel chose to obey GOD by faith and according to His Word, then we can see GOD'S will work according to the love of Messiah, agape' love and not carnal, or erotic love.

Universal freedom is always applicable in regards to GOD'S Word, but not in most religions. But is this really universal freedom that transcends with foreign religions and even foreign gods? The cliche' of religion's universal freedom means what? One world religion that has been trying to be obtained for millenniums. Universal freedom means according to GOD and that each particular people find their own GOD. Revolutions export also, faith should nationally support and the Holy Spirit transports. GOD IS NOT UNAWARE.

As to the TRIBULATION, let us not as believers rely on the assumption that all is well, for it is not. We can disillusion ourselves into becoming self-preservationists. Any people, or nation let alone believers must always be accountable to GOD first. "Love the Lord your GOD with all your heart, mind and soul and love your neighbor as yourself. To do these two things and you have fulfilled all of the Commandments." In the TRIBULATION itself demonic activity shall be horrendous without the Holy Spirit to hold it back. Only the ones who do not accept and take the mark of the beast shall remain GOD fearing, but shall be killed or some few shall be spared by GOD, such as the 144,000 Jews that are Messianic.

Our free will now, as before and shall be, is a double edged sword that we say we need and want, yet again we act as robots by not obeying GOD, but by following Satan freely, or so we think.

Either we use freewill properly as believers, or so we negate it for the robotics of Satan's plan. In socialistic countries robotics always are at work. Man alone by Adam's fall can also do much evil, but also by his relinquishing to self, or ego, or the world.

Fatherhood in America had died, because to us our Father had died, because we refused His son Messiah as a nation. What followed was the no motherhood for displaced mothers who were not able to be mothers first and foremost. Without fatherhood, sons more than daughters are affected because with no bonding or authority to discipline, the male loses his compass in life. Gangs do not just form. They are invented or created by deadbeat dads and hence fill in a distorted way what father, or a father, did not provide at an early age at usually 1-3 years old in a young man's life. That is not to say it ends at that age, but at this age it must start for this is where the bonding takes place. The family correlates and compliments into sound relationships within society itself and extends into the nation this GODLY institution. Even grandparents must be included and must lead this institution and not retire into oblivion, nor over do so that grandparents alone raise another father and mother's child. The mishap family does not work. Adoption was meant as the exception to the rule and not to totally replace fatherhood and motherhood biologically. Foster care in government, or state guardianship. The civil righters instead of listening to the rich and well educated who do not like to raise their own should have had more concern for their own sons and daughters and less concern about free sex. Money and transition transport children here and there and warehousing them creates emotional instability. Families make a nation not mishap families, or dysfunctional families. The collectiveness of individuals is wholesome from the family institution though not perfect. Yet, after all do not all governments quintessentially say, We are perfect?

Why is family so important? It is a foundation, the building block of society. Man is conducive to conduct and animals to behavior. Conduct has reasoning behind it. Behavior has instinct, or patterns that do not reason. Pacifism in a society is not peace, but self-preservation, or let me remain neutral. Either one is for GOD or is for Satan. There is no gray area. Yet most people seem to believe there is. With this pacifism comes apathy. Can this be the peace that passes all understanding? But peace for whom? And this practice that makes perfect, but only if one practices properly, but is not Christianity a participation sport and not a spectator one? What does any ism have to do with the Judeo-Christian faith?

Education without GOD started with Adam and the serpent, or was it Satan in his full brilliant attire? "GOD DID NOT SAY?" A question with a lie is a secular education. Satan audibly spoke to Adam this re-education, or godless chatter of the mind. GOD audibly spoke to Adam so what could Adam have said to GOD after he sinned? Another lie? GOD said this to admonish Adam before he took a bite, because he loved Adam and had given man's creation freewill, but always GOD's will. GOD does not go back on His Word, or anything he speaks, or has written. Did Satan know before hand what GOD said to Adam? After Adam sinned in Genesis it then says about " Messiah's heel being bruised, but Satan's head being crushed. " Provision was made for man immediately. Sin was contagious in heaven and so sin came through Adam in the same way, but also it became hereditary. Meaning all men are born into sin. A kind of two sins. The old man Adam and our freewill to sin not that we should, but we all do. " All have fallen short of the glory of GOD. "

In America the greatest war was against GOD in the 60's. It was totally spiritual. It took afterwards millions of souls silently, viciously and effectively. Who was the perpetrator? Democratic government officials elected and appointed? This greatness became egoism for materialism. A nation that knew poverty and hardship at Jamestown, but later vagabonds came who were Europeanized at too much by Oxford and Cambridge? In 1962 no Bible reading in public schools, in 1963 no school prayer, in 1973 Roe vs Wade and the murder of the unborn of millions, et cetera and the list grew. All those opposed GOD directly by government officials and the rich and well educated and the civil righters.

What had America known about famines, starvation and the gulags? Our Garden of Eden was our materialism. It was a den of thieves, for capitalism knows no limits, because it trusts man's human nature. This boredom of nothingness, or rebellion grew out of not love for our children, but was this a spiritual and not a financial depression? Which one should have been watched constantly? The rebellion under socialism, pure materialism was diametrically opposed to this, yet in essence got it's rebellion from it. Rebellion to authority to supplant not materialism, but morality GODLY morality. Now these rebels who are unqualified hold elite positions, because of POLITICAL CORRECTNESS and because they are affirmative actioned qualified. Thievery did start from the top down and exists till today. It trickled down from Big Business and big government that is this immorality and divisiveness. Morality was gone with the wind. Then Hollywood got involved the ones without a real life, or a real job. Along came these derelicts that preyed on and prayed not for our children. Hate crimes were reverse pathological and indiscriminate laws. The child was to blame.

Since evil is an invention and not original only GOD creates and is the Originator. When theatrical reality ends for the rich and their death is near they seek escape with power, drugs, alcohol, wealth, materialism, promiscuity and sensuality. Reality cannot be faced life had been too good. The rich do not grow old gracefully. Why? Messiah said to the rich young man, "Give all your things to the poor and come and follow Me." The rich man walked away sadly. "To much is given, much is expected. In America it became too much was given and nothing was expected. That is, charity was replaced with delegating one's excesses.

GOD calls all to Him, none come on their own which is different than all shall be saved, or that man's free will alone reaches salvation. "His sheep hear His voice." America had forgotten the purpose the foundation was laid upon? GOD.... "Render unto Caesar the things that are Caesar's and unto GOD the things that are GOD'S", but now Caesar wants it all. Caesar wanted life, always someone else's; liberty, also someone else's, and now private property now that would be our own, or was it ever? And what about a mothers' private property when in gestation? As another year passed we decided to stay in Israel, because Marie and Rachel needed to be in the Holy Land. All of Marie's living relatives were just about here, that is her very closest one. Go worldwide anywhere, or almost anywhere and say the word "Jew" and almost a preconceived notion appears, and sometimes they are right. But why is this so polemical? Are Jews recluse or unavailable for comment even though they are not charitable with faith if they even have one? Do they share their faith no matter how misguided? If not, why not? What is this morbid fear or unconcern between "roots" and "branches"? The "tree" must grow in faith unilaterally, or as one. Not only were they spread apart for disobedience, but maybe in the Time of the Gentiles we could proselytize with love so the "roots" would not separate from Gentile Christianity and Messianic Jewry? So foreign had GOD become that even Messianic Jewry was refused; but again secular Jews only had seen money. Democracy in religion, when a religion or religions knowingly bypass Messiah for the Jews to hear or see in action with conviction. "Stiffnecked" called this by GOD the Father, but not impossible and yet even at Moses' time GOD was ready to eliminate them. There is always an innately Jewish mindset which is not prejudice, which most Gentiles fail to really perceive. The Jewish people assimilate easily, but retain a reclusiveness in faith and do not evangelize about Messiah. Europeanism also coerced Jewry to be either financiers many centuries ago, which was looked down upon, or professionals, because assimilation was frowned upon by the majority. Democracy and Jewishness are an anomaly, but a

Monarch shall suffice. The Jewish people have a Christian nature, but can be the most difficult to love of all the people. Just because He spread them apart does not mean He chose new "roots". In Acts Chapters 10 and 11 is when the Gentiles first heard the Gospel and when Rev Shaul was in Rome was the last time the Jews would really hear about their Messiah.

Only in Israel had I seen for myself the Jewish people as a full majority, even though there is a plebiscite. They fully let others live freely even though it was a Zionist state. Ones who enjoyed freedom were not always ones who were respectful of life. The 12 tribal Arab nations were: the Sudan, Egypt, Saudi Arabia, etc. All other nations are Gentile. Maybe that says something about GOD? Christianity is a Jewish moral concept and the Jewish person does not impose, or share this faith of Orthodoxy like Europeanism did at least 2 times. In America Jews are extravagant with capitalism as the tool and in Russia they are universal and in Poland they are assertive as pioneers and are hard workers, but Polish Catholicism as the ultimate and they are not even a Latin country. They excel sometimes too much in mundane foolishness, or materialistic successes. Maybe they assimilate too much into any culture because they do not know their Messiah. The Law and the Commandments were given to the Jewish people, and Leviticus tells them (that is, the religious Jews) what they must do to be "saved". The Sabbath even comes under the Mosaic Law for Messiah had broken down all rules and regulations in regards to faith. The Jews do not need Gentiles to convince them who Messiah is. They have heard only that many times by the "branches'" side without love and sincerity and with financial strings attached.

The Jewish person is an introverted person according to faith. Gentiles have, I believe, a different mindset. The Jewish people are in foreign countries unaware of their real surroundings, even when danger is around and now it is even in Israel and they cannot see for the most part. The Time of the Gentiles is almost over. Anti-Semitism has occurred from within and without the Jewish community. Pharasaic Judasim does not lead to a spirit of unity between the "branches" and the "roots", and from outside the "branches" do not support the "roots". Suffering has been a constant, I also believe, because GOD'S meaning and their meaning of chosen are quite different and as well to Gentiles. Only to Messianic Jewry is it almost understood in its GODLY form. Without Messiah in the Jew, there is no GOD to worship and they are not really Jews. They were special because they were chosen and not chosen because they were special, and for the most part as obedience of GOD. I can hear it now, "Please choose somebody else."

Marie and Rachel could clearly see Messiah by faith with His love in their hearts. Isaiah 53 was real for them. They knew Truth, "The word that became flesh" because of their opened hearts by Messiah and to believe that there are 3 persons in the one GOD. Why even Islam believes in only one part and not the Trinity. Transformation in the heart of every believer. Does any one think that there are 2 messiahs, one for the Jews and one for the Gentiles? The New Age religion appeals now to most people, especially most Jews without any questions or reserve because he appears this beast as the peace maker and the kingdom ruler and also because it is occurring in Israel itself. "A new broom sweeps good." With each year passing came new dictators and some that stayed. The bickering was growing, but growing toward this beast.

Zionism was in and the secular Jewish style mirrored a Greek democracy. Kosher food was no longer so as it use to be. One could hardly find an intact Jewish People the world over from Anti-Semitism. It was a state by heredity and not by faith and would not GOD bring judgment to Israel during TRIBULATION?

The Wotan Temple, not known as that, was built in Israel. Things in Israel were totalitarian. Marie and Rachel were quite scared, I along with a few other Messianic Jewish Families would meet to worship and discuss the present state of affairs. Many temples and synagogues and mosques and churches were nearly all extinct. All worship would be to this "monarch". The billionaire was over and their war. The millionaires were only well to do follow-the-leaders. People who never had money had it now and it ruined them and society even more.

The American Irish Government Sweepstakes played, or rolled the dice and got three 6's. America was wagging it's English tail. America looked like Brazil, or Argentina now.

A hospital stay was dangerous affair, because of this New Age philosophy. It almost appeared like more people went into the hospital then ever came back out. Most believers children's births were done at home by natural birth. Physicians were all state sponsored employees. Doctors had long ago foregone the Hippocratic Oath and were taught about death and dying.

This so called preventive medicine of monetary care was working to reduce the population. Donors were involuntary made use of and their parts that is body parts were sold to what else, the highest bidder. Never was the cerebral cortex checked for brain activity by a Brain Doppler Scanner, whenever a patient was in a comatose state. Infant mortality rate rose because most women were either fixed for life or used RU-486. Senior citizens averaged about 50-55 years of age. Dr. Jekyl and Mr. Hides could never be found for advice. Always a pre-med student or an intern of foreign descent, or even a physician's assistant would proxy and hospital visits let alone home visits were obsolete. Multiple choices was the system. Malpractice insurance was dropped, because the more deaths meant more money from the world state. The analogy was similar to America's government agencies that had to spend it all or else got a cut in government funds all of course at taxpayers' expense. Male vasectomy and homosexuality kept procreation down, as well as lesbianism. Covert death, predetermined by the state from orders below. Life was worth less than most of the water, food and shelter. Too few could never be fed, only to many. Everything was lend lease. You lend us your house and we'll lease you the property and land to put it on. Everyone had to be employed.

There was no democracy, thank goodness for that, and no constitutional government, only a special kind of pre-nobility monarch. Oligarchy the "rule of law"? The New Age Olympic

Athletic Association was made up of mostly homosexual bodybuilders. The Children's Defense Fund stated no parent could coerce a child of 13 years of age to do anything it did not want to do or the parents could be sued and the child removed from the home forever. This UN treaty had overruled the US Constitution by the Federal Courts which was thought never to happen by the Rutherford Institute. Also all infanticide need not be state controlled, just so that the infanticide was done. Adoption was outlawed. Foster care increased because of state funds. Animals could also supposedly sue under the right of the government and not for cruelty to animals but for civil and criminal proceedings. The rabbinical courts had fun with this. The state had a vested interest in other peoples' affairs and property. The animals had to receive equal or above treatment with children.

At noon each day sirens would go off to remind all that it was time for a 5-minute siesta of New Age meditation, giving thanks to the coming nobility.

I had heard that in America there was a sort of quasi-language of multiculturalism's diversity. Almost a slang like Ebonics were. It was like Hispanic with Phillipino, or French Vietnamese, or even like Pennsylvania Dutch in that only certain individuals could understand it. All this to destroy American English which did not have the many dialects or accents as England's English. Also computers did their best to contribute to a non-thinking decision-making people. South of the border brought with it a brutal and rude culture of the machismo where a married male could commit adultery with his wife's knowledge and the sons and daughters were taught that this was okay. The female had to keep fidelity. Any dead beat dads needed? America had become a conquistador country with luck, chance and gambling and did not World Bank teach the very same thing, to conquer and to divide? Look how far socialist Mexico progressed and engressed into America and the Anglophiles loved it so they could get re-elected. The proof is in the pudding. Collective farming was plentiful. In other words government could not provide for all so it had to mismanage as such is possible in order to claim a 100% tax base, not including state employee thefts. Government jobs were gone and only New Age jobs were available for the right price, but Europe held most of these. America's resources, human and otherwise were just about depleted. Europe was attached to Europe for good. It was like the DuPont's of Delaware, or the Mormons of Utah. A Milton Hershey affect, but with state control. A Columbus, Ohio layout was most affective to separate certain, or all groups from one another with a 52 mile beltway around the city. The cities became also like Jacksonville Florida which took in the entire county to become the largest city in the world in area. Speak about urban flight. In some areas barbed wire, remember where that was used, was in place. The sky and the sun for some reason could not be visibly seen. Almost as if a nuclear holocaust had occurred somewhere in the Eastern world.

The poor needed land, no matter how small, to survive and raise a family, usually believers, but this too was not POLITICALLY CORRECT. Freedom, if it could be called that without land meant no purpose to relate to one's country and more importantly no way to care for one's own immediate family; but is that not what socialism was to do? The Old Testament, Abraham and Lot, plus Caleb at 80 years old did not apply here. Without private property wild life would quickly die off, but landowners could always be blamed for pilfering public lands. Who pilfered more than the political parasites?

Animals did not belong to zoos so environmentalists can worship them as their own progeny almost as if they were their own procreation. Beauty and the beast was now in the world.

Is not Israel at this time in TRIBULATION with a new monarch to be announced? How spiritual then shall Israel be? Roman Catholicism and Protestantism were now playing second fiddle and tended to be less presumptuous, because of the worldwide influence that this new monarch would have. Could this indicate a reason for defending the Antichrist, or to that affect? Europeanism always wanted to be top dog, but in this instance they would have to play second fiddle. Even when Stalin ruled Russia by thuggery, Europe then loved Russia more than ever. Who developed socialism more than the French Jesuits and later the homosexual Weimer Republic? What Russia got was this cancer from FDR and Churchill two Anglophiles with a life insurance policy for their life only.

Did not the Yalta Conference strength totalitarianism in the East and then later in the West far West? The Kings of East: China, Japan, Korea, et cetera now understood how Europeanism worked. Islam would be easy. More and more brutality meant more and more Money and power.

Europe sided with Islam against Christian Russia, when Russia was defending Serbian Slavs and the Islamic Turks were butchering Slavic Christians in the 19th Century. This too was America's fall this taking on of Islam mostly by radical Arabs and Moslems in names. This worshipping of Allah would bring irreparable damage to their own American Negroes. "You shall have no other gods before Me." Judeo-Christian values were gone and church icons were sold as antiques.

Constitutional government could not and did not convey Christianity, because Christianity lies in a people's heart and not on a piece of paper which meant "a living and breathing document" which they said was alive. Were not babies living and breathing? America forgot its history and had no native tongue. Abraham did not pick a land flowing with milk and honey. It was not ready made like America had been in its later years. These rich nomads travelled worldwide with no place to call home. They were the real harlem globetrotters.

After our own Civil War in America many unsavory Jews usurped Negroes' free land from them and in essence stole their purpose for life in America. As time went on the American Negro came to separate themselves from the land, as well as from each other as families and started to intermingle from infidelity and not natural Biblical precepts. A rift grew between Negro man and Negro woman, until in the 20th Century Negro families had been abandoned by non-marriage with their Negro male counter part. Less and less respect was shown for their weaker sex and the very same Anglo-Saxons who endorsed slavery and separated their family units, as well as Africans when they had never even seen Africa then intermingled not intermarried with each other. The American Negro icon became slavery in sports and the deadwood from the civil righters. Slavery was again in and introduced by the rich and well educated. Now the combination of rich as slaves sufficed only the civil righters and, of course, Islamic Jihad.

Any group of males should respect their own women, as mothers and as wives, plus their daughters and especially their own sons. More so called good government was introduced by the Great Society. More out of wedlock infanticized babies more children as mothers having children. Invest in absolute and raw power government. Forced Bostonian bussing did the very opposite of loving one's neighbor. "The ends did justify the means." One cannot coerce one's self onto another no matter how much government promotes and upholds itself. Arrogance toward the other is always what appears as the final affect. If people are not controlled like puppets, they usually shall get along as long as there is a level of playing field with no quotas, or set asides and even those individuals shall choose and not have the rich and well educated for their utopia on the rest of the misplaced people and call it integration or being tolerant, or even diverse as if that meant detente', the lessening of the rope. With full knowledge the very ones who created the Ugly American Big Business and Big Government now living in all the world, but Europe especially, wanted people of different cultures and languages to not get along intentionally so they would that is the rich, look like the so called foreign ambassadors. The New Deal and the Great Society threw our crumbs out to the people and the people said, "GOD save this King, or Caesar" even though it was they who took away their decency and honor, instead of offering land years ago and a purposeful way of life by agriculture to the poor. Idleness, drugs, sports, sensuality, welfare, abandonment became the devil's workshop for the poor and the well-to-do famous and infamous athletes. Instead the rich chose to give to the American Negro a Civil War, or their so called civil rights which did absolutely nothing to remove the facade that racism would instantly dissipate. The union not the nation had to be protected, even with the Dred Scott of 1857. A court that caused a most bitter war. "Is it not the rich who take you to court?" In this case Dred Scott was challenging Negroes as being property, but lost, even though he should have won and the well educated knew it. The rich man's theory was, "if it happens so be it and if not so what?" What poor people in America needed was not war and judicial fiat, but life, liberty and private property, Jefferson's original wording. Jefferson could not include private property, because he too owned slaves which were so called private property.

Land gives a man a purpose, not money, or freedom in his nation to provide for his family, not a way to embarrass and ridicule by ostentatious individuals whose only talent lies in the physical realm. Grown up individuals should put away childish things. To ingratiate oneself, because of talent with the shameless rich and well educated is not complimentary to human compassion, or decency. The enticer is money, or the love of it to the poor and wealth and power always for the rich alone. Nothing is gotten without a reciprocating consequence. If it is too good to be true, chances are it is. The encourage-ment to do the wrong thing for the right person, oneself, or others, or the encouragement to do the right thing at the wrong time. The political ramifications superseded, as usual the moral and spiritual involvement which usually takes much longer to develop completely. Since this did not occur, socialism either through government coercion, or by Islam produced a catastrophic dilemma. Capitalism in Russia did the very same thing. It destroyed the moral idea and agricultural base, because it constantly searches out whatever new era, industrially and technologically that shall and has appeared on the scene and is not capitalism the all with the all in the Western mindset? No technology shall not save us. Living for one's own selfish moment, or this go for the gusto. Drugs and drug dealing worked in America, because reality without convenience, extravagance and laziness could not be faced. Then government became Al Capone and gambled our way into destitution and destruction for an easy buck. Where is crime if government proposes what thugs proposed? Oh yes, it was for a good cause. Again "the end justify the means."

If the rich's children can live with it so can everyone else's, but what if the others may not? I could name the children themselves, but we all know who they are already. First civil rights said, "Protest peacefully, then more boastrous and then get violent and cause harm to humans and private property. Not enough. How about "black" Americans? Still not enough. How about African-American? Still not enough. How about Moslem names and Islamic Jihad and finally how about anti-Semitism being anti-American which had nothing to do whatsoever with slavery? This deathwish for themselves and others sought to free the American Negro, but as for "race" that would be the same and would be played as long as possible by the rich and well educated. Add "social" to it and guess what? You have "social" justice not just justice mind you, but "social" justice? Just ask the peasants in Russia, or the Holocaust victims about "social" justice. Oh, that's right they are all dead, or are they?

Why is it the rich and well educated entertain Saudi Arabia when no American Negroes are allowed there, or no American Jews and no Christians at all? How about our selling the A-WACS PLANE to the Saudis to spy on Israel and which Saudi Arabia has no standing army. How about George Bush, Sr as President celebrating Christmas on a US Naval vessel, instead of on Saudi turf? What about persecution of Christians and kidnapping of American citizens in Saudi Arabia? Oh, that's right for the love of money. Also how does the Bechtel Corporation fit in with the Arabs, since Mr. George Schultz and Casper Weinberger, plus others who worked for them and then served in the trickle down administration? Only blood was trickling down, or should we say after 9/11 our bleeding by the Saudi himself, Osama bin Laden. We needed to contract cancer itself. Being always sincerely apologetic our government that is could forgive 9/11 and all in the name of oil, wealth and power. Israel too could forgive Yassir Arafat, after all there was commonality with the rich, no matter who they were, or what they did. Our Secretary of State found it in his heart to forgive the PLO but was it not the victims' relatives that had to forgive? Oh, forgiveness was based on wealth and the law of supply and demand. The Bible in Y'eshua's words said, "Love your enemy and pray for him." Of course, Y'eshua did not have monetary purposes in mind when He said this.

Is Islam exclusive? Do fish swim? Convert, or else. Money talks and it is in the Arabic Islamic tongue. If one is left with one. Not a peaceful free volition of faith, but ideology which is what Islam is. An ultimate death wish and America chose the latter, but pretended that is government had chosen both. "One cannot serve two masters, for he will hate the one and love the other." Oil, Moslem oil at that and spring water do not mix. Neither does the Bible and the Koran. One has individual faith, the other has group ideology.

Who set up America and what for? No not slavery. Was it for Islam, Buddha or even Judaism no matter the hyperbole' of some sects who are not peace loving? Nothing about one should love your enemy in the Koran. Only death to the infidels. If we, as believers stand behind every word in the Bible why do not Moslems stand also behind every word in the Koran and they do don't they, or they would not be Moslems? As to who set up America were they Mormons, Jehovah Witnesses, Moslems, Hindus, et cetera that decided with their very lives to serve the Trinity with Messiah as GOD in the flesh? Did their gods ever say that, "He was GOD in the flesh?" Could, or would we have been invited to worship freely with which only Christianity allows? Yes there were Deists, but who did they follow? Yes Messianic Jewry is the same as Christianity, or Christianity is the same as Messianic Jewry. Y'eshua was the Forefathers' GOD. Why did Columbus sail the oceans? Was it not to protect against Islamic piracy on the high seas and to understand all the Trade Winds that at that time only the Moslems knew? This we can give credit to the Moslems, as a first. Now America I suppose should never have been discovered except possibly by Moslems, or Native Americans? So much land to burn and destroy, until there would be no forests, yet that is what this New Age replicates itself on, but worse. Along with Columbus, Luis de Torres, a Jew, was the first man to set foot on San Salvador and pronounce it a new nation. Now revival could start, because the "roots" were here to begin with. No one ever mentions about the Conquistadors who founded Latin America, or better yet raped the land.

Earlier in American, not English history would come this new language called American English Lexicon written by Mr. Webster.

Was it secular politicians and gravediggers, or was it a Christian majority? After all in a democracy I am told the majority rules? Was this Protestantism? Did they see "anguish in independence"? Was it Roman Catholicism? Did not the Irish come much later? Was it not by faith and not Europeanism? After all they left there to come here did they not? All governments are raw power. Three forms of government in the world and they are an oligarchy, ruled by the powerful few, a democracy ruled by mob rule or right by might, and a monarch power by authority. It is when man moves from faith and into ideology, or political philosophy that it becomes how could one say it the devil's workshop. Washington chose democracy, power by the majority and a republic documents that get old and were not most Americans Christians as Washington was or subscribed to it's moral base and precepts?

Their church was distinguishable because it was a Body and not a building, or an organization. To declare one's independence does not necessarily mean that one took on a revolutionary mindset. By the way the war of independence was fought as a RELIGIOUS REVIVAL and also 2500 Jews here. So "roots" and "branches" were here. Without the "roots", the "branches" cannot grow. Also to declare independence, it had to be from not only a nation, but from "their" GOD. There would be no set denomination within that particular faith, otherwise why would one die for their faith or the Truth, unless it was ideology, such as Islam, or socialism and nothing in our documents ever eludes to that in the slightest. This was not a so called Revolutionary War, or a Civil War as had occurred in Russia by the Bolsheviks. It was to reiterate a war of independence, independent from British colonialism who was a foreign invader in full military regalia and in red. Their's was a form of a crusade to kill and destroy the sovereignty of another nation and it's people, Americans. Was not colonialism in British blood? There were "Bolsheviks". England even kept it's own criminals in a prison in the state of Georgia. Is that not like the European British? Almost like Communist Cuba that sent their 33,000 criminals, or Communists to America's borders in the 20th Century. In the 20th Century the Mensheviks also appeared, but the catch was too big for their rod.

There was no one to rule here in America, but the British thought there was. Did not Paul Revere say, "The British are coming, the British are coming". Notice he does not equate himself as an Englishman, but as an American, or why else would he say the word British and as an enemy? Following later in American History would come the opportunists of Roman Catholicism followed in part by the Judaizers, not Messianic and then of course Islam, the very ideology of faith that Columbus opposed. None though were turned away, when Christians ruled. One has to again wonder, if we had come to the land under a different faith would they had welcomed us? A nation is made up of a people Americans, not peoples and with one language, American English and with a history which we have in part have already covered, American History.

Again one can hear, "What about slavery?" No, not from the deceased, but from the living. Yes there was slavery by most of the rich, but that should not harm anyone, or surprise them in the slightest. Since human nature, good vs evil, gravitates toward avarice and sin and not always good. There were no Gulags or ovens or Auschwitzs, or Khmer Rouge like in Cambodia, but I know we are not talking about other countries... but the truth must be told, but not relived with distortions or emulations, when separations have been made and the government has hasn't it? Of course no one would want financial reparations, or blood money to dishonor the dead or what would be the opposition to evil itself the love of money? Again the love of money would rule. Would one desecrate for money alone and for what One's ancestry suffered for? By the way John Adams, as well as some others were not slave owners and John Adams opted for a monarch, the only Biblical form of government. One can take note why George Washington might have chosen a democratic/republic and not a monarch, after all the monarch in England became a dictator.

The American Indians needed to be incorporated into a nation not into another nation as Native Americans. They became Americans and did keep for the most part their tribes, but refused nationhood. What can one say about Latin America? Till this very day they still have revolutions and coupes Conquistador style and even Communism. And what about the African continent? Was it too made up of different countries and nations, as well as tribes? The North American continent was not claimed only a new nation, but in a non-gradual process. The only nation that took in the Negro, because of faith, or hereditary faith were the Israelis, when they took in the Falasha from Marxist controlled Ethiopia with "black" civil righters.

Since America was too good to be true, exploiters of all kind followed, as well as hereditary next of kin to find their pot of gold in capitalism. Then in the 20th Century socialism was making roads into America by multiculturalism. It was not for unity, but war between the village. In essence it was to destroy the Judeo-Christian faith amongst the people, because one cannot destroy GOD. This would be another "Yugoslavia".

Big Business raped Latin America like conquistadors which had more natural resources, as well as human, then America did. Mexico became and still is a socialist state. Everything major is owned by the government. Catholicism's Liberation Theology with the help of Dr. Theordore Hesburgh of Notre Dame fame along with his friend in Nicaragua, Daniel Ortega and the Sandinintas who also correlated in part with the American Democratic Socialist Party represented what?

To reiterate in 1857 the Dred Scott Case and then later in 1973 Roe vs Wade, The United States Supreme Court ruled and in both cases that human beings, are certain groups, or persons were property and could not enjoy the breath of life in the second case and liberty in the first case. Why did Blackmun, a Jew, write the major decision for Roe vs Wade? Did he not know about infanticide and the Jewish women during the Holocaust? Did he not learn in Hebrew Law that murder is murder and that judges interpret and do not make law? How come Blackmun did not know about Blackstone? Was it because it was no longer taught in law schools as a requirement, but just as a history lesson?

As America became nuclear that is in the family, many foreigners although rich were leaving their native lands, but not their native culture, history, or mother tongue. In America they would find a ready made government life and government surely needed their oil money to stay out of the red, but the only red that showed was the blood shed by innocent Christians.

One cannot say they sought political asylum, except for 50,000-70,000 Christians in foreign Moslem Jihad nations. The rest from Mexico were not fleeing persecution, but poverty and more machismo, because America would fork the bill and also to dilute the American people. These were not Mexicans fleeing persecution, but illegals who were law breakers. Asylum came for the same reasons our Founders came, religious freedom.

The Negro comprised only about 12% of the American population and American Jewry about 2%, but the Hispanic about 30% and was growing because of Latin American illegals. We were told repeatedly they were needed because Americans were lazy. Then they said we lacked the brain power, but if one looked at the dire need of where these foreigners were coming from one could only assume that they lacked the brain power, since their own people were starving and dying.

Yes, if Islam, the Native Americans, or African Americans had founded America what would they have done that would have been different? Would the brightest be welcomed, or the most corrupt and ignorant? Remember what Lenin said, "Get rid of all the brains in society." Would this group have proposed a democratic/republic, or racial profiling, an oligarchy, or even a monarch? Would they have fought a Civil War, or wrote a Declaration of Independence, or US Constitution, et cetera? Human nature doesn't change with Color, so why suppose it does? It only becomes chameleon like to it's own environment in order to deceive.

As to public land whose land really was it? Government, or the people? Equal access meaning what? No trespassing as well as no private property, even to ranchers and farmers in most cases. Was this envy by the civil righters really believing that they as a whole would come rule and for how long?

In Yugoslavia, Tito kept an iron fist rule over the many different countries contained within Bosnian Moslems, Croatian Roman Catholics and Serbian Russian Orthodoxy to mention only a few who all had a different religion, language and history. Yugoslavia was the ideal multicultural state. Eruption occurred when Tito died and all these groups had no common bond like Americans had. Hence war broke out which it had in years past. So the Yugoslavians never really existed as a people. Tito was rigid and brutal as all Communists are. He did not take orders from Moscow. America that was foreign owned by England through Arab Islamic oil. What did Christianity have to do with Islam? The English wanted this colonialism of America. The Germans who knew from birth their life's story and occupation and wanted in and not as second fiddle, so the Euro-dollar came as well as the Common Market which wasn't so common. Ten nations all as one united.

Religious freedom had nothing to do with America, Europe or Israel in our latter days. This alliance was forming the monarchy. Only in the OLAM HABA would a Monarch work. No Kingdom Dominion Theology would do, unless the beast was in control.

America was trapped in the North by French Canadian Roman Catholicism and Angelican leanings and to the South was again Roman Catholicism's Liberation Theology. Did not America sign it's sovereignty away? NAFTA did just that. Was constitutional democratic government failing again? Why even the Soviets had a constitution.

Benjamin Franklin said, "It is a republic now try and keep it." He knew only with eternal vigilance would it last. We had fallen asleep.

We as believers had to protect and defend our brothers in Messiah first, the unborn and babies were all believers, but we had failed to do that, plus much more. Foreignors rich ones at that Greek style envy, came to America with just that in mind. Jealously would not do, but envy, yes.

America appeared for about 2 centuries to carry for Europeanism and elsewhere, because America's original idea was lost. The English-Irish and the German held for the most part, the Commander-In-Chief position for America's dura-tion. The United Governments in NYC were in control now for the moment in time.

In Europe, not even the Italians wanted Vaticanism, but as far as Poland, France and Latin America it would definitely suffice. "Do as the Romans do" was not followed. Geography for the Vatican was never a problem. Boundaries and continents did not matter, only the Cardinals flight.

In the orient there was another problem such as when to blink or not? These kings would eventually come in full force, but who could blame them for the opium the British gave them?

The time of the Hebrews was coming closer and closer to Daniel's 70th WEEK. The church would not replace, but would be included as an addendum to the "roots" of the "tree". Israel would again be restored to world stature first through evil and then through good. They would be a light unto all nations and not by governments for Messiah would rule from Jerusalem in the OLAM HABA.

My thoughts took me back to America in the 1960's when evil was good and good was evil. There had been step sons in America who felt somebody somewhere owed them a living for their own lives and even relished the fact that they were rebellious and even in their ignorance and lack of GODLY homes they took pride in the certain ideology. It was a certain way to intimidate private property owners. Nobody wanted to be sued and be placed in court. It kept most Americans apathetic. This monstrosity grew and grew beyond control of America's borders, yet controlled America inside and democracy was a facsimile of old Greek days.

Certain groups intermingled, but rarely married and procreated, infanticized their own species that is human being species, once this train was in motion. It had tried to overthrow the American people's government at that time as well as uphold Communism's hold in Southeat Asia. Who could have such power to pull all this off? Would not the American people have to be deceived, or was their moral fiber almost gone? As Americans, we refused to address the moral issues. We heard the constant screeching of the wheel that needed more oil and got it. There is that word again too, oil.

These infringements were wholesaled by our courts and could have been addressed on a one by one basis, but government thought better of it as it always does. Why not incarcerate the whole system and in the way oblige this squeaky wheel by oiling it even more and this time with London oil, or the assets of.

Then came another court ruling of 5-4 in favor of not allowing homosexual pedophiles to molest our male children and youth. What a startling win of 5-4. Who were the five that stood in the way of pedophilia? Hitler's Youth Corps part two was in the making. Then child pornography, how convenient, was approved on the Internet by a vote of 6-3. Now that made all the sense in the world!

Angela Davis now could teach in defense of the terrorists at the University of California as a "history" professor with a full professorship. Yet in Africa there was no mention of Ethiopia, Somalia, Rowanda, the Sudan, Angola, Egypt, but just South Africa and why? Nothing in the slightest about race!

The tape was played over and over again and backwards in time too. Socialism would surely blossom? Hollywood too played its part by inciting evil and proving their loyalty to America. The American Negro hated his own "race". They were not European enough and did look somewhat different, but then a leopard never sheds it's spots. Inner anger said to them, "get even." They could run the country by themselves they would not need the ones who had enslaved them, or their ancestry, because of the way they looked. This self-hatred would surely do the trick. All they needed was another revolution, or so they were told, or to intimidate others for the rich and they would be handsomely rewarded. The Black Panthers, a Marxist/Leninist group, knew what the fist could do as it had done in the pugilistic ring. Make the other people fear you by government sponsored tyranny especially in America and South Africa. Hispanics came into the fray and the poster image by government was asking, "Who shall be first, or next?"

"Me."

"No me first".

"No me," et cetera.

Then the Asiatics picked up the arrogant chant as well as regular household mothers, aunts, sisters, and even grandmothers. The road of least resistance was working, so why rock the boat now?

I remember reading about Dr. Bell, a missionary surgeon who lived his life in dangerous China and pioneered with Christian love even at the risk of his own and his family's life at times. He did all this for his fellow man. This was no one, or two year hitch He was still an American, but his GODLY mission was to serve the Master first. Now why had not one American " black "thought to do just that for their own people in Africa? Africa was in dire need of American Negroes and their expertise. If it has to be " raced " based, then let it be for good and in Africa too.

CHAPTER XI

AN EXCURSION TO AMERICANISM AGAIN

As another year went by Marie, Rachel and myself decided to chance a trip to America, knowing full well anything…

This would be our second trip to America, but probably a more dangerous one. This would be probably our last chance to see what America looked like and for me to see how much it had changed. We would fly EL AL and then stop off at New York City at Kennedy Airport. Our trip would be in the autumn, when in America one could see the leaves changing colors. As we left for America, we notified all close relatives and close friends and told them how long we would be gone for and when we would return, who to notify if we did not return by such and such a date. This was not really a trip for me, it was as a journey into the unknown and Marie and I felt Rachel could make her own decision to go along.

On the day we left the sky was azure blue with a slight cirrus background. We arrived in New York City on time, but could see this Statue of Liberty, or the Empire State Building.

There were other landmarks, such as Central Park that seemed to have some type of installations on them. As we were landing EL AL told us all to remain in our seats. As usual they checked everything and everyone with such professional scrutiny and care. These were minimum wage earners, or government workers, or employees. They knew what they did saved many human lives which had always been precious to the Jewish people, especially in Israel. We exited the plane and went through metal detectors or scanners, and for some reason one elderly man who looked Hasidic was being stopped and they were searching his personal affects like a common criminal. It appeared he has some religious items that were forbidden in New York City. We continued on into the main lobby and saw a host of United States of Nations' military guards about every 100 feet, or so. We did not stop but just followed the other passengers and were treated quite congenial and were welcomed by 2 Butches who were women in military uniforms and were given forms to fill out as to our stay and pictures of us were taken so that if we would be stopped anywhere we could prove we entered the country legally and also for the exact number of visitors in their centralized computer system. I did notice that there was one question that was asked, "if we belonged to any New Age organizations such as Greenpeace, or the Sierra Club, the Club of Rome," as we were required to fill out a questionnaire form? I thought deeply about that one question and knew it probably meant a lot to whomever would be reading over our applications for admittance and exit out of America. We left that answer, or question blank knowing full well that there could be further things involved, because of our blank answer. We noticed every where that we went there were cameras and monitors and came to the conclusion the audio equipment was always nearby. This paranoia by them the authorities was well founded, because of America's new condition. They probably had much to hide from the public and especially Israelis' citizens. All travel was escorted or done in groups, and certain areas were off limits. As we travelled by bus, we noticed more and more the different cultural affects of the village popularized years ago by one of our dear first ladies. Each "village" had its own signs in their own language in large letters with English in smaller letters and separated each village. There were not many children, or elderly seen, but only it appeared strong adult males. There were strangely no dogs, or cats and the ones we did see seemed undomesticated. There was an appearance of communal living with a look alike architectural structures. They were closest to what was called at one time suburbanite developments. There was no common bond of friendship, or camaraderie amongst individuals. A hidden coercion kept people restrained like Tito had done in Yugoslavia. After our long 50 miles journey from the airport with many stops or checkpoints in between we finally arrived at our destination and were shown politely where we could sign up with the proper authorities. Their manners were well coached through reason. After that we went to get a state run cab in English and went to our direct destinations which were Marie's distant relatives and some of her friends lived. Their neighborhood, if one could call it that had many trees which were unusual from what we had so far seen. We also got the feeling that one could easily come in, but not go out. As we approached their single home, we noticed there was no Jewish ornament on the outside of their door. Before we could reach the door it opened and we were greeted by these warm hearted Polish Jews and their Eastern hospitality. As we entered there were other people. They who appeared knew my wife instantly. Rachel and I were politely introduced and sat down in their large dining room with a feast fit for a king. This must have taken some doing to acquire so much food. Their home's interior was very humble and plain looking, but kosher clean, especially the kitchen area. There was no Messiah image anywhere and why should there be? Nonetheless we would respect their religion of Old Testament Judaism. Within this house lived 4 generations and some nieces and nephews along with aunts and uncles. The Jews were always clever with subterfuging the police state of any kind. There was no over indulgence of any kind and nothing was taken for granted. There was no television just a radio which had different bands on it. There was soft Jewish music playing in the background. Why had these Polish Jews ever wanted to come to America, unless they got trapped when the doors closed for Jews to exit America? Within this home we got an uplifting feeling of hope and not Americanism. These were true Americans not what most Americans had become: lethargic, dumb, ignorant, lazy and apathetic, not to mention crude and barbaric. We eventually talked about government and were surprised to find out that America was no longer a democratic/ republic for which it stands... Elections were held only in large metropolis areas, because that is where most of the people lived like cattle. One did not vote as an individual, but on the Internet as a resident. If there were 10 people in a home they got one vote, the same as if there was only one person in an apartment, or room… So if there were say 10,000,000 in a metropolis and say about one half were families and one half were singles that would account for 5,000,000 votes for the singles and a mathematical dilemma for the 5,000,000 made up of families. Just for average sake, let us say there were 5 members in each household who could vote, then the number of votes would decrease to 1,000,000 votes from actually 5,000,000 eligible to vote of legal age which was 14. One can see why being a non-family member held sway, or that of a homosexual. Offices were for 10-20 year terms at all levels. The age to drive and serve in the military had dropped to age 15. More revenue was needed anyway that could be gotten. In dry spells it destroyed fertile land and where fields once were lie only stones and soil erosion in almost avalanche form.

They had a paid phone in their home which the law required a license for if one wanted to use or have a private home phone by Internet. They were like the J. Paul Getty kind. Meters were connected to all utilities including water that ran under the same principle as a paid phone. One could use legal tender for now, but also smart cars were provided free by the government. Bathing, or showering could be quite expensive. Our meals were all Kosher, or from the Union of Orthodox Rabbis' seal. They also had a garden about 2 acres in size to grow all their own crops and raise some livestock, such as chickens, lambs and pigeons for food and otherwise. This appeared to be Jewish community, but with a sort of ghetto affect. Outside this area one could see legal drugs, prostitution, crime, homosexuality, and street children just like any 3rd world nation. There were no firearms allowed, but some citizens had them hidden nonetheless for protection from anti-Semitic thugs in this area. They had a Jewish Defense League that roamed the streets as vigilante' group by car. Usually the authorities left them alone, because of Israel's stand in the world. We were told by Marie's relatives that they had heard that the West Coast was hit with nuclear warheads. So there was a schism in

America, geographically. The elected chieftains had headquarters in New York City and Washington D.C. I knew all roads lead to " Rome ", or Jerusalem.

America's bread basket was depleted. It was no longer an agricultural nation. Food was now the most expensive item. The rich ate at fine restaurants which even made the prices of food-stuffs soar higher and higher. Employment was mainly government jobs, or minimum wage's government interference, so two extremes developed. There were no cemeteries outside the Jewish sector. All bodies and carcasses were cremated instantly.

Our Thanksgiving meal was apropos, but for many it was not, food was at a premium. We had heard stories to the affect that even human cannibalism farther West was occurring in some areas. Fetuses were being eaten as delicacy as they had done in Peking. The Hollywood crowd had evaporated and most people came up with their own form of occultic activity... Big Business was body parts on the black market who were sold to the rich, as they had also done in Peking and from murdered young Christians and Messianic Jews. They were a touch away on one's computer at home via the ever popular big brother of the Internet.

Without special permission no kind of animal could be killed for any purpose not even if it had rabies. Animal parts were in high demand. I had remembered years ago, when they put a baboon's heart into an innocent baby. Severe penalties, if one got caught for killing a part of the human species. Marie's relatives' animals were registered through the Union of Orthodox Rabbis.

Most peoples' clothing had no variety at all. They were massed produced and made to look alike men and women the unisex look. No more Victorian modesty here. Materials such as paper and plastic and cardboard and burlap were used. Uniforms were all in the colors of red, black and white. It was like visiting Mexico years ago where one could see the hammer and the sickle symbols all through the countryside and here all one saw was an elaborate array of rainbows everywhere. A little like Jesse Jackson's Rainbow Coalition with the rainbow, not for the different colors of people.

Hospitalization was very dangerous. The hospitals were like a pig's sty with unqualified professionals in all fields, unionized of course. The hospital director was a New Ager always. Most Americans had a living will which was pro-euthanasia and the Doppler Brain Scanner was rarely, if ever used to measure the brain activity in the cerebral cortex. This was where all the reasoning was done and where the soul was. The middle brain and the bottom part, the brain stem had nothing that separated man from the animal world.

Every young lady down to the age of 10 years was required to have a yearly checkup for gynecological purposes. Even Norplant or hysterectomies were performed unnecessarily on younger girls according to quotas and affirmative action. Every girl and lady had to have a yearly checkup by the state physician. These procedures the patient had to somehow pay for it, if government would not. If a woman or girl was found pregnant then RU-486 would mostly be used to expedite infanticide even at the risk of the mother's life. Infanticide was very prevalent from conception up to age 6 years of age. The Jewish population had to be covert, because if Tay Sachs was found "infanticide it". Muscular dystrophy, multiple sclerosis, et cetera were all to be eliminated, as well as the individual. Most procreation was by test tube methods. Condoms were never used, or sold because safe sex was not 100% safe sex and the government knew it. No margin for error anymore anywhere. AIDS was epidemic outside this Jewish sector which had wisely screened all their blood for HIV antibodies and threw away all blood for HIV antibodies and threw away all blood they were uncertain of. Relatives and close friends usually gave, or donated their own blood for themselves, or family to prevent contraction of AIDS which was also cancer causing. The Jewish sector was highly moral so AIDS was not a problem as it was in the Gentile sectors. There were no universal health precautions according to a doctor or ex-head surgeon of orthopedics at San Francisco General Hospital who was threatened by radical homosexuals who said they would infect her with a contaminated needle while she got into a hospital elevator. How contagious and strong it is, this deadly virus. Government had lied to be POLITICALLY CORRECT. The AIDS virus was .1 micron while the latex surgeon's gloves were .5 microns. This doctor had to wear 3, or 4 pairs of latex gloves to protect her from the AIDS virus. The incubation period is anywhere from half year to 10 years. The AIDS virus stayed alive in dry air for up to 10 days and in bodily fluids for up to 14 days. In Atlanta, Georgia the Center for Disease Control had 3 cases of nurses with intact skin, yes intact skin, who somehow contracted the AIDS virus.

It can be carried by mosquitoes, bed bugs, French kissing, unsanitary rest rooms, homosexual sex which is where it was most prevalent, blood transfusions, innocent babies were born with it because of an infected mother, drug needles, food, et cetera. It is air born or bound, a contact virus with another one who maybe was a carrier and had HIV, or AIDS itself. It is prevalent in the male homosexual community where it started. There still is no blood test, or quarantine for this POLITICALLY CORRECT virus. How insane is that? Even tuberculosis and leprosy has quarantines. The American blood supply had been contaminated since late in the 20th Century. Vitamin k for hemophiliacs made an improvement in science, but still contaminated AIDS blood is lethal and deadly. There is no cure for it, or for any other known virus, yet Hollywood promoted more of this research, or lifestyle, because most of them were homosexuals as well as pedophiles. Pharmaceutical research is going for a cure for this sexual deviancy virus by spending billions of dollars and that is why drug prescriptions have soared incredibly high plus that at the CDC there are homosexuals manning the phones to deceive the American public about AIDS and how highly contagious it is. Other diseases were being ignored while there could be cures for many different kinds of cancers for example. It always had been unconscionable to spread any disease, or illness to others intentionally, but homosexual radicals in high positions keep the lie intact. The Hate Crime lay in the fact that innocent children were also being molested by the homosexual pedophiles and the law protected them like it had in Nazi Germany. The Hate Crime was a reality that the homosexual could do anything just like the Nazis did in Nazi Germany. The percentage of homosexuals who were also pedophiles ran between 60-70%. The United Nations promotes this virus as well as the homosexual lifestyle called NAMBLA, the North American Man Boy Love Association while millions in Africa were dying from the horrible disease and in fact it had a second strain there. Was this a CIA plot? The government also wanted the American Negro to believe that lie. More sexual perversion now spread into the infidelity of the heterosexual community. Why were day care providers, food service employees and owners, law enforcement officers, anything with a uniform, teachers, prisoners incarcerated, foster care, adoption agencies, orphanages, counselors, scout leaders, or anywhere else that babies, toddlers, children, youth and adolescents participated in or happened to be around? This was Hitler's Youth Corps for sure. Why even the Girl Scouts had "women" leaders with one third, yes one third of them being lesbians. Big Brothers and Big Sisters were following suit and the Boys Scouts were also under attack from the ever present United Way. It works for all of us at least if one is a sexual deviant. This was commonly known as tolerance and diversity. Well with friends like this who would need enemies? To intentionally molest, rape and even murder young children and our government gave its seal of approval to it and not only that promoted it in public schools let alone that the Catholic Schools had a 70% proof of homosexual priests in their entire makeup in the US and ones still had the audacity not to call Catholicism, socialism, or at least fascism, or group mentality with the intent to do harm. No wonder the Holocaust spread so fast during WWII. One and one half Million Jewish Children murdered just in ovens or from starvation and one wants to believe that was all there was?

Brian Lamb's C-SPAN was no help.

We were told by Marie's relatives not to eat just anywhere. Many diseases and sicknesses could be contracted. Orthodoxy was heaven sent in this case, because of being strictly kosher food.

One tiny drop just like liquid nicotine, could kill one. Even human bites, or scratches could be lethal.

As I was saying, our eating habits were strictly monitored by Marie's friends and relatives constantly. Most eating establishments were state run, so that meant one had to be aware. Many people sold their homes just to literally be able to survive which meant more "public" land. This is why Marie's people all lived in this one big house. The legal tender was so old like Confederate money, it had ran its 18 month longevity by years and not months.

Doctor appointments were done by rationed, not rational healthcare, HMO socialist style. If one was young and strong preventive medicine worked, but if one was ill or had a chronic condition beware and AARP was all part of it. The nearest hospital was not always used on purpose and sometimes it was good, because of cleanliness, or lack of. Anybody with a physical order, organic, or chemical imbalance could be classified as eventually to be gone. It was heard that drugs were being administered in mental health hospitals to actually rot the brain, especially if they were politicals. The Gulags were here in America. Everyday we spent there we missed more and more our home in Israel. Marie's relatives were wonderful to us, but America had definitely changed. We could see many German shepherds on patrol with prisoners. Many children had deformities because of alcoholism, drug use, lack of proper diet and proper hygiene from previous generations. Curfews were strictly enforced, except for gangs and who could now control them? No group could stand, or talk at street corners, but who would want to for fear of being attacked? The American Negro had been pushed back more than 100 years. Affirmative action went the wrong way. Subcultures were the norm. Major businesses were all foreign owned. Things such as shoes, tires, cars, clothing, furniture and yes even food were all imported from Europe. There was no competition. If a screw to a machine broke one had to buy another entirely new machine to replace the broken one. Planned obsolescence had been around, but not to this extreme. All clothing materials almost felt like paper. Materials were almost always defective. Even the famous

Hershey Kiss was not properly wrapped fully, and Campbell's soup was like salty herring and the chocolate tasted just like paraffin.

The only ones who attended school, public school, were the illiterate and the POLITICALLY CORRECT. Obese students, or vertically challenged (a New Age term) or slightly impaired were not wanted because of their disabilities. Who would protect them? The Jews had their own Hebrew schools.

Many ex-cons had Internet access to personal people's private lives who were on the outside and also held important government positions as well as criminals. These controlled the prisons. If you had no job, you could be hauled in for not carrying your weight for the state. You could also be incarcerated and exiled to Alaska. In some neighborhoods believers and politicals would be harassed by their own neighbors unmercifully. Each village had its public relations problems. Many gypsies, or "half breeds", would steal anything or mug people with the government's silent approval. They were their snitches. One also had to work conscientiously always, which was at the discretion of the employer.

All kinds of sex, even bestiality was permissible. Marriage and sex within marriage was looked down upon. All phones were coin operated or smart card operated even in private homes. All government phones were cellular so that all conversations could be listened into and also could be shut down instantly all at one time everywhere.

There were no longer 50 states, or united states, but individual countries. Individuality was almost obsolete. People had no distinct and separate personalities. There was a New Age vocabulary such as "vertically challenged", "siblings, kids, partners, quality of life, globalism, living wills, quantum" et cetera.

There was diversity, or animosity in all "villages". If one lived in a village, they could get government handouts. There were "too many chiefs and not enough Indians",

If one was a robbed victim, reporting it to police authorities could mean more trouble for you as a victim than for the real criminal. The incidence of reported crime was low because most never reported it, and so the statistics were said to be low under this premise.

One side of the world was plentiful, the other in dire destitution. A cataclysmic event had to occur soon. The New Age government hoarded everything so the world had to be at its mercy for even food, water and shelter.

As we tried to enjoy our stay with Marie's people, we were ready to go home. The past 2 weeks were arduous for me to comprehend, especially how surreal all things now appeared to me. Thirteen years was a long time.

On our last day there we took a small trip in the upper state of New York in the Adirondacks. We were leaving the many villages. We traveled by car on unkept roads. As we approached the Adirondacks, things started to look alike. We proceeded deeper and deeper into the woods until the road became all dirt covered at most places with forest debris and much overhanging undergrowth. We came near what appeared to be a lake of some sort and directly toward it for about one and one-half miles. There was one road leading into this peninsula type of island with water almost surrounding us. The road here was big enough for only one vehicle coming from one direction. The road entirely itself was elevated much higher than the lake itself. After we passed the lake entirely, we came to the other side where a one-car ferry boat was waiting. We got on board and traveled for some miles downstream until we came to a divide in the lake. We proceeded to our left and onto a small type of pier which had sides and the middle where our boat could enter and where we could touch land and drive slightly upward onto the land. As we drove up we finally came to a sort of deep hidden ravine slightly off to the left with a small road that lead to the bottom and brought us to an almost cave-like edifice. There in this like size cavern was an entrance to a building or a house that stood partly above round, but had stories below it in the ground. We got in an elevator by foot with no numbers inside to tell one if they were going up or down. We descended downward by the pull of gravity in the elevator that could be felt. Finally the door opened which lead us to a small hallway and we walked about 50-100 feet until we came to a huge doorway with two large wooden doors covered with the 12 tribes of Israel, six tribes on each door which pulled opened at the center.

In this sanctuary we could see the Holy of Holies up front and the words carved in the wood beautifully Y'ESHUA MESSIAH. This was a Messianic Jewish worship temple. As we approached and entered the aisle and went into a row, men sat on one side and women on the other. In the back of each wooden pew was a rack for books. There were Hebrew books, which opened from the left and appeared backwards, and Gentile books which opened from the right. Both books were Bibles, plus 2 hymnals.

Immediately I wondered why Marie's people brought us here, when all along they appeared only as Orthodox Jews in Judaism. Finally it dawned on me that they were indeed true believers like the Old Testament Saints, but had to keep it hidden from government officials as well as other Jews and neighbors and even friends. It was Messiah that they had in their hearts, hearts of love. They were what Marie and Rachel were, Messianic Jews, but also believers worshipping as one Body and not by Gentile denominations, but the way Messiah and Peter did in Acts 10-11; not as Jews and Gentiles in opposition, but as one just as GOD is one and one GOD in three persons.

I could see the Menorah with the star of David. There was a wooden altar to come to pray as well as to be blessed with oil by the elders of this temple. The first prayer out loud started with "To the Father of Abraham, Isaac and Jacob..." Messiah was in all prayers and hymns. There were no lights or candles for the dead. "Let the dead bury the dead." Songs were in Hebrew and in English. They had respect for America's only official language. We worshipped in silence first before we did anything else. Praying in Messiah's name to give glory to the Father, Adonai, Elohim, Y'eshua Messiah, YHWH, Ruach Hakodesh. Praising and singing would come later.

The sermon we heard was from a thickly bearded Messianic Jewish Rabbi about none other than Daniel's 70th WEEK.

He preached into infanticide, homosexuality, euthanasia, pornography, pedophilia and the New Age occultic religion in such a way that the whole Gospel was presented in love and in admonishing us all, as believers to be true to the faith. The sermon spoke of not to remain silent when evil was taking over, but to speak out against it and to stay away from all Europeanism and its religiosity. Never to take the mark of the beast was the main part of the sermon. "We are our brother's keeper." The innocent had always needed to be protected, and death for us was only passing from this world into paradise to be with Messiah, or heaven. His sermon had no Europeanism in it. The rabbi stressed how important all the Biblical holidays were which did not include Christmas as we knew it as Gentiles or Easter also. Most of the congregation were Jews. It was a powerful 3-hour sermon with no clock, except my watch on me, that I knew about. Time was not important to this rabbi or teacher, while he was in sermon.

After the temple worship he mentioned to us all that he had knowledge to the fact that the authorities were trying to find this almost last temple on a daily basis, but that he was to preach without fear or hesitation and never to entertain for monetary purposes. All tithes and offerings, I later found out, went to the temple upkeep or the poor believers and poor unbelievers to help them to survive. His storehouse for the poor was always full with tithes and offerings. It was like years ago when 98% of the Gentiles gave less in philanthropic causes than less than 2% of all Jewish Americans.

He would preach until he was translated or until …. It was his duty. Messiah commanded all the Disciples by two's to preach to all the world so all could hear, especially those who did not know Messiah. Maybe Messiah wanted the 12 Jewish Disciples plus all other Jewish generations to preach the most after He left to all the world and to Gentiles in their own national faiths? There was no Laodicean consumerism or materialism in his sermons, or a Kenneth Copeland, always health and wealth sermons, but of a life from death here to life everlasting.

One could see his lean body, how he lived his faith and his robust appearance and powerful voice. He got his income from being a farmer and had never attended a seminary like Charles Spurgeon who wrote over 18,000 sermons in his lifetime.

I shook his hand and it felt like a vice, and with eyes of Messiah and a hug of love. No women were allowed to talk or ask questions or hold any authoritative position in this temple of GOD. No men covered their heads, but all women had either long hair or a hat or covering over their heads. All children were well mannered and understood everything during worship. I thought to myself, "Jewish children are so very bright, especially the Messianic Jewish ones." Of course I was a little partial. Afterwards we had a Seder meal as guests on another upper floor. We all gave thanks to GOD for our food after we ate.

After we left this underground temple/house, we would remain silent and be in constant prayer "to fill in the gap and a hedge of protection" for this rabbi and his loyal family. Rabbi Abraham Cohen was truly a priest or "priest" according to the Bible and not to Catholicism.

As we got back to the village area and back to the Jewish settlement, we immediately had to leave for home. We said our goodbyes for indeed it would be goodbye until the next world in heaven or here on Earth. In no time it seemed we were back on EL AL.

What a joy it would be to get back home. Home at least to us. I knew in my heart America was my home, but America had become New Age Americanism. Only when a people exist does a nation exist. Multiculturalism deals in socialism and in peoples, not a people such as Americans.

Whenever self is placed first on any agenda, sin is there. Individualism is self, ego and narcissism. The West had remained too silent for too long and the door was now closed. Ours appeared to be both the churches of Philadelphia and Laodicea.

Political rhetoric was nothing, but pragmatism more so. "Let us have our peace of mind, but leave us alone." A People allowed themselves to be made into a state. Coercive immigration became popular for the right people.

Things to confuse and not bring cohesion, but multiculturalism. It was not important for people to get along or to be able to communicate in the same language at least. That would not do. Clandestine government and Big Business never really told anybody anything. Governments, to them, needed dialogues and rhetoric, but not peoples of the world. Separate all common folk who make history. Human rights could be just talked about, but what other kind of rights could there possibly be? The socialization of the world into an amoeba mass? The human resources was just another commodity on the earth and not in the earth. More New Age Nazi religion said so, so it had to be right. Right?

CHAPTER XII

BACK HOME

As the months passed by I thought about Marie, my wife and her wonderful motherly and feminine ways which seemed in society to have disappeared. Marie's Jewish mindset on medical and mental health issues was excellent, as well as spiritual sense in finances. Marie was a compassionate individual and one could see Messiah in her by her many loving acts. Rachel, our daughter, showed much of the same sharing and caring, even for a 13 year old young lady. How fortunate I was to marry a now Messianic Jewish woman with such benevolence and understanding. My life had certainly changed for the better in regards to my fellow man and Marie played a large part in that. Everyday was a new experience of joy for me knowing Marie and Rachel were such a vital part of me. With my wife's chronic illnesses, she nonetheless always found Messiah's strength to continue to love and nurture her fellow human being, as well as the animal world. Marriage was a lifetime commitment and one had to learn through Messiah as a believer how to love at all times even though we would fail, or the other party did not reciprocate. As I came to understand more and more about real love, I realized that agape' love was the only real kind of true love. In the Greek language, the word love was more explicit, more exact than it ever was in English, but then again the Greek were a very envious people, but what about the Anglophiles? In English people even "loved" cars and things, et cetera. It was invented in this case by the "dukes and lords" themselves.

In America rights were not all unalienable. America had become so legalistic with artificial group rights that it restricted not only freedom of speech, or worship, but also freedom of movement. Where civil rights impinged and they did impinge on rights individual moral responsibility had to take over. GOD'S rights are all that any man needs. Civil rights are always coercive. They represent the group only, hence socialism. Superior rights are what Nazi Germany had and also were based on "race" alone. One's color and physical appearance which is ignorance and asinine in itself and always serves a systematic people. Basing rights on ancestry can in no more way alleviate prejudice itself, nor can it reduce slavery, but in fact increases injustice. Would 8 generations suffice as to pure "race" non-diluted and what and who would determine such criteria? If it is government, then a major form of nepotism would have to respond, because blood would be thicker then water. Since all blood is basically red, one would have to wonder what "race", or race they could possibly be referring to? A non-human one? Of course only religious Messianic Jews and American Biblicals in this case would be eliminated.

With salvation genealogy plays no part, so individuals do not qualify for this by racism. Even families get preference according to genealogy and is not that what sentimentality refers to? The pendulum swings the opposite way with this affirmative action, whenever it pleases the rich and well educated, or the corrupt and deviant. Along came homosexual, animal and children's rights which were all in essence to destroy the concept of family. A facade of this so called equality was nothing more then socialistic slavery. Too bad if you were a human being, but animals had better rights. An excellent example was in the lunacy that babies were inhuman and animals were somehow more human, but did not evolve yet to our level. It was the same in India where most of this New Age mentality came from. Take for example that children would be murdered by infanticide, but the cow was sacred. More insanity came when homosexual pedophiles were even debated about as to their rights as such. NAMBLA said, "The Children asked for it." Again civil rights were anything but. Who could ever take the highest court in the land seriously except the victims they murdered. The first victims of "civil rights" were not by "race" , but by form, or should I say size. Any "race" with 9 months or less and sometimes older with murder as the outcome always.

The inner cities could always have too many unwanted children, because there could never be enough infanticide. Now this affirmative action and racism… Too many inner city children meant more welfare and more taxes to pay, but instead of the courts enforcing the law (or did they on dead beat dads), it chose by fear of race for the easier course and that was the defenseless unborn child. And why not? There was much money to be made! Taxes could be raised, hence a two fold accounts receivable fund for socialistic big government. Our gulags were Planned Parenthood. Just keep having immoral sex, but do procreate until full term and then we shall take over. The rich and well educated got what they wanted wealth. They also sold a bill of perishable goods to the poor and called it civil rights, or planned parenthood. Nothing is ever civil about cold blooded murder. We were like the English. We were Darwinists. Never mind their innocence, just keep reaping in the money and provide more physical freedom in sensuality not marital lifetime sexuality and also convenience for dead beat dads biological and promiscuous and curious young girls and boys and older, but especially the poor since the rich never did like to raise their own children, hence Soviet style daycare with pedophilia. After all it was a free country to do anything or just about anything one wanted to do including murder.

Other groups too had entitlement rights by government decree, such as mother assisted infanticide. Does that sound absurd, or ludicrous? Well so was that Judicial fiat decree. No right that is left outside the womb and then no liberty to be free and own private property, but in this case there would be an exception to the rule for the unborn were according to government, property. Many not to bright government officials would not care when taking a life and remember what Lenin said about the bright in society.

Many handicapped individuals got government taxpayer support by not being able to speak English, dead beat dads, obese ones, prisoners in prison, non-speaking English persons, et cetera.

People with true disabilities had to be exempted because their condition was organic, or not POLITICALLY CORRECT.

Re-election at any cost, especially for incumbents was what was at stake. One had to either go along with the winner, or with the underdog mentality to be for the lesser of two equal parts. "Equality in the cogs of machinery" is what Stalin called it. Well that would be better than anarchy wouldn't it? No cream would be allowed to come to the top for fear that qualifications and not POLITICAL CORRECTNESS would reign. The individual would be hopefully last, but the group was always more important, because numbers is what counted. All groups were created equal.

Did George Mason's Bill of Rights correlate with the 10 Commandments? The United States Constitution spoke of some individual freedoms, but the Declaration of Independence came closer and spoke to England about "get out of our country for good" and now could be included to keep Islam and its money over there in Anglophilia. The Bill of Rights an addition would at first appear to preserve individual freedom, but then even an unconstitutional federal income tax in 1913 was included, but only for the moment, and did not constitutional government make allowances for these kinds of indiscretions? Articles I and X had everything to do with the First Commandment. "You should have no other gods before Me and you should not covet." With capitalism and human nature that certainly… Articles IV and VI correlated with the 9th Commandment. "…not to bear false witness against one's neighbor." The Media had failed this. "Bear false witness" meant to lie. The 6th, and 8th and 10th Commandments were and are" not to murder , not to steal and not to worship materialism. The government was involved in all three so much so that the population emulated the law, or laws themselves, instead of the only LAW. Commandment 2 the media had broken so many times "not to have, or make any graven image." The graven image was POLITICAL CORRECTNESS and to love money and now Islam. Now even GOD was to do for the church what only man could do with free will to choose and act.

The 3 ring circus of government: judicial, legislative and executive had come apart. The judicial was legislative, legislative was the silent royalty and executive was by popularity. Had it ever worked properly for at least the last 2 centuries? If the Commander-In Chief had too many chiefs and not enough Indians no pun intended, what could he do? Even women tribal chieftains wanted in. This could only cause a warpath of the 2 sexes. Custer's last stand with political bull attacking constantly and surrounding him.

In America civil rights went as far as to protect Americans who had committed treason in full view and with evidence, but evidence or not one had to be always innocent or other wise people like Kissinger and Haig and Hammer would all have to be indicted for collaborating with the enemy, an offense punishable by death according to the US constitution "for high crimes and misdemeanor". No preventive medicine here. Always wait till it happens first like 9/11? This absurdity had also given women the right to infanticize their own child or children, because women had gained more then they bargained for, or the feminists. There was no rule of law. Then guilty, until proven innocent by the IRS which got its power from Congress, the silent majority a useless group in Washington. Laws and then more laws and with them their asinine affect on all of society. One could not be guilty, if one President had committed treason and murder and was never even tried for it but did have about 12 grand jury investigations that found him innocent.

I was now an Israeli citizen. Marie's mother and father were both Jewish. Yet I would also be an American in heart always because my faith was American Biblical. I had not given up my national faith part of a collective body, because I sought to help the "roots" of salvation. Make the Israeli nation without faith was the spirit of the age. Ignore Messiah at all costs so the Hebrew could not cross over. Most Israelis Jews, as well as world Jewry, were not believers. Secularism of the Jews, or secularize the Jew so that this false king with his miracles and peace would be bought lock, stock and barrel. Satan was working overtime for his coming kingdom. Hell on earth. The "roots" would have to be ripped out and this "lady" would have to flee during the TRIBULATION.

Our daughter was baptized and made this decision. Rachel was Messianic since 5 years of age and knew both the Old and New Testament, or B'rit Hadasha.

Would Samson learn from Job about past history or would Samson too have to experience it to the end? A repeat inner revolution could occur easily in America. America already had a "Menshevik party and was working on a "Bolshevik" one a second time.

When we made our excursion to America I remember how many names changed from patriots to POLITICALLY CORRECT ones. There was for example Firestone Boulevard which was changed to Armand Hammer Boulevard and even a famous minister invited him to his television show. There was a Mohammed Ali Boulevard, JFK Airport, a JFK School of Government, Cape Kennedy, Martin Luther King, Jr. High school, the Armstrong Center, the GPU, The Dirksen Office Building, Rockefeller Center and Plaza, Roosevelt Boulevard, Brigham Young University, the United Nations, Greenwich Village, The Abraham Lincoln Brigade, the National Democratic Progressive Party, the ACLU, Progressive Insurance, Charles Schwab, People for the American Way, Planned Parenthood, Dubois, NAMBLA, Gay Pride Day, or the Stonewall Riot, Winter Solstice, Spring Recess, Halloween for all saints day thanks to Catholicism, Easter not Passover and many more anti-American nomenclatures.

We, as a family, decided to move to a small farm where we could become closer to the land and felt closer to nature. The city life had become as independent from government as we possibly could. We also rented out land to some of our friends so they too could experience normal living. We dug a well for fresh water and set up irrigation with pumps for our small farms. We knew that for now we could avoid the all encompassing networking of the New Age Movement deceived into believing government, instead of Messiah. Even Rachel was now home schooled by Marie and our neighbors' children too were included. We were living a sequestered and hard working life, but it was well worth it. No television, thank goodness and no phone only a radio for news and emergency alerts. Survival was getting to be most prevalent as the months and years went by.

By the time Rachel was ready for college Israel had become even smaller, then the original size before the War of Independence in 1967. The Mediterranean Sea was Israel's outlet to water, except the Gaza Strip which was fenced in with about 2 million Moslem Arabs and the West Bank also was fenced in about the same size of the population as the Gaza Strip and one could see that Jerusalem was gradually being surrounded on nearly all sides. The Golan Heights were still Israel's, because of shellings in which even school children had to hide in bunker like shelters to protect them. The Sinai too was getting smaller. Jerusalem was still Israel's capital and was in Israelis' hands for now with the East and West part of Jerusalem.

The sin unbelief is the only sin that cannot be forgiven. Life is a series of choices. So many millenniums for the Jews not to know Messiah, or even have a nation. Messiah came in love and not in power and most Jews could not understand that. Nomads to the world, until GOD would decide when to return. The time of the Hebrews was soon approaching. To man it was ions, but to GOD just days. GOD had chosen and that was final. The Jews could not identify with Messiah, because of Moses' veil. The Father and Son is a relationship, but the Jews had had bad sons, as well as bad fathers, hence Messiah was not seen now as a personal relationship. Time is relative, but eternity is forever, because time ends and eternity does not. Only choice, or freewill makes time have importance after time the watch stops. It is pertinent to see this life in time as not the end, but as a trail with two paths and only one of two choices. Some things have many answers, some have a few and some only one. In this experiment for man, or his experience in life and man must experience life, man had to learn through Messiah about agape' love which is a commitment, or an ongoing thing. Unconditional love is what GOD's love is all about. Unless transformation of the heart occurs, man shall not understand what the Spirit is saying, because the spiritual heart has a void which should only be filled by Messiah, or life has no purpose. Messiah has not gotten older, or aged. He is the same. Who can ever get away from Messiah in time? Even in death which is where it actually starts, this timeless period shall not cease and neither shall any of us. GOD has no time, He is eternal. Time has opened for man through Adam, hence fallen man needs Messiah in this world to get into His next world with GOD.

In the Old Testament, Isaac and Ishmael, Semite brothers, not by faith in most cases, but by the same father in the flesh. Did GOD not love both, but gave His blessing to Isaac? Anti-Semitism is not to mean against Islam, but against the Jewish faith.. with the "roots" as the Jews. With Ruth and Naomi, Ruth chose a Semite Jew, Naomi, instead of Gentile heathenism. Ruth chose faith over "races" or culture. The Old Testament always is based on the Jewish people and their dealings and not about the secular world. Ruth was a saint through faith and not through blood which meant Gentiles too later could and would come in by Messiah. Ruth also became the lineage of, or to David which leads to Messiah. One cannot be inclusive with all Jews, only past Messianic Jews. Is the Jewish faith then totally exclusive? No. it depends on Messiah's grace from Calvary. These the above, are the "roots " of salvation. Unconditional love and not for ones who tried to reach for GOD with good works, or Levitical regulations. This gift is free to men to the Jew and to the Gentile. There is no two way religion, or separation, because He is only one GOD having come in the Flesh. This is agape love which the world knows nothing about. Death to sin and Adam's old man and only through Messiah. Can one literally find faith in the Scriptures themselves? Only in Y'eshua now at present through faith to believe what the Bible said He would do. Isaiah 53 and what He did John 1. A gift is not a wage, but something that's given freely. There is no condition either in receiving this gift. Y'eshua can save without man's freewill. It is His will to say,you are mine.

After some years our daughter met a fine Israelis' Messianic Jewish man who was also quite an athlete, of course with brains and had made the Israelis' Olympic Wrestling Team in Greco-Roman wrestling. Alexander Roseman was quite a competitor capturing a bronze medal for Israel. The games were being held in Jerusalem for the first time ever and security was in place from beginning to end. Alexander also served in the Israelis' military, because he was Messianic Jewish which was not recognized as being religious in the Jewish state. Alexander's family had come from Kiev, Russia to Israel only recently. Moscow was still in Soviet control of the Russian government and had never relinquished control ever since 1917. The Russian peasants too were also persecuted along with the Old Believers in Russian Orthodoxy. All churches, temples and synagogues had to be state registered like in 1720. Most believers stayed cleared of those worship centers.

The time of the Gentiles from 605 BC till the Second Advent was still in affect. The image in Daniel of the 4 evil Gentile Kingdoms started in Babylon with King Nebuchadnezzer, then came Media-Persia, then Greece and them Rome. At the top of this statue was a head of gold, Babylon; chest and arms of silver, Media-Persia; the abdomen and thighs of bronze, Greece; and the bottom legs of iron and feet of iron and clay unmixable as Rome. With each empire in the chronology of time and with more degradation each time came a lesser valued metal.

The Second Rome would also have feet of iron and clay meaning dictators (iron) and democracies (clay). This would form the 10 nation Confederacy and the Common Market and the Eurodollar.

In Egypt before the Semites (Shem) Ham's relatives settled there and had built the great pyramids. I believe this is where some form of change took place within Northern Africa not mentioned in Scripture, because it had no dealings with the Israelites. Were UFO's involved with the pyramids? The sons of gods? One's faith and freewill was a burden if one was a believer. Believers, though, had joy and did not seek this circumstantial pursuit of Deist happiness. Sadness also was a state of mind. These states of the mind, reasoning with feelings, but reasoning and feeling do not save, but by faith in the spiritual heart the acceptance of Messiah's death and resurrection (Romans 10: 9-10). It is impossible to please GOD without faith in Messiah. "I shall never leave you." Deism came to believe that GOD had created, but left for good so that is why Deists had to pursue happiness. This would be their last chance here on earth almost like the Sadducees. Only GOD'S grace through Messiah can joy come into the Spiritual heart and happiness need not be pursued.

Who gave man his freewill, but not his fall? Hardly would man himself give anyone else his freewill, or freedom. Human nature must oppose this. Only in Messiah's love was freewill given and not to have it over us as a hard taskmaster for did not GOD leave Adam and Eve alone in the Garden? Does man not seek always to control over another human being by coercion and not through love? The more the merrier, or how else would one attain fame and fortune and power? The ego, or the "I" in man, or the old man to always revert back to Adam. Did not Eve pick Cain as her favorite progeny? Cain willed it over Abel by murder.

Man does not respond well to freewill, because after he had sinned he will not own up to the fact that he, his own freewill chooses to do what God said not to do through the Law, yet being unable to control this sin he continues time and again his involvement in the whole thing and to escape goat as Adam did about Eve. Man's own invention, or he has this notion that freewill is something he has invented and hence sin through the mind reasons and the conscience is seared eventually. After Adam's fall the conscience was formed for in innocence why would one need a conscience? That was the first sin of mortal man. They consciously were aware of their nakedness, hence no innocence any longer. GOD shall choose even in freewill.

This "GOD is dead" from a diseased mind, such as Nietzsche. Adam, through sin in a physical manifestation, changed in essence a perfect environment. "Which came first, the chicken or the egg? It was not his environment that caused sin, but his own freewill to want to sin. He was not coerced for who could do that not even... Satan? Adam was still innocent, hence no conscience. Created beings want to always be equal with GOD, either in power, or in knowledge. Satan chose power through his own pride and Adam chose rebellion through knowledge. Both knew they were sinning, but Satan's equality was much worse, because of himself as a god but Adam wanted to know good and evil like a god right? Adam wanted to have GOD's knowledge for himself, Satan wanted it too but in a different form and not one in which his species could repent. Nonetheless one was thrown out of his position in heaven and one was thrown out of the Garden. Now Adam would toil hard. Did Adam's environment change Adam? No, Adam changed his own environment and for the worse. Now this New Age as asinine as can be says change the environment and man will really change. Adam did the opposite, or the opposite occurred. Man changed himself which affected his environment and a perfect environment at that. Why, if Adam who in a perfect environment sinned, would one tend to believe that the opposite was true? That to change now the environment would change man from the outside, when man in his innocence and in a perfect environment changed his own environment in disobedience which in essence meant man's human nature now that must be transformed by Messiah and not his environment.

New Age worship of creation in all its evil forms animate, or inanimate, but not Messiah who created it all. Environmentalists say, "Let us make man in our image that is like the beast with no real freewill, but coercion with no such thing as good vs. evil, since it is environment not man that needs to be changed." This is Satan's New Age lie.

GOD'S original creation, the Garden of Eden was for good, but according to secular man it was backwards. If only man could have been a robot, then he would not have sinned? Man cannot have freewill as such, but must be regimented to obey by another master and once he sees the "light", then he shall know what is what.

If man would have been left to himself and no discipline by GOD once out of the Garden, he would have probably lasted no more than 3, or 4 generations. GOD disciplined Adam, because he loved man, but not his sin. A father always disciplines a son that he loves.

What are all the isms in political theories? Are they not all lies? Don't tell that to our human nature, heaven forbid. Self delusion, or believing in our own lies is better. We want it and we want it now. Fellow man means to secular man, "follow me for I am first in line and must always lead." "Our wisdom is not GOD'S wisdom." Just eliminate evil, or man? You can lead a horse to water, but you cannot make him drink it. Of course you can. All animals are created equal and coercion only need be applied for this POLITICALLY CORRECT behavior. Oh yes behavior, hence totalitarianism.

The miscarriages in justice are ones who are infanticized. What appears as freedom, luxury and extravagance is actually slavery to this world system. The constant interruption of family is too much. Progress must continue, as well as profit.

Back to Daniel and the 4 evil Gentile Empires. Babylon the lion, Media-Persia the bear, Greece the Leopard and Rome the Iron beast. All 4 had already occurred. The TRIBULATION parts 1 and 2 with a remnant to be saved who would go into the OLAM HABA with Messiah after Armageddon. After 1,000 years, Messiah gives back the kingdom to the Father. The unbelievers resurrect after the OLAM HABA. They would one by one go to the GREAT WHITE THRONE JUDGMENT and then be thrown into the burning lake of fire forever. Satan would be released to amount another attack, but be defeated again and he too with his cohorts already there would also be thrown into the burning lake of fire.

Yes even the King Nebuchadnezzar did not give GOD the glory and for 7 years was struck by GOD with an animal's brain called lycanthropy and then later was restored to his kingdom and became an Old Testament Saint. His grandson was not so fortunate. He had literally seen the handwriting on the wall, but it was too late. To this very day Babylon, Iraq (Mesopotamia) has had no Christianity ever.

In Daniel "a little horn", the Antichrist eats the three other horns. Antiochus Epiphanes was a forerunner. He brought a pig into the temple to desecrate it. This "lady", Israel shall be hidden from the enemy, probably in Petra with 12,000 from each of the 12 tribes of Israel. This 144,000 would be preserved. All believers in the FIRST RESURRECTION would go to the JUDGMENT SEAT OF MESSIAH, individually not to be judged, but to be shown what even more GOD had in good for them while on earth and their past life would pass by, but be forgiven, and 24 elders sang, "Holy, Holy, Holy, Lord are you LORD GOD ALMIGHTY, who was and is and is to come."

GOD wants man to be saved. "Y'eshua in me loves you." It is HIS love and not our love.

We started to see in Israel more and more demonic activity in people and also this abstract modernism in architecture, art, literature, entertainment, church, education, et cetera. Technology did all of man's thinking for him.

In education "look say" and phonetics were taught in America in public schools to actually create dyslexia in young children, self-induced dyslexia. English is a phonetic language and Chinese is "look say"; as far as the East is from the West.

The "ram", Media-Persia with 2 horns represented a shared empire and the "goat" represented Greece and Alexander the Great who died at age 33 and probably was one of the greatest generals like Antiochus Maccabee was ever, considering they did not have the technology we have today, but their minds were strategic enough that even today at West Point Antiochus Maccabee is still studied. Four generals, mediocrity again and 3 major other groups - Macedonia, Egypt and Syria - formed. Then another "small horn", not the "little horn" in Daniel, refers to Antiochus Epiphanes and not the Antichrist.

Only in Scripture by Ruach Hakodesh is history an exact science. The Gutenberg press was not like the old Hebrew Scribes who always changed pens whenever the word GOD, YHWH, was written in Hebrew. All scripture was written by Old Testament Saints, or Messianic Jewry with its 39 books. "Faith without works is dead" does apply to grace which is always first before works, but is something we do not deserve, or undeserved merit, hence grace then works and never vice versa.

It appeared Europe was deceiving Israel, or at least their Iconoclast was. Israel would be blinded for three and one-half years and until it was too late. This "little horn" makes an alliance with Israel for three and one-half years. This is the time of Jacob's Trouble the next three and one-half years. This would be Daniel's 70th WEEK, or 70 WEEKS which is broken into 3 parts. PART ONE was from 445 BC – 396 BC, or 7 WEEKS, or 49 years, when the Temple was rebuilt in Jerusalem. PART TWO was 396 B.C.-39 AD when Y'eshua rode into Jerusalem on a donkey which made up 62 WEEKS or 434 years. PART THREE would be the 70-th WEEK of TRIBULATION which had 2 parts. The first three and one-half years and the second part, another part of three and one-half years, or 1,260 days and another 1,260 days. This is in essence 42 months plus 42 months, or a total of 7 years. In the TRIBULATION this "little horn" shall sit on the throne in Jerusalem having deceived Israel. He would help bring in Armageddon in Megiddo, Israel. North, South, East and West would come to do battle with this ANTICHRIST. Israel would be a non-participant. All these forces would forget the ANTICHRIST and attack Messiah. With the world system being defeated, Messiah shall reign for 1,000 years. All previous years are based on a 360-day year, but no day has exactly 24 hours in it. The very laws of physics, natural law would be broken and Messiah, then GOD the Father would transform the earth and rule forever. GOD would be our sun and the Son.

The 4 HORSEMEN were out already and much more was to come. "Nation against nation and tribes against tribes, but still not the end." One needed now more than ever to keep Y'eshua, not even one's wife, as his first love. "Treat our wife as Y'eshua treated and took care of the church."

To carry someone else's burdens as Messiah carried the cross. Isaac was spared. Jonah too, but not Messiah. Messiah gave up

His life willingly. Y'eshua was the only Full Revelation ever. No one shall escape Truth. "Every knee shall bow."

As Rachel grew older and was ready to wed, Marie and I understood that our little girl had grown up so quickly and that life had still much to offer if we let GOD LEAD. Everything belongs to Him. Our spouses, children, finances, worship, home, money, career, or occupation, et cetera all belong to Him. We were only stewards as believers. Only one thing we came into the world without and that is Messiah.

Our daughter was ready to be yoked to another believer in a lifetime of marriage, GOD willing, and both were remaining in their physical state, as Jews. This young man who had courted Rachel honorably and caringly would be a good provider and a priest for his family. Alexander Roseman had finished his 2 years of military service, then had gotten a degree in archaeology and hired himself out to institutions as well as government.

Marie and I had prayed years ago before her birth that our child would find a believer as a spouse and would be one in Messiah. Only believers believed in family life and for a lifetime in one marriage to one mate of the opposite sex and the only faith.

Natural law could kill and most often times did and man's law had already done so and would do much more, but GOD's Law laid in love always.

Well, Rachel and Alexander got married and spent their honeymoon just outside of Jerusalem. They did not want to go to atheistic Europe which controlled from the Artic to the island of Crete in the south. Rachel and Alexander had a chosen family, meaning the blessing of having children. Rachel, bright and aware, even though strong willed like her mother and at times obstinate would live in a patriarchal household, and Alex would treat his wife like Y'eshua treated the church. We had truly gained a son.

At times we could feel tremors under us, a 3-4 on the Richter Scale. Our weather was climatically changing. Our winters became more brutal and the summers much more humid and hot.

One's health was vital to staying alive much longer. Death was all around. We had heard of stories to the effect that patients who had living wills were taken to emergency rooms, left there for hours and then finally expired, because of a living will's worded statement as to who had authority or final say. Some patients were taken off of feeding intravenous tubes for nutrition and not life support systems only. This was hospitalized starvation by involuntary methods. This was not natural death but murder. The doctors had no Hippocratic Oath and the mental health field was even worse.

The Hemlock Society of death by murder through being euthanized became another evil instrument for POLITICAL CORRECTNESS. While this occurred on the other side of the spectrum, transplants by chips were being used on the very rich and some on patients against their will. Why did not the rich want to die? Mental health was sexual orientation, hypnotism, self esteem, id, Freud, et cetera. Already big corporate executives had had this occult New Age mental indoctrination. Anesthesiologists were like gods. Comatose patients were goners unless a believing physician well informed would be treating such a patient. Comatose patients are known to hear, but have no motor functions sometimes. Some use the blinking of the eyes when the eyes are open to respond. Nonetheless the cerebral cortex is alive and so is the person still a person, which means the soul is still here with the patient.

Our smart card covered with interest all things, or a consumer tax on them even medical care. This was HMO preventive style medicine and did apply to cover all things from food to cremation and we had plenty of deaths. Medical students were taught death not life. Some patients were not given pain relievers, but instead a final solution syringe to end their whining. Hospital personnel had criminal and nefarious backgrounds. Also, not too bright of individuals worked in these non-profit morgues. Businessman physician was the name of the game. Anesthesiologists were usually given total charge of a patient after they read the patient's medical sheet and life history by computer. Human resources came to mean just that, extra donor parts as resources for the rich. Quotas in hospitals were for bed space, but not for the living.

Blood banks were all contaminated from the AIDS virus. Hemophiliacs and ones with surgery were dying off unless they used their own blood or knew someone who had good blood. Special blood was kept for homosexuals with certain antibodies which dried up the blood banks. Preferential treatment went to New Agers then unbelievers. Even veterinarians would donate their time when hospitals got too full. In some cases, children could request that their parents donate blood and body parts for them. Blood was 100% profit. Years before, America and Germany had agreed to throw away all unsure and tainted blood. Germany followed through; America of course, did not. Also, the Center for Disease Control in Georgia was manned by the POLITICALLY CORRECT. Blood though at Calvary was never spared by the Romans. It was given freely, but Satan had fooled the Romans into extracting GOD'S blood profusely and so hence he too was fooled.

"Social" security was a thing of the past. There were not even suppliers to meet the demand and Congress needed no longer to add billions into the fiscal budget automatically without debate in the House of Representatives. They had found a better way, euthanize the elderly whenever so. Rarely did a citizen reach the age of 65. Life expectancy was to be about to 80 years old.

Judges were criminals like at the Nuremburg Trials. The death penalty was outlawed because they needed the real outlaws so believers and others could be eliminated so many other ways. They said it was immoral to have a physician inject a convicted DNA criminal with lethal poison, but said nothing about infanticide by the millions.

If one entered a hospital, they could not take any valuables because rarely were any personal items returned, because of staff theft and even other patients. Even Gentile non-believers were treated in Jewish hospitals, but Messianic Jews were not.

Many believers never went to the hospital unless under very extreme and severe circumstances. Some of our friends who were all believers cared for other believers and the poor whenever they needed it and according to the charitable pro bono of medicine and the Hippocratic Oath. These people were professionals or had been professionals in the medical field. They had refused the medical schools' death courses and so used their skills in a charitable way. These included pediatricians, obstetricians, midwives, osteopaths, MD's, nurses, and even a few surgeons and technicians. In mental health a rare few psychologists and psychiatrists gave of their assistance. They even helped some homosexuals come out of their own deviancy. This not so well known community of medical professionals was only known to believers and the very poor. This group had become an underground subculture. Regular medicine was death wish warrants. Most in the hospitals were unqualified. No one had to be qualified any longer in any field or position, because of affirmative action years ago.

Private property meant only one's home, but not the land it sat on. One's wages were mostly paid through a smart card account unless one bartered items for services rendered.

I had to be thankful for the State of Israel founded on May 15, 1948, because it had probably kept alive millions of Jews, my wife being one of them, but now it appeared her own nation was turning hostile to other Jews, such as The Messianic Jews, even more so. Israel had been an ambivalent nation in spirituality. In one way it blocked the Gentile evil world powers from eliminating the Jews even more. Yet Israel in the future would in fact hurt some of its own "roots" as well as "branches". The Iconoclast would do that from Jerusalem. The world would eventually scape goat all Jews in Israel for what the Antichrist from Europe would do and Europe too would eventually attack Israel; hence anti-Semitism kept getting worse. This thorn to the Gentiles would also be more of one to Messianic Jewry and worldwide believers. The Jew would never be completely eliminated, but the carnage for such a minority in the world would probably be devastating. GOD'S absolute will would intervene, but when?

In the surrounding Arab countries there was much homosexuality as there had been protection for ex-Nazi war criminals years before. In fact, Mein Kampf was studied by Arab Moslem terrorists.

One day an Israeli Arab, a "social" Christian, invited us to dinner, my wife and me. He was a neighbor by acquaintance only. After a most unusual conversation that lasted a few hours at the restaurant, he just got up and left, making us pay the entire food bill. I thought a little about this and came to the conclusion he had acted just like a socialist at heart. Was he not a Christian and not part of Islam? In our conversation earlier at dinner, he mentioned how he felt that Y'eshua was only a prophet. We went on to discuss how Y'eshua was impregnated by the Holy Spirit into Mary's womb, a young Jewish woman. Y'eshua, we said, had lived off of the Father's blood while in gestation. We also discussed the issue about men and women and marriage and how that homosexuality wasn't innate, maybe a proclivity. We said that medical science had proved it to be not innate because identical twins have the same chromosomes and genes, and if one was homosexual later in life, so would the other twin be. Since this didn't occur, it proved homosexuality was not innate at birth. The same two babies from the same egg. This is an environmental issue and in some way related to "bridge brain" children if they were lead that way by no father or mother bonding from 1-3 years of age, or abuse from pedophilia or even by miseducation by experimentation. Young people usually have a normal dilemma about their sexuality and can easily be lead to believe a lie, especially if a daughter does not bond with her mother and a son does not bond with his father, or biological father, or other normal male figure. Some young boys being effeminate does not mean that they are homosexual, but have an environment persuading them in the wrong direction, whether at home or in school or church or anywhere else. Most young people have a complex about their own sex and sexuality so deviancy is an influence.

We also said, "Why would GOD call it an abomination but yet allow it at birth?"

There was inconsistency on this and GOD never went back on His Word. Old and B'rit Hadasha both speak of homosexuality's pernicious and pusillanimous nature, the act itself. Life is a series of choices and coercion, or influence plays a major part, especially the former one because it is by force and the lie and a mental health problem. It is a powerful addiction and makes the mind turn to reprobation. The individual can leave this unnatural or abnormal life if they seek Christian counseling for 3-5 years, but it is not easy. The entire person must be treated as in Teen Challenge where non-recidivism is at 86%, the best in the world for addiction. (Pedophilia and child pornography are a major part of it; just ask NAMBLA.) After that statement he asked the following question:

"What is NAMBLA?"

I said, "The North American Man Boy Love Association. Even Hitler's Youth Corps leaders were all homosexual pedophiles, or Butches. Homosexuality holds fascist brotherhood above everything else, even loyalty to one's own nation. They are clones in the sense of their reprobation. This is not to ridicule or make fun, but just a fact. Bad blood in this case is thicker than water.

He then said, "I totally disagree" and that is when he got up and left our table.

It is always honorable and proper, when one invites others out to dine or otherwise, to a least pick up most of the bill, if not all, even if the other party should offer to help pay it.

The earlier part of our conversation had to do with carcinogenic foods and a moderate intake of them.

He said all food, no matter how much, was good for one. It was better than starving.

I said, "If one eats any one of 5 different foods every day they shall contract cancer by carcinogenic chemicals in them, or what causes cancerous tumors in the body proclivity or not to cancer. They were sugary cereals, hot dogs, soda pop, bacon and potato chips. Not all foods are carcinogenic in nature and do not contain these harmful preservatives in them."

I also said, "Cancer can be contracted through what is called the "birch tree theory" when cancer can be contracted by a traumatic experience in life, so severe that it actually, through the thought process, is a kind of metamorphosis through the brain which activates dormant cancer cells in one's body, which cancer cells we all have and pass at the base of the skull through a...."

He then said, "That is totally insane. What kind of fool do you think I am to believe such a thing?"

How had so many Islamic Arabs gotten a foothold in American business when homeland security was supposed to protect us and the enemy was right here amongst us?

Later that night I was reading Scripture and came across some particular part of Scripture that caught my eye. It was in Daniel Chapter 10 where all 4 Gentile evil empires were demonic, but the one real Jewish empire, the OLAM HABA in which Messiah would reign would be wonderful. I thought had not Europeanism brought a Druid heathen holiday to America by All Saints Day? Also, the 111th Pope would or could be the antichrist and we were at the 110th Pope starting from Pope Celestine II in 1143 AD till now. The present pope believed after him shall come this 111th Pope which correlates with the Antichrist maybe at this time, but it is not, or he is not the antichrist. America opened the door willingly to Satan and he had a stronghold now through Islam too.

American Biblicals had their own American Christianity and did not need Europeanism. Daniel 10 referred to the king of Persia. Daniel prayed, but for about 21 days Michael (the archangel) was held up by principalities from the enemy. Daniel's prayer had gotten through right away, but an answer from GOD was delayed by the enemy. Daniel 10 is a prelude to Daniel 11.

Constitutional democracies, I thought to myself, do not work at least for longevity. America had certainly proven that with its short lifespan. Israel now appeared to be changing from a parliamentarian Knesset to a monarch. Satan chose to emulate the third one. Sometimes governments would adopt names or a nice sounding euphemism, but would in reality be that only in name and not in content. I knew that after capitalism came socialism and America had been one of the great ones just like Russia before the Revolution. America also was mismanaged by incompetents and women and homosexuals. "And you shall be ruled by women."

If any nation, let alone government was not GOD fearing, then it would fall under demonic oppression as a collective or by GOD'S judgment.

In Daniel's 11th Chapter King Cyrus is taken over by demonic influence. The king of the North, Syria, or the Seleucids both attack the Antichrist and lose. Michael, the patron angel of the Jews, responds to the prayer of Daniel and is always sent by GOD'S will. This king of this chapter is the antichrist himself. Antiochus Epiphanes again is the so called "other horn" of this Antichrist. Satan has been judged at Calvary, but not yet sentenced.

America could not, for all it was worth, separate itself from England in all its history. America was a place to make money and always anxious about everything. American Biblicals were the only ones that stayed away from John Locke's materialistic view. Anybody who was against Messiah was real anti-Semitic such as the Gentile Palestinians. Samson was once strong at the beginning, but soon thereafter opportunities from Europe brought this enlightenment with them that had no spiritual renewal. The Western world had gotten half the message, the Mosaic Law, but forgot about Messiah. That is why probably more Jews, except for the Soviet Union and that was totalitarianism, took hold onto this materialism. It was a faith that was not heard about that of the entire Bible and it had never been the so called right time. Old Testament Judaism of works the same as Catholicism and with of course Protestantism protesting Catholicism, so nothing original was really in the plan. Our Founding Forefathers knew that the Old Scripture had to be lived not just written. Along came eventually this multiculturalism of Marxist/Leninism which only had to usurp capitalism which was a natural occurrence.

This kingdom on earth was an illusion of a so called Promised Land, but essentially there is only one PROMISED LAND. Another non-original idea confused itself with GOD'S Holy Land. Is emulation in futility to bring a utopia on earth which could never occur, hence America's idealism could not last for long like

Russia's monarchy and Christianity had? Not having forgotten about the Book of Daniel, I recalled that Michael the patron angel of the Jews, was answering Daniel's prayer by repatriating the Jews to their homeland from Babylon and again King Cyrus was used by the enemy to stop this. This epilogue to Daniel 11.

Rev Shaul's missionary journeys were as follows: Attalia, Cilicia, Derbe, Ephesus, Galatia, Iconium, Lycaonia, Lystra, Macedonia, Mysia, Neapolis, Pamphylia, Paphos, Perga, Phenice, Philippi, Pisidia, Rome, Samaria, Samothracie, Syria, Thessolonica, and Troas and not necessarily in that order.

The Prophets in the Bible were: Aaron, Ahijah, Amos, Balaam, Daniel, Eldad, Elijah, Elisha, Ezekiel, Gad, Habakkuk, Haggai, Hanani, Hosea, Iddo, Isaiah, Jehu, Jeremiah, Joel, Jonah, Malachi, Medad, Micah, Moses, Nahum, Nathan, Obadiah, Samuel, Shemaiah, Zacharias, Zechariah, Zephaniah.

The foreshadows of Messiah were: Abraham, Daniel, David, the dove, the eagle, Elijah, Elisha, Ezekiel, Ezra, the heifer, Isaac, Jeremiah, Jonah, Joseph, Joshua, The Lamb, the Lion, Melchizedek, Moses, Nehemiah, Noah, the ox, the pigeon, the ram, the sheep, Solomon.

The 7 Bowls of Judgment from GOD was climax to an evil world system. The second half of the TRIBULATION, or the GREAT TRIBULATION for three and one half years, or 1,260 days was called the time of Jacob's Trouble (Jacob was called Israel) and Satan would pursue the "lady" Israel, since he was thrown down to earth. There is again this mention of the 4 Gentile Evil empires including the Roman one. It would be a physical resurrection of the Old Testament Saints, such as Daniel, who would rule in the new OLAM HABA and also a remnant saved Messianic Jews who would also pass from the GREAT TRIBULATION and ARMAGEDDON into the OLAM HABA. All unbelieving Jews and Gentiles would resurrect at the end of the OLAM HABA and be thrown into the burning lake of fire. The 7 Bowls in Revelation would occur during the GREAT TRIBULATION. The FIRST BOWL would be moral and spiritual affliction. The SECOND BOWL would pour out upon the sea like blood. The THIRD BOWL would be fresh waters to become blood. The FOURTH BOWL would be solar heat and its intensity. The FIFTH BOWL would be darkness over the Antichrist's reign, or the beast. The SIXTH BOWL would be drying up of the Euphrates River 1,780 miles long, with Turkey now being able to block the water so that the kings of the East could cross over and the 3 Frogs were the unholy trinity. BOWL SEVEN would be an earthquake starting in Israel and affecting the whole world with the words "it is finished", the same words that Messiah said on the Cross. After this from GOD'S throne in heaven and from the Temple on earth this would be spoken. The first 6 BOWLS would all emanate from GOD'S temple. There is a difference between 1260 and 1,290 days and also the 1,335 days which would mean 75 days needed to be accounted for. In other words, 1,335 days minus 1,260 equals a difference of 75 days.

In the Old Testament, the Book of Genesis was the beginnings, the Book of Exodus was redemption, and the Book of Leviticus was the atonement. What can one discover in foreshadowing? George Washington wrote to the Newport synagogue that they had a right by GOD to free religion in that the Old Testament is part of the Bible even though not nearly the full part with Messiah. King George was a dictator that George Washington and other Americans fought against for religious freedom.

This hodge podge of the world's multiculturalism or "Tower of Babel" invaded America and inundated it with barbarism of the worse kind, first with its so called "medical science", which was nothing more than what Josef Mengele instituted in Nazi Germany. This New Age was Nazism again worldwide. Americans had done themselves in by following the lead of the rich and well educated who had either a guilt complex or love of avarice from the pockets of others not their own. Share and share alike, said government and all will be well. Let foreigners who have no loyalty and even sometimes no Christian values take over and who are unqualified, take the land. This was the blind leading the blind. None needed to be qualified, just affirmed by affirmative action, set asides, quotas, New Age philosophy socialism, reverse discrimination, et cetera. The Trojan horse was let in again by the rich and well educated along with drugs and other nefarious stimulants and depressants. How else would third world countries pay back loans to World Bank? No one had ever told us what was in Fort Knox.

Many official foreign languages to uphold for confusion, dumbing down and bringing resentment and animosity for all. So many illegals that one wondered why we had immigration agencies. Since most of these hated America but not its wealth, one then could understand their ever sincere patriotism…. Who promote this hatred for America and its own GOD? Government officials and the rich? “Do America in”? Did they know that someone would know?

Campaign finance reform was a façade for restricted 1st Amendment Rights, so the status quo could stay in for life like the Politburo and then call it republicanism. Mr. Richard Gephardt made the quote that, “Either there is freedom of speech, faith, or our desire for healthy campaign in a healthy democracy. You can’t have both.” What was he suggesting? Now this was the minority leader in the House of Representatives who felt we could do without the 1st Amendment. So liberty is not important, but a regime of regulation is? With donations and spending, he says, James Madison is wrong and that this cure is better than the disease, but really meant to say that the disease is better than the cure. Right of property and liberty do not go together and are not compatible, according to Mr. Gephardt. He knew more than James Madison? The Supreme Court also said, “Donations and expenditures were different.” In other words, spending and contributions were different, which they were not. If I pay for my own expenditures it would be okay, but contributions for other candidates were not the same. Representative meant if it were my own money and candidacy it was all right, but if for another it was not. Contributions were struck down, but not campaign expenditures. Another wonderful ruling by this magnificent 9. The media loved it because they controlled the parties for POLITICAL CORRECTNESS. Then later a court decision was made by Judges Alfred Goodwin and Stephen Reinhardt in the Ninth Circuit Court of Appeals who were both unelected and said, "Under GOD" was unconstitutional in the Pledge of Alliance. Senator John McCain also stonewalled all of Mr. Bush's nominations of U.S. Marshals, thus lending a hand in removing GOD totally from our country and in effect put our national security at risk. Remember this is the man who broke under pressure while in Vietnam and whose father and grandfather were both admirals. This was the opening of Pandora's Box.

Yes, anything but Messiah. Group therapy for an entire nation would do the trick and constitutional government would fail, especially since the masses thought alike in one thing: "more for me this free materialism with no holds barred." Free to do as one pleases. If one can commit murder and kill GOD, then anything was possible. The sky was the limit. Insanity then reigned in America while political speeches were made that meant absolutely nothing. Hot air balloons that ascended to nowhere. America was high on socialism for all. It gave more than it took in. Free handouts, especially to those who were deadbeat dads.

America's hair had been cut, and Samson lost all of his strength. There had been subcultures such as the Amish, a quiet religious cult; the Hasidim, unsaved; and revolutionary cultures such as Hell's Angels, neo-homosexual Nazis, New Agers, the Communist Party; no un-American House Activities in the House of Representatives, Harlem's racism, et cetera. The homosexual subculture was the worst. It was totally demonic in nature.

Monoculture meaning only one Judeo-Christian GOD, the American GOD in America, not multiculturalism meaning any god or gods in America. Some groups did not want to assimilate because the rich and well educated found it to their liking that is picking pockets and certain groups liked it because of past historical failures, not by Americans but again by the rich and well educated which had created these atrocities from Europeanism.

For example, in Peru children were starving, but Big Business took 70% of Peru's fish and made American dog food. Buildings in Latin America had infamous names such as Rockefeller on them, especially in Puerto Rico, but why Puerto Rico?

This was the ugly Americanism, the Anglo-Saxon of Americanism, something the Hispanic could not differentiate or did not want to, with government urging. Blame the average American. This was truly dedicated to the rich who coerced the average American through way of government to accept colonialism and for even immigration and a foreign language and an anti-Semitic Latin culture such as in Paraguay's Nazi haven (WW II) that set up or was set up by Elizabeth Nietzche, sister of the infamous homosexual Nazi, Fred. It was to create havoc and chaos and melt down Americans into a Pan American slave mentality. A sort of Bostonian school bussing, another cruel act against our own children.

These billionaires who are abnormal thinkers bought out Latin America and their people without the people's knowledge and felt they had to reciprocate and integrate at least North, Central and South America. After all, they were all Americans, right?

Our own State Department supported anti-Semitism, such as General Powell with foreign brutal regimes as the PLO, Aristide, the Viet Cong, et cetera. This was not "We the people" but "we the peoples". The rich are always needed to sell their avarice to someone anywhere. There is always a buyer and their commodities are anything and everything from socialism to drugs and even body parts. In this case the English language had to be dissolved because it meant cohesion and discipline, or self-discipline in America. But where were the crimes and poverty? This was most disconcerting to the courts and trial lawyers. What about the filthy and corrupt inner cities proposed by big government and Big Business including Hollywood? From Cain's lineage of the urban settlers, plus "garbage stew" and of course "poetry" if one could call the rappers that. Should not this cancer also expand there?

Once again it reverberates the sound of the jungle elite to take the money and wealth and run and leave the violence, the lies, to us, or our posterity so that we could take the crunch of violence on the chin. "Lies upon lies produce violence." Shift all the blame to America and Americans, a people and subterfuge all guilt away from the elites. No crimes really occurred at Harvard, Yale, Dartmouth, Brown, Princeton, Colombia, Cornell and Penn, only POLITICALLY CORRECT ones. Also Hollywood's atheism along with Pontifico Falls, Southern Jersey, Vermont, Tennessee and the 49'er state one could not overlook. Other states and infamous cities included Washington State, Oregon, New York State, Maine, Florida, Colorado, Nevada, Nebraska, Oklahoma, and Virginia. Cities included: San Francisco, N.Y., Miami, Orlando, Atlanta, Detroit, Chicago, Boston, Alexandria, Fort Knox, Los Angeles, et cetera. It was all just environmental pollution.

Along came Islam, just like that out of nowhere and it's socialism of a different kind. Oh, it had the same death wish, but Americans patronized and worked their hearts out, not for the Moslems, but for their money. Americans weren't only ignorant but apathetic to what a true American was, but just wanted Hollywood's infamous fame and fortune.

The Bechtel Corporation was a major part in all of this. Maybe that is why in all sports they always felt obliged to accommodate only the fastest, quickest and shiftiest to compete, as they do and also to have a camaraderie amongst the amoeba mass. Chinese ping pong anyone? Their hidden gamesmanship, though always had to be won. It was not how one played the game, but only that you won, no matter how. The ends did justify the means. They flooded funds by coercion upon the poor millionaires for sports, business, education, government and even churches. All had to remain silent. Civil rights, or superior rights, had an avalanche effect. "Civil" did not imply diplomacy or peace loving but burning cities, except possibly for one city in the Northeast and everyone knew which one that was.

This brown shirt mentality would take over the gray shirt of the union, yes gray. Emulation was in the polluted air. It was as if Mao himself was America's fashion designer or at least one athlete thought so.

Bushwhacked by the south-of-the-border mentality and not too aware of the average person and also too young and one too

New Aged with the younger one opting for 3 million Mexicans on board by a stroke of the pen, until 9/11 and also wanted to reduce citizen statute from 10 years of work in America to 5 years in residence in order to be able to collect government welfare. Over one half million came to America in one year already. Fair play had to be, or did it? Lower wages for all, even in America not to only make it poor but also to make a profit for someone. The Spanish conquistador promised new hope. Main Street America became gang family oriented. The subculture had become the so called "culture". The moral idea did no longer precede the civic responsibility. "Do your own thing" later became "for the good of the cause", but what cause nobody said.

Even the Communist Party was represented in congress. Ron Dellums and Pat Schroeder and Hollywood had Ed Asner and education had Angela Davis. They were all card carrying.

We kept holding Israel by the throat as all good anti-Semites do until Israel no longer could restrain herself or its soldiers or its own sovereignty. Soldiers are taught to kill, not to enforce the law. This all started with the New Ager, Churchill, when in 1922 and after the Balfour Declaration he gave away 78% of Israel, Jordan, which was all Jewish land. The Arabs have 22 countries. Israel has one and it is not Islamic or dictatorial, but all 22 Arab nations are. Why?

The billionaires could they have said, "Here, come to New York to commit Islamic Jihad" or was it an 8-year fiasco of indecency before that?

"Now I am fantasizing, right?"

How many Israelis must be slaughtered by Islam to please Europeanism and capitalism and Jihad? Now even their own are not spared among the rich and well educated.

We told Israel, "Just hold back until…." But for how long and from what? Against their own sovereignty? Israel would have to pay for not listening to Samson too.

Even in schools in Israel weapons of all kinds were brought to protect the students, Jewish from Arab terrorists students in their "bi-partisan" schools. They were second to 28 countries listed in weapon carrying to school. Belgium was first, but the other countries did not have Islamic Jihad to go to school with. The kibbutz was dying, but in one sense this kibbutz effect, or loss of it, was bringing families back together again, wasn't it?

In America, 40% were Orthodox, 26% Reformed (pro-homosexual), Conservative 23%, then Reconstructionists and Humanistic, yet only 10% Orthodox with 6,000,000 Jews in America which showed how far the Jews in America were from GOD. There were about 100,000 Messianic Jews though in America who were believers.

The Gutenberg press, or printing press, produced the Gutenberg Bible which contained from Latin the Old Testament from 1455 AD which diluted it from the original Hebrew.

Israel had no constitution but a parliamentarian Knesset. This is one body with 120 members of many different parties. Sixty-one is a majority. It is a democracy which is problematic and the prime minister is the head and the president is a sort of figurehead or is less well known. The Sanhedrin were figureheads in archaic times. The President signs treaties and laws passed and appoints judges and meets foreign dignitaries. The president is elected by the Knesset in a majority vote and serves 5 years and can serve for 2 terms. The following in chronological order were all presidents of Israel since its founding: Chaim Weizman (1949-1952); Yitzhak Ben Zvi (1952-1963); Zalman Shazar (1963-1973); Ephraim Katzir (1973-1978); Yitzhak Navon (1978-1983); Chaim Herzog (1983-1993); Ezer Weizman (1993-2000); Moshé Katsay, et cetera. The prime ministers were more well known to the world such as David Ben-Gurion (1948-1954); Moshe Sharett (1954-1955); David Ben-Gurion (1955-1963); Levi Eshkal (1963-1969); Golda Meir (1969-1974 and American born); Yitzhak Rabin (1974-1977); Menachem Begin (1977-1983); Yitzhak Shamir (1983-1984); Shimon Peres (1984-1986 and a graduate of Harvard); Yitzhak Shamir (1986-1992); Yitzhak Rabin (1992-1995); Shimon Peres (1995-1996); Benjamin Netanyahu (1996-1999 and also an Ivy leaguer); Ehud Barak (1999-2001); Ariel Sharon, the lion of GOD et cetera. The prime minister picks the Cabinet and the other ministers.

Margaret Thatcher pleaded with George Bush, Sr. to stop Saddam Hussein from going into Kuwait while the U.S. Ambassador, April Glass told Saddam it was all right to enter Kuwait earlier. England has a lot of Arab oil money in accounts in London much more investments for Islam into buying out America than Japan ever had.

In 1933 FDR sent the first U.S. Ambassador to the Bolsheviks. Since Israel's existence, Satan and his earthly cohorts have attacked Israel to liquidate it completely. Do as well as Churchill and FDR did at Yalta and oil wells shall end Israel. If Israel was America's ally, the State Department had a funny way of showing it. American Jewry would not now visit. Russian Jewry would wait for Aliyah and Islamic Jihad there was growing under communist rule some even from Turkey with Iranian influence from the Ayatollah. Saudi Arabia was supplying the funds.

In America, Nazis were being still caught and extradited like Nikolaus Schiffer (1 of 50 since 1959). Nikolaus was born in America but grew up in Romania. In San Francisco Arab homosexuals attacked with violent words Jewish students.

In New York City their own New York City Jewry defended child sexual abuse as if they were part of Hitler's Youth Corps. Even the ultra-Orthodox had an incident in Brooklyn, the Hasidim, but Reformed Judaism was blatantly homosexual.

Three major groups in America were anti-Semites no matter what. The Black Islamic Moslems, The German Judaizers, and of course the Anglo-Saxons more this time than the Catholic Church and Latin America. One proclaimed to be the "roots" one proclaimed their defense of Hitler's Youth Corps and the other murder in cold blood. While they only spoke but could never hear, it was like talking to the wall. "What was life and liberty compared to campaign finance reform?" said Mr. Gephardt to reiterate.

Who supported infanticide, besides the white male? How about 92% of "blacks" who voted for Clinton? Or a higher percentage of American Jewry who voted for Nazi infanticide which was even higher in percentage than the American "black".

One can remember in the Soviet Unin that a minority too kept all those republics and Russians under totalitarianism by a number of about only 18,000,000 communists. The "Mensheviks" in America had their "Bolsheviks" to please. As had occurred in Russia with the monarch and the Duma, they too saw their Mensheviks as their saviours, but the Bolsheviks had other plans and so a repeat of history was occurring in America. Lenin's Bolsheviks like Solomon Lezosky and Ehrenburg the journalists were anti-Semitic Jewish Communists.

CHAPTER XIII

HIDDEN HISTORY

Frederick Krupp, an industrialist, was a homosexual. How many more businessmen of the super rich fit into this category? This subculture had some outstanding cultures from which to follow.

For example, the DOUBANS would allow a father to abandon his child at birth. Sound familiar? And where sorcery and witchcraft, Vermont and Tennessee, were a "good" thing. Stealing was honorable as well as adultery. No-fault divorce trial lawyers and judges though were not needed. They had no sense of humor, our liberals and did not trust anyone, the IRS. They learned all this by so called equal cultures. Another example was the ALARESE where mothers did not always feed their babies. Does this not too sound so familiar again? And after age one a child feeds himself; A FDC's day care soviet style? It is a culture where the parents almost try to deceive the children, Hollywood and the NEA. The KUKUKUKU culture terrorize other tribes and dismember them, Islam and are eaten. Peking's Communists do the same with fetuses; hence cannibalism. The giraffe women of BURMA place a rod or a brass rod is placed around all girls at the age of 5. As she gets older she stoops more and more. Up to 20 pounds were put on. It elongates her neck. After a while they cannot drink water but must sip it through a straw. If the nice brass rods are removed, if she commits adultery her head drops and she suffocates.

In Africa there is female circumcision where the girl's clitoris is removed and also her outer labia as well as a girl's genitalia and are sewn together until the vagina is closed. Here in America we are much more civilized. We let procreation happen through mostly infidelity and otherwise lust and then extract the "cavity" much easier through RU-486, or infanticide. The above female circumcision, by the way, is done in 26 African countries, Europe (how European) and yes, none other than in the red, white and blue.

In India, when a husband dies a widow is burned at a husband's funeral pyre. One man, aged 24 and his wife aged 18 chose to be burned alive with his corpse. This is not uncommon. There are also rat temples to worship in India.

The Aztecs of Tenochtillan, now Mexico City, were a warrior people who acquired prisoners for human sacrifices. Their chests were cut open by an obsidian knife and the hearts amputated. The head was strung up as a public trophy (like the British Mandate in Palestine with real effigies) and severed arms and legs were taken as souvenirs and for cannibalism amongst this tribe.

The Auca Indians dig a hole in the ground when a baby cries. They put the baby inside it and the trample on it.

The Siriono Indians argue about food. Does this not sound familiar also? Food can be hidden, even in vaginas. Human excreta surrounds their houses.

The Chuckee have their women skin their reindeer and prepare the meat while they only get leftovers, and American women complained about not being able to vote and doing household chores.

In Latin America, far richer in natural resources and human resources than North America, they go hungry many times.

When our founders were setting up a Christian government, the Spaniards from Spain and the Portuguese from Portugal both encouraged luck, machoism and heroism, a macho status as opposed to a Christian beginning.

At the Beijing infanticide conference they did condemn female genital mutilation, but blackmailed – or they tried to blackmail – all third world countries by making or coercing them with an offer they could not refuse, which most did though and kept procreation alive.

One can see that all cultures and peoples are not equal but mostly inhumane and immoral. This is multiculturalism many diverse cultures. Multiculturalism has 5 reasons to deceive: (1) To deceive their real intent, (2) to destroy, (3) to destroy America, (4) to make America ignorant and feel guilty and to desensitize America, (5) to promote an ideology and not faith and to use this euphemism, "multiculturalism" to sound harmless and all encompassing for more civil rights. This ism deals in lies, and hence its roots are all socialistic and this utopia of theatrical reality lies in all isms. Phrases or words such as "only if", "but", "what if", "but, yes, but" always fail to render the truth because it is the lie that all socialisms must deal with or not deal with, no matter what. Lenin took the Russian church and replaced it with the religion of Marxism where state, not GOD, was worshipped as well as its thugs.

Satan invented the lie because of pride. Here is a lie conceived years ago.

"It was our Founders who invented all or the worst kind of slavery and the first to bring it to America."

Now the truth. American Indian tribes dealt in slavery in 1565 by holding Cuban Indians as slaves, and in 1616 Henrickson encountered slave arming Indians in the Schuylkill River area of Pennsylvania. Also, the Illinois Ottawa Indians, Iroquois Indians, the Puma Indians all enslaved the Apache and the Yuma Indians. Also, the Pawnee Indians were enslaved. The Atlantic slave trade grew out of and was rationalized by African high societies, or chieftans who had complete control over it. Ethiopia did not outlaw slavery until 1942, and the Falash Mura were dispered, India in 1976 and Red China never. The Mohawk Indians ate human flesh as well as the Chippe plus the Sioux. Yes, the rich and well educated also lied about all this or did not tell the truth but once again want to reinstitute socialism in America to a further degree. This is, make no mistake about it, part of their diversity and tolerance for America, this time by other non-ignorant or civilized individuals as the method.

Arafat's Koran says in Sura XLVII "death of the infidels". Now Israel had to be tolerant and emulate the 60's riots in "black" America. What about Arabic nations or tribes hiding ex-Nazi war criminals under Islamic names?

CHAPTER XIV

IN ISRAEL AND THE COMMUNITIES

Our immediate family was growing, and Rachel had a set of identical twins named Abraham and Jacob and blessed us so much with these two beautiful baby boys. It was our faith in Messiah and our family's closeness that kept us going on, even though times were getting more severe for all believers. We kept a small trust fund within the family made up of legal tender, though most legal tender was not used by government. We replaced it with whatever commodity or foodstuff that was in high demand. Then we sold the commodity for credit on their smart card. We knew we had to help the young ones try to prepare for the future. Alexander was an excellent provider and priest. All of Alexander's family had come to know Messiah. How rare that was indeed. We also saw the sadness of friends and neighbors who were torn apart by the enemy's new religion. We always prayed standing in the gap for our daughter Alex and the two twins. We celebrated all the holidays and feasts such as YOM KIPPUR, the Day of Stonement; ROSH HASHANAH; HANUKAH; THE FEAST OF TABERNACLES; PASSOVER, not Easter, et cetera. All holidays were only Biblical and even some not out of the Levitical Order. PASSOVER was the crucifixion, death, burial and resurrection of Y'eshua Messiah. Messiah worshipped as a Jewish man in a Temple and spoke Aramaic. The synagogue was Babylonian. Now the "roots" were starting to be pulled out, then the "branches" would be next.

UCLA, Cornell, Grinnell and the University of Michigan all promoted homosexuality. USC was the biggest employer in LA. Talk about big government. In relation to the above deviancy, there was a 1984 report in the Journal of the American Medical Association that said the following: "The human rectum (why that?) was not made for sexual penile intercourse. The female vagina mucuous multi-layered skin to protect it from abrasions. The rectum canal has only one layer of columnar skin (epidermis); thence cannot protect against infection (HIV-AIDS) by sperm antigens enhancing exposure to the immune apparatus in the lymphatic and blood circulation. "The outcome is the HIV virus, or full blown AIDS.

One day I was traveling east to west in Israel and I marveled at how small a distance this was of about 50 or more miles.

As the older generation died off, the younger Sabras became more and more secularized for the most part. Some Jews no longer even come to visit let alone live in Israel. Messianic Jewry was illegal. "Protocols …" was brought up a gain and again.

The 38th Parallel in Korea had its similarity now in Israel or the DMZ zone in Vietnam. The New Age was this: (1) the occult, (2) the Antichrist's system, (3) Anti-Messiah, (4) world government and world religion, (5) death and destruction, (6) one evil source, (7) networking, (8) hoarding all food and water, (9) creating wars and feuds in the "villages" and chaos so totalitarian order would be chosen as "peace", (10) no families, (11) to worship Satan and to take his mark, (12) Israel to be deceived and destroyed. There was nowhere for them to turn or look to for peace except Messiah, and that was out for now.

The city on a hill was nicknamed Pork Chop Hill. Products to America had at least 40 languages on them. American English was dying in America. English was not like Russian, a universal language. The West wanted Europe to weaken by dealing with China. Latin dealt with too much romanticism and no compromising even though it had America's medical terms. Greek was homosexual or of sort "oriental" the music and democracy was all it knew. French was outlandish and happily displayed the French Jesuits.

Franco-Germanic political philosophy was bad news for real life, liberty and freedom. German composers were the best in quintessential and ageless music. "If you don't first succeed the first time, try and try and try again."

One could see why Soviet Moscow took Russian or its language by raping it. Devoid all human compassion if they could. Pure Russian was indeed rare. Fool the world to make the world believe Russia and its language and all its people were innately somehow barbaric Communists. What better language to use than universal Russian? Communism could be spread much more easily this way to the world.

Another phenomenon is the Russian Jew who is probably out of all world Jewry nothing short of being brilliant even though past history has poor racial and political relations. These foresighted people are acutely cognitive of many hidden things in life. Only the well educated and the ones who served their military duty were allowed to move anywhere in Russia; otherwise it was the Pale of Settlement. Russia, like America, had many nationalities but one nation. The Russian is a cousin to the Ukraine. Russia had a Christian monarch ... America had a Christian democratic/ republic and too went totalitarian.

Russian Jewish children as immigrants to America learn English better than any other immigrant in the world coming to America. Purebreds are for show dogs.

In America, pastors and priests and rabbis were plump when you cook them, and the Anglicans lived a life of Riley. The professionals -- we all know them -- needed degrees and degrees for what? Money, fame and wealth? "Who is it that takes you to court? Is it not the rich?"

America had little or no legal tender so "e pluribus unum" and more importantly "In GOD we trust" no longer could be seen. Access, not excess, to food, clothing, water, shelter, medicine, et cetera in America was all by microchip. Even when we had traveled to America it was strange not to see any cash transactions when even buying food or going on public transportation. Everything was by 64 K Verichip with a higher K infusion. People were ignorant robots. No more robberies for money, but food was another thing. One could not barter; it was illegal. The world was not overpopulated but condensed in certain parts of the world with a lack of clean water and food that was edible for human consumption. Agriculture worldwide was literally dead. With 6 billion people at one time one could give each person about 1 acre of land in Australia. The problem was not so much the land but was it agricultural and did the people have access to the market or the fields? All gold and no bread.

Mob rule by thugs put Putin in office and tribal groups would not rule under the Antichrist. Hoarding of edible food items meant now that so many had lost their lives or life savings as well investments for the future, since all was being controlled from a single source, even though networking was throughout most the world. Even if one network went out, it did not affect the others. The cataclysmic catastrophe was imminent. The West and Israel had hoarded much, but the rest of the world had none. Two extremes, hot and cold, to hit each other soon. Advancement in one region and starvation in another, and the advanced society wanted even more and more and would not share. The church was part of it, that is this religion. Israel was leading and would let a "light" shine. Satan can come in the form of a light.

We grew more uncomfortable as Israel started to look like the bad guy and was against Messiah and His land. Would the "lady" be consumed by the "ocean of water"? Pets were becoming a thing of the past. No extra source of food was being allowed. I had heard that in Vietnam they ate dogs and cats for food during the conflict. The worse it got, the more man cursed GOD. Satan was searing more and more consciences and hearts. Demonic activity was increasing. Hearts had become like Pharoah's heart by GOD at the time of Moses. We heard that some had turned over to cannibalism. Life had no purpose for unbelievers. When did it ever? It was literally dog eat dog in most other lands. Red China was rattling its saber. The Euphrates was getting drier by Turkey's implementation. The East appeared strongest next to the West with the North and South next. Would the logistics play a part for the North or the South? Nuclear armaments would do no good, only if far enough away from Israel.

The aggressor in a military battle must attack first in order to win, but the oriental mind might for sure keep coming and coming.

Who educated the first Communist Chinese? Was it not Europe and America? Remember Ho Chi Minh? The East would be willing to die for their cause or ideology, but the West had refused to do the same. Did not the Yalta Conference become a albatross around our own necks so that Satan got all he wanted? This was pure insanity by the West to waste thousands and millions of lives to fight a war against just Nazism, but not soviet socialism. And why? In turn make peace at the end of the war with another form of socialism? One must ask the Anglophiles about self-preservation, or their animosity against the Russian Christian people as well as the Poles, Hungarians, Chinese, Koreans, Vietnamese, Cambodians, Laotians? This did not occur all at one time, but nonetheless it did occur in due time by a domino effect that destroyed many lives unnecessarily because of old age and senility and most of all self-preservation with a little sprinkling of good old blue blooded arrogance and coldness and higher than thou attitude and the socialistic New Deal, philosophy of homosexualist Lord Keynes and his Keynesian Economics from good old Harvard the poison Ivy of world business and law. Harvard once was a seminary, but now had become a cemetery.

The Fords, the Krupps, the Hammers did more for socialism than even for capitalism even though capitalism did more for socialism than anything else. While people were tortured to death in the Gulags, these above individuals knowingly wined and dined with the Kremlin and the Nazi thugs enjoying the good life. They also took part in tearing America and Latin America apart. Where did the Soviets get their technology from all those years except from some of these infamous whippersnappers who became un-American in every shape and form. Whippersnappers that know too much and share with anybody else a nation's soul. Now their children get to do more damage in the world like Margaret Sanger's grandson did in Planned Parenthood, though

22 grandchildren of the Rockefellers refused any kind of will from the wealth of their ancestry that was accumulated.

The Franco-Germanic mindset was also helpful to destroy millions of earlier lives over and over again, but all was to be forgiven and forgotten so quickly and easily and the Jewish issue was not even Jewish in the sense that Judaism and materialism never did anything to transform the Jew with GOD except through Messianic Jewry. Israel, too, for the most part wanted nothing to do with the real GOD and their real purpose. Western materialism stole the other Jew's heart who was not of the family of Abraham, Isaac and Jacob. Too many opportunities to do good, but the mundane Jew chose wealth in this world over wealth in eternity. These Pharisees of today's synagogue had gone too far in claiming the rights in the business and educational world. They had missed the Messiah by about 2,000 years and were hoping, just hoping, for what would be a restoration of Israel for all those who someday would believe and did not already believe. This spiritual suicide always has been, but GOD is in control and not man's free will.

Our Founders in American English had accomplished much while in the Spanish language there was no word for "compromise" or "dissent"; hence coupes and revolutions in Latin America. And why the arrogance in America?

Whenever lies and absolute power get together, mankind is ravaged by violence and avarice along with all kinds of evil. In the 8th century the Papal State came into being. Violence for most and wealth and comfort and safety for the infinite few. Free will? The New Age movement involved all the cults and organizations and why not all rolled into one. Christianity is not an organization but a living and breathing spirit. The Masons, the Templars, the Mormons, et cetera all combined to make the world anti-GOD. The world now had become tribal and factions and nations fought against each other, creating animosities and there appeared no end in sight. People were shifted as Stalin had done by the millions and became nomadic because of lack of food and fresh water and other necessities. Only the rigid totalitarian states kept control of their borders but were experiencing some inner turmoil due to a lack of food and fresh water. The Middle East was becoming a hot bed more and more, and nuclear proliferation was becoming more because even small states had been armed with nuclear weapons of smaller sizes from the West. There had to be a ruler who most people thought could control the anarchy in the world and preserve peace and bring about this world utopia, and since Israel appeared as one of the strongest nations in the world and was logistically located in the center of the world, it appeared that Israel with in the limelight. Somehow destiny or fate was bringing to fruition this leadership role in the world.

Some earlier Russian economic scholars had spoken about a 60 to 70-year world depression that was part of this cyclical economic world. This era, though, appeared it was here to stay and would not be cyclical this time. It appeared that we were coming to the end of an age when political ramifications and spiritual events were coming to a cataclysmic debacle. Uncontrollable amounts of anarchy and famines – manmade and otherwise – plus mass starvation in certain regions in the world. Man's innateness to sin.

Abraham and Jacob, our two twins, were getting older and had reached the ages of 3 with 85% of their personalities set. Both were constantly kept with Rachel, Alex, or us. The Jacob in the Bible blessed Joseph's two Gentile/Jewish sons with Ephraim, the younger one, getting the blessing and Manasseh, the older one who did not. As Jacob crossed his arms, it was a symbol that the Gentiles too would come in.

Time was appearing to move faster because of man's anxiety and the darkened severity into an abyss of immorality. Home schooling would be what Alex and Rachel had chosen, since any public or secular school would never suffice. Students were coerced to accept atheism and most people were unbelievers and were following Satan who was hell bent on destroying this world.

Abraham and Jacob were not bridged brain children. They both were all boy. Wrestling with dad and with each other and so helpful as little boys who loved Rachel and me as dad and mom and all of us as family. At this time it was usual for young children to be exposed to all kinds of evils. We sheltered Abe and Jacob, but did not keep them from what life presented to them, but guided and nurtured and answered many questions with the most importance. We also differentiated between Abraham and Jacob's personalities.

Abraham appeared more stoic and had the ability of leadership unforcefully. His choleric qualities were as such. He was confident, decisive, persuasive, competitive, and strong-willed. He also was affectionate with a little sanguine, or upgoing.

Jacob was more melancholic, analytical and loyal with phlegmatic tendencies such as patience, a good listener, a peacekeeper. Both boys were identical, not fraternal, twins, the same egg. They were by natural birth and both boys weighed about 5 and one- half pounds each and were born at about 3:00 A.M. in the morning on May 15.

My own background had been half-Italian and half Polish. I remember ex-mayor LaGuardia had been half Italian and half Jewish. Marie was all Jewish even though her background was Polish-Jewish. The Polish culture had a reflection on her family's Jewishness, hardworking and pioneers. Alex was Russian and Polish Jewish. Alex's Israeli name was Moshé Alexander Roseman. His mother's name was Sonia Cohen. Cohen meant priest in Hebrew, and Alex was both priest and good provider for his family that GOD had given him. Rachel was like her mother, Marie, my wife, affectionate and very compassionate. Marie was from the Levite tribe and so was Alexander. One from the Gershon family and one from the Kohath family of Levites. Both were Ashkenazim with a little Sephardim.

The Biblical holidays or Holy Days were as such according to the B'rit Hadasha and the Old Testament. PESACH was changed from the first month to another month when in Babylonian exile. PESACH involves 7 days of unleavened bread (no sin) which corresponds with PASSOVER, Y'eshua's resurrection (Exodus 12). This represented in part the 10th plague on Pharoah and his kingdom. John the Baptist, Yohanan said, "Behold the Lamb of

GOD." Rev Shaul also mentions in B'rit Hadasha, "Y'eshua our PASSOVER is sacrificed for us." (1 Corinthians 5:7) Afikomen, the one who came, was the Greek term used for Y'eshua for the first 2 centuries in A.D. In Leviticus 23:6-8 THE FEAST OF UNLEAVENED BREAD related to PESACH, or PASSOVER week. Then the CEREMONY OF FIRST FRUITS Leviticus 23:9-14 continues the 50th day period and occurs immediately after PESACH. Y'eshua was the "first fruit" of those who died (1 Corinthians 15:20). Then came SHAVUOT, or PENTECOST, THE FEAST OF WEEKS. This takes place 50 days after the "first fruit ceremony". The giving of the law was also included. Two loaves of bread represent Jews and Gentiles. "Your people are my people."

GOD placed His Ruach Hakodesh onY'eshua's follower on SHAVUOT, Acts 2:4. SHAVUOT was the completion of the 50 days from first fruits (the resurrection). He would write His laws on our hearts (Jeremiah 31:32-33). Ezekiel 36:25-27 mentions His placing Ruach Hakodesh in our hearts. The blowing of the trumpets (Leviticus 2:23-25) the new Year. GOD created the world on this day. To eat sweet things. The shofar is blown, the coming of the OLAM HABA. The Day of Atonement, YOM KIPPUR, when only once a year the high priest could enter the most sacred part of the sanctuary. This day is to repent for one's sins. ROSH HOSHANAH and YOM KIPPUR services refer to Isaac almost being sacrificed which foreshadows Messiah's death, GOD'S only son, like Abraham's only son. Also, Jonah spending 3 days and 3 nights in the stomach of a whale. (Matthew 12:39-40)

SUCCOT, the FESTIVAL OF BOOTHS or TABERNACLES is an 8-day period. GOD'S faithfulness in the wilderness. When Peter, Shimon HaShaliach, awoke he thought the kingdom had come and Messiah was going to rule. The booths remind us to depend on GOD and not material goods, a lesson for America. (Matthew 6:25-33)

To briefly review the above, PASSOVER week's atoning events: Y'eshua's death and resurrection. PESACH, Y'eshua's blood shed for us. Unleavened bread, Y'eshua's body given for us. First fruits, Y'eshua's resurrection. SHAVUOT visible coming of Ruach Hakodesh (the Holy Spirit) at SAVUOT in 32 A.D. All these have been fulfilled. ROSH HOSHANAH, translation of the temple or the church, YOM KIPPUR, national and then world atonement; and then SUCCOT, Messiah's reign.

Holy Days outside the Leviticus Cycle, such as PURIM and the evil Haman. Haman was the first to try to exterminate the Jews. HANAKAH is a victory won by the Maccabees in 165 B.C. to preserve Jewish identity. The Temple was cleansed. Antiochus had defiled the Temple like the Antichrist shall. This shall be the 3rd Temple. PURIM means preservation from our enemies while in exile and HANAKAH our preservation while in the land. These are the FEASTS OF THE LORD, Messiah (Leviticus 23:4).

Do any Gentile religions come close to these rich Jewish festivals and holidays? Messiah, a Jewish man, "the roots of salvation" with their "branches" hence the failure of Catholicism-Protestantism.

Our surrounding countries worshipped a god or gods who they called GOD, but when has Islam ever worshipped the GOD of Abraham, Isaac and Jacob, or for that matter most importantly Messiah? Islam never had anything to do with Messiah. It has always been non-Judeo-Christian. It is not a cult like Jehovah Witnesses or the Mormons that emulate Christianity and never recognized the Trinity or Messiah as GOD in the flesh. Islam, though is violent and much worse than most Westerners know. It told one without GOD (which meant no salvation) who to worship by indoctrination from Satan. It, too, like Judaism forgot Messiah, GOD which meant no salvation or grace or faith or paradise or Truth.

Now that America had embraced heathenism, GOD no longer needed to shield America or heathenism. He, though, could protect His family, which was quite small. The enemy was worshipped instead of GOD by the national soul. GOD can remove His blessings and take them somewhere else just as He would any church that claimed it represented Y'eshua alone or used apostate sermons. "Be careful GOD shall not be mocked."

Whether one said, "to the left" or "liberal", they meant socialist or socialism. Whether one said "to the right" or "conservative", they meant Big Business, capitalism, avarice.

Groups were plentiful in America except for believers and they were not a group but a part of a worldwide Body. The American Spiritual civil war would prove to be more destructive than any other war in America. Was it good vs. evil to the core? Even after American Jewry helped the Negro, the American "black", an anomaly started to become now anti-Semitic and anti-American for whatever reason and judicial infanticide followed Dred Scott of 1857. Now American Negroes had to reform or conform to the image of the American "black"; almost an opposite of each other and had to be anti-American. Yes, but also of being a superior "race", "black", hence the inconsistency of peace and the one human race. The Mensheviks did their best behind the scenes, and it appeared to draw the most attention because of physical differences like no others had. The "Bolsheviks" were waiting to come on stage for theatrical reality.

Did something transcend amongst our beginning as to why Messiah (roots) was never mentioned, but only the Old Testament or was it GOD? Reference to Providence was what? Colloquialism? What Father could a Deist be referring to when Messiah has always been, is and shall always be?

The first believers in the first century A.D. were Jewish and none left their Messianic faith. Most Gentile religions diluted or removed Scripture and then tried to emulate Judaism, but lost their way. Salvation is of the Jews started to mean very little. Along came this church that would retain, as government would, private property and claim to be of Peter and then Reformation, not transformation, with both having much anti-Semitism. How could GOD bless anti-Semitism when in the first place He came as a Jewish man? The Bible never upheld slave trading, but told the truth as it was. There is a difference. Rev Shaul told his friend to accept a slave not as a slave, but as a friend in Messiah first and as no slave and in that order and that context.

Messiah knew man's evil heart so that in addressing slavery He wanted the slaves to know their plight and that He would defend them by His death, crucifixion, burial and resurrection. GOD does not uphold evil, only good, even though in each man is good vs evil. Universal freedom for all men no matter the age, poverty, or "race". GOD has no favorites. GOD'S permissive will would allow man to continue with man's fallen nature because man was not a robot, or a perfect being, but a free agent for Him put there by GOD in men, yet He knew all men would not be saved and some were at birth or shortly thereafter, because He knew His own. Yes all infants in and out of the womb were saved and children up to the age of accountability. The sin of man was innate and his committing of sin in thought, word and deed. It was the Jews who wrote the Bible, under GOD'S Holy inspiration. What could be added by the Gentiles, except Luke the great physician? The Ruach Hakodesh was to lead man, if man would first know GOD personally in his heart.

In the Old Testament Ruth, Ephraim and Manasseh all were showing the Gentiles entry through Messiah into this faith. It did not mean GOD did not love man, but that His church was just that His chosen church.

In about 32 AD our Palm Sunday for Gentiles, The time of the Hebrews had stopped. The time of the Gentiles began. The Disciples represented a few Jews and could not represent the entire nation of Israel, GOD was emphasizing to the Messianic Jews that the Gospel was now opened to Gentiles, but on the part of disobedience of the Jewish nation.

The mixture in Russian was for the Russian Orthodox church to lead, I believe, since it removed itself from Europeanism proper during the Byzantine Empire. What occurred in Russia was to be a blessing from GOD, because of the almost 6 million Jews in Russia, but man intervened into GOD"s will until an ism took over. There was nothing in Europeanism. Germany too had a chance as a Christian nation to get GOD'S blessing, but chose to follow Europeanism. Without Messiah, The Jews and Gentiles would be thorns to each other. As for the Jews alone they would be thorns to any nation, because we failed as Gentiles to show the way of love. After all the Times of the Gentiles to proselytize the same as Shimon Hashaliach later was told to do by GOD was nearly wasted.

The time of the Hebrews would begin. A remnant, the nation, would be saved to go into the OLAM HABA not seeing death with Messiah ruling from Jerusalem. Would all Jews be saved then? Could all Jews, the elect be saved?

Possibly if to the Jew it would have been presented in a Messianic way then that might have been more in with the will of GOD even though they were a stiff necked people. Transformation is an individual thing, not individualism that Martin Luther taught, but GOD does the saving no matter the human restraint. Was Judas Inscariot a demon and not just demon possessed?

CHAPTER XV

AMERICANISM VS. SCRIPTURE

America removed most "roots" and years before that had removed almost all the "branches". What about inalienable rights? We correlated a position to that of a Second Rome. We were seeing but not believing as a people, as Americans. We gave Most Favored Nation Status to Communist Red China for our own services. MOST in and of itself expresses with highest honor. FAVORED to look upon with such benevolence. NATION, Red China now is anything but a nation as 80% are poor peasants, because of socialism and its run by criminals and thugs. And of course STATUS is to rank as officially recognized. Four words so ludicrous in this sense for any normal person with a brain would see the "tom foolery". Trading bodies for money and Christian ones at that. Our neo-pagan government in action.

The Sudanese also got from Clinton the red, their shed blood carpet treatment. To defend one's own ungodliness, but not fellow believers? Another "Yalta conference", but this time to the sell out of America.

GOD'S family of saints cannot be ignored, if we want GOD'S real blessings and not Satan's materialism. Being that I was part Italian, I know how the Sicilian mob immigrants with Turkish blood had ruined it for the other immigrants in America with their Mafioso, La Cosa Nostra, et cetera. Vendettas, pimpism, drugs, prostitution, child slavery, slave labor, murder, et cetera all culminated from this nefarious Island. What Moslem rivalry lie here?

In the Old Testament from Daniel 2:4 to Chapter 7 is all for the Gentiles and is written by Daniel in Aramaic, Y'eshua's language but translated from the original Hebrew. Daniel was bilingual and not two different people. Chapter 7 had been called the greatest chapter in the entire Bible. In Chapter 2:39-43 of Daniel the power of GOD leaves the Jews and goes to the Gentiles. Between Chapter 2 and Chapter 3 at its beginning was a time period of about 16-20 years. Daniel had to learn the Chaldean language, or the Magi's language. Daniel served 4 kings. King Nebuchadnezzar who he respected, Belshazzar, a grandson who he did not. Darius the Mede and Cyrus the Persian King. Daniel 7-12 are all chapters in prophecy. Daniel had four dreams over 22 years. Each kingdom had a beast which indicated that kingdom's nature. The FIRST BEAST a lion with gold as the head was King Nebuchadnezzer who also had wings. THE SECOND BEAST a bear with silver arms and a breast of silver was Persia (Iran) with 3 ribs; Libya, Babylon (Iraq), Egypt. The THIRD BEAST was a 4 headed monster with brass the metal for the belly which was Alexander the Great in Greece, the great leopard. The FOURTH BEAST had 10 horns and had iron which was Rome. Isaiah 61:1-2 is Messiah's two comings. Chapter 7 "the little horn" is the Antichrist. The language in Chapter 8 changes from Aramaic to Hebrew. The FEAST OF DEDICATION is Hanakah, John 10:22. From March 14, 445 BC-April 6, 39 AD this time period was 69 WEEKS, or 483 years, 173,880 days. Daniel 11:36 is 200 years in the future to 2,000 years in the future. Babylon fell on October 11, 539 BC. The Gentiles are Chapters 1-7 and the Jews are Chapters 8-12. Alexander The Great Hellenized the world. He conquered the civilized world in only 12 years. Again in 144 BC Judas Maccabees is when the oil lasted miraculously for 8 days, hence HANUKAH. With Pharaoh, Passover; Haman. THE FEAST OF PURIM; Epiphanes, THE FEAST OF DEDICATION.

I had remembered that the paganized ACLU in America, the atheistic hereditary synagogue of the Satan lawyers wanted to have freedom from all laws. The Judeo-Christian faith had to keep private because it, too, offended these American Pharisees. One's private was their public life, hence these "Bolsheviks". New York Jewry was notorious for opposing GOD, if they even cared.

What would America become in the final analysis? Enclaves of tribalism and "villages" isolated totally from a national being? This sort of occultic blood line... Could America now escape this BEAST and Europeanism? America maybe, just maybe, could find it's own GOD? Did not our Founders mean to find their own GOD that is the Pilgrims and the Puritans? American Biblicals?

A new nation with it's own personal national GOD, not the one from Europeanism not the Spanish Inquisition of 1492 with anti-Semitism and homosexuality. This monarch, Isabella and Ferdinand had such problems from where else, but Roman Catholicism.

Should George Washington again have chosen a monarch a family of Christians? Christianity by family and not be Greek democracy or Rhodes' republicanism on paper parchment. The "king" George Washington would not have had to please special interest, only his particular view which was GOD given. "Queen" Martha and their children would have extended America by and through Y'eshua. America would have inherited American Christianity, not Europeanism, because the Americans then would be making original history to find their, if you will, American GOD. Immigrants here would have seen the difference and accepted America's GOD and not Europe's and European prejudices, just as Russia had accepted their Russian GOD for 1,000 years. American Biblicals would have retained positions of authority in all walks of life and immigrants would not have brought old luggage from Europe that was totally alien to America in a new land. When one leaves their birthplace, it is not such a good thing to come to a foreign land with old luggage. They relinquish, or at least should, that sovereignty for their old nation and also the language, religion and history, or in whole should want to, or why come to America but possibly to run wild, or for a ready made life of luxury. American Biblicals did not do that and did not have to conform, because assimilation was not needed. Russian Orthodoxy was just that, Russian, not exported to Europe, or imported from Europeanism even though they were a part of the European continent physically, but not spiritually. Why even

Shimon HaShaliach misunderstood GOD'S call for him amongst the Gentiles. "Be as one." GOD had all but closed the door to the Hebrews, until all the Gentiles came, or would come in. was Christianity foreign to our Founders? Only possibly in the sense that they did not and perhaps could not at that time find another land and later in American history refused to work the soil with their own hands, but this should not surprise anyone. The Deists again believed they needed to help GOD in all His ways and went too far in rights and not enough in responsibilities even for themselves. Progression was from George Mason's Bill of Rights not all now unalienable and why need Amendments if it was a Christian Bible that one should follow as in a monarch it could have? Now with so called children's rights rebellion in America did it not have socialism and not children in mind? Civil rights, or superior rights not equal members in Messiah. Did not Negroes have conscience rights? Animal rights followed and what could that possibly mean that man was an animal? What was Adam a nomenclature for? The Bible does not talk about man's rights per se, or his will, but GOD'S will and GOD'S laws. GOD'S rights and grace and His will for man, hence universal freedom. GOD is an authoritarian GOD not a democratic take a vote on it GOD. American Biblicals understand how GOD applied to America not to Europeanism. Americans were to be an individual people, one nation under America's GOD. American Biblicals and Messianic Jewry understood at least for the most part about GOD'S liberty justice and life that one individual at a time had. Were Washington's slaves "indentured servants" as Abraham had which were a part of the family? It was to be the moral idea that set up the foundation for America. Messiah's turning over the tables meant that the moneylenders should barter equally not lend with usurious interest, for Caesar's coins could not be used, only a Hebrew one. "Render unto Caesar the things that are Caesar's and unto GOD the things that are GOD'S." They were not a bank with interest to rob GOD'S temple by making profits or otherwise in the exchange for after all what does a bank produce? Should money be borrowed with interest? Caesar's coins could not be given in the Jewish temple, hence the moneylenders had to exchange coins in Hebrew of equal worth and had to be there, but not for Caesar, or avarice. The moneylenders, or money exchangers let GOD tell them what to do, but Satan told them how to do it.

Later through the centuries consumerism entered Catholicism and more than tithes and offerings, as well as donations took on a different meaning. Caesar again was brought into GOD'S affairs. Many American television mini-series of ministries kept reiterating for only a "donation", or a "contribution of", when the price was always a certain amount of dollars. A price is something that Messiah paid for on the cross. A price is something I would pay not something I would voluntary just give. There must be profit but in the church too amongst men? Tithing became not heart felt but by guilt, indoctrination, follow the leader, or even fashionable profit. Offerings were left go. "The lady gave her last two pence and gave more than all others, because it was her last 2 pence and not her surplus even though the other gave more and also she gave with all her heart." It was Abel's offering not Cain's offering, because Cain gave not his best "first fruits". American ministries on television more of GOD'S money used for mundaneness and selfish purposes and innocent victims too gave and GOD would use their money for His will and not for an organization's will, if an organization can have a will which it cannot.

The Crusades welcomed their form of Christianity like Liberation Theology as today in Israel which is a secular state and not a light unto the nations, but a fighting army, or better yet like in Latin America.

More land means more Jewish deaths by Europeanism. To revolt by religion by blood letting such as is mentioned Latin America. "Those who live by the sword die by the sword." The aggressor must export its wares so sovereignty plays no part in a nation's own GOD. Israel's sovereignty is at stake.

Messiah shed His blood for a most just and perfect love that only GOD could give. This was this grace, or underserved merit. The Ruach Hakodesh does not reform, or perform, but transforms in peace individual by individual into each one's own accountability. Messiah shall set up His kingdom and not Dominion Kingdom Theology Now. Man must, as an individual and as a part of a collective body, find a national way to worship his GOD in the context of no foreign cultures or foreign religions. "What does good have to do with evil?" In this case, "do not do as the Romans do." Faith to a person and a nation should be a personal, national thing. America was not Constantine's state of coerced religion. Christianity does not coerce, but GOD'S will shall be done.

Remember free will is by GOD. The moral idea preceded the state in America, but was it original when the state said, "Let us make ourselves a democratic/republic"? If GOD does not lead, who shall lead, but Satan? Did we let GOD lead?

Rule of law meant the Mosaic Law, the 10 Commandments. With law must come GOD'S grace which would instill in man compassion mercy and pity. Is grace wholesale? A nation's soul must be preserved by honoring it's GOD faithfully through Messiah, hence a Christian nation. Christianity must enter both public, as well as private lives, or else that nation is not a Christian or GOD fearing nation. Atheism, or communism allows a public immoral life, hence privacy is non-existent and a people do not exist as a nation, or as an individual in the way GOD meant them to be.

We as believers are commanded to preach in love GOD'S Word and always to show a faith in action as James says in his Epistle. It is not necessarily free speech that the ACLU is contentious and violent (lies) about, but only when it refers to Messiah GOD and the Father of Abraham, Isaac and Jacob. GOD in the flesh and that a pure form of free speech the Gospel and to worship as a people.

These "Pharisees" and "Sadduccees" want not only atheism, but to gag and totally silence the worship and preaching of Messiah. Who are these sons of Satan and not of Abraham? They are not known personally as GOD'S children, or as even Jews. They are devilish and evil in their spiritual thinking. The more physical a people the more kind of freedom they need. They need much which can become a danger. Not all peoples are the same in this regard. The same as individuals are not. Should freedom be lead by anarchy or totalitarianism? Both have lawlessness in them, or no moral idea. In the first scenario anyone's head tends to come off quicker. The rule of law is gone, and the rule of the fist, like in America's 60's and into the new millennium, was their rule of rebellion, always rebellion, in the second scenario.

Families are non-existent and only a group can one enter the fray, or now the democratic majority. Also families cannot exist, because families have individual relationships as one unit like a nation. There are honored private lives. Homosexuality had nothing private in fact the whole life is obsessed with sexual perversion, or evil sensuality, or carnal love. Everything is exposed. This addiction to sin can only be broken by grace and counseling. "My grace is sufficient for you." Sexuality is sacred only in the Biblical marriage scene for a lifetime between a man and a woman. Sensuality is not agape' love, but is always lust and deviancy no matter what the world says. Children become playthings and not GOD'S intention as children. This mental health issue not treated as such, but is POLITICALLY CORRECT called group, or civil rights. The out care patients are left to themselves to self destruct, but also more importantly left to our or GOD'S children. Hollywood has plenty of these vaudevillian entertainers. There is no sacred intimacy, just infamy.

In Arab nations among the hierarchy especially is homosexuality. The restriction of family by Messiah's way, or the way created by Him is ignored. Mistreatment of all women and girls showed an innately anti-family decorum, hence socialism. Just as the Nazis outlawed school prayer in 1935 and in 1941 all religious instruction was banned in America in 1962 and 1963 by the United States Supreme Court. In Nazi Germany it too was for students, but for students over 14 years of age. No longer crosses were seen anywhere.

The homosexual Butches were the first to persecute the Jews by camp confinement. Only Judeo-Christianity is what these Nazis, sexual deviants feared just as the Soviets did about their

Gulags. It could defeat their atheism one heart at a time, but why did it not? Transformation not reformation and by a man who was anti-Semitic. It took decades to remove GOD from the German people or perhaps centuries. No, it did take centuries, hence the Holocaust with 13 million murdered not killed and not soldiers, but as civilians and citizens. Germany had become a nation possessed and replaced the church with this homosexual Nazism or sexual deviancy. Homosexuality, occultism and drugs have to be included for such barbarism and where does America now stand? Individualism was the word for self-salvation.

In the Book of Revelation at the end of the B'rit Hadasha there are 7 churches. The Messiah sends a letter to each. The first one EPHESUS which lost it's first love, but was not Nicolatian. The second church was SMYRNA where no rebuke is given by the Messiah. The Jews there were a synagogue of Satan not a Temple and were not believers, but Jews only in ancestry. This was the persecuted church. The third church was PERGAMUM the worldly church which accepted the Nicolatioans, or the papacy of Roman Catholicism. This was Satan's throne and the Jews there were anti-Messiah. The fourth church was THYATIRA the paganized church like Ahab's wicked consort. The fifth church was SARDIS, the lifeless church. There were very few believers and it was called by Messiah to wake up. The sixth church was PHILADELPHIA, the missionary church and one of brotherly love. There was no rebuke by Messiah. They kept Messiah's name with vigorous Messianic Jews that won many Jews in the city, but were opposed by other Jews. This was called the "Day of the Lord", or what is known as the TRANSLATED church. The 7th church was LAODICEA, the lukewarm church, the church that ousted their Lord and Savior Y'eshua. There is no commendation for this church. Those are the 7 churches ages and 7 churches for the 7 areas in the Book of Revelation. What a fearsome warning to most all these churches. Sin is contagious and always affects others. We are accountable for what we think, say and do and "we are our brother's keeper." Whether we believe it or not, consequences are always there. When we sin the Law applies to all; ignorance shall be no excuse. GOD'S laws were not meant for groups, but individuals. The Messianic Body was just that, a Body. The Israelites were a people, only one who also had freewill choice. Even though GOD chose them as His People He required more out of them and they had to obey. It is the same today with B'rit Hadasha's Saints. We too have to obey GOD. Grace is not a license to do what we deem, or what we need. With GOD there is always restrictions, because His will is not our will, nor should our will ever exceed His will. "His thoughts are not our thoughts." Innocence was left in the Garden of Eden and since then man needed grace. This innocence was not perfection in man, but environmental perfection. Adam had to simply obey GOD audibly. The B'rit Hadasha did not change obedience itself, or free us to do as one pleases for Adam also had this same freewill along with GOD'S will. Sin was so bad only one time because it was pollution in a then perfect environment and a sin to a perfect GOD. Never was obedience and disobedience changed, but that Messiah's grace would transform us, believing as Adam had not. His responsibilities to obey GOD, BUT GOD was not surprised. Does not GOD give us our faith? Freewill choice, yet He knows our response always. The gift of salvation is free, but is not from government, but from Holiness. This means accepting Messiah's crucifixion, death, burial and resurrection. Who has ever seen the Father? In the Old Testament, and what was there grace, it had to be faith? For without faith one cannot please GOD. "His sheep hear His voice." Abraham pleased GOD by faith. God chose.

Quintessential man would be this beast, or what it leads to when man says, "That he is god." Nephilim to be pure evil.

In the OLAM HABA when Satan is put away will not man sin? Each individual must choose, but there is an elect to obey GOD also. Unrejuvenated procreated man cannot still understand it is in the heart, since sin starts in the mind and yet it is the heart to be transformed, then the mind and back to the heart. "If you confess with your mouth and believe in your heart, you shall be saved." (Romans 10:9-10).

The "thy's" and "thou's" are a foreign English and a foreign religion. It stressed the "I" too much, too easy to reason but not too hard to believe for GOD supplies the faith no matter how small. " His Kingdom come, His will be done" is about GOD, as GOD. We know GOD in Messiah's strength. It is our own sin that needs forgiving for us, but let us now seek His forgiveness by His gift that he gave. If Adam sinned one time and he did, was it not in a specific way that he sinned? Was it not from only one tree that he could not eat? Was there any other way he could have sinned against GOD? Man's senses came into play to do evil and not good. Man was to live in paradise, but now a better promise lies in heaven even though here on earth we must do His will. If Adam would have thought about it and not done it would it still have been sin? The thought of sinning at that time would not have been sin, since GOD knows our thoughts and Adam would not have tasted from the Tree of knowledge. In other words to think of sinning Adam would not have sinned, because he would not have done the physical sin, hence no conscience.

Individual responsibility before free will means accountability to God first always. Rebellion had complicated man's reasoning that is why his heart must be transformed. GOD already knew Adam's decision. The more we become independent from GOD the more destructive we become. The Trinity in Genesis says, "Let us make man in our image." Plural personalities, but one GOD. God is not a respecter of persons, yet he can choose. Who can earn GOD's respect by anything, or work it out? Only by grace unmerited, or undeserved favor that GOD provided through Messiah. "Our body is the Temple of GOD."

In Israel we appeared to be in the church of Philadelphia's translation. Most the Gentiles now came in and soon it felt as though "The Times of the Hebrews" to cross over would begin. Was it near Daniel's 70th WEEK with 69 WEEKS fulfilled? Not all Israelis were believers, even though all were nationals. "Look up for your redemption draws near." Duty to Messiah, family and country and respect for yourself and all others had dissipated.

All this self-esteem or ego to make one feel better, not morally do better.

Growing Generations was giving quadruplets to two homosexuals who were males by in-vitro-fertilization from an unknown woman. Now I could understand why cloning, embryonic stem cell research et cetera would be used for by the enemy. To produce a whole generation of Naziphiles, Jew and Gentile. Even psychiatry with Christian counselors could help, but at this rate it would be unbearable. NAMBLA was celebrating along with the United Nations and the media what had occurred in Nazi Germany, but now in America. With 3-5 years of counseling one could come out straight. According to GOD'S laws and natural order of things this homosexuality is an abomination to GOD. "The rain falls on the just and the unjust."

Woman as Eve wanted to usurp Adam's role. Wife, mother, sister, aunt, grandmother, daughter and niece were all females. Adam was free not to choose wrongly, or why would GOD have admonished him not to? Woman was deceived and Adam was not. He allowed woman, as a companion, to maintain authority over GOD'S audible voice. Adam used Eve as a scapegoat. Did not Pontius Pilate do the same thing?

The 12 male Disciples, the 4 Gospels and all the Epistles plus Revelation were written and directed to man first as head of household. The woman was to be subservient to her husband and her husband to GOD.

The Israelite kings from Israel and the Kingdom of Judah were just that earthly kings and in the Davidic Kings there was even one interruption and that was by a wicked queen who had no lineage to David. Yes, women add much compassion in the world perhaps more than man, but woman are to hold no authority in GOD'S church. This is an authoritarian GOD, not a democratic pick-and-choose GOD. Man today, as Adam had, did not take his responsibility seriously. "The spirit is willing but the flesh is weak."

Back to the family issue of a devoted wife and mother at home with her children and bonding as only a mother can in a home environment. The husband must also bond especially to his sons and see a father's role, and where the mother must relinquish to the father the sons or son at an early age so that this male child sees his father and the FATHER and can relate to a personal relationship as does the Father and the Son. This is agape love.

Our family was getting older, but much quicker an ambience of evil that surrounded all of us. "Be anxious for nothing." Abraham and Jacob were seven years old and home schooling was showing a plus in their lives. Marie and I continued as always in our faith, but now with more concern for the younger people, or children especially. Most children did not have a childhood, and it was not through poverty that all this had occurred.

When I had left America years ago 80% of the American people got some kind of socialized welfare. These included farmers, teachers, professors, postal workers, AFDC, deadbeat dads, the retired, the National Endowment for the Arts, Medicare, Medicaid, Soviet day care, infanticide facilities, politicians, college grants and loans, doctors, lawyers, corporation executives, government employees, government pension, banks, et cetera. All of the above had received free handouts from other taxpayers and not from private enterprise, and more were asking for more, plus new ones were added. Government said, "Come to America for free handouts." Americans emulated the rich and well educated by not working for a living. The taxpayers were getting something in return for their money: more and more socialism. At least with socialism everything was taken care of, even one's death, premature or not. This was the redistribution of money, but not of wealth. Private property would be next. Collective farming and day care could not possibly be referring to capitalism. What was capital in the hands of "children"? People who had never had money now had it and it was destroying them. It was like giving a small child a $50 bill to go to the mall and spend it as they liked just to get them out of the house. These were the so called millionaires. Pure materialism or, in other words socialism for all in America.

In order to establish a more perfect union -- but what kind of union and why a union? One can easily remember the Union of …. Yes, the Clintonites borrowed from Lenin quite a shortsighted idea such as the propagation of cinema for propaganda. Susan Sarandon's defense of the PLO and its terrorists in Israel, generals on pensions (except Haig and in so called leadership; Powell's anti-Israelis' view; Kissinger's (which one) pro-communist's view towards Red China and his business associates replacing the church with the US Supreme Court's POLITICALLY CORRECT agenda as well as the entire Democratic party; the New Age Nazi agenda; inciting the darker "races" in society.

Housewives short of housework but not of feminism, adolescents running wild and emulating Hollywood and the rich and well educated; socialism, capitalism into socialism; et cetera. – this survival of the misfittest had inundated America with so much decadence that there was no longer a foundation holding the nation up. Now it had spread like cancer or AIDS everywhere. The all inclusive cornucopia of languages and cultures that worked hard to oppose the Judeo-Christian faith.

Yes, with that of "eat, drink and be merry" became the Western "Babylon" with "social" Christianity a kind of pretend to play church. For a while it worked, but then something happened. The charade was over and the party was late, but the other "Party" knew what to do with the event.

In America, race, not always human or humane, was used erroneously as "race" to promote group thought by appearance first, then by age, and then by sexuality or sensuality.

Did not fellow Negroes own other Negroes as slaves and in most instances were very brutal and fought for the Confederacy? These Negro slaveholders had many assets to lose. If they lost the war, it was as before. If one was a poor Negro, then slavery. Slavery was not "race"-based, it was the poor in slavery first, not "race" alone. Lincoln said, "We must preserve the union." Why? Is not a civil war the worst kind of war? He knew full well that whites had white slaves earlier and that Negroes had other Negroes as slaves. Our public socialized schools had made slavery a black and white issue and not slavery itself, which is always an evil depending, of course, on which side one happens that day to be caught on that day. This was surely, even then as now in its earliest stages of so called "civil rights" socialism or "as long as I was not one", such as in infanticide or a pedophiled child who had been murdered. Slavery of all "races" was in fact always a crime which could also include pimpism, prostitution, drug running, et cetera and their use of young children to addict them to drugs and to indecency. Man's human nature (meaning it is not skin-based but heart based) was to most always promote slavery and its evils. Even in one's own family in America one could see brother prostituting his own sister and mother and hustling his own daughter and breaking her virginity. Europeanism through avarice and vice, plus laziness did not invent slavery, it legitimized it in the so called civilized world. It carried this virus to America and infected each Negro in one way or another and every white as well as all the other "races". Then Negroes, of course, in Africa played a part, and Negroes in America got on the bandwagon. Negroes in America had Negro slaves as well as whites having both. The first Negroes to America were like Russian peasants or serfs who had no education and were brought to America as early as 1619. By 1790 one fifth of the US population was or were slaves, or 20%. In 1860, four million Negroes had been slaves. Also, in 1790, 25% of American families had slaves, but by 1850 it was down to 10%. American Indians owned slaves which were once free Negroes. In 1830, more than 3500 Negroes owned more than 10,000 Negro slaves. In the South, one half million Negroes were free in 1860.

Free Negroes could buy property and did such skills as carpentry, masonry, tailors, butchery, shoemaking, blacksmiths. In 1640 a Negro man named Anthony Johnson owned Negro slaves. Virginia courts upheld this, and the US Supreme Court in 1833 affirmed Negroes to enslave other Negroes. Why not? The rich and well educated did it. Up until the Civil War white Americans, Negroes and American Indians had legal rights to own Negro slaves. It was bad enough whites did it, now blacks did it too; hence "black" America started, instead of the American Negro. Another "black" slave owner, William Ellison, owned slaves and was very brutal with them even though, yes, he once was a slave himself. Incredible? Not really. Human nature has not changed since Adam's fall. Mr. Ellison learned well the technique from the rich and well educated. Ellison sided with the Confederacy. What else? Yankee Negroes fought Rebel Negroes in the Civil War. The conclusion is that human nature and not "race" is the thing that is not kind, and that John Locke's Enlightenment, capitalism, the contribution that the West took on along with Europeanism and not solely "race" based. Why should one do heavy labor when they had slaves to do it? This is where Marxism would work on America because it made the proletarian understand that physical labor with mental insight is what needed to be done away with. But they only charaded it so that socialism's slavery would come into being, and it did. The chains one would never break. Would the Industrial Revolution make a difference as to physical human labor?

The same occurred in Russia. The rich and the elite and the sophisticated said one thing in such sincerity, but in their own lives lived another diametrically opposed to the Judeo-Christian faith.

In 1807 in England, Evangelical Christians did fight to abolish slavery and won. After this slavery, Darwinism came along and did say in essence that Negroes were an earlier form of human specie, or why else the idiocy the Neanderthal man, or Nebraska man (a pig's part), et cetera? Bringing this to America, good old evolution could possibly start a revolution eventually in the 60's and thereafter.

All men are GOD'S creation from Adam and made in the image of GOD, Messiah physically and spiritually.

Why not teach only the truth about Creation? Why also the lie? Would it show how diverse America was especially by emphasizing the "races ", and their different appearances and not that man was one that is the human race? Who were the primates? Was it not the rich and well educated?

It took GOD 6 days to finish. The Anglophiles again promote intellectual universal slavery that is to say it is only some of the human species such as the darker " races ", with Russians too who else, or why would Darwin more than insinuate that physical appearance had to be his " pseudo-science " that those humans different from him were less than human and why bury Karl Marx in one country that condones this type of idiocy? Even Stalin read Darwin and see how much Mr. Stalin accomplished with over 30,000,000 million murders. Darwin though was fascinated with the eye and how it worked and was amazed by it's function.

In 1863 the Emancipation Proclamation along with the 13th, 14th and 15th Amendments had given the Negro slaves full rights, or did they? Also on April 30, 1863 President Abraham Lincoln after becoming a Christian, one does not grow into it grace, designated the day a National Day of Prayer and Humiliation. Also when presented in Baltimore with a Bible President Lincoln said, " The Bible is the best gift GOD has ever given to man. " this was an excerpt from the President's " Reply to Loyal Colored People of Baltimore upon Presentation of a Bible. " President Reagan in 1983 called that year The Year of the Bible. In the same year in the Congressional Records it lists the 10 Commandments on February 2, 1983. The Mayflower Compact invoked the name of GOD and said their journey was for the Glory of GOD and the advancement of the CHRISTIAN FAITH. The above rights should have always been there. GOD given. Did some United States' citizens somewhat belated believe that other Americans did not know that the other side knew that they were human beings and Americans who too had a heart, mind and a soul? Common sense came to be allocate private property to some of the "race". If not private property and they were not then how comes private property was given to them, but the " Pharisees " swindled them?

Does not socialism treat all human beings like property of the state and as objects as if people do not have should? Yes, oh yes, this was not oligarchy, but a democratic/republic, but for whom? For all?

Maybe too many English "thee's, thou's and thy's" were self-serving and part of egoism?

Later on another issue came to the fore and it was firearms, the Second Amendment, the right to keep firearms in case of government tyranny. But would that not be another "Bolshevik Revolution"?

In 1878 again the United States Tribunal Court ruled that socialized egalitarian segregation became another wonderful judicial law. Would this have made human beings human? So much for constitutions and where were those all impressive unalienable rights? The American Negro, not " black ", nor African-American, but American Negro still could not be a human being and civil rights did not address this, but that superior rights is what was needed.

Fiasco poll taxes, literacy tests, all white primaries and now all socialists' primaries. Segregation infected funding by " race ", such as in hospitals, schools, et cetera. When the American negro for the most part was humble and Christian America was silent about the freedom with the land, but when socialism and Communists promised one " food and water " like in Red China the rich and well educated felt it was their obligation to support " black " not Negro organizations. It always had to do with racism in some form, all socialisms do that.

This had nothing to do with life, liberty and justice, rule of law, or universal freedom, but everything to do with quotas, affirmative action, et cetera of which the latter all could be reversed, the former could not so easily. Another slavery called civil rights was installed so that reversals could be made at any time. They were written in granite. Oh, how the rich and well educated sold this bill of goods, perishable for freedom and land lovers to instigate and agitate animosity and some had more than others between the " races " which lead into other kinds of enemies and opponents such as the young vs. old, rich vs. poor, male vs. female, amongst their own "race".

Their agenda was not freedom for all. It was recruitment to overthrow the entire government, but why do that when in so many years they would be in power and then they would know what to do? Already America was sold to the highest bidder. Americans wanted this "social" justice would work for it would be different than in Russia. This philosophy of world utopia needed another chance, but in America? It was called utopianism with the same WASP in control as before only with government called "civil rights democracy". it would be like the POLITICALLY CORRECT Black Panthers with a new "black" racism that was almost innately tribal. As long as one was "black", they were recognized by government and some churches and mosques joined in with the rich and well educated. Government though would not support the right of private property, but their right to riot, revolt and seek revenge which would eventually leave no other haven for the American Negro to go in the world.

This tokenism would be used for all it was worth oh, how much Paul Robeson wanted the East Moscow Communists to accept him like they later would Angela Davis. No matter this sincerity they would not. Was it "raced" based, or ideology? The Western Socialists, "but what if" as their insecurity and if not wholesale by government, it could always be given away at anytime but if it was real individual freedom such as private property well that was another thing. No, that would never do that is to own it and individual thought could never be controlled by this pied piper. The Negro family or what was left of it after the Great Society was decimated and it had to be kept that way by the elites. The foundation of any civilization that is GODLY is the institution of family. The elite needed more slaves to do their work in fact they needed a whole society. Without the majority first to deceive how would this movement get started? It was not unalienable rights, but government decreed civil rights which would appear to most American Negroes, or now "black" and "Africans " that it was the rich and well educated that was going to give them their financial not universal, but group freedom that was so long awaited for. But if it was group and not individual freedom was that still not racism? It was already there, but only needed to be egotistically inserted into government, business, sports, education by Commissar officials. What elite Ralph Bunches proclaimed one in a million like Hamilton Jordan? These were the "black" belts that mastered over "race" and not for the Human Race.

Certain "black" leaders had nefarious dealings with the Communist Party, or the "social" justice of the peace, as well as illicit sexual liaisons edging on the border of divorce, if married. Others had openly admitted to raping women. He said, "I became a rapist first to my own women then to others" hence deadbeat dads had its start, but with a criminal act. Others emulated and succeeded with government approval. The rich's children turned soured and rebelled, but somehow they would get a billion dollar reprieve to inherit and possibly more if they could destroy another person's life. For after all, if the rich served why not all? Then an athlete was acquitted for being "black". His attorney needed bodyguards, but why? DNA was overruled and "social" justice was served. Even one "black" juror raised his fist like an old not New Black Panther that he used to be. Why was he not screened out? The MC of ceremonies had not done her job. There were 9 blacks, or "blacks", 2 Hispanics and one "white" elderly lady who had to decide "in defense of the terrorist ".

The most infamous was Louis Farrakkhan the "black" Moslem and virulent anti-Semitic racist supported by Howard University and sponsored by Brian Lamb's C-SPAN. " A mind is a terrible thing to waste. "

Unions came into play with coerced contributions from it's own members. No scabbing here. Before anyone can say I am a non-proletarian, I need to distinguish one thing and that is collective workshops do not work.

The Jablonski family paid with their very lives because of Tony Boyle and the Teamster's Union. More time off, more vacations, more benefits, shop stoolies, or stewards but no quality and here is where the word quality is apropos' such as quality work and quality control. In the car manufacturing plants, some as big as small towns there was a "dealer" (not car) in all kinds of pills as such. Nothing about quality workmanship, reliability sobriety, conscientiousness, honesty, et cetera. It was again group mentality vs. corruption and party ideology and dues owed to a POLITICALLY CORRECT party and in this case for most workers who were highly ignorant, it would be okay. They never had it so financially good ever, appeal to self and fruition would occur. Mass production by the amoeba mass. Higher wages not really, for much toys, such as chain saws, pick up trucks, booze, drugs, guns, gambling, illicit sex, abnormal sex, et cetera. " The one with the most toys wins. " it was the old " me myself and I." Now this was mundane man's trinity. Sentimentality with no normalcy. Their children would pay dearly through immature idiocy.

Even in public schools movies were shown without parental permission in class such as FRIDAY THE 13TH. Substitute high school teachers were male strippers in the evenings. Even day care for high school girls was provided so that it would encourage them to have illicit sex with the public school's approval. Yes companies were even buying life insurance policies for their employees without their approval and knowledge.

In 1973, no not Blackman's Roe vs Wade but another infamous event, or statement, or false proclamation was made by none other than a Harvard Professor who said, "Every child in America entering school at age 5 is mentally, yes mentally ill, because of belief in GOD, respect for parents, respect for some of our Founders, et cetera" and this professor was American born.

Maybe this nutty professor with poison Ivy needs psycho-therapy or psycho-analysis, or needs his head to be shrunk by a secular "head shrinker". A repeat of this insanity of "GOD IS DEAD" from another diseased brain like Nietzche, a homosexual deviant and Nazi who had contracted syphilis. Another fine institution UCLA contributed to revisionism in text books by not mentioning Paul Revere at all, or Robert E. Lee, one mention of the Gettysburg Address, many mentions of the homosexual anti-Semitic KU Klux Klan, Harriet Tubman, and Tip "the bottle" O'Neil. Jonas Salk was not mentioned. The atheist Albert Einstein and the agnostic Mark Twain were mentioned along with the occult dabbler Alexander Graham Bell. America's only natives like Sabras were Native Americans and not Americans, which meant America was tribal not national and was non-inclusive, that is to the inclusion of a majority of egotistical individuals from the Far East and not all were Orientals, nor intellectuals, meaning they had not GODLY morals but were well educated and rich otherwise. It was multiculturalism "Yugoslavian" style with a "Tito" in the White House most of the time who also did not take orders from Peking or Moscow. Also Ebonics or "black" racial slang meant to offend was introduced into the party, or Party. Hollywood's vaudevillian tactics came into play here. All to disrupt, mesmerize the young and simple minded, confuse the Senior Citizen, which was not too hard to do, separate whatever families were left, discourage many Americans who now appeared not native enough but only aliens at least to America's ideals. Our children would be piped into this Pied Piper of "garbage stew" by most baby boomers who never grew up or never stood up for anything that was moral. This format of so called savage colonialism would be called anything but by it's real name, as in Woodstock where the youth smoked pot and were not arrested and slept on homeowners' lawns, but yet a man selling T-shirts was arrested.

The Democratic Party endorsed the drug lords in Colombia, because they opposed helping the Colombian government. The blue and the gray started to appear brown in more than one way. Who was not the master of his own home? Government with a capital G was trying harder. It became almost normal in 1973 -- there is that infamous year again -- for homosexuality to be "good". Just like that, or so it appeared, as if schizophrenia was a figment of one's imagination and not a chemical imbalance in the brain, or cancer was just a hypochondriac's paranoia and nothing more, and of course with universal health precautions and AIDS awareness. If only there really had been.

Why was there no universal blood test in any American hospitals for this deadly and lively in the "heir " virus? Privacy? POLITICAL CORRECTNESS? Even the butcher, Castro, had isolation for people with AIDS. Also the Legionnaires' Disease was air and water borne and could incapacitate the elderly and the sick and even be fatal to them.

In Colorado in 1996, 53% of the citizens, a majority nonetheless as far as I still knew, but still scary at such a slight margin, voted though in favor of Amendment 2 which said, "No special or superior status for lesbians, bisexuals, pedophiles, homosexuals". Of course I am paraphrasing, but then a great tribulation occurred and the leviathan opened it's mouth and said, "Sodom and Gomorrah could be rebuilt and a 6-3 vote by judicial fiat." So it struck down a state's voters' referendum. "States shall receive all the powers not specifically mentioned in the US Constitution and not given to the federal government." The only disability that would not be addressed was that of a mental origin called homosexuality and also posed a problem for procreation, but not a lack of the AIDS virus or child pedophilia. Heaven forbid! How strange that should have by passed these robed jurists! Of course 47% voted for Nazism in the state unknowingly.

Thomas Jefferson, a Deist was in France when the US Constitution was written. No Danbury Baptist Letter here to open and propagandize as fact in our official documents by the ACLU. Jefferson believed in no Trinity like Senator Orrin Hatch. How could he not believe? But then again he did own slaves right that is Jefferson? The Ruach Hakodesh is here and has been since Messiah ascended. The rich and well educated can explain it? Was there no original sin, no virgin birth, no resurrection and ascension and no infallibility of Scripture? Even Christians and Jews in name only would almost render this much. Was there Judeo-Christian morals, or only metaphysics and reasoning alone? Why were some people acting like there was a Holy GOD and not just mimmicking with motions like politicians always do?

Why had the Party's choice, Angela Davis a "black" Communist had Gary Nash another comrade to organize the Angela Davis Defense Committee and who had then written from UCLA the standards for a revision of historical perspective of America in 1992 be allowed?

Alexander Solzhenitsyn, the Russian Christian historian had said all they heard about in the Soviet Union was about this poor poor Angela Davis (forget about the LA judge) for months on end and without stopping.

Some Hungarian peasants and dissidents had pleaded for her to help them against Communist brutality.

Her response, "You get what you deserve." Now this is the true color of all Communism. Now higher education has rewarded one of it's own by giving her a full professorship at the University of California and guess what subject it is in? History. "In defense of the terrorists" (Alexander Solzhenitsyn) and by our own government officials.

In California some firefighters start fires, yes arsons, because they only get paid as firefighters when fighting fires. How diabolical that provision must have been to legislate, or unionize in the wacko state of California?

In Europe a Soviet bloc country at the time that a famous individual was in part mainly responsible for the ... Of course he spoke but in broken English and I could have misinterpreted what he said.

Mail searching after 9/11 was American approved by 40%, 75% approved of neighborhood video surveillance, 62% random car searches, 52% approved road blocks to search vehicles and the Pentagon was initiating a new computer system to follow Moslem terrorists instead of deportation and internment camps. This was government's way to be Big Brother by excuse of "it has to be done". Also wiretapping could be done by a non-federal judge and it could include more then one phone and for any one time and all in the name of Islamic Jihad by the way which had no symbol. The main cities Mecca, Medina and Jerusalem started in the 7th Century, et cetera. Tony Blair was Clinton's protegé and supporter of cameras and approved them. In England no one opposes the government and America it's tail would follow. Also on February 14, 2002 the House of Representatives passed the campaign finance reform BILL which violates the First Amendment. This legislation states that no individual, or group can extrapolate on the politician's record within 2 months of a general election, not a primary. Only the media and the politicians would be allowed to make political speeches. Even publishing the truth could be punished by incarceration. Any US Senator could launch a campaign to revoke the Second Amendment and if a conservative private organization spoke out within 60 days of Election Day, they could be guilty of a federal crime. These laws were to protect the socialists, anti-American incumbents, especially in New York State and Massachusetts. Any corporate advocacy group could be banned from advertising 30 days before a primary and 60 days before a general election all electronic communications, including the Internet. Big Media Corporations would be exempt. And who were these? Viacom, Disney, AOL, Time-Warner and General Electric.

The war on terrorism after 9/11 can be restricted in 3 ways as Benjamin Netanyahu had said. First there must be moral clarity which means that terrorism is always evil like the PLO and Hamas and they are never to be equated as so called "freedom fighters". Terrorists always attack the innocent and the defenseless. The second is strategic clarity which means attack, or shut off any sovereign state that supports, funds, or gives refuge to them. The third principle is for victory. GODLY morale and GODLY laws supercede, or always are before any totalitarianism of any kind Cuba, Iraq, Iran, Saudia Arabia, Lebanon, Syria, Egypt, Libya, Afghanistan, Peking, Moscow, North Korea, Mexico, Red China, et cetera. None of the above are free lands, or free cities.

Now the New Age United Nations with it's Nazi NAMBLA had come full swing and government by the governments, businessmen style. How comforting that was to know that through the UN and Washington DC had confiscated for self, or owned 80% of Nevada, two thirds of Idaho and Utah, the Mormon State, one half of Oregon, Wyoming and Arizona and California, one third of Colorado and Montana. A back door approach to environmentalism-ecologyism, while Americans lived it up in the East and wined and dined. There is no life, infanticide, liberty, the UN, or private property, environmentalism. Jefferson's original wording again was private property and not "pursuit of happiness".

Big corporations, Hollywooders, and Pulitzer-Hearst news were opponents of private property for others, especially in the West from the 100th Meredian to the Cascade Range (although they owned a museum in San Diego made mostly out of solid gold objects).

Celebrities such as Carole King, John Oates and Daryl Hall of Private Eyes had gone public by contributing their talents to stop all logging and even their song's lyrics one could hear of Big Brother. Too much physical labor to endure called hard work and real work. Local and state governments do not own the land. "All rights not specifically given, or mentioned in the Constitution go to the states." So much for Constitutional government. One story that stood out in the entire West was about a man named John Shuler who in SELF-DEFENSE, yes SELF-DEFENSE, shot and killed a bear and was CHARGED, yes CHARGED, by an ADMINISTRATIVE LAW JUDGE, what else with a $7,000 fine, because he broke the Endangered Species Act. But for the animal? Talk about inordinate affection. Incredible not really but insane? Yes. You decide animals included? Was this not more animal rights? This was the FIRST TIME EVER IN LEGAL HISTORY THAT CRIMINAL NOT CIVIL LAW IN SELF DEFENSE STANDARD WAS APPLIED TO AN ANIMAL. No not the man, but the ANIMAL! Karl Marx from the English grave.

Greenpeace and the Sierra Club, both New Age organizations, are deeply concerned, you bet, about your private property, or should I say, as they do, ENVIRONMENTALISM.

Mankind, it has been said "is the biggest menace to the face of this earth", the Discovery Channel.

Also "mankind is the biggest blight on the earth" Sounds more like Karl Marx. Other phrases such as, "6 MILLION (REALLY 13 MILLION) DIED IN CONCENTRATION CAMPS, BUT <u>6</u> MILLION BROILER CHICKENS WILL DIE THIS YEAR IN SLAUGHTER HOUSE." Get ready for the hoarding of New Age food. Or, "THE DEATH OF YOUNG IN WAR IS

UNFORTUNATE, BUT NOT MORE SERIOUS THAN THE TOUCHING OF MOUNTAINS AND THE WILDERNESS AREAS BY HUMANKIND." Apropos for a John Denver's TAKE ME HOME WEST VIRGINIA.

Maybe Randy Weaver, an ex-Green Beret, was shot at by Reno thugs because of his military hero stature. His wife and 14-year-old son were murdered in cold blood. His son caught these thugs shooting his dog and reacted as any normal 14-year-old boy would and then ran up the hill. Janet Reno could not be found; neither could the Japanese sniper who also showed up at WACO.

Why would a Green Beret betray his own country? We knew Clinton had in 1973 and thereafter and ever since and was seen by 6 Congressmen and the wives in Moscow going to the Kremlin by invitation only.

Who are these monsters? We cannot call them that for to do so would give them an excuse to do and say just what they did and now others are doing in daily life as if they did not have the ability to reason, or reasoning alone was the answer. To do so would be to remove them from the human race and categorize them into the animal world which could, or would be false, but yet they appear as such, or worse for animals do not reason, but rely only on instinct and have not done what these men have done along with Stalin, Trotsky, Lenin and Hitler. They loathe mankind just as Karl Marx and Engles did. The Nuremburg Trials were all about man's inhumanity to his fellowman and not about legendary monsters and, or animals. It was to sentence and judge what these evil and vile men did to their straight fellow man, but the Orthodox Jews first, because of their faith in an Old Testament. GOD and His Law and their stand against sexual deviancy. It was also to show the world that justice had to be served and show evil for what it really was and hopefully have repentance for their evil deeds. The Orthodox German-Jew controlled the media, but the German officials refused to expose this high official sex scandal and so two major journalists by the names of Samuel Igra and Harden did so eventually bringing down Nazism on all the Jewish people first in Germany and then elsewhere, plus 7 million Gentiles.

As man we are all accountable to GOD, each one of us. We have a soul, a cerebral cortex in our brain where all reasoning is done. Animals have neither and were created as a separate species by GOD. The creation was to be enjoyed and not worshipped as New Agers do.

It was once said by a very famous Russian author in the 19th Century, "The Germanic people were in actuality very ignorant and depressing and not too bright people" and history I believe has confirmed this with two World Wars.

What people, an entire nation, would allow homosexuality to flourish in the nation or put people in ovens, or spread now AIDS in America, or think as a unit for the non-sovereignty in the nation they happen to be in and with no compassion, or their follow the leader mentality, or go along with the winner, or I must rule it over you and yet be so squeamish about manhood and fatherhood in the home? To cover up a sexual deviancy scandal by the German elites is one thing, but to again knowing full well what was happening in their own country is beyond comprehension. Somewhat like America had done also. One would have thought they would have upheld normal sexuality and love of their fellow man after all this was the home of Protestantism. Nazism did declare openly like the Soviet Union did that it's people were slaves. Also if Germany's Wilhelm would not have helped Trotsky and Lenin financially as well as England and America the Revolution might have failed in Russia. Nationality not only is based on one's origins, but also one's loyalties. To equate Communism with the Russians is a racist view. In America evil was covert which meant that evil would spread and the people would become more corrupt, but when evil is out in the open then the people regenerate to overcome that evil. There appeared to never be any remorse on the part of this nation. Maybe Stalin knew this and decided on a two part Germany to subdue their warriorlike aggression. Had not Nazi Germany inherited by choice India's swastika and their Masonic Arab Patrol or was that part vice versa? This "Aryan" from India was also part of the New Age reincarnation mumble jumble of Shirley McLaine, John Denver and ex-Senator Hatfield in America. It is dangerous and it was all occultic this worship of Satan, or Wotan. Both Germans and Indians at least in America had that same touch of arrogance and coldness with hardly any regard for benevolence. Ghandi had already sold out her people to the Soviets before her death and the West gave India nuclear power.

Wages and private property are one's individual wealth. Socialism does not promote either one, nor can it provide for either one. Wages are something one works for at a fair labor price and not by government's dictate of the minimum wage fiasco and for work done properly and on time properly and of course waitresses need not apply for this utopian "Minimum Wage." Unions are not needed, if capitalism is all that it is suppose to be.

There is this gullible Americanism that listens to such garbage as Atmospheric or New Age music. This is the coming of the Antichrist. Demonic activity is increasing more and more in America and in the world. Demons even clinging onto believers on the outside and being usually believers who uphold their testimony for GOD. Witchcraft as one man from the Congo termed it "garbage stew" with beats summoning the demons. Rock n' roll and this hard rapper song and New Age Music. Whenever one hears this they can usually see how the occupants in a house, a car, or when they walk as to how they conduct themselves and how they dress and especially how immoral they live in most cases. Usually alcohol, drugs, illicit sex, violence, noise and no peace accompany all of this evil. If one plays music from the 40's, 50's, 60's, 70's, 80's, 90's, et cetera and takes each decade individually...

One week one can easily discern how distorted and violent each gets with each passing decade, until total insanity with Wotan worship and the occult, drugs, alcohol and sacrifices and not always animal with much more from the very pit of Hell.

Our government in America instituted reforms to destroy agriculture, farm land, the forests, humans and yes even the animal world; hoarding land and destroying it, so that there would be no drinking water, foodstuffs and even clothing and shelter. Preventing farmers from growing crops, raising livestock, loggers from supplying building materials, as well as no real paper products. Unnatural destruction of our American land by government started with the Clinton Administration. The New Age was not only a subversion of a nation, a free people, but of GOD Himself who shall not be mocked. We are to take care of the animal world in the priority that human beings always come first. Insects are not animals, but a different species. Man was not the problem alone but his worship of false idols and ideologies, instead of to an Almighty GOD in the present Messiah.

Israel once had a strong leader named Ariel the lion of GOD. He was not Messianic, but would suffice for now. "Praying for the peace of Jerusalem "was an ambivalent thing, knowing that GOD was allowing this city to be where the Antichrist would make his throne. Israel's enemies of course one could not be for because socialistic Islam had a deathwish to destroy Jerusalem and all Jews. Yet Israel would rise by evil intent by a Nephilim Jewish leader with all of Satan's powers and would come out of probably Europe to deceive not only Israel, but all the nations. The 10 Nation European Confederacy would present this Hellish impostor as a messiah and who would at first bring stability to that part of the world. The battle ground was forming for the second 3 and one . . half year period, when all Hell would break loose with Israel as a non-participant. World War I and II would not be or had not been like this real World War. Just as Stalin hated Russia, so the Antichrist hated Israel and Clinton hated America.

"Satan came to seek and destroy, devouring about like a roaring lion." This roaring was to trigger man's freewill to do evil. All believers are like sheep and need a Shepherd. They go astray, get lost, or fall down and need to be literally picked up. Satan's roaring was just that. Messiah had defeated the works of the devil on the Cross.

The real wealth of any nation is always spiritual, but the necessity to barter has always been land to own, or private property, if one so chooses. Israel was GOD'S private property from the Euphrates River to the Egypt River which included all of

Jordan. Abraham got to choose his own land from GOD. Abraham took the lesser part, but GOD made it flourish while Lot took Sodom and Gomorrah the better part at that initial time.

With government in the job business, socialism in America took hold and nothing was said, because the wages and benefits were usuriously high as opposed to the private sector and one could not be fired in this Union. It is all mediocrity.

"Anything with government is mediocre" was the statement made by Dr. DeBakey.

All capital was wasted in Arab oil, foreign hostile countries, government approved. The rest was what appeared to most Americans as a nice round sum. Government would not stop, even murder, but endorse it. Only socialism, or an oligarchy does that does it not and of course some "democracies"? Government was in everybody's business, except for what they were intended to do and we had no elder statesman anywhere, even including the White House and in fact least of all. What had they really known about the experience of life? With each decade officials became younger and younger. These were the whippersnappers in business, education and religion also. When 9/11 occurred the damage had already been done by the Clinton Administration. Everyday in his tenure meant more socialism and anti-American sentiment here and abroad.

Even the demons shudder at the name of Messiah. The Angelic world understands what warfare is all about, it is man who must see more judgment, or see it to the end, or even see miracles of faith to be convinced that there is a just and Holy GOD.

Nuclear warheads were computer controlled so principalities would play a vital role. It was not in man's hands any more. Chernobyl, or a Wormwood had occurred in the Soviet Union. This was only a touch of the iceberg. Even America had it's meltdowns on atomic energy that could release Alpha, Beta and Gamma Rays that could penetrate 7 feet of solid steel. Dr. William Teller described briefly how during a nuclear holocaust electric and gasoline motors shut down, magnetic force fields are altered and repelled and water is boiling hot.

The New Age was barbaric and involved in: astrology, Ouji boards, psychic readings, tarot cards, hypnotism, Dungeons and Dragons, superstition, luck, chance, gambling, the occult, animal and human sacrifices to Wotan, ESP, transcendental meditation, acupuncture, holistic healing, out of the body experiences, seances, white and black witchcraft and magic, clairvoyance, UFO's, astral projections, prestidigitation, defying death, crystal ball gazing, levitation, horoscopes, Masonic chants, Mormonism, Jehovah Witnesses, pseudo-schizophrenia, demonic activity, health food stores, New Age books, music, false resurrections and healings, artificial anything, et cetera.

In Revelation the Father is holding a scroll that nobody can open with names written on both sides. Only Messiah though could open it. There are 24 Elders: 12 Old Testament Saints and 12 B'rit Hadasha Saints. No one shall ever see the Father even in heaven only shall they see the Son. The angels have no gender and hence do not procreate and neither shall man after a New Heaven and a New Earth. The 4 Creatures are angels with eyes on them. The 7 Bowls are GOD'S messengers to do His work and have a hierarchy. As the present became the past as well as into the future one could see the antagonisms of buffer zones with different languages and cultures, but the same one system to have to deal with in the economic sense, if one wanted to remain alive. No one could hardly bypass this economic system without being ostracized from almost life itself. Yet so many diverse and different and heathen cultures that did not assimilate with Judeo-Christianity nor could they. Even stronger buffer zones were in place to separate in an apartheid manner. This made networking even more powerful. Divide and conquer village by Hillary village.

Satan was promoting disorder and evil upon the world scene and America would not be spared. Envy, envy, envy was promoted and if one could see it, it had to be believed, if one was a non-believer.

The 7 SEALS OF GOD in Revelation are an omen of things to come upon the face of the earth and some of the 4 HORSEMEN are out now. The FIRST SEAL is the FIRST HORSEMEN in the white horse which deceives everyone to think it is Messiah, but it is the Antichrist. Israel is deceived as a nation. The SECOND SEAL in red indicating world Communism and blood and wars and is the SECOND HORSEMAN. The THIRD SEAL is the THIRD HORSEMAN in black representing famine and pestilence already in Africa and China and elsewhere. The FOURTH SEAL is the FOURTH HORSEMAN in pale and represents death on the earth, probably one third of the population. The FIFTH SEAL is the martyrs of Messianic Jews who die in the Tribulation period. The SIXTH SEAL is the world government of the Antichrist in Jerusalem.

One of Satan's direct temptations, but Messiah answered these three out in the wilderness to refuse Roman Catholicism. "Man does not live by bread alone, but by every word that proceeds from the mouth of GOD."

The West glorifies food, the East does not. In Red China the Communists gave 80% of the people who are peasants food and water or bread and water and that sufficed. The East does not need our capitalism, only more time that is in Peking.

People such as Alexander Haig, yes the General and Henry Kissinger opened Pandora's Box into Red China and now the leviathan is more hungry for power than ever the Soviets were. Our weakness is their strength. After capitalism comes socialism. Armand Hammer supported the Soviets, but not the Russian peasants or people and he did it for pride. Red China shall be 10 times worse to deal with then the Soviets were.

In one Indian (India) village alone they killed or murdered 7,999 females and allowed one birth of the female gender over a period of time and the rest all boys they let live. Maybe that is why Bill Gates went there as a billionaire?

One young Jewish girl went to New York City with her father to worship in a Reformed Synagogue. Looking down into the front row this young Jewish girl told her dad to look at something despicable and beyond belief.

She said to her father, "Look dad, now how can a young Jewish girl like me find a nice young Jewish boy?"

Ira Glasser, the German-Jew more German than Jew contends he is of a Polish background, but then again homosexuality was legalized in Poland, the German Democratic Republic and Czechoslovakia all in the 70's. This ACLU atheist president first is not any way Jewish in the true Biblical sense, but another unbeliever. He had brought more Nazism to America than any Nazi ever could have, ever. Nadine Strossen now holds that infamous post.

With Presidents, such as Carter, Ford, Bush, Sr. and the infamous Clintons who would need enemies?

Noah's 3 sons were at each other's throats in America by Marx's multiculturalism. "Race always spoke in the past hardly the present. Socialism had to subterfuge the truth of the present time and hold on to future "closed time". The future "closed time" to all socialists was played upon. This constant obsession with diversity, alienation and animosity. Beat it like a dead horse till the lie was believed by most Americans.

The government kept almost everyone busy with induced crimes, higher taxes, fear for family and loved ones, want, desire, avarice. It was not about inflation, but good vs evil, but the dollar was valueless which with any raise in pay was a facade because the dollar had devalued so much that one was always going down, or backwards and not forward and imagine the poor and the waitresses as such that did not even get minimum wage? Forget about the over inflated stock market, or the roulette wheel which had nothing to do with the American economy. Americans could not restrain the temptation from this opium addiction this time in 401 K's their wealth and retirement. They were in some way like Freud who was addicted to real cocaine. Capitalism had them hooked for sure.

Entire good neighborhoods crumbled into government Section 8 villages. If it appeared to be too good, it probably was.

Imported slavery from Mexico would do the trick since we were told that most Americans did not want to work. It would accelerate poverty only to many more American born citizens send much quicker which meant lower wages and a lower standard of living as in a 3rd world country not to mention a socialist country like Mexico. The middle class was dead and even cars and property were being leased and many Moslems had other reasons for leasing. The airwaves into one's own home were polluted with "garbage stew". The criminal in one's home was sometimes more dangerous than on the street, as well as the educated criminals in society. The spirit of in the game of life was death.

The law never required one to help one's neighbor, but the spirit of the law now said, "Be not benevolent and do not help." It was like the trucker who would only stop to help, if one was only in need. This is heartless and by indoctrination.

"Please do not try to be too human or humane."

Then these two phrases of guilt. One was real, which Messiah took care of and the other was false guilt which is what America thought about constantly, till it made them for the underdog always. Satan dealt always mostly in false guilt. Calvary did not cover false guilt.

When my European grandparents came to Ellis Island many years ago, one could be turned back for a speck of dandruff and if one could not recite in English the Preamble, the Pledge of Alliance, or any other well known English quotation. It was for asylum and religious freedom and not handouts, or a ready made life, or because they envied America. They taught my aunts and uncles as children the English language at home very proficiently, because they were invited guests into a new land. Whenever in public the courtesy was to speak English and always be polite and thankful to the American people mostly for their wonderful way about them.

There was not "me no understand English", but "thank you, do you need help," etc. It was not because of poverty or wealth that they came to America, but religious persecution, because of their Christian faith. In years to come all that would change into POLITICAL CORRECTNESS from the White House down. What had their relatives known about religious persecution when the number for immigration was in the millions per year, but the number for asylum was between 50,000-70,000 people? Why the disparaging inequality of the numbers? Now America was taking in 80% of all the world's immigration, but that was still called unfair by the Socialists in America and now even illegals, or law breakers were coming to America by government decree to reduce our living standards and separate more the rich from the poor and eliminate the middle class altogether.

Our government indoctrinated an already hostile Latin America to ask Americans, "How they treated the Hispanics and never how the Hispanics as guests treated the American people?" There was 1 Hispanic counselor by government for every 4 Hispanics, because of Big Business and Big Government and was not that what NAFTA was all about? Never had my grandparents heard of such a thing or would have thought of such a thing. Was this an apology for the rich and the well educated's raping the lands of Latin America. Did our governments make reparations to the Russian peasants, because of FDR? We know the American people did help send charitable items in the millions of dollars to Russia, but which the butcher with the moustache claimed it all for the Communist Party.

When we give anything to Mexico it is to uphold socialism and of which the Mexicans now only understand, because Mexico is a socialist country. The same as Ginsburg had to learn how to get a job when he left the Soviet Union and came to Israel. Does anyone believe Vincente' Fox is sharing any of this with their peasants, or Indians? The government owns all the oil wells, plus much more. Is that not socialism? Ivy Leaguers never fought, or opposed totalitarianism so to them it was all "business as usual". This is why Harvard Business and Law Degrees were given out and recognized the world over for their clout. "How Harvard Hates America" had to be read by me.

The American government only in name turned on America and told these hostile foreigners, "Do as you please and cry discrimination and we shall protect and support you financially out of the American taxpayers pockets, they shall never know or care."

The government also said, "It is all free, take what you can et cetera."

This was that thing called DIVERSITY.

"Take America apart and then blame the Americans for being prejudice."

"Was not Lenin too a robber of the taxpayers by robbing all the banks?"

After the Russian Revolution the Russian peasants revolted but were killed on the spot. The founder of the Russian Communist Party not Lenin, but was Shliapnikov was murdered by Lenin.

In America anti-trust laws were almost nil because of trial lawyers and corrupt judges and politicians, and Bell Telephone and Hershey's Chocolates were disbanded because the first one worked so well and the second one represented America period. They also represented the very heart of working America and free enterprise, since Mr. Hershey owned everything to produce his products and no socialized unions could intervene to destroy free enterprise. At one time it was reported that Sanka Coffee gave you cancer, or that Tylenol cyanide scare, or the tobacco families who would not sell out, but the breweries were left alone as well as the drug cartel by government at 5 levels of government. It was not because tobacco gave you lung cancer, or that seat belts saved lives, but that it was a loophole for government and trial lawyers to later infringe on one's private life.

The Monroe Doctrine was one because of President Ford and America looked like an embarrassment to the rest of the world with Communism only 90 miles from it's own shores and the fact that since Communism was no threat and was "benevolent in business" we had nothing to worry about, because the "oligarchy" in America had nothing to fear, or so they thought. The Monroe Doctrine had a down side and that was it did not care about the rest of the free world out of the Western Hemisphere which was an indictment against our government. President Ford's reasoning had nothing to do with this by the way.

The Democratic Socialist Party was waiting for a Panamanian, or Nicaraguan coupe' to occur so that Communism could be in this part of the world and spread like cancer and be welcomed even in America openly.

President Clinton had a rap sheet as long as one's arms so he was not as smart as the media played him out to be. It was more like that there were no laws, or that all laws were legal. Among his endeavors of 12 Grand Jury Indictments was treason in 1973, David Brock in Little Rock and his reports that murders transpired as was also reported by the 700 Club. Drug trafficking out of the state of Arkansas in the nose of small airplanes. While in the White House inviting well know terrorists such as Jerry Adams, as well as the Beijing Conference with Hillary and Bella Abzug that promoted infanticide. Also while in the White House treason this time with Red China along with infidelity and pedophilia and then the $8 million dollars he got when he left office and not incarceration "for high crimes and misdemeanors". The worse he got the more Hollywood and the media glorified him as their poster boy for socialism. After Oxford which he did not graduate from and was not a Rhode Scholar he went directly to the Kremlin from England by invitation and the London Tribune, or Times wanted to know why the American media was not releasing all this news in their press releases? A conscientious objector? Hardly!

After 9/11 Americans had to question Caesar about "Mohammed" but Caesar was nearly dead and Islam kept coming. To repeat as before were the super rich playing games with American as well as other peoples' lives?

At the end of the 20th Century only 2 one hundredths of 1% of America's total land area was used for mining. In Nevada where government owned 80% of the land and mining use amounted to only 1 tenth of 1% of the total land for mining, $81 billion in state and local, not federal taxes were collected. Notice that none went to Washington DC, or to the UN. They did try to rob Peter to pay Paul. Our 18,000 airports used up more land than did all American mining. More noise pollution to deafen the soul and the spiritual ears.

The West too had an economy, but DC and the media and Hollywood needed that, or their land to also provide for more of the welfare state with slave labor, plus they had to destroy the forests by letting the underbrush remain as such so when lightning struck major forest fires would occur and how many arsonists and Clinton put into office or in positions of authority? Lend lease was again on their minds, just as it had been in Stalin's time.

The only Platinum and Palladium mine in the entire Western world was in Montana. These are only found in 2 other places in the entire world and they are SOUTH AFRICA, one can now see why that country was so important to the Communists here in America and the other country was Russia. Moscow's African National Congress had gotten what it wanted with Nelson Mendela. And was not South Africa a tribal and not a racial war? Even one of the Zulu Chieftains who was a Christian wanted to make peace between all tribes with the Zulus, but America refused him to speak, except for one time shortly in the UN and then he was ignored. After this failure AIDS and Communism, or national racial socialism took over in reverse.

Back again in America in Brooklyn one man continually filed lawsuits for every mining effort to oppose in the West.

Mr. Dan Quayle who wonderfully phrased the term, "dead beat dads" something more important than "potato" also got a missile defense system while in the Senate in Israel which came into play when Saddam Hussein shot Scud Missiles over Jordan and hit Israel during Desert Storm. Mr. Quayle also suggested that loser pay all in all law suits which the American Bar Association went ballistic on as well as all trial lawyers. This would definitely reduce such law suits as a woman spilling hot coffee on her own lap, or an obese man eating too many French fries.

Moving power to the executive and the judicial relieves the deaf and the dumb in Congress who refuse to address the moral issues. Judicial legislation was nothing new. The US Supreme Court had been doing all this important law making not interpretation that appeared always to tear at the core of America's foundation. The U S Supreme Court hears less than a total of 3% of all court cases brought to them. How did Roe vs Wade in 1973 with Norma McCorvey get to be one of them along with no school prayer in 1963, or no public school Bible reading in 1962, or oppose Dred Scott in 1857 which went the immoral way not to mention the Internet and it's child pornography that also became legal, or the Boy Scouts of America that won only by a margin of 5-4: How many on the bench were actually homosexuals, or homosexualists?

The U.S. Supreme Court does not like to make declarative judgments at least the majority 5 or more and do not like to review premature cases, or "premature life" in the womb. Where else do normal marital lifetime heterosexual couples procreate, but in woman? Was it not the U.S. Court of Claims that ordered the federal government to hand over the compensation? How much is it for 42,000,000 human beings? Justice Blackmun another "Jew" wrote the majority decision in Roe vs Wade in 1973. How much did his wife help in this? Did she not know about Jewish women who were in gestation during the Nazi rule and who were coerced like in Red China now to have abortions, but of both sexes of Jewish children? Something like Martin Luther's anti-Semitism.

In regards to private property which included one's wages the TAKINGS CLAUSE is what socialists, or environmentalists feared most and yet taking a baby's life was not. Someone's private property became another's profit and their "pursuit of happiness", or so they thought. "Made in the image of GOD." All parents are only stewards from conception with egg and sperm and GOD is their Father. Herod's Planned Parenthood though had other ideas, but Rachel could be heard crying. Human resources became just that resources, or revenue from the Wasted Resources.

The New Agers worship the creation and Wotan and the UN is their church. The forests are off limits, or their outer limits to timber, hiking, fishing, or even flying over. These forests that restrict all the timber industry would include the areas large as Norway, Sweden, Denmark, Austria, Holland, Switzerland, Belgium and our tiny Israel combined. More than 90% of the land classified by the Federal Government as grazing land is not suitable for farming or growing crops. About 80% of wildlife in America depended on privately owned land for food, water and shelter. About 1200 mines supply 90% of the free world's mineral requirements, but the Shirley MacLaines, Clintons, McCains, et cetera made us still depend on hostile Islamic Oil and resources. The question is why? Is not America's Anglophilian-reptilian interest in the Middle East driven by anti-Semitism, destruction of America from within and lack of ready used resources here to serve the one world government as well as strengthen our enemies and also a part of the Senate's greed and re-election campaign even if it meant selling America out.? It was nine tenths of the law as possession but the super rich had much invested in Islamic oil to give up what they or should I say what our own American forces fought for and gave their very lives and not for our own sovereignty, or why else ignore the Northern and Southern Borders with 25,000 Al Qaeda in Canada? Would the super rich and government been so anxious to assist Kuwait if the largest export had been corn and the fact that Kuwait uses slave maiden labor with barbaric cruelty.

As for Desert Storm, this had nothing to do with America's sovereignty, but everything to do with reaping the havoc of their POLITICAL CORRECTNESS, and there had been an eye for an eye according to Osama bin Laden since they lost in Desert Storm and the retribution for him was the attack of 9/11 and much more before and after along with all of Islam. The New Age Movement could now find their "peacemaker" for the coming New World.

CHAPTER XVI

THE HEAVENS AND THIS EARTH

Now to the 7th SEAL in heaven in the Book of Revealation.

There were 4 Angels holding back the 4 Winds and an Angel from the East came and said, "Do not harm the land, sea, or trees until the 144,000 Messianic Jews are marked on their foreheads emanating from the 12 tribes of Jacob, or Israel, excluding Dan and Ephraim."

There were to be 12,000 exactly from each tribe from Judah, Levite, Napthali, Joseph, Zebulun, et cetera. This is the time of the Great Tribulation the second half of the 70th WEEK which shall equal three and one half years, or 1260 days. Then the saved Gentiles with unglorified bodies brought up their prayers in this half of the Tribulation period. Both groups would not die and would enter into the OLAM HARA. The 7th Seal was the preservation of both these groups of believers for one half an hour. There was silence in the heavens and 7 Angels were given seven Trumpets and another Angel brought incense to the altar of GOD and of which the Angel took fire from the throne and threw it upon the earth which created lightning and thunder on the earth.

"Put on the whole armor of GOD", Ephesians.

The BELT OF TRUTH is to hold the entire armor of GOD on and to come to salvation and live life honorably and to read Scripture daily. The BREAST PLATE OF RIGHTEOUS-NESS is to protect the organs of the body, whenever the enemy lies which is always, or to tempt us into sin. The SHIELD OF FAITH that protects us from the fiery darts of the enemy to confuse our minds. Our FEET ARE SHOD IN THE PEACE OF GOOD NEWS to carry the Gospel at least one person at a time to all others that we possibly can. The HELMET OF SALVATION is to protect our mind from the enemy and the SWORD OF THE SPIRIT, Ruach Hakodesh which is our offensive and defensive power in His Word against the enemy which cuts to bone and marrow. Verbal and mental Scripture that defeats the enemy through the blood of Messiah and His name said out loud, "Y'eshua".

The Scriptures that Messiah used directly to Satan, when in the wilderness when Satan tried to tempt Messiah was, "Man does not live by bread alone, but by every Word that proceeds from the mouth of GOD."

Messiah's body would be that bread.

"Do not tempt the Lord GOD."

This Tribulation of three and one half years is the 70th WEEK in the second half called the Great Tribulation. It would be the 144,000 Messianic Jews with a mark on their forehead and the Gentile believers in the world who came to know the Lord during this period of time hearing it for the first time with Gentiles who would die for their faith. Again their bodies are not glorified because they were not part of the age of grace in the TRANSLATION of the church into heaven at the Father's command. They shall remain the ones alive after Armageddon in the OLAM HARA. They worshipped at the temple.

In the 20th Century, Trotsky and Lenin had invented the concentration camps and the taking of hostages which meant no matter how brave one was they had to fear for their loved ones. The opposite of peace not war, but violence which meant that behind the scenes all peoples had to be free and not murdered, or tortured. Freedom is conditional in the sense that it is based on religious responsibility. It started with liberals then radicalism then socialized society, or socialism and then Communism. FDR had given away other countries such as Latvia, Estonia, Lithuania, Moldavia and Mongolia to Stalin. America was travelling the same path as Russia before the Revolution which did not settle down until about 1928 because of peasant turmoil. The West was counting on the rift between USSR and Red China where the Soviets believed in page 533 as opposed to the Red Chinese that subscribed to page 335. Russia still could survive by transforming the Northeast the European part, the North of the Asian part and main Siberia. Untapped lands that were valuable were Russia, Australia, Canada and Brazil. One had to watch the turmoil coming from the Flemish and the Walloons. Americans such as Senator George McGovern, Averall Harriman, George Kennan, Kennedy, Henry Kissinger, Robert Kaiser, Chris Wren and Marshall Shulman all helped to contribute to the Soviet empire.

I could almost see this compilation of events somehow coming into being but as to the exact time nobody could know for sure. These were all saints saved by Messiah and protected in the Tribulation period. I thought about how Christian Negroes since the 6th Century in the Sudan had been murdered, because their faith was in Messiah and not Islam. GOD does not recognize foreign gods, or in actuality the worship of demons. He calls and they respond. There are no multiple choices with grace. Even Judaism misses the mark. We defended a foreign god with Islam in America. "You shall have no other gods before Me."

Who would call on Mohammed's god, Allah and have their sins removed by a free gift? GOD does capitalize the G in GOD Himself. Messiah is worshipped through His grace which He provides once saved by Y'eshua's death, crucifixion, burial and resurrection and His shedded blood at Calvary. The Trinity 3 persons in one GOD. This is GOD and in no other way.

Christian names and organizations do not make one a believer for the Messianic Jew, or the American Biblical, nor do Hebrew names. They depend only on Y'eshua's done work at Calvary for their salvation. It had never changed, since Y'eshua walked the earth.

The Truth stays the same eternally. New Age's says, "Look at this, it is new!"

Y'eshua says, "I AM the same yesterday, today and tomorrow.

Eternal timelessness and not more time. Time is limited.

In America it had become comfortable for Americans to become comfortable with sin. It was not always that way. America had been desensitized, even the church.

Shimon HaShaliach said, "Judgment begins with the household of GOD."

A dying civilization without GOD does always die. GOD does not go away like Jefferson and Franklin thought, no matter their sincerity, honesty and genius. GOD can use unbelievers, if it is in His good plan to do so, but is under no obligation.

Rabbi Levin spoke for all Orthodox Jews, yes unbelievers, in America when he addressed his congress.

"Nazi homosexuals, sexual deviants, have nothing to do with the Holocaust victims, in fact, it was they who were on trial and were the criminals. One is a people, the other is a criminal element of thugs that were homosexual pedophile Nazis, "to paraphrase. No ACLU, or Ira Glasser here? The Nuremburg Trials were anti-hate crimes, if there be such a thing?

America had become sick in the heart and ill in the mind with carnal sin. The body, or the collective body of America became infected with cancer that was terminal and ate out America from within. "The handwriting was on the wall."

David Geffin a billionaire and good friend of Mr. Clinton supported homosexuality in America every way that he possibly could. Sexual promiscuity was allowed to decay into sexual deviancy. Man had to have his god given rights. It was the Hollywooders and the vaudevillian decadence. Hollywood was true theatrical reality not only on the screen, but in a family's own home all across America. Never to work the American soil with their hands or use their minds for Messiah. America's jobs became nothing but subservience to technology, or heathenism. There was no longer America's own purpose for GOD or to have a life. We had forgotten about GOD. Even when one said marriage, which marriage did they mean? Sodom and Gomorrah, or GOD'S? Live and let live, or let us live as we want for the moment, or die and help us die as we want was this death wish. GOD turned us over to a reprobate mind as a nation. For a GOD we felt we could not see we chose the visible senses alone pure materialism and our burning lustful flesh. Marriage vows who needed them? Why should one make a lifetime commitment? Egosim and vanity soared. The elderly forgot to age gracefully and senior citizens meant, "I lived my life and you live your's." Instead of praying on their knees, they were spending their retirement how many times has one heard this word money on gambling and other mundane things. They soon would face GOD all of us do in this winter of their life. There was hardly any generation that in particular stood out, except possibly the children which were being abused maliciously in society. Only tiny sporadic porous holes of true Biblical faith here and there. The American Biblicals had gotten much older and there were, but a few left. The ones remaining still continued to read Scriptures and pray without ceasing not for themselves, but for others and worshipped GOD the same way they had done for many years on their knees before a Holy GOD. They were ostracized by most others in society, because they would not yield and collaborate with evil in silence. Time in America, or for America was running short and the hour glass was almost all run out. It was only death that America now sought, plus slavery and not freedom. It was no longer, "Give me liberty, or give me death," but just the latter. Once again the gay old 90's at the end of the 20th Century was completely different.

Europeanism had drilled "success, success, success" to the point of egoism and vanity. Yes, America had become a haven for Hell. This was the "Valley of Jehosophat" and the Mosaic Jews in the wilderness wondering for the "PROMISED LAND" that was rich in "silk and money". Everybody had a gay old time, except the babies and our small children.

In Israel and National Liberation Front was the casue of death for many innocent lives. Ishmael did not get GOD'S spiritual blessing, but His love and it is Islam more than just Ishmael that promoted this evil through Mohammed. Ishmael was from the mishap or accidental family and born through disobedient sin, because of Abram and Sarai's lack of faith.

Later both religious non-Judeo-Christians were not Biblical, because one did not know their own Messiah and one never recognized that He was the ONE. Judaism lost it's bearings after even Messiah had resurrected and the nation refused to believe.

The Jew was Christian in nature, the Arab had become anything but, except for a small minority. Islam is a worship to demons and New Age a worship to Satan.

The worst of all scenarios is when Satan gives all his powers to this Antichrist who is probably half man and half demon. This BEAST can be amongst us mortal men now and could do more damage because of his physical body and power now in a different dimension the same as mortal man. A mutation of man/demon. Then the FALSE PROPHET shall probably also be a Jewish man like the Antichrist's mother shall be. Satan's emulation of the Trinity and of course Mary a Jewish woman who carried the Father's Son.

When Messiah came to earth the Ruach Hakodesh came upon Jewish Mary and Y'eshua was BEGOTTEN Not made by man as in procreation. He is the Creator. "One in being with the Father." Satan's son shall be this Antichrist. This mutation of total evil. GOD has no beginning and no end, but this unholy Trinity shall have had both, when GOD'S absolute will is finally done. This Tribulation is GOD controlled. Satan has been allowed in the permissive will of GOD to do evil things, because from the beginning he was a liar. GOD'S absolute will shall be this burning lake of eternal fire.

In the OLAM HABA the lamb and lion shall lie down together with each other. Man shall die in this 1,000 years, only not all? Satan is for the time being out of the picture in this 1,000 year period. GOD'S absolute will shall control all of His Judgments.

The 7 Trumpets now appear in heaven and the FIRST ANGEL blows the Trumpet and hail and fire come upon the earth and causes a worldwide drought. The SECOND TRUMPET sounds and the seas and oceans have their seafood die and it affects oceanic transportation. The THIRD TRUMPET sounds and all the fresh water is turned bitter or deathly bitter by Wormwood. The FOURTH TRUMPET sounds and one third of all heavenly bodies go dark affecting the sun and other stars and planets. Man still does not repent, but curses GOD even more.

Sudan had come and gone and nothing was done by America where the Southern Sudanese were murdered by crucifixion Roman style with child slave labor, raping of women, torture and millions murdered. We too were doing the same, except for the crucifixions, for now at least.

Kuwait, an Eastern nation where Islam is the state religion, no separation of mosque and state here and domestic servants, mostly Christians, are treated as slaves and are raped, yet we defended Islam in Desert Storm, because of Thatcher and Bush, Sr. These maids, or slaves came from the Philippines, Sir Lanka and India, plus Bangladesh. These 250,000 Asian maids were treated brutally and confined, but yet a Desert Storm by George Bush, Sr. who said not to kill Saddam Hussein. This Kuwait is a country that is the richest in the world per person not that it is equally shared, or even near that. This is our, or the elite's Western financial ally called the Persian, or Iranian Gulf. "We are our brother's keeper," but Americanism meant not for good, but for evil. We would fight another conflict. Who were we protecting, or what? Another ally was the virulent anti-Semitic Saudi Arabia with its Islamic monarch that is 100% Islamic to their death, or others, and are really dictators.

Pakistan's militant Islamic forces attack Christianity and Christians, but yet America upholds this totalitarianism in this state. There is a death penalty for one who blasphemes Mohammed. Yet no American evangelical church responds for their brothers in Messiah. Tear gas is used on Christians who peacefully demonstrate. The 2-3 million Christians there live in constant fear of cleansing. Moslems raid Christian villages and plunder homes dishonor their women, kidnap young Christian girls and force Islam on them as our US Supreme Court forced infanticide on America. The police do not respond, even when women are raped. Only ten churches have been built since they separated from India.

Thirty years they have tried to build a church in Islamabad. Christians are denied housing and jobs, but Pakistan and

Afghanistan get American funding and moral support with taxpayers' dollars.

In Egypt up until the 7th Century, it was a Christian nation. The Copts have even helped Egypt from invasions and war. Anwar Sadat increased Islamic rule. Hosni Mubarak does the same, but still America gives billions to Egypt. Moslems attack Christians constantly. If one converts to Christianity, death is imminent by militants and the police. Now that is police brutality never heard about in the media. In upper southern Egypt Christians are murdered, assaulted, stolen from, or have their property destroyed. Nothing like totalitarianism, Jihad style. The local police stand by and look and why shouldn't they, they are Moslems too? Christians have been massacred. Christians are second class citizens, worse than the "blacks" were ever in America and Christians there can be discriminated against. Education is a no for all Christians. No church has been built since 1982 when Hosni Mubarak came to power. Nothing can be fixed, or repaired no matter how little in or on church property. Penalties and fines are incurred when this happens. This is not fascism, but good vs evil in a different context.

Sudan, Iran, Saudi Arabia, Pakistan and Egypt all discriminate torture and kill Christians. Why do Moslems come to America? Why do "blacks" in America such as Mohammed Ali, Louis Farrakan, Kareem Abdul Jabbar, Dula Abdul, Ahmad Rashad, Jamaal Wilkes and 30% or more of "blacks" in America become Moslems and how can anyone trust as to whom their loyalty belongs? Nationality is not blood alone, but the spirit or consicousness of a nation. Mixed blood does not determine everything. After 9/11 does any of them change their names to their birth names? Do they apologize or offer condolences to the families at the World Trade Center Buildings? POLITICAL CORRECTNESS, Lenin style. What does this have to do with "all men are created equal," when each individual has their own talents, or potentials and is not this in search of "social" justice? If theirs is Islam then maybe they should reconsider and travel to Saudi Arabia? Oh yes, no

American "blacks" are allowed there. One could call this racial implosion or for the good of their cause.

Why does our government entertain these terrorists and their sovereign states? Why does Big Business keep pumping their oil for them and keep us hostage? Other fuels could be used, or oil wells here could be dug safely, but then again totalitarianism would not thrive and the New Age would be stifled somewhat. Some cultures "never say die" and some say "you must die" America had acquired this in it's final hour.

Let the party and not the State pay for government pensions. Prices in our economy should be stabilized for at least 20 years. Russia at one time did it for 1 whole century. Banks must not become usurious growths just financial institutions who produce nothing the same as the government. With less productivity comes higher prices in America? Even so called Christians in America worked for Moslems even after 9/11 knowing full well their brothers and sisters in those foreign countries were being murdered and tortured.

One must really read the entire Koran about infidels and are not all Moslems reading their Koran like all Christians read the Bible? But then again "social" Christians in America did not read Scripture and the ones that did would pick and choose.

In Afghanistan one can face death, if they leave Islam, yet we praised Karzai and his relatives who are in power and are Moslems? All Moslem states that are Arabic and are not Arabic cannot have tolerance, or diversity of any kind in their dictatorial states, yet Moslem "blacks" in America would have us believe that their diversity is any different then over there.

In Turkey where we have US military bases could be included with the above and some Sicilians might even entertain their own Mafioso Jihad which is centuries old too.

Kurdish rebels have also murdered Christian village chiefs. How we cried, when the Soviets were attacking at least our government and Big Business was the Kurds. Indonesia has more Moslems in their country, than any other country in the world and they are not Arabs. There are about 190,000,000 people in

Indonesia. Why are there so many different Arab states and only one Jewish state? Could it lie in the religion and the nature of the beast?

Ninja gangs, sound familiar, attack dissidents' homes at night, as agents of the government in East Timor in East Asia.

The southern Philippines have a large Moslem population and also Communists' insurrection. How socialisms tend to attract each other. In this country one can also see the influence of outside interference. When Ferdinand Marcos ruled as a dictator there were no insurgents to deal with like this, but since decmocracy came and Aquino took office she has been a downfall toward a more vicious totalitarianism and again democracy has proved to be too unstable against transitional types of governments that go from one extreme to the other. Am I upholding socialism? Heaven forbid... King Ferdinand Marcos is not one size that fits all and our government leaders knew that from the start.

Most of the world today lives under socialism. The National and World Council of Churches says not enough and in fact support socialism.

All freedoms are conditional. Islam originated from nomadic pagans and the continent of Africa had natural socialism which does not mean socialism is either racial, or geographical. Socialism spans all of human history and has state socialism and a doctrine which are not to be confused with each other. The state is outward and allows for no private property. The doctrine stresses also no family, or marriage and is a theory in accord to it's utopian future. Socialism means that the human will does not determine history, hence the destruction of man. Fatalism is what is preaches and renders no individual responsibility, Marxism is an atheistic religion by Lenin which he used to replace Russian Orthodoxy and allows for no human personality. Wife sharing is allowed publicly, no tax reductions ever. Socialist non-Marxist is a sexual revolution outwardly. (Families produce private property and inheritance.) In Mesopotamia in about 2200 BC they had in this order peasants, temples, units, the state in unification and people were cells. Workers worked for food only and bought from the state stores. No family only units. State officials allocated land. State workshops were in affect. The heaviest work was left for children and women. The Incas in Chile and Ecuador before Spain took over in the 16th Century (1500's) had no money, no private property, no trade, etc. The Inca governing class was military or civilian. Bureaucracies trained in state schools. They had more than one wife. Nine to 16 year olds were shepherds and 16-20 year olds were servants. Peasant girls were used as human sacrifices and peasant marriages were arranged by the State. Each village had to wear a special cape and a distinctive hairstyle so that they could not leave the peasant villages. In Paraguay the state allowed for no private property, no money and no trade by the Indians. In Egypt the Pharaoh was first then the owners and then the peasants who were the workers. The Scribes were like the Soviet Commissars and it is here that this gave birth to the state and not the nation and there is a difference. The other part of socialism is the socialist doctrine which is about 2,000 years old and there are 3 periods. Plato was the first and it was Gnostic and had master race breeding, no family, no private property, doctors treated only certain people and the disabled were killed there was no Catholic Church here. Then came the medieval heretics and philosophers with their revolutions and different groups. There was absolutely no material world and marriage was a sin. Again no private property was allowed which also included the Reformation and the English Revolution in the 17th Century (1600's). The third one was John Locke's Enlightment which had no preachers, but just philosophers in the higher strata. This was in the 18th Century (1700's). What was also influenced by this was in 1516 Thomas More's *Utopia,* the European West with it's compulsory work and bureaucratic rule and no private property.

In the year of seventeen eighty-six in Paris the first ATTEMPT to put socialist ideology into practice was used and all work was by the state and there were punishment islands. Then "equality" with no hierarchy came and the amoeba mass this equality in slavery came. This brought about the two different individuals. The anonymous which were the "herrings" with no identity and had state control and made man as animal and the individual which were the "wild geese" with personal relationships such as family and made man human. With this the educated/slavery came a split in the nation's personality. No one moment is missed in a nation yet no historical situation goes to the full depths of it's personality and here personality is not a metaphor. Freedom and equality have NEVER yet existed without despotism. Equality in the herd has all that has so far appeared. There was to be no brains or geniuses in society as Lenin later quoted. "Equality" was turned into equivalence which meant a part of the machinery and the common denominator was total equality and all slaves, or all are slaves and equal in slavery. As I said before all freedoms are conditional by GOD and it started in the Garden. Socialism does spout it's policies openly, then when in power watch out. Many times religion and socialism are confused with each other because they have the same elements, but are in a different context. In one GOD is the highest sphere and with socialism the destruction of man. GOD in religion is the highest in human existence. In socialism private ownership of marriage to collective prostitution, hence woman becomes a lower form of social property as in Nazi Germany. With the New Age came this scenario and knowledge that without soil, water, fuel and air there would be no human life and if only one of these were taken away it would be catastrophic in nature. The chief source of inflation was blackmail by unions on employers by strikes. It was like too much potassium in the brain over the amount of sodium in the brain and since potassium must never exceed the sodium death shall incur.

When J. Paul Getty died, a man worth $50,000 a minute, all of Africa went topsy turvy and when Armand Hammer died, owner of Occidental Petroleum (what else?), the Arab sheiks found another Western Billionaire and then the oil wells became explosive because Israel could not be exterminated, and even some thought that Islam would eliminate Communism.

In Red China it is most normal for Communists to eat, as a delicacy in Peking, aborted fetuses. If this is not cannibalism at its worse glorified in "sophistication", then nothing is. Yet Most

Favored National Status? The Communist Chinese also use young Christians as slave labor. See the mark that says "MADE IN CHINA" not Taiwan on your next Wal-Mart purchase. And Kathy Lee Gifford was brutalized by the media for her ignorant mistake, but the merchandise from China keeps coming in. One can thank Mr. Kissinger and Mr. Haig for their businessmen's minds. The Communists also kill young Christians and then extract body parts as donors to be sold to Western businessmen. So that is how the billionaires live so long. I wonder why (or should I?) that all this should be enough to cut off this blood money with a totalitarian group of thugs? There are many Gulags, or laogai camps or 1100 Gulags to be more exact. This is all brutality by forced slavery on mostly Christians yet again the US Senate the millionaire suite in pure materialism likes their new business partners. No other time in human history has so many Christians been murdered in such a short period of time. This was the so called Mao Cultural Revolution, or the mass murder of. It was nothing cultural, but plain cold blooded murder. There is a famous "black" American boxer with a Mao tattoo on his forearm, but then again he is a Moslem with a lot of brain damage. How socialisms constantly meet.

During the Mao mass murders in the millions, or Cultural Revolution, the people were buried alive. Then they were dismembered and eaten by their tormentors. There was mass cannibalism. Dong Xiapang increased religious persecution in the 1980's. Married couples were sterilized. There were forced infanticides for all female babies. This could be their oriental mindset of a vast army from the kings of the East. Don't blink an eye...

Hillary Clinton visited Romania to incite and stir up problems there. There are many gypsies in Romania. Were these the same gypsies come to America that were in the Gulags who tormented and tortured the politicals and Christians while in the camps with Soviet approval, or were they the small group of Christian gypsies?

There are about 50,000,000 Communists in Red China and about up to 100,000,000 Christians with a total population of between 1.5-2.0 billion people. Majorities do not rule in an oligarchy and in most short lived democracies, only thugs and murderers and too eventually are done away with. America was the opposite, or was it from China's socialism? After all we could also claim we murdered 42,000,000 believers of our own and did not democracy allow that too?

Mikhail Romanov was the first Czar elected by the people with much power, but respected the peasantry's local governments (1613-1645). With the second Czar, Alexis, the local governments were ignored and he was an administrative, not a practical Czar who was to set in motion a downfall for the Russian people. His Code of 1649 brought more enslavement to the peasantry. He emulated the West in authority even though he did oust the Poles from Russian lands. Along came a church schism between Greek and Russian Orthodoxy. This too would weaken Russia's spiritual quest into the 20th Century. The dissenters who stayed with Russian Orthodoxy at that time were called OLD BELIEVERS. His reign was from 1645-1676. Then came Fyodor II, 1676-1682, followed by Ivan V with his brutal mind on the throne from 1689-1725. He did away with a national representative body and instilled a Western mindset. He raised taxes and he had no feeling for the peasants. The Decree of 1714 turned the peasants over to property by the landowners. He also created unworthy ruling class. This monarch was commonly thought to be the Antichrist, because of his murder of 1,000,000 peasants between the years 1719-1727 which was 10% of the population. Peter was like the Bolsheviks. Then came Catherine I from 1725-1727 and Peter II from 1717-1730. Next in line was Anna 1730-1740 who brought German influence into Russia. Her rule was one of unnecessary and unsuccessful wars. She wanted to place a Saxon on the Polish throne. Next came Ivan VI, 1740-1741 followed by Elizabeth 1741-1762 who did have faith, but bitterly was against the Swedes. She outlawed the death penalty. She was easy on crime with lesser punishment. She did not support though the OLD BELIEVERS. Serfs could be deported to Siberia for their conduct, or lack thereof. Her concern was more about Europe than her own Russia.

Peter III 1762 was a nephew of Elizabeth who ruled for one half of a year. His 1762 Decree brought about more serfdom and filled the army with foreign officers. He did not like the Russian Orthodox, but yet protected the OLD BELIEVERS, Muslims and idolaters. Catherine II 1762-1796 treated the German colonists with more respect than her own people. She promoted the gentry. The peasants could not complain against their landowners. She was out of touch with the peasants. Voltaire was an adviser to her. Her sinister plots in the Balkans started this trend so that Europe became suspicious since. During her reign Prussia and the Turkish Sultan met secretly with Spain, the Netherlands and yes of course Sicily as their allies against Russia, but the French Revolution stopped this so called Russo-Turkish peace. Then came Paul I (1796-1801) who too got involved in shedding Russian blood for Europe, as well as Napoleon to fight England. England had a plot to remove Paul I of Russia. He limited the serfs work week and the work on the Sabbath for them. Serfs now could lodge complaints against landowners. Russia's rulers were colonizers and with this the St. Petersburg Period which was between the 18th and 19th Centuries. Alexander I (1801-1825) permitted serfs to marry without the landowner's consent, but no land for the peasants. He knew about the plot to remove his father, Paul I. Bureaucracy was his trademark with the young gentry allowing to be idle and live in comfort. He had pro-English advisers. The Patriotic War could have been avoided if not for Paul I. Nicholas I (1825-1855) who was a Russian Monarch, or thought he was. He supported the Hapsburgs. He was in everybody's business, even Pushkin's death was blamed on him. He was almost assassinated but refused to fire back even warning shots. Even Poland exonerated the Decembrists and Nicholas went along. He was diligent, precise and hardworking, but thought he could do it all alone. Serfdom continued to expand. At this time there were 17-18 million state-owned peasants and also 25 million privately owned serfs in a country of 52 million. He stopped the splitting apart of peasants' families. His military was very weak. Alexander II, 1855-1881 lost the Danube River and the Black Sea. His 1861 Emancipation Act left only homesteads as private property for the peasants. This was a foreshadowing of Stalin's collectivization. The peasants did not and could not understand this system, since everything they paid for was through their labor, or it's product. Peasants could not use the forests and common pasture. The Emancipation Act of February 19th granted personal freedom, but no land and its fruit, and the latter was more important to the peasants than is the land. This separated them from the rest of society. The open market only confused the peasants more and with no money to pay the taxes loan sharks took their properties. The elites kept moving away from the peasants. Slavery grew stronger. Bureaucrats became even stronger. The agricultural base kept the peasants in obedience in the family and gave them self discipline. Serfdom was better, because it had a better relationship as to the land. The serfs had twice the land and the landowners had to support the peasant in all that he did to the land much the same that George Washington did. Even in serfdom the drunkards and good-for-nothings were drafted first, then children from large families that did not affect the agricultural labor of the peasant. The rich also paid more taxes than the poor under selfdom. Education was in church schools in the villages, turning ego into an all-grieving heart. It did not promote benefits and unnecessary knowledge. No drunkenness, confusion, mischief and disrespect for elders occurred. Patriarch Nikon and his reforms helped destroy Russian Orthodoxy earlier in Russian history, except for the OLD BELIEVERS. Labor from peasantry declined in quality at the end of the 19th Century. Woodlands grew thinner, agriculture fell. There was no agricultural training, only Ancient Greek and Latin. Horses became scarce. Next came trial lawyers, permanent judges; the jury system et cetera all borrowed from the West. Crimes were transferred from the individual to Russia as a whole.

Alexander III (1881-1894) promoted idle gentry at administrative levels, unqualified. There were no more peasant courts. Peasants could buy out their land in full, if they opted out of the self-governing organization unit which existed from medieval times, until the 12th Century in communal agriculture. This blocked the path of the most energetic healthy and industrious peasants and gave more power to the elites. In 1863 Russia sent her fleet to America to support the North against the South, but for what reason? To oppose England? Why not help the Ukrainians and the Belorussians? The Russian elite and rulers did have messianism. The multi-talented personalities were almost extinct. Only Alexander III in nearly one and one half centuries understood the importance of inner health to Russia and not foreign wars. He did not wage a single war in his reign, but Wilhelm abrogated, hence the Russo-German War at the beginning of the 20th Century. He had to stay conservative with the murder of his father on March 1st. Russia started to export grain, taxes were lowered, but local peasant government was weakened. Village priests lived in poverty and abandoned the church. Muslims continued to enjoy the same tolerance as before, sound familiar? Alexander III enlightened Russia, but he died early tragically. Nicholas II his son (1894-1917) began to dismantle what his father had done that was good for Russia. The colonies had more freedom than did the Russian peasants. They did not have to serve in the military, they paid less taxes and the Finns filled all the high posts in the Russian government and even in the military. The Russians had to speak Finnish even when only miles from the Russian capital, since the Finns were the inspection officials but refused to speak Russian, that is the Finns. Does this sound very familiar? Finland was a haven for revolutionaries, such as Lenin's Bolsheviks and thugs. Also Asian nationals received money transfers from the top. Even the Kazakhs and Central Asians did not have to serve in the military nor pay the military tax. Another analogy? More was given to indigenous nationalities, than to the Russians. The English had the gold mines, the Belgiums the ironworks, Nobel the Baku oil fields, the French the Crimean saltworks, the Norwegians the fishing industry, the Japanese the Amur Delta. Two thirds of the factory owners were foreigners and their names filled the revolutionary annals of 1917. And a fait accompli? Russians and foreigners alike took their profits out of the country. This monarch was on a collision course with Japan. Hostility grew between governments and the people while the revolutionaries stirred the brew. Even students in Moscow and St. Petersburg wished the Mikado victory. Sounds Clintony doesn't it? Only Stolypin saved him until Stolypin died. Wilhelm II was insincere and theatrical about Bjorko and this treaty. England had for 90 years kept up its malevolence towards Russia. Nicholas II lost power on the throne. England sided with Japan. Nicholas II did not opt out a war with Germany, remember the homosexual scandal, but instead allied himself with Russia's worse enemy. England by signing the Anglo-Russian Convention of 1907 and this war spelled doom for Russia, because 1914 would come and Lenin's Revolution in 1917. Russia never annexed tribes, or aborigines. In Siberia in the 18th Century navigational, medical and mining schools were opened up, plus libraries, printing houses were established. Such was the wealth of the people with only 50 years out of serfdom ... Russia was 5th in the world in industrial production with exports, such as Siberian butter and grain by their own railroad constsruction. Private economic activity thrived in Siberia. Even the Jewish Pale of Settlement was on the out. Generals rose from the lowest ranks. Russia was democratic in upward mobility and not wretched men of noble birth. There were no class barriers by the 20th Century here and rights were by qualifications. There was an open court system with no censorship and from 1906 a true government and multi-party system. There was always high quality medical care and workers' insurance was introduced. Women's education excelled all of Europe's and population growth. Then 1917 and totalitarianism. From 1906-1913 there was prosperity for the peasants and Russia. The media felt otherwise and hence the monarch and his relatives were all executed along with the Duma, The Mensheviks, the peasants, et cetera. Now Lenin only wanted Moscow and offered America through a delegation in 1919 West Belorussia, half of The Ukraine, all the Caucasus, The Crimea, the Urals, Siberia, Lenin was in a panic. Lenin's thugs took later the diamond fund and all of private property.

Yes, a nation has a personality pre-designed by GOD to fulfill His will and is not an individual nation as well as a person is an individual, but has a personality as GOD in 3 personalities in One? All the nations or personalities make up the whole and not individual parts which would never bring together the fellowship of man. At Pentecost the Disciples each spoke unknown tongues as personalities. A nation is not created by a people's history but again by GOD'S plan for them. The nation is a personality and an individual nation, not just a people as an amoeba mass. The Triune GOD is 3 personalities, not 3 individuals in GOD. No one individual historical period makes up a nation's history to its fullest depths. Just as He has for a nation He also has one for the human personality and of which neither can themselves destroy the roots. The higher personal being is what is known as the church or the Body of Messiah. The one world government, or the nationalism in Nazi Germany is never GOD'S plan for mankind or for a nation, or the individual personality. The "schizophrenia" of a nation such as Russia and America came when the rich and the well educated separated themselves from the people, hence a "split personality". To serve GOD they served man, "the people" while subconsciously not serving GOD first; hence the 60's in America. In America nationalism became universalism. Man is single in nature, but plural in personality. Nazi Germany and Soviet Russia appeared as extremes, but both desired the love of a tribe only in the first instance and the second the love of mankind in the mundane only. The insanity of man fallen man through the Old Man Adam.

The churches in America kept emulating the agnostic Hal Lindsey's term of "Rapture". Why Hal Lindsey? To put the church to sleep in America and not the sleep Rev Shaul spoke about? His "Late Great Planet Earth" was a bestseller in the secular stream.

Most all television ministries were entertainment asking the going price for items, usurping the local churches' tithing weakening American Christian communities by delegating to them and by wholesale give away programs that emulated the government. Nothing to remind one, as American Biblicals who had loyalty to their finding of their own GOD. Extravagant monostrosities for religious purposes and even one claimed to have a personal horse worth $500,000. Of course his father had been a US Senator too. Most of these shows came out of the south, so one had to be suspect as to their validity. People were healed who could have been missed diagnosed? Celebrities of all kinds would entertain, but real little prayer, or Scripture lessons. This was a new kind of Europeanism via the satellite. No longer did one have to attend church and be with the Body of Messiah.

It appeared that the church in America was looking for more civil rights socialism, or "social" justice with "race" relations through affirmative action, monetary retirements and future investments, but not about the poor or the abused. Why were we also silent about our own brothers in America? Self-esteem is a big thing. It is called ego. Also, in American churches pacifism a way to get out or around of seeing no evil, hearing no evil and speaking out against no evil. Protestantism certainly was isolationism. Yes, do not become mundane and secular, but speak to the evil in one's own nation. Even preaching about immoral issues was outlawed. Where does theatrical reality not touch? Even unbelievers such as Don Feder, a conservative Jew, spoke out directly. Who had silenced the church and who were the real believers? Only GOD really knew.

Cardinal William Keeler had received an award from a well-known terrorist organization and said that, "We needed to avoid Muslim bashing?"

Is this more of Roman Catholicism's anti-Semitism as in WW II, or just two socialisms meeting once again?

The caste system in India has a system that says, "In another karma you could be something," but here even in America?

Maybe that is why India's Indians who came here were from New Delhi where the rich and well educated came from and are like our own elites, the unbelievers. These Hindus and Moslems do not assimilate and do we want to be unequally yoked since Catholicism is what entered the foreign country? Theirs is to get rich for their religious freedom was never in peril in India and the United States Government gave them the nuclear atomic bomb just so Big Business could get hold of their resources. They were some of the ones who persecuted the real Christians in America, as well as in their own countries and we allowed them through the rich and well educated to do just that. If it was democracy, the rich worked through right by might in an oligarchy fashion.

Survey upon survey and polls upon totem polls were the barometers for most Americans especially the media and the government politicians who did not have leadership skills, plus no morality. It was called follow the leader Germanic style, no matter who that so called leader might be. The English were good at making others follow them, especially the elites in America. English and German were founded languages but the Russian Cyrillic alphabet was discovered by St. Cyril for Christianity who brought Christianity to Russia along with St. Methodius. This was similar though to Daniel's Webster's Original Dictionary in America, when good meant good and evil meant evil with no revised editions. Russian, or pure Russian is a Christian based language as well as a universal language. The American modern English had been revised to mean just about anything and was fused with foreign colloquialisms.

German music (except for Wagner) and their art too is excellent but their political philosophy was utopian in an oligarchy form. English is logical, factual, concise, but not expressive enough to even differentiate the 3 kinds of love. There is a carnal love, a phileo love, and an agapé love. Writers such as Dickens, Shakespeare and a few others did a masterful job with what they had to work with, but then again in their day English itself was not so distorted. American English derives, of course in part from England's English but is less restrictive and more at ease with itself. The monarchial English was different than the Democratic English in America and it had to be because the original idea in America was to be one language with no different extreme accents like they had in England which told others exactly where one was from and from what class of people they were. American English was an original idea and it had to be because the original idea in America was not from a dictatorial monarch, but a democratic/ republic. One must dress for the proper occasion England knew colonialism and holier-than-thou aristocracy among the rich and well educated. America at its beginning knew Christian freedom and "His will be done".

As my mind oscillated back and forth again and again, I had remembered that in America a Sudanese Christian one like Francis Bak was denied asylum and a Pakistani Christian who feared mob retaliation also was refused entry. Iranian Christians -- are there such a thing? Four of their colleagues were gunned down and were not in our news media. Chinese Christian women were even refused asylum by Clinton because these women refused to murder their own unborn children by Communist decree in Peking. Mr. Clinton also had them incarcerated, something that should have happened to him long ago in our own prisons. These were real hardcore criminals according to Lenin's POLITICAL CORRECTNESS. They had to be dealt with. Mr. Clinton also had bombed, before 9/11 a medical pharmaceutical company in the Sudan and 4 Mosques in Afghanistan not to instigate but incite Islamic Jihad. He also watered down the CIA and FBI and encouraged military personnel to leave the armed forces because they could not serve under such a Commander-In-Chief who had committed treason, murder, adultery, child molestation, drug running from Arkansas, terrorists' training. You name it and he did it each and every day while in political office in Arkansas or in D.C. His loathing of the military was well known even in many foreign countries. Medical records of him were never found.

Religiosity in certain cases goes far in human history. There was a German King, Henry VI in 1070 AD when Pope Gregory VII summoned a crusade against him. Catholicism somewhat like Liberation Theology in Latin America.

Many Middle Eastern Christians had no part in this. Eastern Christians are not for the most part Catholicized or are they? The Immigration and Naturalization Agency had turned away so many evangelical Christians coming to America, but not the Islamic Jihad under Bill Clinton. Asylum and immigration are not the same thing. The first is because of religious persecution and the number had to be kept low for Christians to about

50,000-70,000 a year while Latin America had about 3 million a year and France 4,000 a year. Even David Dinkins allowed the Dominican Drug Lords into America and held a parade and party for them as Mayor of New York City. That was real affirmative action. Today's immigration is nothing more than saying anyone subversive, or otherwise can invade our land with government approval just so they meet POLITICAL CORRECTNESS criteria. Latin America is not to dominate no matter what the rich and well educated propose for America. As the Russians tried to remove the Communists in their government we too would have to remove Marxist/Leninism multiculturalism from America's Government. Latin America had a different mindset with a non-Judeo-Christian base. The Conquistadors were their founders and their religion was Europeanism's ultimate "do as the Romans do". They do not understand compromise or dissent, but only coercion or if one can get away with it because of their multiculturalism. It has been ingrained into their psyche to respond that way for centuries. Their spiritual and political are so different from America's even though they are only literally miles apart from us. It is as urban flight, where no geographical boundary such as a huge river, sea, or ocean, or high mountainous range is to offset the tide of this multiculturalism. The rich are hoping the dam breaks and NAFTA was the first blow they used along with bi-lingualism in America.

GOD in the Old Testament, "Stay away from unbelievers" or at least their world, and heathen culture. Mexico was a socialist state. Poland accepted Soviet supervision because 98% of Poles had Roman Catholicism ingrained in them and was a border against Western intrusion for the Soviets and yet could not hold off the Soviets, yet tiny Vietnam was told to do so.

Why would I want to leave America, unless I wanted to go to Israel? Why do Latin Americans seek America, yet refuse with government approval to assimilate and speak English and be an American but wanted to be conquistadors here in America? When I entered Israel, I became an Israelis' citizen even though my faith was an American Biblical. I still obeyed and respected their culture and did no violence to it and why should I, unless I had a non-Judeo-Christian motive? No, not "Love America, or Leave It", but to them I would propose that they first learn to love their own country first and then America and for American born to love America.

GOD is a jealous GOD. America married other gods, such as materialism and heathenism. Our Founding was founded on Christianity and the Bible and not the Koran, or Islam, or whatever the colleges, or universities preached in POLITICAL CORRECTNESS. Even Jehovah Witnesses, Christology, Mormonism, the Christian Science Monitor, Hinduism, Buddhism were all carcinogenic growths to the main body of America and all demonic.

Christianity does allow all others of America to worship freely, but never let that be any kind of prerequisite for heathenism or for the worship freely of demons to take over in any authoritative positions.

Nationalism, Zionism, was hurting Israel spiritually. The collective body were mostly unbelievers. It was secular and had always been. Israel was not at liberty to give away GOD'S holy land to Islam, or demonic worship. Israel was not a warrior like state, diametrically opposed to GOD'S will, but now necessary until Messiah would return. Messianic Jewry would inherit the future Jerusalem. The enemy was restricting the Jews from hearing His voice through His Son Messiah, "The Word That Became Flesh". Whose blood would be shed for disobedience? Messiah had already shed GOD'S blood. Messiah would return for His Saints, Jew and Gentile and then again for Armageddon to defeat Satan and to set up this long awaited OLAM HARA.

The Israelis trusted man, when they could be trusting Messiah. Too much trust in Americanism and Europeanism. The Gentile evil powers were still in affect. Messianic Jews were the saints and all before them, plus the Old Testament ones and up to the Translation. Then in Tribulation more Messianic Jews, plus the 144,000 would be all the real Jews that GOD spoke about and knew personally.

To proselytize was illegal in Israel. The 10 Commandments were propagated falsely as to save one as in the BOOK OF LEVITICUS. The Israelis were also killing their own through infanticide, 50,000 a year, but fought like hell to defend others? With only about 5 million Israelis' Jews with a total population of about 10 million why would one kill off such a high percentage of Jews? The figure came up to be about 1% of all Israelis that were Jewish. There were about 6 million Jews in America. The Arabic aliens in Israel had, since 1948 tried to inhabit foreign soil with the Jews. They were not wanted in any of the Arabic nations, but why? Why were these Arabs not taken in? Could it have been that there was a plot to destroy Israel, even before it's inception as a state? England did not want the Israelis' State, nor did Germany, or any of the Arab nations. Little did the United Nations know that Israel would remain now forever, but of course the New Age, the UN was going to try to destroy the Jews once and for all, because Satan was in charge of this anti-Semitism. The analogy could be seen between the 60's "blacks" and these Arab terrorists living in the Israelis' Sovereign State.

The Hasidim were the only ones who did not believe in the now State of Israel until Messiah made His "first" appearance but would be too late for them. With Israel's secular state and it was secular, it would not be a nation, or a "light unto the world" for only Messiah's second return could provide that light. The nation would be individual, but not personal the way GOD the Father, the Son and the Holy Spirit is. In the OLAM HABA the Messianic Jews would rule with Messiah from Jerusalem. Right now Israel was an apostate state losing time, people land and most of all faith in the GOD of Abraham, Isaac and Jacob. It still was a home land for Jews, such as the Ethiopian Falash Mura and not to please the West's Multiculturalism, or Enlightment. Whether Ashkenazim or Sephardim, Reformed, Constructionist, Conservative, Orthodox, or Ultra- Orthodox it did not matter. Only that soon the Tribulation would begin and they all would be lost. What had the Jew known about the entire Bible and it's rich heritage about them, except for the Messianic Jews who did and yet did not even address the infanticide issue in Israel and in America which was indeed a sad affair? Did they too believe that this could be ignored, or did they know, or did not care?

"Let the little children come unto Me."

Was not Messiah at one time a little Jewish child also? What did most Gentiles know about Passover, instead of paganized Easter, or of Biblical Hanukah, instead of paganized Christmas, or for that matter any of the other Feasts and Holy Days that GOD only recognized by His Word in Scripture? Yes Messianic Jews were to worship and keep all these Holy Days, but as Gentile believers we too were to worship as to only the real Holy Days that were in Scripture. No it did not bring salvation, but GOD was to be remembered in this way. It appeared the real Holy Days were lost, but would be celebrated in the OLAM HABA. No more Europeanism religiosity well intended, or not.

Charles Spurgeon was right when he said, "There are more people in heaven, because of infant mortality rates", and now with our new infanticide and this crusade against Christians in the 20th and 21st Centuries.

Christians in the West could not get angry, not even about murder and also pedophilia, but apathy was certainly no problem. All conceptions, egg and sperm whether in laboratories, through miscarriages, infanticide, or any other process were all in GOD'S saved family. A human being was formed by GOD. Up until the age of accountability they were all protected, and only GOD knew with each person what that was. For most it was early in their childhood when most children understood what Messiah in the heart meant to them. (Romans 10:9-10). All the above are saints of GOD. John the Baptist never baptized infants, only ones who understood their planted seed through Y'eshua. Also, no unbelievers should take part in the Body and Blood of Messiah during Communion, or if one was not right with GOD and if one was not saved by grace and grace alone, or they could become sick and ill and possibly die. About 250,000,000 Christians were persecuted, and another 700,000,000 live in severe discrimination and all these numbers were increasing daily.

Who is a believer can be discussed, but GOD only knows who they are for sure and His Word is quite clear about it.

Catholicism and homosexuality and pedophilia in it's order.

Lenin said, "A Communist should tolerate a priest that violates young girls."

Hezballah was Iranian backed and a Shiite part of Islam. The PLO terrorist organization was formed in 1964. After Communism some post-Communists along with Moslem backing sought to exclude a role for the Greek and the Orthodox minority.

In Laos the Communist Party welcomed Buddhism, but persecuted Christians. The first "Christian" to step foot in Korea probably occurred in the 16th Century when a Catholic chaplain attached to a marauding army from Japan's Shogun came. This was a most tragic event in history.

The Greek Orthodox militia in Romania set up to terrorize religious minorities. Many Romanians were invited to America again under "Prince Charming".

Protestants have the best record for allowing religious freedom, Catholics only protect their own and the Orthodox are the most persecuted. If the nation of Israel had repented after Peter's second sermon and after Y'eshua had resurrected, "the lame man had been healed" then Israel would have seen the Kingdom. There was this short duration still. Unfortunately the nation did not and hence the Second Advent is a waiting expectation for Messianic Jews. Shall there be more Jews in heaven then even Gentiles? "Repent for the Kingdom of heaven is at hand."

The 5TH TRUMPET was blown, this is the 1ST WOE. What appeared in metaphor is the following. Without a star the angel to the Abyss was seen falling from the sky and was opening the Pit to release the worse demons that GOD had locked up and now would release them to torment all men, unless they had the seal of God on them. In Scripture these were described as "locusts". This is the same angel that shall confine Satan to the Abyss for 1,000 years, or the OLAM HABA. No one in America then seemed immune to this Americanism.

Even the iconoclast Billy Graham had made anti-Semitic remarks and also had said that churches in the Soviet Union in 1982 had no religious persecution.

He was a graduate of Wheaton College with an elderly friend of mine who said that in one of their classes Billy had fallen asleep and the good Dr. said, "Please wake up Billy, he is a good boy."

There was also a booklet published called the NORTH KOREA JOURNEY which passed over government repression. One would have to ask as to the why to some of the above? Maybe he believed once they got in they could then preach the Gospel? Or perhaps they trusted the National and World Council of Churches? Mr. Graham had admitted he attended one Communist Party meeting by mistake. "All have sinned and fallen short of the glory of GOD." Even Carter's friend, Fidel Castro the butcher got into the act by courting Jesse Jackson and the "black" churches to his island of Communism, or utopia.

Were America's "blacks" becoming a master "race"? Thirty percent of Moslems in America were "black" for whatever reason or excuse. Even Michael Jackson, the pedophile like Madonna is, went to entertain Islam by being invited to the world's richest sheik's birthday party. Could this sheik also be?

The World Council of Churches chose to focus on civil rights' socialism like the Black Congressional Caucus in America and not the crucifixions in the Sudan in 1996. The Black Moslem Congressional Caucus was also anti-Semitic, but that should come as no surprise many were Moslems themselves. This Caucus was also an offshoot to another party within the National Democratic Party called the Progressive Party with it's own set of by-laws and regulations that they swore to uphold. How far would political subversion go? There were 53 members already.

If "white" is the presence of all colors meaning all inclusive, why is any human being regarded as a "black" and not a Negro meaning with "black" which is not all inclusive, but the absence of all other colors, hence reverse racism one could contend would be in affect and be disguised as a wolf in sheep's clothing? Why the racial term "black" in a positive light?

Y'eshua, GOD in the flesh and a Jewish man said, "We are all ONE RACE the human race," so why the new term of "black" music, "black" athletes, et cetera, when integration not by force in government and Big Business was meant to assimilate not discriminate by either side, or sides.

Our Founders forced integration to an extreme and now the other side wishes to do the very same thing and to the fullest extent by government and popularity, but also by the way of Islam? "One nation, one personality, under GOD", not under man's dictates. Two wrongs do not make a right.

With man's rejection of GOD'S Son for the most part in man's entire history this odium in man remains until death, then there is no more choice to reject, or accept Messiah and Hell which is temporary now, but a reality just as much as you can see your hand or my hand in front of me. Man's sin was forgiven, but only through Messiah and "many are called, but few are chosen". One prayer that GOD does hear from any unbeliever (Romans 10:9-10).

Cain slew his brother Abel and since that first human murder man has been hating or killing. Remember, this was a biological brother who Eve chose that is Cain as her favorite and "if one hates his brother he is a murderer."

In Communist countries, if one is thought to be thinking about GOD then that person is found guilty as charged by reasonable insanity on their part and are to be considered not normal. They never are wrong and in America we use to relegate, or did relegate to the fact that the real criminal has broken GOD'S Law. Probable cause never enters, because the environment is always to blame and so it is not man's old man in Adam in Communist countries. Even George Bush, Sr. interfered with double jeopardy and finding the defendants guilty because of what they thought (mind reading), hence more POLITICAL CORRECTNESS. These conclusions reveal socialism and fascism, as well as the criminals who administrate justice, or should I say "social" justice.

There are 6 kinds of socialisms mentioned by Karl Marx, plus many more not mentioned just like there are many kinds of democracies. Nazism is first of all socialistic deviancy, plus anti-"Semitic, anti-GOD racism against the Jewish race. It was not necessarily in economics but in the group homosexual mentality that put brotherhood first, even before the sovereign state. Can democracies evolve into socialism? Most often times they do, because the majority never know what's right and voting does not seek the truth. A monarch under Biblical Christianity is the best form of government, because the authority figure needs to lead and has an personal view and not an ideology like all parties do. Family and monarchy are Biblical, democracies and oligarchies are not. Oligarchy is by a powerful few. Democracy is mob rule and a monarch is one person. Man must have someone rule over him morally for anarchy is much worse and anyways man shall choose totalitarianism over anarchy.

An elected Hitler by the Reichstag put Hitler in total power. His friend Stalin inherited from Lenin class socialism, or full fledged Communism, not yet come to fruition. Hitler and Stalin the Georgian were friends and that should come as no surprise since both were socialists. Lenin chose Trotsky, but Stalin eliminated Trotsky in socialist Mexico.

Many consider Saudi Arabia a monarch, but it is not. It has dictators who rule through Islam another innate form of socialism. Even America elected a socialist at the near end of the 20th Century and who won by only a so called majority of about 25% of the popular vote, because all who were eligible to vote did not register to vote, or did not vote if registered. Many others voted a multiple amount of times, plus other parties ran to get him in appearing to oppose him, such as Ross Perot the billionaire. One can already see why democracies have no longevity to them. Most do not understand democracy, let alone it's idiosyncratic ways and means of mob rule. It does sometimes strive for hope with good intentions, but human nature usually prevails.

Free will, which Satan hates along with GOD'S will means one can choose good over evil with GOD in control, but man must rely on GOD'S will and the faith He gives to one to do so. Love vs disobedience. Satan's tool that he uses is discouragement and also apathy, pride, ego avarice, vanity, power, envy, jealously, the old man Adam, et cetera, if we allow him to and if GOD'S permissive will concurs. "You can do anything to Job, but you cannot take his life." Would not GOD use his absolute will if we would obey Him?

Many people like socialism, because there appears to be no responsibility only giving up one's freewill to the party ideology. Dead beat dads and big government are both promoters of this father to families, or mishap and dysfunctional families. These groups sell everything out, even their own soul and rarely, if ever come back from this eternal Hell. Only grace can save them, or us. No government works perfectly, but without Messiah there is no hope whatsoever. America once had that hope at it's inception and now would go protect a heathen nation for avarice?

The Founding Fathers had a moral idea before they had a government. The Pilgrims and Puritans were Christians not European zealots of religiosity. The Law was Scripture. The poor in America now have been materialistically destroyed. The land had a moral and an economic issue. Education is secular as Dewey and Mann chose. Getting high and stealing is tops in the world in America that is why the rich and the elite wanted to legalize drugs and did not support Colombia and other nations to fight off their drug lords. What is our nationality? Is it not where one's loyalty lies, as well as one's national origin? To say Americans had become a dirty word. Islam cannot live with Christianity just as Messiah and Satan cannot share the same space. Why are military bases in Islamic countries and not Christian countries? Keep the morally best and brightest down. The Democratic Party's patriotism was socialism. Why do we hold Puerto Rico or Guam as territories and why do we allow 101 different languages to be spoken with government approval? Give them their freedom, of course with conditions. The size of a nation is not as important as the spirituality of a nation. Where were our Christian origins from? The Scottish Enlightment? Who were these historical Americans and what does capitalism's hold on Arabic Islam have to do with America? World Bank? Socialism is pure materialism and capitalism feeds into that every time. The major denominations lost site of a vision and became more political than spiritual. English and the Judeo-Christian faith is the cultural religion and no other to hold authority ... The real minorities must have a say, but no longer was that so. The socialists introduced America to devisiveness. Can Harlem be an island from America? The local elections should have remained no bigger, then a county in area who then in turn would send a representative or representatives from their appointed group to the state with no parties. We do not need a Portuguese flight from Angola. We need no more dump sights, or space programs and fathers need to make enough so mothers can stay with their children. Sports should never be 7/24 and 365, or state sponsored, or even professional. About 80% of committees and ministries could be done away with in government. Who shall work the land? Make private property and zero real estate taxes. Does not government and the rich deny private property to the poor? No joint stock companies as private land owners. Foreigners should be restricted to buying land in America. Limited amounts of land to be bought and not Ted Turner's 68,000 acres in Montana. This restriction would encourage city dwellers to raise their own food. This should be free. An administration is loaded with bureaucracy. Foreign investments should never exceed internal exported profits. Real families should get all real first benefits. No atheism taught anywhere, such as evolution in any taxpayer public school in America. Teachers must be taught Founding Forefathers principles. Americanism in filth must stop from Hollywood, Washington DC and New York City. DC is not an entity unto itself. The structure of government is secondary to a nation spiritually and we can see that in our Founding Forefathers. No system works without morality and how much the Germans love their systems. Too much political activity means lesser spiritual activity in a nation. Crimes increase, because the paths to honest upwardness have been blocked for the young.

Let us use self-restraint, or self-discipline, instead of more rights. Communication bombards the mind with nonsense, such as liquified radio and television.

Each nation has a uniqueness about the type of government it needs. Cloning is not necessary. The size of a nation plays a major part in this. Democracy is for a small city state as in Greece. A monarchy can turn into tyranny, an aristocracy into an oligarchy and democracy into mob rule. No new governments have appeared, but only the additions of a constitution. National security over human rights. Democracy is to limit government, but has done the very opposite. Inequality means different talents, ages, life's experience, loyalty. This is quantity over not quality. An apportioned representation is a ticket, or candidate drawn up by the party with no personal responsibility to the voter only to the party ideology. Lenin chose this form to gain votes and control government. Plural voting is pre-election alliance. If slightly ahead the Winner can take all which leaves a high part of the population unrepresented. A candidate with lesser votes can actually win. The decisive majority where voting is not a search of the truth and mediocrity comes to the fore. Greece rejected the oligarchy because of it's small size as a country. Government has less rights than the people do have GODLY rights always with conditions the same as freedom. Separation of 3 parts is not good for the American body politic. No lawyers would be quite affective. Our Pilgrims and Puritans had Christian responsibility and self-discipline. "A party is first and foremost a power," as Trotsky said. Party struggle is worse than natural catastrophies. The cream at the top turns sour in an oligarchy and in a democracy. Outside control of constitutions miss. Citizen assembly works for democracy. The right to bear arms (Aristotle) by an open display of votes. Township government, or district, a large city, a region and a state from the bottom up and starting at the local level and not vice versa. America is too big to elect "foreignors" in a national election. Vote for the person and not a party ideology. Short campaigns not state funded. Local funding could be decided by local authorities. Ages to vote should be 24 years of age for the national level. Residency should be for at least 7 years. The local politicians elect an executive board from themselves to serve, or run at a higher level. Local elections are by direct vote only. The executive will be upon the size of the area. This must be a 4 level system with each one rising gradually and not jack in the boxes as surprise candidates that nobody knows. Local self reliance not career politicians. A strong presidency is good with laws covering all restrictions. The House would nominate a candidate. Two rounds of voting would do. No long election campaign. The Cabinet must be authoritatively trained for their positions at a 2, or 3 year academy. A government does not have a bureaucracy, an administration does. Petitions from the people can be sent to the House. Common occupation and shared territory equals cooperation.

The 6TH TRUMPET was blown and this is the 2ND WOE. Four ANGELS met at the Euphrates River at an exact day and hour to be released to meet the 200,000,000.

There was a "little horn" which was the scroll with a seal which stood for the mystery of GOD and was not to be opened by Daniel until the end time.

Annanias and Sapphira lied to the Holy Spirit in regards to what they promised to give to the church a living body. The property was theirs and they could do with it what they wanted and could sell it for whatever, but made a promise for a certain amount and lied to others to impress others others who probably gave more and then they rescinded part of the original amount and lied to the Ruach Hakodesh. When Shimon HaShaliach asked them, "Why have you lied to the Ruach Hakodesh?" They both one at a time dropped dead literally at Shimon HaShaliach's feet and were carried out.

Job, or Russia and Samson America both had lied to the Ruach Hakodesh too. This was the personal "collective" body. His protection for these once Christian Nations had gone. They were no longer glorifying the Father through Y'eshua. It was people that GOD was concerned about one by one and as a nation. The death of two nations, or civilizations by man's will not GOD'S.

A nation can remain physical by the state and die spiritually. I was born under capitalism being oblivious to real freedom with conditions. The accumulative process of evil continued and took over and the nations took on wills of their own, or of the enemy and not of GOD'S.

This personality is spiritual and is not a group. A family is an institution. Families make up neighborhoods and neighborhoods make up a nation. Other institutions such as cities and towns are governmental endeavors, or enclaves started by Cain's relatives. Villages are communes set in Socialistic government attire. Villages in Russia were different in that they were neighborhoods, until the Soviets were established.

Self-esteem and self-preservation go hand in hand. Egotistical self with individualism at the core. Sentimentality as in Nazi Germany keeps families apart and hence real neighborhoods never form and family becomes a possession and so does everything else. Gangs like Hitler's Youth Corps formed into militaristic groups and criminality reigned and father is hated, hence homosexuality ... as in Germany's case developed. In the USSR the Kosmosol formed the wrong fatherless state. It is not innate for man to do good. Man must learn honor and respect and love as a commitment and not from passion, or odium. Made in the image of GOD man has a soul, spirited heart and a mind to reason to decide, but without Messiah man always decides wrong. Agape' love the third love in Greek is GODLY love. English does not express love in three's.

The West took John Locke's socialism and made everything consumer driven, hence consumerism. Even the churches have gone along with this. What many called so called blessings were actually materialism's want.

"Without faith it is impossible to please GOD."

When man suffers he grows usually, because self must be rendered useless. To get something in return is GOD'S business. In the West consumerism took over for a faith and these "blessings" were proof of it. They could be seen so they had to be blessings, right?

Any man's clock in time can stop, or in the realm of mortal time and in an instant physical man, or his physical being is gone and the ability to now believe is gone forever. This too is in the twinkling of an eye and GOD knows when and how long and why and why not. "Not works lest any man shall boast."

Theatrical reality has only one curtain call. The stage curtain shall close on each of us one by one.

The lie, an invention by Satan which meant he was never original, but only emulated good, but always as evil. The charade is passing and with this New Age it too shall deceive, because man chooses to believe the lie and GOD HAS NOT CHOSEN ALL.

"Satan is the father of all lies."

GOD created Lucifer with free will just as we have free will, and also gave him a high role, but was not surprised by Satan or Adam. Wanting through pride to be equal with GOD, he chose Hell for himself and his cohorts. Their fallen nature has no repentance, they are doomed. With man, in part, GOD gave us His undying love for all mankind. This invention has been mechanized in the machinery of rebellion. Sin is contagious, sin is never intended for man, but GOD knew what was in man's heart. Theatrical reality has already been known by GOD, not written by GOD, so GOD knows the scenario to be played out on the stage of life but does not interfere and only encourages to do right according to His will, and His absolute will becomes His ...

Free will - such a misleading word to man's fallen nature. Are we free to do as we want? Heaven forbid... GOD is an authoritarian GOD, not a democratic GOD in His ways and freewill depends mostly on GOD and not on man. GOD wills us to do good. His undying love for us. Are we yet not responsible for obedience?

Adam and Eve were innocent before sin in a perfect environment. Only GOD could be perfect. All were created angelic and human. GOD audibly spoke to Adam and Eve and both chose to ignore GOD'S voice. This is not a metaphor. Just as Moses received the 10 Commandments by the finger of GOD, Moses too heard an audible voice. GOD spoke the universe into being. Adam was tempted, but Satan was not. Adam though allowed Satan into his world by being disobedient to GOD. Satan could not have entered man's world in any other way, but GOD allowed Satan to be there. Adam was not possessed before sinning. Neither had the ability not to sin, but then if they would have GOD would not be GOD. This New Age is like Satan that says, "There is no sin and this invention, or lie of Satan. It again says man's environment is the innate problem such as poverty and never too rich. Why the contradiction? If it is environment alone, then there can be no other variables. It is the complete lie. No good vs evil. This is socialism's false utopia to make it better by man's freewill alone which means in closed time and ignores GOD'S will completely.

The 7TH TRUMPET sounded but before that the End of the Gentiles must be with the SECOND ADVENT from Judah which started in Babylon in 605 BC.

The witnesses are polemical, because in a sense most believe they are Moses and Elijah, or Elijah and Enoch, because in the Old Testament the latter two did not see death. Could it be that the above scenario is wrong? Could these 2 Witnesses belong to the latter day remnant? These 2 Witnesses are killed by the enemy but after 3 full days and on the 4th day they stand up and come back to life and are resurrected and then ascend into heaven.

Now the 7TH TRUMPET and the 3RD WOE is the remaining judgments before the establishment of the OLAM HABA OF MESSIAH. Armageddon judgment of the dead, the destroyers of the earth are destroyed and rewarding of the prophets and the saints in the OLAM HABA with positions of rule and domain occur. In the Tribulation: PERSON #1 is a woman, Israel; PERSON #2 the dragon, Satan and PERSON #3 is the male child, Messiah; PERSON #4 is Michael, the Archangel. Satan tries to persecute the woman with the water like a river, the Gentile nations who are wicked. PERSON #5 the remnant, Israel, the Jews who did not escape to safety during the Tribulation, kept GOD'S Commandments; PERSON #6 is the beast out of the sea; PERSON #7 the beast out of the earth and the False Prophet most likely a fully possessed Jewish man. The mark of the beast is unknown. Babylon's Fall means not to worship the beast, but GOD. This "Babylon" is Satan's world system, New Age. To reiterate the 7 BOWLS OF GOD. The 1ST BOWL is spiritual and physical affliction to all unbelievers. BOWL 2 is a godless society. BOWL 3 is fresh waters that become blood. BOWL 4 is solar heart. BOWL 5 is darkness over the beast's kingdom. BOWL 6 is the Euphrates River that dried up. BOWL 7 is Satan and his cohorts drive onto the earth and out of heaven, because Messiah is there and Messiah and Satan cannot share the same area. The "harlot" is the corrupt religionism. The "beast" shall turn against this harlot..

The marriage of the Lamb with the Judgment Seat of Messiah for believers. Invited guests are the Tanach Saints. Messiah's Second Advent. He is on a white horse, this time no emulation by the enemy.

The 1ST COMPANY from Abel to the Translation of the church. The 2ND COMPANY is the souls of martyrs in the early part of the Tribulation in their disembodied state. The 3RD COMPANY is the souls who did not worship the beast and belong to the martyrs of the GREAT TRIBULATION. The martyred in the Tribulation is the so called 1ST RESURRECTION. This RESURRECTION occurs after the marriage and before the beginning of the OLAM HABA. The 1ST RESURRECTION includes the 3 above COMPANIES. These COMPANIES shall reign with Messiah in the OLAM HABA. After 1,000 years Satan is released and the POST OLAM HABA is as the PRE OLAM HABA Rebellion was and is metaphorically named "Gog and Magog". The Resurrection of the dead, the Second Resurrection is for all unbelievers. Unbelievers, Satan and his cohorts will all be eventually thrown into the burning like of fire forever and not Hell and shall not die.

The GREAT WHITE THRONE OF JUDGMENT will be just before the burning lake of fire. Each unbeliever is face to face alone with GOD. Death and hell are down away with after the FIRST RESURRECTION. After the Second Resurrection there shall be people to rule over on the New Earth.

Judas Iscariot was believed to be a demon because of the implications of what he was to do to Messiah. No man could be trusted to do this alone since man could almost always repent while an "angelic being" could not. "Go and do what you have to do."

Y'eshua in the wilderness with Satan. "Be gone Satan. I shall worship the Lord my GOD and only Him shall I serve."

"Change these stones into bread."

"Man does not live by bread alone, but by every Word that proceeds from the mouth of GOD."

"Jump down from the top."

"Do not tempt the Lord my GOD."

"Worship me and I shall give you all the kingdoms on earth."

"Be gone Satan."

Y'eshua sent them out two by two, a Body. The Disciples were all Jewish. The church Peter received was the Body of Messiah. In the B'rit Hadasha Rev Shaul talks about the TRANSLATION of the church almost as if it was immediate and today the same also appears this and of the world, or the coming of the Tribulation was somewhat hysteria in that America had a proclivity for earth's total destruction which is another lie and that if America fell that must mean the end was near. GOD gives prophecy little by little and America disillusioned itself to believe with it's demise came so the world's demise. This consumer driven church but near Philadelphia Church as soon coming, but not because of America, but because of Israel and the events that surrounded Jerusalem. The world ruler would come from Europe probably. GOD'S timing was His own and not ours, nor His thoughts our thoughts. The Eastern Church was growing by leaps and bounds but the Western church was dying. The Ruach Hakodesh was spreading out before the TRANSLATION. America called for this "Rapture" or at least this Kingdom Dominion Theology Now to setup up the OLAM HABA. America's poor were affluent to the world's poor and destitute that is why everybody and anybody wanted to come to America. America's demise did not create this world system, but fell prey to it, hence America was playing New Age follow the leader. Europeanism and Israel were mundanely growing. America was falling both morally and spiritually and nobody could turn back the hands of time. This American Apochalypse was not anything in the Bible.

During dying, as in life man must have the courage to face the truth. If one as a believer would see others literally die, this would give that believer the courage to at least face their own death with courage as a Christian. It would help the believers to overcome this fear of death not that one hated life, or wanted to seek death, but that while in the trenches of death all around GOD'S courage would be seen as a testimony to others and bring them comfort and give glory to a Holy GOD. A support system of family and friends is important. One must come to understand that dying is a process and can come to face natural death with GODLY courage. Suicide, to commit murder could never provide that and was the easy way out in almost all cases. Materialism holds too to self-preservation.

The human brain is remarkable, but does not have a predetermined make up internally. When one thinks about that it is incredible to know that freewill in essence forms the genetic code for each brain. GOD'S miracles is this freewill thought that cannot be emulated and this part of man makes him different from the animal world. GOD'S cerebral cortex is where all reasoning is done. Man's soul as opposed to the animal world's lack of a soul.

Relationship with GOD first not rights, but responsibility for oneself in regards always for others. Not to do for them, but to show through GOD'S love what they can do through Messiah and that through faith with obedience it is to GOD's glory. We confuse ourselves with too much self, or too much doing for others what they should want to do for themselves and can do. Our rights are given up for others and not nonsensical animal rights who cannot reason, hence have no soul and are accountable to no one. With man's rights should always first come accountability. "We are our brother's keeper, but not through government, or what this brother can do for himself. Self-discipline is a habit with obedience to Him as our Teacher and has to be learned like honor and love.

GOD is the only Original. All others emulate and in some instances it is okay to emulate, but never with the heart. Energy can be neither created, nor destroyed, neither can man, except by GOD and He only does the former and never the latter. Every angelic and human being is eternal. None shall be missing from one of two places. The correlation of "good" of human and angelic beings and the correlation of the evil of human and angelic beings.

In original America, GOD over government was important. Now government was god. Was government imported?

In the sense that it was not original but baggage was brought with it through John Locke's materialism. Religion tried to be monarchial in the sense it was messianic as king over all men in America. Equal members in Messiah, not equality of government by man, which is communism. Unalienable rights mean only given by a Judeo-Christian GOD who is a Monarch. GOD never gives civil rights, because it had to do with socialism and superiority. Always superior rights in the sense that talents and abilities would not be recognized. Who is superior but GOD?

In America for centuries during slavery homosexuality was prevalent as it had been in the French Reign of Terror, the Roman Empire, Nazi Germany and the Spanish Inquisition. It appeals to man's lowest nature always.

Was this original?

The 13 colonies were with few colonists. Denominationalism in the First Amendment is established as not to be, but also in the way one would, or could worship Messiah that was to be left alone by all of government. America's English founded by Mr. Webster the slang and England's colloquialisms dissipated. This was a new nation made up of not only Englishmen, but of many nationalities with this American English as it's only language but more importantly only an American GOD. Quakerism, knights in shining armor (those who live by the sword die by the sword) or at least a sect tried to make their denomination more important within the Christian faith. This fatherland became a motherland through the years and foreign cultures who lacked the Father bowed down to Eve's deception. History is an inexact science since most all historians write in the past and not from the present.

Medical science exploded in the 1940's and went beyond what we call humanity well beyond and became pseudo-science and medicine. Uneducated in America as a democratic/republic is suicide to a nation. This use of people, weapons, organizations and money is what equals power. The power of communism in Russia was to strike with no reason. An answer to solve the solution to bring about the Revolution and civil war to destroy a nation.

GOD rested on the 7th day, why? Was He tired? Was not the Sabbath made for man and not man for the Sabbath?

The usuriousness of the Pentagon gave them power to purchase screw drivers that normally cost a few dollars for about $40 a piece as well as thousands of other items. What would all this unionism lead to? Would first the police then the military be used against the American people with first the workers incited to then overturn a government from within in a subversive manner?

If George Washington had become a monarch he would have lead a Christian nation being that he was a Christian and not by denomination but by being an American Biblical. If one seeks Christianity through a Christian, can it be achieved? The Biblical mode was a monarch not a President but nonetheless can be authoritative even though no president is mentioned in the Bible. Servants not slaves could have become indentured servants with the ability to buy land. The Scripture in an individual view and not a political party's ideology. Hired workers for others with wages. George Washington left a will for his slaves to provide them with for 40 years their health care provision. Not even government can make a will in a democracy even though some try to. Washington was born in America. The Articles of Confederation did not work hence Constitutional government not a monarch, not another form of government outside of Greek democracy which is mob rule in such now a huge nation, or country. This could not last for a long time. In the French Revolution Hamilton favored England and Jefferson favored France. Even Lenin studied The French Revolution. Remember Washington kept our nation out of it, because France was exporting it's revolution, hence socialism. George Washington prayed one hour in the morning and one hour in the evening each day. Deists don't really pray? His Presidency was from 1789-1797 and he was elected by the Electoral College, even though the people wanted him to become their king.

With slavery came Biblical sin, knowledge and grace. The collective body is the nation's soul and slavery and slaves were part of that collective body no matter what. Brought to Scripture by Love? America supplied the nourishment for future generations? No human government is perfect, but many are evil.

A Christian monarch would have been the best, because outside interference would have been stopped. The people too would have fought for the monarch a real person and not an inanimate government, such as parchment paper. This was not Catholicisim's state religion by coercion. GOD is of love, not power. New Age is state religion always, or world religion, but that is okay for New Agers now in America, because this god appeals to the flesh always. Constantine, Caesar, was the first part and religion the second, hence government with a capital G. The secular over the moral idea. Not a monarch, but an oligarchy the Vatican.

With a monarch Americans would have more understood today that George Washington was a Christian king not apolitical archaic leader which some have rendered him as such and would have brought a correlation to America as a Christian nation. A king would have ruled with Queen Martha. America with a Christian King a monarch like our Messiah as far as being authoritative in the Biblical sense. This would have instituted the first family as Christian which government in two other forms could not do.

John Adams was for a monarch too and owned no slaves. Also born in America he went to Harvard seminary school, but as a lawyer in Blackstone's Law. Congress passed the Alien and Sedition Act. He also was a Christian (1797-1801). He probably was the 3rd best President we ever had.

Thomas Jefferson was the third President who was a Deist. Now already we see a falling away from Judeo-Christianity in the form of this democratic/republic. Jefferson was a writer not an orator. He was for small federalized government, but rights for states. He eliminated the whiskey tax. He owned slaves. (1801-1809).

James Madison the 4th President was a Mason and attended Princeton another seminary school who studied history, government and law. He help write the Federalists' Papers. He enacted the first revenue legislation. He help start the war of 1812. He was for the Union and bigger gov't. Another turn away from Christianity (1809-1817). No creed, but Y'eshua.

James Monroe the 5th President was a politician, but barred all slavery north and west of Missouri forever. He formulated the Monroe Doctrine, protectionism, and too was a Mason and Christianity continued to move further away from the leaders in America. He served from 1817-1825. He was for the French cause.

John Quincy Adams the 6th President went to Harvard as a lawyer. He got the Floridas, plus formulated in full the Monroe Doctrine that would keep all hostile enemies out of the Western Hemisphere and served from 1825-1829. What about freedom for all nations?

Andrew Jackson the 7th President was self-educated and rugged. He was for slavery. He tried to eliminate the Electoral College and served from 1829-1837. He tired to put in term limits. He was an aggressive executor-in-chief, was against banking and the government, but sponsored monopolies. He was a soldier type President.

Martin Van Buren the 8th President from 1837-1841 was of Dutch descent, one of the few outside the Anglo-Saxons and a lawyer. He destroyed government's bank and made hard assets to be used to buy land. There could be no state banks. He also was against slavery. (No college)

William Henry Harrison was the 9th President and served about one half of a year. He was self-educated and studied medicine, but also fought against the Indians. When he was a governor he was for settlers obtaining Indian lands. He died in office of pneumonia. The Indians never found America because they never had founded a nation. They existed as separate tribes.

John Tyler was the 10th President from 1841-1845 and was against nationalist legislation and against state banks. He was almost impeached. He was for states' rights and slavery. He worked at a Southern Confederacy and was a Constitutionalist.

James K. Polk the 11th President from 1845-1849 was again another lawyer who wanted to annex Oregon (North), Texas (South) and California. This annexation was causing more of a dispute about slavery.

Zachary Taylor was number 12 and served from 1849-1850 and was against slavery and he was a military man though he owned 100 slaves. He encouraged that the state constitutions to decide the issue of slavery. In Washington D.C. slavery was still legal. He also died in office. (No college).

Millard Fillmore was number 13 and served from 1850-1853 and was a lawyer who filled in for the remaining term of Zachary Taylor and he was for slavery. (No college)

Franklin Pierce, number 14, served from 1853-1857 who too was another lawyer and whose son died at the age of 11 years old in a train wreck. He was for expanionism to include Cuba.

James Buchanan the 15th President served from 1857-1861 and was the only President from the state of Pennsylvania and was the only President who was never married. A lawyer and a debater he leaned for judicial fiat in slavery. Dred Scott in 1857 was decided against Negroes and the United States Supreme Court said that Negroes were not persons, but property. Buchanan became wishy washy on issues especially slavery.

Abraham Lincoln the 16th President served actually two terms or was elected twice and wrote the Gettysburg Address and too was self-educated, but was a slick lawyer. He would protect the Union at all costs. His mother died when he was 10 years old. Mary Todd his wife and he had 4 children or 4 sons and only one lived to maturity. He issued the Emancipation Proclamation on January 1, 1863. The last 2 years of his life he became a Christian. He was assassinated in Ford's Theatre by John Wilkes Booth, an actor, on Good Friday. He was for centralized government. He had to know Civil War was the worse kind of war. (1861-1865 and no college)

Andrew Johnson the 17th President served from 1865-1869 after Lincoln was assassinated, and was for states' rights, but against aristocracy's slavery at that time. HE was for the common poor man and opposed the rich. He wanted to provide land for the poor. A Civil Rights' Act was passed in 1866 which said that Negroes...were citizens and said discrimination was illegal. The 14th Amendment was passed. He was almost impeached, but one vote saved him. He violated the Tenure of Office Act. (No college)

Ulysses S. Grant the 18th President from 1869-1877 was a general who went to West Point against his will. He won the battle of Vicksburg, Mississippi and divided the Confederacy. General Lee surrendered to Grant at Appomattox Court House.

Rutherford Hayes was the 19th President and served from 1877-1881 and banished all liquor from the White House by the Women's Christian Temperance Union, another Union. He went to Harvard Law School. He too was a general. Mark Twain, an agnostic, supported Hayes as President. He chose his cabinet according to qualifications. He upheld freedom and promoted self-government locally.

James A. Garfield was the 20th President and served in 1881. He was fatherless at the age of 2. Another general and also he was a college president. He was shot in office by another lawyer. He served only 6 months and was a friend of Alexander Graham Bell who dabbled in the occult.

Chester A. Arthur was the 21st President, served from 1881-1885 and finished the rest of Garfield's term. He was the son of a Baptist minister from Ireland. He was a lawyer and a teacher. He believed in the spoils system of party politics. He was a jet setter. He set up the Civil Service Commission which meant more government waste. He enacted the first general Federal Immigration Law which included no lunatics, or criminals, or paupers into the nation.

Grover Cleveland was the 22nd President and 24th President and served from 1885-1889 and 1893-1897. His father was a Presbyterian minister and he was one of 9 children. He was a lawyer and he got married while in office the only man to do so. He was against farm subsidies, or special favors, no pension bills and no railroad owned lands by the government by way of grants, or free money. He help start the Interstate Commerce Act to regulate the railroads. He maintained the Treasury's gold reserve with the Federal Reserve's help and he stopped railroad strikers. Later teachers and nurses were to strike in America's history. (No college).

Benjamin Harrison was the 23rd President from 1889-1893 who too was a lawyer and started the first Pan American Union in which billions of dollars in government funds were spent on business. He signed anti-trust laws and was the grandson of another President.

William McKinley was the 25th President and served from 1897-1901 and he too was a jet setter. He also was a lawyer. During his term William Randolph Hearst printed lies about the Spaniards brutalizing the Cubans and hence started the Spanish-American War. He seized Puerto Rico as President and Guam and the Philippines. He was shot in office at a Pan American Exposition.

Theodore Roosevelt was a Blue Blood who was the 26th President and served from 1901-1909 and became President at the age of 43 and the teddy bear nonsense was named after him. He broadened all executive powers and was born in New York City to a wealthy family. His first wife died and he later married a woman from London. He established the Panama Canal and was involved in foreign politics. He won the Nobel Prize for mediating the Russo Japanese War. He had 5 children and ran on the Progressive Party Ticket which came to life again around the new millennium of 2000. It had its own by-laws and was properly known as the Socialist Party within the National Democratic Party and Jesse Jackson, Jr. was one of 53 members. He, that is President Roosevelt was shot in office but survived in Milwaukee which was one of two cities in the United States ever to have a city socialist government.

William Howard Taft was the 27th President and was also a Chief Justice. He graduated from Yale Law School. He was not for executive powers, but judicial powers. He initiated 80 anti-trust law suits. He established the Federal Income Tax and the Interstate Commerce Commission and was president of Yale Law School. A falling away from the Judeo-Christian faith. His years of service were from 1909-1913.

Woodrow Wilson was the 28th President from 1913-1921 and established a new world order in America. He got into World War I so democracy was safe (mob rule), but we must remember why Germany's elites created this scandal which turned into a war and that was to cover up their sexual deviancy from the German people at large Sarajevo was just the excuse to do it. He was the son of a Presbyterian minister and graduated from Princeton Law. He was also president of Princeton. He stressed individualism and states' rights. He established a graduated Federal Income Tax, the Federal Reserve, and the Federal Trade Commission and was big government President. The 8-hour work day and child labor laws he initiated were actually started by a socialist in Russia, that is the 8-hour work day. He got involved, or endorsed the League of Nations which was a prelude to the United Nations or United Governments.

Warren Harding was the 29th President and served from 1921-1923 but was unsure of the League of Nations and opposed Franklin D. Roosevelt on this issue. He was involved in church and charitable organizations. He slashed taxes and held tight limitations on immigration. He wanted less government in business. He died in office of a heart attack. No Wonder... He was the 4th best President to serve.

Calvin Coolidge was the 30th President from 1923-1929 and was sworn in on a family Bible. He too was a lawyer, but was for tax cuts and limited aid to farmers. He was a friend of Bernard Baruch, a Jewish Wall Streeter. The 1929 Depression hit in America and insurance companies were suspect.

Herbert Hoover, number 31 from 1929-1933 was a Quaker like Nixon. He graduated as a mining engineer. He extended aid to Russia in 1921 under the Soviets. He was for bigger government. Truman and Eisenhower appointed him to different commissions.

Franklin D. Roosevelt, number 32, served from 1933-1945 and was elected for 4 terms. He went to Harvard and was taught by the homosexual socialist Lord Keynes in economics of whom he adored. (Keynesian Economics). He also studied Colombia Law. He got polio in 1921 at the age of 39. The "New Deal" of socialism was started under him. He took us off of the gold standard. He initiated the socialism of Social Security. He wanted to enlarge the Supreme Court to more justices. He watered down the Monroe Doctrine. He did not want to go to war with Europe even after knowing what was going on in Nazi Germany and he appointed Joseph Kennedy as Ambassador to England. Only until Pearl Harbor on December 7, 1941 did he enter the war or he may never have. He supported the Soviets and the United Nations and failed miserably at the Yalta Conference. His wife Eleanor visited the camps of the Soviets and came out no smarter than when she went in to visit the conditions. He died in office serving his fourth term and that is why a President can only serve 2 consecutive terms. He also was a Blue Blood.

Harry S. Truman, number 33, served 2 consecutive terms. He also was a farmer. He ordered the terrible bombing of innocent civilians in Hiroshima and Nagasaki and let the Emperor dictator go. Before they were bombed, US planes dropped leaflets from the planes saying something terrible was going to happen, but did not say what, only days before. He supported the United Nations and Social Security and public housing. He backed down to the Soviets and Red China. (1945-1953).

Dwight D. Eisenhower, number 34 from 1953-1961 was also a 4 star general and only settled for a truce in Korea. He went to West Point and was president of Colombia University and headed NATO, which meant that America would defend Europe, our "stepfather", even when Europe would not or refused to defend itself. He too was a New Dealer. He loaned the atomic element uranium to other nations. He was anti-Semitic and refused to allow a Jewish ship to stay in America's ports.

John F. Kennedy, number 35, served from 1961-1963 and was assassinated or nearly assassinated in office in Dallas, Texas, but was accidentally killed, not murdered, by the rifle bullet of a Secret Service Agent. He was the first Roman Catholic President and was a womanizer and was married twice. He was of Irish descent. He also went to Harvard and did not initiate civil rights, but it was Eisenhower. He served in World War II and was not Joseph Kennedy's favorite son. His Bay of Pigs was a disaster. He was the youngest President to be elected and the youngest to die in office. He was allegedly involved with the mob because of Lansky, Roselli and Cuba along with a fling with Marilyn Monroe.

Lyndon B. Johnson, number 36, served from 1963-1969 and was another President for big government with his Great Society. He was a flaky teacher who taught Mexican students. He supported Eisenhower's measures. He started Medicare. He limited the bombing in Hanoi and major depots in North Vietnam. He used to sign all his billboards down South with his own original signature whenever he came across them in travelling. He owned a construction firm in Vietnam during the Vietnam War. He was outlandish and was known for the unmentionable.

Richard Nixon was the 37th President and served from 1969-1974 and was a Quaker. He ended the Vietnam Conflict disgracefully, but Moscow and Peking always had their door open for him. He was a lawyer for Pepsi Cola in the Soviet Union. He graduated from Duke University (the Blue Devils). He ended the draft and increased the EPA. His infamous Secretary of State was Henry Kissinger who was, or had a twin brother. He was almost impeached for Watergate, and Ehrlichmann and Haldemann went to a country club type prison, and Chuck Colson resigned and Spirio Agnew was removed from the Vice Presidency for a banking scandal. Gerald Ford the House Minority Leader was appointed President with Congressional approval and Nixon's first choice along with the majority in the Democratic Party in the House and Senate.

Gerald Ford was the 38th President from 1974-1977 who was chosen under the 25th Amendment. He went to Yale and later became a lawyer. His vice president was Nelson Rockefeller of New York State. He gave much aid to Egypt and continued with Soviet detente but refused to meet with the famous Russian Christian dissident Alexander Solzhenitsyn.

Jimmy Carter was the 39th President and served from 1977-1981 and supported homosexuality, even though he was raised as a Baptist. He also was an environmentalist and was for Habitat For Humanity and sent his daughter to the Washington D. C. Public School System. He created the Department of Education, hence the National Teachers' Association or Union, the strongest in the entire nation. He had peasants as slave labor on his peasant farms. He decimated the economy to almost 23%. He also visited the Middle East and since then there has been no peace.

Ronald Reagan was the 40th President, a Biblical Number, and served from 1981-1989 and was elected by both Republicans and Democrats and was at one time president of the Screen Actors Guild and was an actor on Death Valley Days, as well as motion pictures. He understood the common man probably better than any other President ever. He was Governor of California. His second wife Nancy (Davis) Reagan came from a well to do surgeon family. Nancy would seek the astrology charts plus an astrologer for information to give to Ronald. Reagan did almost as much as Solzhenitsyn to bring down the Soviet Union by increasing Defense Spending. With every good defense is a good offense. At one time he was pro-infanticide and then later changed and apologized for it and turned pro-life or pro-humane. He too was of Irish descent. He was a Chicago Cub announcer. He belonged to none of the elite organizations that all the modern day Presidents belonged to such as the Tri-Lateral Commission, etc. Even though his father was alcoholic, Reagan always had sense about who he was and what the Presidency really meant. He had 4 children. He was against Communism and Communism in Hollywood, which upset the Civil Righters. He chose the New Ager George Bush, Sr. as Vice President. He was shot by a .22 caliber pistol, but survived with only 69 days in office. He actually walked out of the limousine and into the hospital on his own and into the emergency room behind closed doors and then collapsed so that the nation would not panic as to how much blood he had lost and how severe it had been. He wanted the Strategic Defense Initiative, but socialists in Congress did not want it. He was one of the few Presidents that was not a lawyer and was not controlled by the rich and well educated even though Reaganomics was made fun of because it did not appeal to socialism in government. Next to George Washington I believe he was the next best President to ever hold this position. He put America back together after the previous President had mismanaged our economic system, the Middle East as well as how to deal with Communism. Bitburg and the name "Dutch" created Jewish problems for him.

George Bush, Sr., the 41st President, served from 1989-1992 and was a graduate of Yale and also a member of the Skull and Bones secret New Age organization the same as William F. Buckley. He was the youngest pilot to fly in the Pacific during the War. He raised taxes, and when Margaret Thatcher privately came to him to stop Saddam Hussein from invading Kuwait he started Desert Storm and refused to kill Saddam Hussein. April Glass was then US Ambassador to Iraq and had told Saddam Hussein it would be all right if he went into Kuwait. Desert Storm was a conflict over the rich and well educated's financial ends, since trillions of dollars went through London who in turn invested this Arab oil money in America to control and own America's economy as well as sovereignty. He played on Yale's baseball team at first base.

William Jefferson Clinton was the 42nd President and served from 1992-2000. He also graduated from Yale and Georgetown's Catholic Institution and the school that lead to politics in Washington, DC. He did not graduate from Oxford and so was not a Rhodes Scholar and was one of four students who did not. Dr. Bork had both Hillary and Bill in one of his classes while teaching at Yale. He left England to go to the Kremlin by invitation and what other way could one possibly go since he was not affiliated with the US government? He served as Governor of Arkansas with many strange stories from womanizing to murder. The Ku Klux Klan's national headquarters was in Fayetteville, Arkansas. After committing treason with the enemy, he was put on the Democratic Partly's Ticket and was run as a dark horse in the Presidential Election. He also was a homosexualist and had appointed 24 homosexuals to his cabinet and other officials around the White House. His real father was alcoholic, and his medical records, that is Bill's, could never be found even after becoming President and did not have top security clearance in regards to the nuclear button. His mother, Ms. Kelly, was involved in a suspicious death of a patient. His brother was a derelict. The death of Vince Foster was not suicidal but murder because when the body was found by the Park Security and not the FBI, the stomach was empty which is highly unusual in a suicide. The gun was in the wrong hand, the blood was flowing against gravity, and polyester fibers were found all on Vince Foster's clothing, and 3 important witnesses were ignored by the FBI as to their true testimony because two of the people were meeting through infidelity. He received only 22% of the popular vote and most "blacks" (92%) and Jews voted for him. This President always loathed the military and that is why many loyal and good military people resigned. He became Commander-In-Chief and the head Supreme Court Justice, William Rehnquist, stayed on the court when Clinton won a second term. He and Hillary are anti-Israel, but pro-Communists. Hillary's village was a code word for multi-culturalism which had its roots in Marxist/Leninism. Also Hillary's United Nation's Children Defense Fund meant that a child could sue their parents if their parents chose to discipline their children, and the Beijing Conference needs no explanation. Mr. Clinton, by far, is the worse individual to have ever served such a high office, or for that matter in the federal government. Both he and Hillary are lawyers and their daughter Chelsea had gone to the New Age University of Stanford. Vince Foster was very close to Hillary when Clinton was Governor of Arkansas. He was indicted 12 times by grand juries and each time he was "exonerated". "Kenneth" backed off from his investigation.

George W. Bush, Jr. was the 43rd President and served from 2000- . He was a Yale graduate and had a drinking problem and could not control his two daughters. His wife was pro-abortion.

Just before 9/11 he was going to sign into law the admittance of 3 million Mexicans who were illegals as citizens and then decided not to. He also wanted to reduce the qualifications for citizenship and federal funds from working 10 years in America to only 5 years of residency. His brother Jeb Bush, governor of Florida, was married to a Mexican. He was his brother's keeper. He was too young to be President. He was much more sincere than his father had been, but he too was a millionaire and owned at least half of the Texas Rangers, a baseball team in the Major Leagues. He also always seemed to be campaigning for office and would procrastinate on foreign affairs because he chose the wrong Secretary of State, Colin Powell, who was a Colonel in the Americal Division in Vietnam when the My Lai Massacre occurred. Only Lieutenant William Calley and Captain Medina had charges brought against them. This was probably the reason he was not picked for Vice President, because the CIA would have brought this to the surface and Bush would not have been elected President? Affirmative action followed Colin Powell all the years in the military. Colin Powell was anti-Israel and the Israelis knew it. He upheld Islam and Jihad terrorist organizations such as the PLO and Hamas.

Orthodoxy goes back to the Roman Empire the 4th Gentile empire. The Western part fell in the 5th Century and the East continued for another 1,000 years in the city of Constantine of which state religion was sanctioned. This Byzantium was close to the emperor but had different tasks no separation of church and state. This lasted until 1453 when the Ottoman Turks (Islam) conquered Istanbul, or Constantinople. Orthodoxy had already been accepted in Moscow 500 years earlier, but Orthodox authority then too moved to Moscow, because of Islam. Russian rulers intermarried with the Byzantine Emperor and Ivan III got the name Caesar, or Czar. Islam took control of the Middle East. St. Cyril, the Cyrillio Alphabet, formed through this alphabet the spread of Christianity in Russia. Two years later this too fell under Islamic control. The word Slav comes from slave which the Muslims made them. The Ottomans were from Bosnia, hence today Bosnian Moslems. The Serbs, or Russian Orthodox relate to these Moslems. Religious bodies had to set controls in Orthodoxy, because of Islam. Under Islam this was okay. In other words church was state. Also Jewish communities came under this affect. Only external relations did Islam control. Nationality became the church such as Russian Orthodox, or Greek Orthodoxy. They only survived because of this method against Islam's brutality. The monarch in Russia reinforced this. The monarchs and the church sought both to govern the people with church closer to the people than the Monarch. This later brought about, or help bring about the state and church of totalitarianism, but Orthodoxy needed all those horrible centuries.

CHAPTER XVII

WHOSE HISTORY?

An individual, as I said many times before, has a view, but all parties have an ideology. One example in American History is John Adams who owned no slaves and was for a monarch. Some things in history must though be let go of, or else it festers and brews inside the heart and becomes carcinogenic in nature. This was an individual view and not popular at the time with any political party, but yet if he would have been followed there possibly would have been no need for a Civil War, or any type of civil rights, or harsh race relations up to the present day?

So called monarchs, such as Arab Islamic Nations are not monarchs, but dictators, or an oligarchy of the few who rule through Islam with an iron fist. In Russia in the 20th Century they had all 3 forms of government, but ended up with totalitarianism. The Christian King must please GOD first and not special interests, or even a minority, or a majority. In Russia the monarch had all power with the local peasants forming small governments which the monarch respected for to do otherwise would be totally foolish for him.

From generation to generation Biblical kings transfer by family their values and in democracy here is little search for the truth mostly popularity contests. Even some of America's Founders spoke about GOD, but as a non-personal Deity without Messiah and that man does not have the fluctuation of good vs evil in them, but the more one goes beyond the threshold rarely if ever do they return. There are not just evil men while the others are good for we all have this constant battle of good vs evil. "No man is good." Only through Messiah can grace be bestowed. The foundation of government must have an authority figure and in America's "later" documents there was one kind of inanimate object. We are not an amoeba mass. Personalities have personal relationships. It was a system of checks and balances and a separation of government, instead of coming together. Does that mean that monarchs are perfect? No, but Christian monarchs usually want to please GOD first with the people in a humane way. As one reads our list of Presidents not too many had that in mind. It was ego and power that they sought, because they could not rule but only execute as in the executive with a division in the 3 separations of power. The Russian peasants fought for the monarch a living being a king not by popularity. Making pledges democratically upon parchment paper and not in the present time period to a living people who must always be shown self restraint, as well as self discipline in America's democracy. There were constant "parties", of two, or more kinds. The first was for holidays just about every other week and the second and third for all kinds of extra ideologies. The Christian monarch does not rule to be popular, he has a much more vested interest in ruling authoritatively.

Who found favor in GOD'S eyes? Was it not a king, but by the name of David? No mention in Scripture ever about any kind of democracy just a monarch along with judges who did what they wanted to do. Even Messiah is King of kings and not of Presidents, or Premiers, or prime ministers, etc. There is a hierarchy to GOD'S thinking and man fails most times to understand that. Many in democracies fight for a cause, or ideology and not to uphold the King, such as Messiah. A democratic/republic no matter how well intended, fails to meet the criteria of longevity and eventually dissipates very quickly and with capitalism it is only a matter of short time that man seeks himself and not GOD for authority. George Washington for example could not transcend his Christian faith to a nation because man's law obstructed GOD'S will eventually. Yes, GOD can use unbelievers, but that is rare and not long lived and also shall keep those Christians that believe that they can leave His family whenever they want to. The family as exists in a monarch or as it should Biblically be, has almost all been dissipated. It was when man tried to serve self and not the King that corruption evolved into depravity, but shall not occur in the OLAM HABA. America served a purpose as a nation all nations do, but that had ended some time ago. After democracy comes socialism especially with capitalism as an economic system and then atheism and America originally chose a type, not a form of democracy. It stresses self always. John Locke's socialism without GOD, or the spiritual absence of a Christian life. The light of truth is not shed upon a majority of people. After the initial Pilgrims, or maybe 3, or 4 generations, or much less did America lose it's Christian majority, so hence democracy took over with republicanism. In a monarch only the family need be Christian to maintain rule. It actually works from the bottom up, because all decent men want to obey their ruler who is Christian and not in elitism where it starts from the top down. With time words are revised to mean something different because of this urge to do what one wants to do and not to obey the will of GOD. Republicanism is not a whole form of government. It was a check and balance system to hold mob rule in place. Man must always be governed but the question is by whom? Republicanism bases it upon esoterical and pragmatic philosophy which does not work. Our own US Constitution makes no mention of sex as do the Ten Commandments.

King Nebuchadnezzar became a believer after he almost lost his entire kingdom and his mind. He was the first Gentile king. Groups like to vote themselves in. This is this party ideology that leads to socialism and man's ultimate his human nature.

After 2,000 years and Israel was still waiting for their Messiah, a King, a Monarch, to rule over them. Right by many, or a few can only bring eventual short, but quick disaster. Rule by a Christian monarch with a new American English by Mr. Webster would have been a complete and original plan. Original ideas must conform to Biblical precept and according to GOD'S will which is His Word.

In Russia the monarch, or monarchs took it upon themselves to forget their own nation and people and also became too

Europeanized til eventually an administration, or a bureaucracy and not a monarch started to rule which in turn brought in socialism and then socialism's ultimate goal totalitarianism. The rich and elite had separated themselves from the peasants and the land and private property and loyalty to one's land was gone. If the upper elite would have stayed close to the peasants, then the country would have stayed free, because it was the people individually that make history and as a collective body, or how else would anything move forward, except by force which was brutal? Being not well educated and learned the peasants though were GOD fearing and honored the monarch and their homeland and not foreign cultures. If the ruler and the people could be separated or destroyed then the Bolsheviks would win their Revolution. The peasants were close to the Russian soil and the elites to Europeanism. They did not know their own Russian language, or culture, or their own land and hence the Same happened in America. The soviets and the bureaucrats had to destroy their villages and make room for the large cities such as Moscow and St. Petersburg that were failing already under socialism called soviets and which started in at least the 19th Century. The Russian monarch had devious relatives who orchestrated their own deaths. The Duma fell and the rest is totalitarianism. The police were told to fire on the peasants, workers and veterans, whenever a Bolshevik was in the crowd and yelled, "Up with the revolution." A few Gephardts, Clintons, Kennedys, Dellums, Schroeders, Davis', et cetera and our "Bolsheviks" were doing the same. Someone had told the American "black" that Prison was like wearing a badge of honor. Even New York State Supreme Court Justice Leibowitz said, "There was dignity in the Gulag sometimes afterward." As the peasants fought for Russia so will our government have the poor fight too for their cause.

In my own home town there had been elected for 3 terms a socialist candidate who promoted showing movies on a Sunday and was a member of the Masons and the Teutonic Lodge as well as the Tall Cedars of Lebanon as well as a union. It was at a time when the Nazis won in the German elections and Mahatma Ghandi marched for Indian independence from Britain to remove the badges they had to wear and the time when Pluto was discovered and the Federal Bureau of Prisons was established. The city tax was $1.10 and the County Tax was $.30 and the State Tax on property was $4.80.

The Gulag was scattered from the Bering Strait to the Bosporus which was quite a range. The Bolsheviks not only killed the monarch, the rich and elite, but also some of their own and they gladly died as long as they could be members of the Party. Their turn would come. The only thing Stalin did different then Lenin was to kill members of his own party, he was too ignorant, brutal and asinine to think up anything different from Lenin. Lenin had not known the Revolution had started his being in the West most of the time. He and his entourage were transported with millions in gold on a train from Germany to Russia to set up his totalitarianism with a little help from his friends. This Western shortsightedness would eventually even come to America. Self-perservation has a way of taking the shortsighted route into destruction. The West kept saying, "take this country, or that country, but leave us alone. Please leave US in peace." This kind of Peace I would not wish on my own enemy.

The Yalta Conference was the Anglophilian clincher against the Russian people. Give up everything for our own peace. Illusions of grandeur are prominent amongst the Anglophiles in leadership.

To Israel were coming many Jews until reality set in for the non-Sabras. Tourism was over and Israel's true purpose was coming to fruition. GOD was calling His people back, but for how long and how many would respond and how many really knew as to the why? As the beginning would start like never before. Faith was not Zionism's nationality only a secular mind set existed.

A secular state now, but soon to be a religious state as heresy and then GOD. The Gentile power was ending.

The Antichrist was on the scene ready to take his place in Israel. He would promote anti-Semitism for Messianic Jews and a world system from Europe where he came from. America and

Europe would ally themselves with him. Would Satan have had power, if Adam did not sin? Did Satan have power, unless GOD had allowed him to? Satan could enter into a human form with this Antichrist. As Adam and Eve would procreate always through sin. Satan needed the physical to promote and emulate his evil through man. Adam and Eve were innocent in a perfect environment with Satan there in a visible countenance, yet with no power over man but over demons, or did he? Satan could tempt, but man's own will to sin was just that his own for GOD does not tempt anyone. The dialogue with Satan was deadly and even today until a New Heaven and a New Earth would be transformed. Audible voices then and now a spiritual dialogue in seared and unseared consciences.

Was Adam afraid to die after sinning? Was Messiah afraid? These were all foreign sins from created man and not from a Begotten GOD head. GOD'S absolute will Calvary had then been spoken. At the Feast Of Weeks the Messianic Jews knew about the Ruach Hakodesh "for even the crumbs that fall off the table the dogs shall eat". Zionism would fail, even though it looked like it would succeed and Messianic rule would forever prevail.

As Margaret Powers so wonderfully described with her poem called FOOTPRINTS IN THE SAND.

The Biblical holidays, or Holy Days were PASSOVER for the resurrection and what meal did Y'eshua have in the upper room with the Disciples? Was it not the Passover Meal? PESACH the death of Y'eshua, unleavened bread, no sin. The sacrificial death of Y'eshua. The FIRST FRUITS OF UNLEAVENED BREAD was part of PASSOVER. To eat the unleavened bread for 7 days. After PESACH comes the CEREMONY OF FIRST FRUITS. This is a harvest. The beginning of a 50 day ceremony. Y'eshua was the FIRST FRUIT who rose from the dead. This FIRST FRUIT is Y'eshua's resurrection. The PASSOVER LAMB'S blood, Y'eshua's shedded blood. PASSOVER WEEK is his atonement for us. Then comes PENTECOST, THE FEAST OF WEEKS, the church. 50 days after THE FIRST FRUIT CEREMONY, the Resurrection. SHAVUOL, the giving of the Law at Mt. Sinai with the reading of Ruth, the Gentile. Jews and Gentiles come into His kingdom free from sin, SHAVUOT, Acts 2:4. Ruach Hakodesh served as a completion of PASSOVER to overcome sin and our tendency to it John 16:7. SHAVUOT the completion of 50 days from FIRST FRUITS during PASSOVER WEEK. To write the Law on our hearts. Jeremiah 31:32-33 and Ezekiel 36:25-27.

Then comes ROSH HASHANAH, the blowing of the trumpets, a New Year that now appeared to be near the 6,000th year according to the Jewish calendar. GOD created the world on this day. A day of remembrance, the eating of sweet things. The shofar is blown. The coming of the OLAM HABA. The TRANSLATION OF THE SAINTS not ecumenical, I Thessalonians 4:16-18. A new creation, I Corinthians 15:50-53. Creation and TRANSLATION at ROSH HASHANAH, YOM KIPPUR, the Day of Atonement, to repent of one's sins for the year. Once a year the high priest, now Messiah had taken care of that could enter the Holy of Holies for the whole nation. A goat died for this day Abraham's foreshadowing of his only son, Hebrews 11 Yom Kippur's book is the book of Jonah, 3 days and 3 nights in the stomach of a whale, or a big fish, Matthew 12:39-40. Jonah was as Y'eshua would be resurrected on the 3rd day. National redemption of Israel YOM KIPPUR in the future II Corinthians 13:5, Romans 11, Zechariah 12:10 and 13:9. Now SUCCOT comes, or the FESTIVAL OF BOOTHS, OR TABERNACLE an 8 day period of rejoicing. GOD'S faithfulness in the wilderness, Leviticus 23:43. The 7th day to save now and the 9th day SIMCHAT TORAH rejoicing of GOD'S GIFT OF THE LAW. The living Torah Y'eshua, Zechariah 14:16-19. All nations shall celebrate this. SUCCOT is to come. PASSOVER, PESACH, UNLEAVENED BREAD, FIRST FRUITS, SHAVUOT all have been fulfilled. ROSH HASHANAH, YOM KIPPUR and the SUCCOT have not been. In PURIM disorder is the picture with cross dressing as a sinful act in the Book of Esther. GOD'S preservation in exile and against the evil Haman. Then HANAKAH, THE FEAST OF DEDICATION, won by the Maccabees, when Antiochus desecrated the Temple, John 10:22. Y'eshua's proclamation of the New Testament. Antiochus in

Daniel 8 and 11. Also used to represent the Antichrist. This shall be the 3rd Temple, Jeremiah 30:4-7 and Zechariah 13:8-9. The preservation of Messianic Jews during the TIME OF JACOB'S TROUBLE in the GREAT TRIBULATION of three and one half years, or 1260 days. PURIM AND HANUKAH are not in the Leviticus Cycle.

The 12 Apostles all later to become Messianic Jews except one were as follows. ANDREW THE FRIENDLY APOSTLE who was Peter's older brother. ANDREW was crucified on an X cross and is the Messainic Saint of Scotland. The Scottish Enlightment started America's eventual founding. PHILIP, THE PRACTICAL APOSTLE his death was uncertain. NATHANIEL, THE VISIONARY was untidy, introverted and was not judgmental. He was flogged to death and tied up and thrown into the sea. MATTHEW, THE RESCUED APOSTLE who was a tax collector and wrote the Jewish Gospel of Matthew. SIMON THE ZEALOT was crucified. JAMES THE UNKNOWN APOSTLE also was crucified. JUDAS, THE STEADY APOSTLE died a martyr's death in Persia, or Iran. JUDAS ISCARIOT, A DEMON who betrayed Y'eshua and hung himself for 30 pieces of silver. SHIMON SHALLIACH, THE MAGNIFICENT APOSTLE extroverted who hung upside down on the cross for his death. JAMES, THE AMBITIOUS APOSTLE the brother of JOHN. JOHN, THE APOSTLE OF LOVE the one who Y'eshua loved and who saw the vision in the Book of Revealation who was to starve to death on the island of Patmos. He died a natural death and was the last to die. THOMAS, THE DOUBTING APOSTLE was shot by a shower of arrows. Then there was REV SHAUL who was not amongst the 12 original APOSTLES, the one that replaced Judas Iscariot later on and who had two names. REV SHAUL wrote most of the New Testament who was a Pharisee from the tribe of Benjamin and a citizen of Rome, or the Roman Empire. Converted on the road to Dasmascus who was later beheaded in Rome.

Now comes America's ultimate successes in the mundane and blasé business and avarice for self world and the most secretive, or covert part of American society. All 8 supported capitalism and avarice for self. All 8 also met in 1923 and were successful financiers. Charles Schwab was in steel and died a pauper and then committed suicide. Howard Hobson went insane. Arthur Colton died abroad and went insolvent. Richard Whitney served time in Sing Sing Prison. Alfred Hall was released and pardoned from prison so he could die at home. Jesse Livermore, a Wall Streeter, who also committed suicide. Ivan Krugar committed suicide and the last man was a president of the Bank International who shot himself which was another suicide. Not an auspicious ending and with most all doing what Judas Iscariot did to himself for 30 pieces of silver. These names are not well known by all, but I did say that America's business world was the most secretive part of America ever at that time. Now they were being exposed to the public, but why?

I picked up one book by Solzhenitsyn and it cost $3.95 only and thought, "Where is capitalism when you most need it." The average American worker had forgot what the word work really meant. Our Socialism was different then in the Soviet Union, but came to the same conclusion, no GOD.

Out of the above two groups the first group, except for one followed Messiah and the second group followed Satan and State, because they did not know Messiah. The second group ended up doing themselves in. The first group died giving themselves up. Surrender is better in faith than to surrender in vain one's will to the enemy, or any ideology, or an economic system. "What would it gain a man if he would obtain the whole world, but lose his very soul?"

As to war, there were 13 years of war for one year of peace since recorded history. In 320 AD Roman Catholicism adopted December 25th, not Messianic Jews, as a Christmas, or Mass holiday under Constantine. Remember them, state religion of a particular denomination?

The followers of Germanic Protestantism from the Celtic and Germanic, or Teutonic Tribes came from north central Asia Minor.

The 5 Cosmic World Ages are: #1 the fall of Adam which lasted 2 weeks. The second one was after the flood. The third one was the Church of Grace. The 4th one was, or will be the OLAM HABA and the 5th one will be a NEW HEAVEN AND A NEW EARTH.

America's correlation to GOD by American history we have seen in part through the individual Presidents which mostly were iconoclastic lawyers. The origins started with the Pilgrims and the Mayflower Compact with 2,000 families and 138 scholars included later.

Biblical Christians, the Pilgrims, understood grace and not the English "dictator", or the Anglican Church. Even England had it's own church Anglican, but it too had "anguish in independence". The Pilgrims left first for Holland, then when intermarriage with unbelievers occurred, they left for America and also Holland allowed for no proselytizing which meant Holland kept Europeanism and did not find their own GOD individually.

Reverend John Robinson a Christian Biblical scholar lead them to Holland, but died there. The Puritan Movement, Pilgrims that were separatists in 1606 left Eastern England (Scruly), because King James I persecuted them. He was a secular monarch. These were the Pilgrims that first went to Holland. These Pilgrims sailed later to Cape Cod by sea to America in 63 days and one half of them died the first year. After them came Elder Brewster to America who lead 8 hours of worship service in America on the Sabbath. The Pilgrims were finding their own GOD in America. Original? In America they could witness, or spread the Gospel if one would listen or could understand them. There was no nation here at that time, but only tribes with multiculturalism.

Some would later contend that slavery was the worst form that existed ever, but Lenin, Stalin and Hitler would prove them wrong. There were warring factions only. These Pilgrims celebrated Thanksgiving, as one would the FEAST OF TABERNACLES with the Indians who helped them survive and the Pilgrims who shared their GOD of a new nation which was all inclusive in Messiah. Later on humanity appeared in the way of hospitals and GODLY medicine, colleges as seminaries, the Ivy League and their national GOD of Biblical Christians and not Roman

Catholicism, or Europeanism. Most Pilgrims had died for their new found faith as American Biblicals.

In 1620 the Mayflower Compact included church covenant into the government. The moral idea precedes civil responsibility. This occurred in Russia with St. Cyril and St. Methodius who brought the Christian alphabet and Christianity another original founding of the Russian GOD and not of Europeanism. The Great awakening occurred for spiritual revival. In 1962 America rejected Messiah for He is the Word. Not beautiful, but bestial, not noble but degrading; not precious, but perverted; not sublime, but sordid; not encouraging, but discouraging. Sensuality had indeed replaced marital lifetime sexuality a sacred bonding. Then Naziphilia's homosexuality marched into Skokie, Illinois, San Francisco (remember the World Series earthquake), New York City's cancerous tumor, Beverly Hills and it's filth, Orlando (the indecency of Disney). America's 5 fold Christian Heritage of apostles, prophets, evangelists, pastors and teachers were gone, or done. Y'eshua taught more than anything else to His Disciples.

Rebellion always tops spiritual maturity. It was their own anti-Semitism that created more anti-Semitism. The 60's generation was both. Universal freedom means freedom first for others and not civil rights socialism. GOD could have crushed Satan, but justice was first, or at least the judgment of. Therefore Y'eshua died that justice. Satan was found guilty, but not sentenced to serve his eternal punishment, yet. GODLY justice first in society, or no longer GOD'S protective shield. If GOD would give all our justice we would all be going to hell.

Martin Luther's grace without works also included "anguish an independence". James in his epistle says, "faith without works is dead," meaning the fruit should appear after grace for it cannot appear ever before without grace. It is always through Messiah's strength. Anti-Semitism is not fruit bearing, but something demonic.

In the Soviet Union Stalin was married twice. One woman was a Nadexhda Sergeyeyna Alliluyevs. His daughter like so many other Soviets came directly to America as well as Nazis through our government and Big Business. Even in the Soviet Union at one time all abortions are illegal. Now that does sound hard to believe. The father of Communism was Lenin who was, as repeated before, only one quarter Russia. What slavery was ever worse than 66,000,000 murdered human beings from 1917-1959? Where was Hollywood which did not film any of this at all, because names such as Trotsky, Marx, Liebowitz, et cetera maybe made them back away? They too had a religion called Marxism which the state promoted with luster and in America the same had occurred by way of Capitalism. The state would support all and there would be no unemployment at all because many lives were not needed.

Back to America's history. John Witherspoon, a Presbyterian (many Presidents were this) was president of Princeton Seminary and the only pastor to sign the Declaration of Independence.

Samuel Rutherford 1600-1661 wrote Lex Rex GOD'S law not the secular king's law.

Thomas Jefferson our Deist GOD is one a slave owner did not write any of the US Constitution. He was in volatile France at that time. He believed GOD left man to himself.

Benjamin Franklin another Deist believed the same and even said, "It is a republic; now try and keep it."

Not very promising words. He also believed that without GOD education was dead. Mind you he was a Deist... He also was a Utilitarian and an inventor and had one son out of wedlock. He opposed the Penns of Pennsylvania, because later Penn's relatives become scoundrels.

The first Thanksgiving Day was called by Congress, yes Congress and also 12 of 13 original colonies had state churches that taxed so the Gospel could be preached and churches could be built. No room for Ira Glasser's atheism here, or his loyal ACLU socialism from the 60's.

Massachusetts, of all places, till 1853 had taxes for churches. Now they have Barney Franks, A congressman who is a homosexual pedophile and only a "Jew" by birth. For 30 pieces of silver.

Christianity the faith not the religion, or denominations should be respected always. Other religions, or better yet cults and cultures cannot be embraced as ever being good in America. To respect an individual, or a group of people who worship another religion within Christianity is proper, but never is a believer or an American to ever participate, or even slightly encourage any religion based on the lie of Satan. After all foreign gods are the worship of demons no less and no more. It is indeed a sin and a false witness to that individual, or group. "Social Christians are worse, then atheists and agnostics. This is the religiosity of "Christianity". In America Christianity and not socialism should have only been preached. The same happened in Russia. If one respects the right of worship of another that is proper and non- violent in public and in privacy, but not in the public arena of government, or for that matter conducive not to a cult, or the occult and in Judeo-Christianity since government in America was in the business of education then that would be American or was American. If otherwise in so doing we bring judgment, or abandonment upon ourselves according to the First Commandment. Individual liberty is only found in the Judeo-Christian faith. America was founded by Christians for Christians not for atheism or heathenism. Christianity is the only faith our Founders could be referring directly to. Only one faith with different denominations which would mean and still meant foreign worship of GOD and not the American GOD. No Islam, Buddhism, Mormonism, Jehovah Witnesses, or even Judaism, but only Messiah. Why believe a lie? Christianity is the only faith, not a religion that allows all others to worship freely, but not usurp authority in government, education, et cetera. One must carefully read the First Amendment and First Commandment.

In 1811 utterances against Messiah were blasphemous in New York which was upheld by the, now listen to this, the Chief Justice. Today if one does not mock GOD they are blaspheming in New York. One can only hear His name used in profanity constantly.

William Blackstone was a must to learn in all law schools and colleges. Now it is read as a history lesson only. Common Law from England had Christianity as a foundation. The Constitution was written to restrain the Asners, Dellums,

Schroeders, Glasssers, Davis', et cetera, or their usurpation of state power into totalitarianism. The 4th Branch of Government the media, incognito as a party, or the Party has no truth and does not swear to uphold the US Constitution with any kind of oath and has no truthful objectivity, since at least Pulitzer. Their's is commercialism and POLITICAL CORRECTNESS.

Wesley revivals saved England not personal salvation alone as in America and in Germany. The neighborhood and not the "villages" was involved. There were two Wesley brothers and their mother had many children and would put up her apron upon her face when she was praying and all the children knew not to bother her at that time.

William Wilberforce (1759-1833) changed England from slavery long before the United States did, but Churchill put Russia and Israel into slavery. The state is a delegated authority.

Tyndale was executed in England in 10/6/1536, but first was arrested without a license. He believed the Pope was the ...

John Knox of Scotland taught civil disobedience, not civil rights, if leaders do not obey GOD and follow His Word, then the people could have civil disobedience. The 60's racial riots were anarchy and not civil disobedience and were next to revolution if it could have pulled it off.

Germany's Martin Luther and His Reformation "anguish in independence" was to reform Roman Catholicism, but had no original idea of it's own. Martin Luther did not preach grace alone, but anti-Semitism in him transcended which was more of Europeanism. Also it was in protest of what?

John Calvin limited civil disobedience to rulers, or leaders alone, hence the American War of Independence, but not the Russian Revolution? (He believed the Pope was the Antichrist).

Samuel Rutherford also agreed with Luther and Calvin. To protest to use force, to defend oneself is okay. Did anyone imagine infanticide at that time? Ones who can neither flee, or fight.

King David was against force. He never killed King Saul his nemesis, but respected the king's authority, because it was personal and the king is not a "free" man. The Russian peasants had done the same. What made the American "black" feel he could take things into his own hands and that went against the 10 Commandments and then to contract AIDS knowingly and then blame it on the CIA? King David believed one should flee, as he did from King Saul who wanted to kill David not for any crime David had done, but because he envied David. He was to flee which is not always possible with others especially the unborn, or when one has to defend themselves to avoid another committing murder a malicious intent. One should not flee though if one can protest and back we are to protestation, or Protestanism and if one cannot be heard how can they protest? The two levels of resistance, when against a corporate body such as in America. Moscow was not corporate, but thugs and gangsters and America went the same road. Nonetheless force could not be used which is always political and not spiritual in the sense that subversion shall not seek out...

Local government years ago in America was the church, a duly constituted state who were not autonomous to do whatever they wanted to do. To protest, self-defense, a distinction between a lawless uprising and lawless resistance. The 60's was a revolution in America that failed at that time to America's weak moral fiber that opposed it.

Force and violence are not the same. Legitimate reason for force and a vigilant precaution against it's over reaction in practice. Protestation, or to protest is a form of force not violence, hence picketing infanticide clinics is legal and moral and if one does not as a Christian then they have failed the true Gospel. There should be no so called buffer zone, or the racketeering clause involved. The racketeering clause was not written for that intent as stated by the author himself.

James Madison said, "Powers delegated by the United States Constitution to the Federal Government are few and defined. The states are numerous and indefinite and he was a Mason. When any nation is too politically oriented then the spiritual part fails because instead of seeking GOD man seeks in secular humanism.

The American War of Independence was not a Revolutionary War and was preached as a religious revival. The 60's generation was a revolution, or the attempt of, or one as such.

In the middle of the 14th Century many groups entered America which did not have the Reformation base, though they too enjoyed the freedom and luxury to become rich. Their base would not have produced most likely freedom with conditions, but possibly another Constantine state.

Whoever shuns evil becomes a prey as well as the innocent since they refuse to oppose it in a Biblical sense. When the Reformation being Europeanism failed to discern that American Biblicals were different, because America had found it's own GOD already as a nation and not as Germany had done with Martin Luther, or the Italian Vatican, or Roman Empire. With the Reformation came excess baggage to America in the form of the Franco-Germanic political philosophy which was part of the French Revolution, socialism and later on travelled to Nazi Germany, hence a foreign way to worship GOD. Yes Russia became the first Communist State ever through Lenin. Socialism was not new, but Marxist/ Leninism was in the form of Communism which was the totality of "social" justice. It is peace vs violence and not peace vs war. The lie is the underlying thing.

At the end of the 1st Century all New Testament Books were accepted as Divine by believers somewhere, but not the Catholic Apochrypha which came later.

The Catholic Church, or any church shall not replace Israel, because it was from Messianic Jewry that the Scriptures came to be through the work of GOD.

When did America not become a Christian majority? Could it have happened after our Founders, the Pilgrims, because of European baggage of negative influence to America's own GOD and it's anti-Semitism?

In regards to Catholicism the Roman Vulgate in Latin for the New Testament was Roman Catholicism's Bible. The Eastern Church chose the Cyrillic Alphabet. When the Roman Catholic Church in 400 AD chose Jerome's Latin Vulgate, the New

Testament by Divine Inspiration by Messianic Jews had already been completed. In 200 AD the Tertullian Church was the first to use the term the New Test. In 367 AD the Alexandrian Church and in 385 AD and 397 AD two North African Church Councils, confirmed the Protestant Bible, but reformation only reformed and Biblical interpretation was essentially the same later in regards to anti-Semitism. It was an original version of one nation's Bible, or was it? Earlier the Messianic Jews a nation of Jews in the sense that everything was given to them and that their scribes were meticulous in how the Bible was written and how it started in the 1st Century which was original.

The Roman Empire's Caesar through his influence made Latin the official language of Roman Catholicism, hence Jerome's Vulgate in 383 AD. What happened to Greek and Hebrew?

Bede translated the Bible into English.

In the 14th Century John Wycliffe wrote the English Version of the New Testament and two and one half years later also wrote the Old Testament. This was the first completed Bible not to be in Latin, but in English. Each language is different.

The CHAPTERS in the Bible were developed by Stephen Langdon in 1227 AD.

Wycliffe later was condemned posthumously and his body was burned for being a heretic. Remember Wycliffe wrote the first English version which deviated away from Roman Catholicism and with their Church tradition replaced actual Scripture and when Rome said that no priests could no longer get married, because they were leaving their land and estates to their relatives, hence Catholicism claimed all the land and the celibacy of pure …

Erasmus a monk wrote in Greek the New Testament in 1516 AD. Martin Luther in 1534 AD wrote from the original Greek the New Testament and Hebrew but in German not Latin, or in English. Germany's founding of their German GOD.

William Tyndale was the father of the English Bible which he translated from the original languages Greek and Hebrew to German and then into English in 1526 AD. It was not translated from Latin which has 3 genders. This was the base form for the flamboyant King James' Version. Tyndale was later strangled and burned at the stake near Brussels, Belgium in 1535 AD.

Miles Coverdale fled England and went to Germany to complete that first English Bible to be printed on the Gutenberg Press in 1535 AD which was probably to present a major problem, since all Hebrew Scribes wrote by hand the original Bible, that is the Jews or Scribes and America's Bible it was.

In 1560 AD John Calvin and John Knox transcribed the Geneva Bible in Geneva, Switzerland. Robert Stephanus created the Bible thing called the VERSE in 1551 and 1555 AD. Puritans brought this Bible, the Geneva Bible, or Breecher's Bible to America influenced by John Calvin and John Knox. Was there a founding of an American Bible that was translated from the original languages into American English on American soil? Salvation by grace and GOD'S right to choose GOD'S chosen family chosen by GOD.

Roman Catholicism still uses Jerome's Latin Vulgate Bible and their followers were not allowed to read Scripture until late in the 20th Century, but only the priests. Who did the Vatican think the Bible was written for? Also confessions are still today given to another mortal who has sin like in the Old Testament and not to Messiah Himself directly. Y'eshua is the Great High Priest and no where in Scriptures does it say that anybody should proxy for Messiah.

In 1941 then in 1952 the first Catholic version based on the original languages Greek and Hebrew were written. It was called the New American Bible the only Bible Catholics use today that is in English, as do most Baptists only use the King James' Version. In 1965 in America Catholics were reading the Revised Standard Version and the Good News Bible. Without the Holy Spirit who would interpret? Roman Catholicism was more than just a denomination.

Some consider Erasmus, the monk, the best text.

All through history there are 4 different scenarios that can be subscribed to and they are as follows. The rich writing about the rich which means the well educated and wealthy either through inheritance, or education and who do not work with their hands in hard labor. Then there is also this free time so much of it to do what one wants to do which is contentment and kills the spiritual part of man. The second stratum is the rich writing about the poor. They cannot connect with the lower stratum because they have never really lived it and only through experience can one obtain this. The third stratum is the poor writing about the poor with an inexperience in life itself which comes from folklore and legends and individual know how is lacking. The fourth stratum is the poor writing about the rich where much envy and hatred come from because class is confused with the sin that all of humanity has and that the poor too have these same vices. Only when the rich write about the rich and when a rich person gives up his wealth and writes in the truth does great literature appear. To bring a war to America the scenario can be used for example the rich writing about the poor and the poor writing about the rich. To bring a war on domestic soil a foreign enemy, then with forethought to create a Civil War in America is what the 60's revolution was all about.

The infamous National Council of Churches endorsed none other than the Revised Edition, or the Revised Standard Version and the Good News Bible for English as a second language and of which both were approved by Roman Catholicism. What did all this have to do with American Biblicals?

The Living Bible paraphrases all the way much like Pat Robertson's version of The Book.

The first entire Bible for missions' work was by John Elliott in England, but for America in 1663.

Today there are 1700 different languages with 1279 languages to go for the Bible to be translated into.

Since 1982 laity Catholics could read the Bible as I just mentioned before.

Churches have been started without missionaries only the Bible and the Holy Spirit.

There are 550 different English versions. One would have to ask as to the why? Are there not many languages which have never been heard let alone read the Bible even for the first time? In Hebrew there are 750 original manuscripts for the Old Testament and in Greek there are 5,000 original manuscripts for the New Testament with 0.1% or 1/10 of 1% in variance and 99.9% accuracy for both transcript types as opposed to Homer's ILIAD which has 5% corruption, or 50 times the inaccuracy of the Bible. The Bible is for transformation not reformation, or catholicism. Other books are for information only and do not breathe, because the Holy Spirit a third living personality in the Trinity which is this personal second by second relationship with Messiah and not some far away GOD that others do not know, or who they cannot converse with in their own living spirit. One must decide had America been deceived and was our founding Messianic for American Biblicals, since English in America was used?

Remember Martin Luther and most Popes were anti-Semitic or anti-Semites even though Jewish people by nature are Christians. Only Messianic Jewry appears now to be proselytizing to it's own people properly, since the Time of the Hebrews and then all of Israel.

Only the Holy Spirit spreads the Gospel, for GOD is not limited. This is a mystery of GOD until He reveals it Himself.

CHAPTER XVIII

CONTINUING THROUGH?

Now the Antichrist was in the world and soon coming to Israel. Israel was in turmoil and so was the entire world, including the island now called America, since America lost its Biblical base and was just another fallen civilization in such a short time. GOD was not protecting America, nor was He giving it His will, except for possibly American Biblicals who were continually praying, but also doing what GOD would not do, but what man had to do. "We are our brother's keeper." In Russia from 1917-1959 about 66,000,000 people were murdered and out of them about 32,000,000 were children. In America the number was approaching near 50,000,000 and that number was daily increasing quickly.

This Antichrist somehow was creating more and more chaos and anarchy in the world so that he could be the knight in shining armor. His rise had to be growing in Europe, but his name was not in correlation to this beast as of yet. Well educated, rich and handsome and of Jewish heritage, this Nephilim would soon come on the scene in his first 3 and a half years and Jewish rabbis would adore this messiah that was deceiving, or going to deceive them, but not only them, but most all the Jews and Gentiles. It would go from one extreme violence and wars to this Satan's peace and back to judgment by GOD Himself in the second part known as the Great Tribulation when all hell would break loose literally and Antichrist would show his true colors of evil. He first was to be loved by Israel, Europe and America and this would be his domain since all the world's wealth and most valuable land was mostly his. That did not mean it would be easy for believers in this area, but maybe even worse, because they would need the mark of the beast, or die. So much would occur, but so quickly after the church would be TRANSLATED. Maybe America thought too they would be spared by Translation, but it did not appear so. "The rain falls on the just and the unjust." "Judgment begins with the household of GOD."

IN A DREAM CAME THE FOLLOWING:

The church, the Body of Y'eshua translated just like that with no warning whatsoever. Only the signs on earth that Messiah spoke about leading up to this. He came as a thief in the night when most were "asleep" and unaware.

America had become insane with strikes of all kinds from laborers to doctors and nurses and teachers and there was no morals. Something seemed to change that everyone who came to America's shore even back in the 1930's and 1940's as to money. This lingering slave mentality to get rich at any cost and the constant talk about money and materialism as well as the weather. Foreigners for many years coming to America took on capitalism and Americanism.

I found myself alone in bed and Marie was not aside of me. Later on in my findings I could not find her anywhere in our home. I called, but the number would not go through to my daughter's house, so I walked a few miles to her home and on the way everything appeared normal, except there were more sights to see in the streets and almost complete abscence of morality with some abnormal sights to see in the streets. I noticed for whatever reason that certain people were dumb founded as I appeared to be and at this time in the early morning certain deliveries were not being made, as one would usually find at this time when I would drive to work. Certain systems such as mall lights and office lights and building lights were still left on in what appeared to be from the previous night. This was quite strange to me, but somehow I blocked all this out of my mind. I finally reached Alex and Rachel's home and found the front door slightly ajared. I wondered why and immediately thought there possibly could have been some foul play, or that even the suspect, or intruder ... I entered quietly and cautiously into the house and went room to room and found no one inside. It was too early for the children to be out of bed but not for Alex to be at work. There were dirty dishes in the sink and on the table, but it appeared they were from last night, because of the main course of food which did not look like breakfast. As I looked into each bedroom I noticed something about all the beds that appeared ever so strange. The beds were in a made position with the pillows at the usual top, but somehow the blankets had been gotten out of without disturbing the covers, or the mitred sheets. Rachel always mitred her corners. There were also a few small dim lights on, but only on one side of the bed and with a light on in the hallway and one on in the living room and in the kitchen. Nobody was to be found anywhere. Now Marie, Rachel, Alex, Abraham and Jacob were missing. I again used the phone to call police headquarters and a voice at the other end answered the phone after many rings. This voice was not a tape as I began to explain my dilemma.

The person at the other end said, "Our phone lines have been jammed since early morning in regards to missing persons."

I then got this strange feeling all through my body and refused to believe what my mind logically tried to tell me, but also another part of me that said that all this had to make sense. Things though were so surreal that I could not blend, or coordinate in my mind as to the why. Finally it dawned on me, but I still refused to..."How could that be possible? It can't be? Why then was I still here and what about others I knew?"

Immediately I called again, but this time I called Sal my friend to ask him what was going on. "Would he answer the phone and if he did not, what did that really mean?" Finally I heard the receiver pick up. But who would answer?

"Hello"...

It was Sal's voice. What a relief. Now I knew my imagination was running away with me, because Sal was a believer, or was he? I asked Sal about my wife as well as Rachel, Alex and the twins, since sometimes they would visit Sal and his family for overnight camping stays on Sal's farm. My inner thoughts kept saying, or asking, "There are no notes, messages, or anything to indicate such a thing occurred, but maybe they forgot?"

Marie always told me whenever she went somewhere always.

Why not this time?

Sal said, "Nobody is at my home, but they all had gone to a kibbutz yesterday and would be back sometime later tomorrow."

Finally I decided to relax again and thought that explains it. They forgot to tell me where they were going. It probably was with Sal's family to get away for a few days on the kibbutz?

I waited late the next day and still no sign of Marie, Rachel, Alex or the twins.

I then called Sal and he said, "My family will be here any minute."

I said. "Oh!"

But quickly explained to Sal what my dilemma was now that none of my family was around and I had to wait at least 72 hours to file a missing report with the police authorities. Sal was convinced everything would be all right. I then hung up and had the strangest thoughts about terrorists, Islamic terrorists.

"My relatives, my family had been killed, but if so why no phone call by the authorities, or the IDF?"

I again called all the officials and authorities and reported them missing, but was told there was a long list of missing persons being filed with them in such a short time and I would have to wait.

Then it dawned on me. My body became cold and chilled and I could not move. or even think, but only about one thing, the word t-r-a-n-s-l-a-t-e-d over and over again with an obsessive compulsiveness.

"They had been Translated."

That is why their beds appeared so strange and the lights in their house were on at certain spots as well as the abnormal activity out on the streets and the full lighting of some buildings so early in the morning as if it was daytime. I thought also about their door appearing to be ajar, Marie with no note, but Sal and his family they were here, but why? They were like me unsaved? I could barely get the word out of my mind let alone even to try and say it. I was home alone, but for good. A sickening feeling came all over me. I would never again see my family ever again and I was doomed. Unless, unless I did not take the mark of the beast, but then that would mean almost certain death for me and how would I survive?

Finally the phone rang and I was still in my daughter's house. "Who would call here, now?"

"Hello?"

"Sal, this is Sal, your friend."

"Oh, I thought it was possibly the authorities." I knew it was not, but did not tell Sal that.

Sal said, "My family has disappeared."

I said, "Disappeared?"

"Yes disappeared. Nobody at the kibbutz could find them anywhere and then I thought of you and what you had said about your family. What is going on?"

"Sal, come over to my daughter's house now and I shall try to explain what I think happened, okay?"

Sal just hung up, but was at my daughter's home in no time at all and I started to explain what had occurred and in detail.

Sal had something to confess to me.

"I am not a believer, I am Cuban-Jewish not just Cuban, and I never believed what my wife and children ever told me about Messiah.

I said, "This is Messiah's second visit, which means that only believers will not be here and we are not believers, since both of us are still here on earth." I thought to myself I had accepted reformation and not transformation.

He looked at me dumbfounded, but for now could not come up with any logical conclusion of his own that was better. We were not part of Romans 10:9-10.

As each day went by, I could see out in the streets violent disturbances of all kinds. Worship places had become heathen like and Wotan was being mentioned more and more all the time.

People were totally heathenistic, except for a very few individuals and Sal and I were two of them. Finally Sal and I stayed at his farm to live and went about our daily lives, both as farmers. We did not say too much about our families and if ever rarely mentioned their names. There were no graves to visit, or flowers to place, or tombstones to see. They were gone for good with Messiah in glorified bodies and all this time I thought, yes thought, I was saved.

GOD'S calendar had come quickly. A new moon marked the beginning of the month and a full moon marked the middle. The Jewish lunar calendar was more accurate than the solar, or Gregorian calendar. The Gregorian calendar begins at midnight and ends, or extends to 24 hours. There also was another Jewish calendar called the civil calendar which was based on the agricultural seasons. I should have not so much celebrated ROSH HASHANAH, but YOM KIPPUR which was the soon coming of Messiah and not just a New Year. This New Year was when the Jews returned from Babylonian exile and was of the Babylon calendar. I had chose the civil before the sacred calendar. All GOD'S children Jew and Gentile alike should have been celebrating YOM TERU'AH (THE FEAST OF TRUMPETS), YOM KIPPUR (THE DAY OF ATONEMENT) and SUKKOT (THE FEAST OF TABERNACLES) all of which had not been fulfilled. The Time of the Gentiles had ended and the Time of the Hebrews has begun. The Messianic Jews read the Scriptures according to the calendar so on any given Sabbath all Messianic Jews read from the same portions from the Bible, now that was incredible. This was occurring throughout the world by Messianic Jews. The Scripture readings were from the miraculous birth of Isaac and his miraculous salvation when his life was spared by GOD and Abraham trusted GOD. What wasn't asked of Abraham GOD had asked of Himself. Now Y'eshua had a choice to make in the Garden of Gethsemane. And yes there were no names for any of the 7 days of the week except for the Sabbath in Hebrew, but were referred to as the first day, the second day, et cetera. It was over the year 6,000 in the Jewish calendar, because the Jewish lunar calendar had 354 days, while the Gregorian calendar had 365 which meant we were far in time according to the Bible.

Sal and I did not talk a lot about politics and this one world order and the Antichrist. We now knew after one half year that this Antichrist was coming to Jerusalem for a special ceremony. A huge and magnificent temple was being built, but Sal and I had yet to see it. We had only heard about it. We also discussed in detail Sal's Jewish background that I never knew about and why he never told me. It came to be that Sal knew how I felt about Israel years ago and when we decided to come to Israel he knew he could trust me, but not enough to tell me that he was Jewish. He could not take the chance that I would let slip when inebriated back then in America if I would reveal this. Cuban Jews were rare indeed, but also in constant danger, because of Castro back at that time and as the years passed in Israel he felt no need to share such information, because he felt I might no longer be his friend, if I found out that he was Jewish and a non-believer.

I explained to him, "I always choose my friends very carefully and did not let them choose me. Friendship is a very important part of one's life that is true friendship."

Sal just smiled with his dark complexion stretching in his face.

Now the Ruach Hakodesh was out of the world and Satan was thrown out of heaven unto the earth and all hell would break loose in about 2 more years, or so. People everywhere were swallowing the bait hook, line and sinker. All lies and Sal and I knew it. He and I would not bow to this false messiah, but most all would. One could usually tell who the ones were that did, but one could never be absolutely certain.

He was coming from Europe to Israel to work out peace with the support of Europe and America and all it's Arab oil wealth and power. Little did the rich and super rich know all would be his to control and even the billionaires he would usurp to the bone, unless they did exactly what he said to the tee and then no one would know for sure, since this Antichrist had killed his own mother. He would have these Satanic powers and all the demons would obey him and we had to watch out, Sal and me, what we said to each other, or what we wrote down on paper. We could not pray for protection. The age of grace was over. We were on our own. It was "give me liberty, or give me death" as Patrick Henry had once said. Death was more imminent.

After about 2 and one half years into the Tribulation, times were odious, depraved and of such decadence that most thought of this as peace. Here we were a Jew and a Gentile, but on the same side, but a little too late. We thought religion and good works would get us in, or at least I did. We did not consciously think about it that way, or at least I did not, but I did not really in my heart access GOD'S saving grace by faith, by mental ... Messiah would have never let go of me.

I thought back about things that had occurred in the 20th Century that had happened in Communist countries, such as Russia. Socialism had started in Russia in the 19th Century with the Monarch and continued especially when Nicholas I died early just when Russia was getting its freedom. Nicholas II was too lenient with the revolutionaries and Germany and the West had contributed to the downfall of not only Russia, but also China, Korea, Eastern Europe, Latin America, et cetera. The Yalta Conference was a disaster and with Hitler and Stalin, the Georgian as friends that made for more disaster leading up to the 21st Century. Millions and millions of innocent people in Russia and elsewhere were murdered and tortured by a group of imbecilic thugs such as Trotsky, Lenin and Stalin who were not Russian at all except for Lenin who was only one quarter Russian and whose brother tried to assassinate the monarch. The Anglophiles had always done a number on Russia even choosing Islam over Christian Russia and the same happened to in regards to betrayal. Time and time again Europe chose socialism over Christianity, but professed to be a Christian continent, but was anything but. Capitalism had grown socialism into a leviathan. Give away another nation's freedom for one's own self-preservation. Churchill had made deals with Stalin many times and Roosevelt too added poison to the pot to build up communism in the entire world. Universal freedom was not considered a factor only power and avarice. Israel too had suffered at the hands of Churchill and the English. Big Business always wanted national boundaries. Lenin at the other end loved countries like Switzerland, because they spoke 3 different main languages which could export a revolution all throughout Europe and that is why Yugoslavia had gone up in smoke, because of the different nationalities and languages as well as religions. Lenin also wanted no national defenses which sounded much like the American Democratic Party in late term 20th Century. Lenin also wanted the minority to rule which was an oligarchy, or totalitarianism and got Jewish financing. He knew all politics lead to war. Lenin had taken on this name before leaving Munich when he was young and Plekhanov was his friend. Later on in Lenin's life Malinovsky brought in Stalin. The Moslem Arabs like Saddam Hussein wanted to liquidate Israel and so Israel wanted to stop Hussein from shooting missiles over Jordan. England and America just did not want Saddam Hussein to bomb the oil wells in Kuwait to begin with, because Arab oil money was being channeled through Banks in London and buying out America daily and was another reason our Federal Government would not deport all Moslems of Islam and use internment camps since 9/11 and that our own borders were unguarded in the south at Mexico and especially in Canada where there were 25,000 Al-Qaeda some crossing the Canadian and American border daily so what good did sending our troops to Afghanistan and Iraq really do to protect the sovereignty of America? Even small American businessmen were making trips to Red China to have their products made by slave labor in a closed country where at anytime the door could close on these small time businessmen while there. Nonetheless the dragon in the East was getting fed more and more and they became more and more defiant and would be much worse than the Soviet Union had been under Lenin, Stalin, Khruschev, et cetera.

In America there were no more American Negroes because they either had been destroyed or incarcerated or were part of the same system of socialism and therefore called themselves "black" or African American which also gave the label to Marxist/ Leninism.

Would Sal or I make it through the OLAM HABA or to the OLAM HABA? And in such a case then we could procreate, but not have bodies.

We were older now and farm work was lessened, because of government's interference into what to grow and what not to grow as well as confiscation of about 2/3's of Sal's farm for this Antichrist. I had sold all my property and kept the cash, or hard assets which could mean incarceration and capital punishment and did not bother with any type of stock market that was totally controlled.

All believers were gone, or dead and I thought about Sal and me and how much longer before they would coerce us to take the mark of the beast?

Sal had become somewhat sick and ill and I was afraid I would lose my only friend I had here left on earth. I still prayed on my knees for Sal's health to recover from his illness and he did. I knew GOD was in control, but the Ruach Hakodesh was not here to protect us.

By Jewish Biblical tradition it was the Torah first and then repentance and the Word was before the creation of the world. Yes Y'eshua was with GOD and He had no beginning like the earth did. (John 17:5). Y'eshua was the Creator, Ephesians 3:9. GOD the FATHER created everything through the WORD. "And the Word became flesh."

Would I ever get to see my loved ones ever again? I still asked Messiah into my heart, repeating it almost 50 times. I confessed this out loud to Sal and he prayed too this prayer. Did GOD hear us anymore? This was the Tribulation and not the age of grace. We would not renounce our faith in Messiah no matter what even for a crumb of bread and for me a Gentile I would eat the crumbs that fell off of the table.

As the months went by the Antichrist named Wotan Cohen came into power in Jerusalem. He was all knowing as to all mundane and evil earthly things. He came from a Jewish background with a Jewish mother and an unknown father. His mother disappeared for about a year somewhere in Europe. Some said it was Germany and others said it was Russia. She was, that is his mother, some sort of white witch and had dabbled in the occult. She had made trips to Berlin, Moscow, Rome, Peking, London, New York City, Washington D.C. and Jerusalem before her gestation. Legend had it that her life was mysterious indeed and in fact it was believed that somehow she had become pregnant with a Nephilim somewhere in Europe and that after a certain age, as I had said before, her own son Wotan Cohen did away with his own mother. Of course nobody could prove this to be so. I believed that his father, or so called "biological" one, was a demonic being as had occurred in Noah's time before the flood. This half man/half demon was accumulating much world wealth and power and was respected by even Israel. Blood is thicker than water. The Knesset had actually fallen apart and only were a skeletal body taking orders from him voluntarily, or should I say in some cases involuntarily. It appeared that Europe as a nation would support and did support this reign as he lead them successfully through finances and so called peace treaties of one kind or another. Another Jewish businessman was his agent known as the False Prophet. The unholy trinity according to me and Sal was in place and all that needed to take place was the finish of the first three and one-half years into the Tribulation. After that all hell would start to really break loose for the next three and one-half years that the world had never known since the beginning of time, and this was called the GREAT TRIBULATION, or the Time of Jacob's Trouble. He had already deceived almost all into who they thought he was as either a great world peacemaker or, to the Jews, their own messiah. There were parades and royalties who paid tribute to him. Many were donating fabulous amounts of money and gems and jewels as well as gold and silver for the Temple in Jerusalem. The country itself was lead by a rabbi who really believed this was the real "King of kings". There were different paranormal activities such as false healings and false resurrections. Signs appeared in the sky from astral projections which made things seem miraculous, as well as demonic UFO's that had been around for ages.

America was hardly heard from and was in alliance now with the old or new Roman Empire. The New Age Movement Empire covered a part of the world and the Far East appeared more hostile due to famines and pestilences and because their world seeking power was diminishing quickly and Jerusalem was now that world power, or world ruler. This emulation of the real OLAM HABA was in full swing.

With my own health deteriorating from lack of proper diet and clean water and Sal's too, he appeared sick again, but this time much worse, we both had to find ways just to survive. We did not attend worship services, because they had nothing to do with Messiah but only Wotan Cohen. Hymnals glorified not GOD the Father but this Antichrist in the flesh. It had all started back near the end of the 20th Century when churches began to perform "musicals" on stage where the altar was and did not address the moral issues of the day and only spoke about self-preservation and self-esteem. The Gospel had been watered down so that the pastors and priests gave anything, but to do for one's neighbor which is where real...

There was a strange story to the effect that there were some Messianic Jews in Israel, but as to their exact whereabouts I did not know. Their number was an incredible 100,000 or more.

Sal and I stayed together most of the time and my work ethic was almost at a nil due to my deteriorating health. From old type sources I had found out that in the Vatican things were stirring. Yes most all people were deceived by this man of immense stature and handsome appearance. He was not crude not yet, but very educated and refined in the finer things in life when in the public. More than that about him I did not know.

In Berlin there were innumerable amounts of Nazi homosexuals in positions of high authority and another holocaust this time amongst believers was being perpetuated. Executions were carried out day after day as they beheaded these believers for their faith and then transported to execution camps. I had to deal with some German-Jews years ago, when I worked for Israel's government to secure their safe passage to Israel. Germany always had demonic oppression. Whenever I was there I had to be very careful not to let slip who I really was, because again as before I would find Messianic Jews hidden amongst the crowd of other unbelieving Jews. Even fellow unbelievers, or other German-Jews would turn them in thinking they were doing a GODLY thing.

What nation had not been anti-Semitic especially with the Messianic Jews? Nation after nation would not allow Jews of any kind for ages to settle, or be lead to Scripture even if it meant only a few at a time. They would protect them that is a few but to witness had not become the church's function at least they felt that it was not. Who could know the mind of GOD?

At all times in Israel Sal and I had to be very careful how we spoke, or what we wrote as I said before, because demonic activity was all around and could inform on one by networking to higher principalities. One time such an event occurred, when I ran into static about my marriage to my wife, Marie and someone who had by chance known her as a Messianic Jew while they were not, but who as a Jew, or unbeliever did not believe in Messiah.

I told this person my wife had died so that they would leave me alone. I did not want to die and so I hid my faith inside of me. As I had said before this was not a world that had the Ruach Hakodesh in it, and I was not about to offer any assistance for self-preservation was too important to me.

At that time is when I decided to stay at home for good while Sal kept going about his daily routine. Many people and neighbors were very arrogant and crude and would profane GOD'S holy name repeatedly. There were many occult symbols on most all public buildings and the New Age symbol 666 was marked on just about everything that Sal had seen on his excursions to the outside world. Sal and I knew that the enemy could not read our minds but was an age old psychologist when it came to human nature.

One day with about almost three and one half years into the Tribulation I found myself alone because Sal openly professed

Messiah and was quickly removed from his old house of worship, or his wife's and would not worship this beast or take it's mark and was sentenced to death and was beheaded about 2 weeks after the coronation of this new king in Jerusalem.

I asked myself why had Sal done such a foolish thing when he could have remained silent, and anyways most likely now they would be coming after me shortly.

I remained secluded, waiting for the knock on the door. Now I was, or would be next, I surely felt. Sal had a glorified body and I would have grief from now on.

Why had he not talked about it with me? Now I had no one to talk to or to trust in any longer.

"Was not Sal's action suicidal?" I thought to myself.

Sal had been such a good athlete years ago and played semi-professional sports in America until the Moslems came on the scene and then he got out completely.

After this traumatic experience for me I contracted cancer of the brain which I was told was terminal.

I was diagnosed by a doctor from their hospital and how could I tell that they were not lying to me, since they knew Sal and I had lived together and would they inject me with a mind destroying drug, or lethal dose of hemlock? This might all sound like paranoia but to me it was as real as could be. I could not trust them at all no matter which doctor, or doctors examined me, because my own doctor did not make hospital calls.

Without anyone to confide in, or talk to I stayed to myself for the most part and was becoming bedridden and I felt myself dying slowly and becoming weaker and weaker. I stayed in the little cabin by myself and was starting to become paranoid because I knew I might die all alone with no one with me and no pain killers to relieve my pain which was increasing. Never had I imagined I would die in this incapacitated way and all alone with no one I could trust. I was beginning to lose my will to live. Now I felt I was in the clutch of death itself, and if it was my time to go I really did not have anything to do with it, since I myself was refusing medical help completely.

Had I waited too long to get medical help?

If I did get medical help would it make any difference?

My body was getting emaciated and appeared to be wasting away. I kept refusing medical help or help from the New Agers at the hospital.

Finally I called the hospital because I could not commit suicide by not receiving help if there was a chance, still however so slight, to get well. Also the pain was becoming unbearable. I was admitted as a patient voluntarily because I once worked for the Israelis' government as an official. All I saw were mostly New Agers. Their eyes were searing and evil peering and their laughter quite wicked. This was near the time of, or at the time of Jacob's Trouble. The Great Tribulation was beginning, and now it would get even worse. My memory was short lived and my childhood memories would come and go and my marriage to Marie. With my ankles being swollen from chronic heart failure, I knew my body was shutting down. I had requested to be removed of any artificial life support systems but not intravenous feeding tubes.

My body was to shut down naturally and go to a quiet death in my sleep like Dr. Bell had in China as a missionary. When my neo-cerebral cortex or my physical body exhumed then would I be with the Lord. I would, under no circumstances though beg for food in turn for the mark of the beast. My intravenous feeding was lessened to exacerbate my condition. I got just enough to sustain me and remain alive and little more than that. Oh, they were so ... I would not rescind my love for GOD. Messiah was worth dying for. He had died for me. Would it be by natural causes (which I was hoping) or starvation or some other horrible way? My appetite had also dissipated quite considerably, but I kept this to myself afraid that they might force feed me with a tube down my throat. I still refused their great king. This would have to be voluntary and a freewill choice and along with GOD'S will, but I would not surrender. Always believing in GOD, even in my early childhood, I had always feared Hell, but I never knew Messiah or about Him being in my heart until I got much older, I thought. When Marie disappeared I knew my heart had not been right with GOD in a personal way. There were too many "reborn" phrases with no fruits, or no works to bear after salvation that I had seen in so many so called "reborn" social Christians. This salvation that was preached was always for oneself and not for His will, or by His will in my life and to care for others first, especially the believing poor, as well as unbelieving poor and as James had said in his epistle "First faith without works is dead." One had to show that Messiah was working through each individual in order to receive their crown or crowns at the Judgment Seat of Messiah. I had to surrender all of me to Him.

I went into realistic events that were very clear and dreamt of the way America had fallen so fast in regards to morality. I could see before me the fatherless children and mothers who grew cold to their own children. The elderly acted like teenagers and could care less about the young. The people were dressed in black and were constantly doing evil with no regard to GOD. There were marriages of all kinds and to all things. I would have a cold sweat realizing that now it was no better in the state I was in.

For some unknown reason I had made it into this world so far, so I continued to battle as well as observe, whenever I was strong enough. I believed I had contracted ...

The birch tree theory is when a traumatic experience such as Marie's disappearance and my family's, plus the fact Sal was beheaded for his faith. In everyone's body are dormant cancer cells, and by a tragic or terrible event in one's life, one could contract cancer through the thought process, almost like a metamorphosis that would in turn become organic. With these cancer cells in my body now active I would eventually die or, if they so chose to eliminate me quickly. I would try to die naturally if they would let me, but my faith given by GOD would remain.

I had already seen lethal injections into patients who gave in, or who wanted to die prematurely, or ones who did not want to die at all, but the worse to see die is an atheist.

I had remembered that in the Netherlands and in Oregon both had induced death involuntarily some years ago which was to open Pandora's Box. Yet, now I was still alive or conscious and dying ever so slowly. My history was no longer relevant, but how I died had to be with courage and faith and unafraid to meet my Lord. "I once was lost, but now I have found."

I also did deeply think one-third of my life was in growing up, one-third in maturing, and the last one third in not remembering in what the first 2/3's were even like, or for that matter yesterday, and it all started 4 scores and 7 years ago, or was it 3 scores and 7 years ago? I would be amongst the dogs that ate the crumbs off of the PASSOVER table.

In my remembrances my town at one time was nice and safe, and by the time the rich and well-educated destroyed it we had illegal criminals from all over the world plus from the New Age City and this one time borough from March 16, 1847 till the turn of the 21st Century was a so called city. It was not the poverty but the immorality that destroyed the city and the surrounding area and government, all 5 levels greatly contributed to it by its mob rule of democracy. There was no honor among thieves. Drugs were sold on just about every block and children were predominantly illegitimate and dead beat dads roamed the streets supported by government welfare very young in age in adult males to the not so young and with no disabilities, but only POLITICAL CORRECTNESS. Homosexuality was so bad that everywhere one looked one could see the sick perversion that brought along with it AIDS, pedophilia, bisexuality, transvestites, cross dressing, violence, drugs, diseases of a multitude that lead into the heterosexual community, transsexuals, et cetera.

My contemporary thoughts were only for minutes at a time. What I once was I could hardly remember and theatrical reality would almost soon end and perhaps eternal security would soon begin for me. The tragedy had been in not remembering fluently my own and not being able to remember who, or what I was. Without my own history and my own language and background to remember my neo-cerebral cortex only thought in the present state of things. My bodily functions were shutting down. My middle brain and lower brain stem were almost dead, so more functions were inoperable. I had so far survived, if one could call it that this zombie state without any premature death. I could then possibly see Marie and my family in heaven in their glorified bodies hopefully. Marie and I were no longer married, but I certainly would know her in heaven. All loved ones would appear in a mature and perfect state that is the ones that knew Messiah. I would get to see the twins in a mature state, as well as other babies that had been infanticized whose mothers I had known, plus all the other babies who had been murdered. I would like the chance to rule and reign with Messiah and meet the Old Testament Saints, such as King David and Moses, as well as Jeremiah.

My body would be different and possibly just by thought I could transfer from one place to another, I knew that all of my family could. Not prestidigitation, but a spiritual being with a body like Messiah. I would have to go through Psalm 23, "The Lord is my Shepherd......."

"He knew of me before I was in my mother's womb and before the foundation of the world." He also knew that I would come to Him and on His part and I would depart not when it was my time, but when it was His time.

As soon as I leave this life's journey I shall return here to Jerusalem with Messiah as King of the world and where His government would reign for 1,000 years.

Life is "extensive" so to do away with millions upon millions is the easiest way to eliminate the problem and to do away with some of the brightest people who were GOD fearing. How many times had GOD spared my life when some times I would see a car accident just before me when I myself was running late that day for work, or when I was learning to hunt with a shotgun and the safety was on and it could have blown up in my face if I would have pulled the trigger in that old shotgun. Or the time I had triple pneumonia, was rear ended at 70 miles an hour by another driver at 2:00 AM in the morning, when I fell down an entire flight of stairs, when I got hit by a car at the age of 5 years old, when I almost got frostbite in the winter waiting for a school bus that never came, when I had severe appendicitis for almost an entire day, et cetera. There also was a time I went over the lawn of a synagogue on a tractor lawn mower and there was a hole about 40 feet deep.

Then I could recall seeing in New York City's Bowery men of all ages and background including doctors, lawyers, businessmen, et cetera dying everywhere just like it was a third world country. This was the way of success and wealth and even education that came to destroy America quickly that is according to time itself. What could my own...

Could we really teach to the young ones except the evils of the heart that grew more grotesque as the years went by? The 60's generation had basically stood for nothing and had accepted anything that came along to fulfill their heart's desire and Civil Rights meant freedom with no limitations in order to self-destruct and destroy more than ever before. Civil rights became spiritual civil war against GOD Himself. No shots had to be fired because this or my generation had done themselves in at an early age and had no compass to guide them because the previous generation had already accepted socialism readily. The battle was won, but the war had only just begun in America at that time. There were no statesmen, or writers of literature that came through with the truth. It was all ego and materialism and social materialism the things that one can see and the spiritual realm by faith could not be seen, hence memories for GOD did not exist at least the GOD of the Bible. What had the entire life of America from beginning to end stood really for, since no history could be remembered?

Yes, the OLAM HABA I shall see. A new heaven and a new earth shall appear shortly thereafter. No more of Adam's fall for me, or my sin, or of Satan's temptation, but there would be sinners on the earth during the OLAM HABA and they would die in that time or would they? I shall know of GOD'S original plan for my life, instead of what I wanted to do. There shall be no time, or clocks or even a sun in the OLAM HABA for He shall be the light of the world. There shall be streets of fine gold and a vast array of most precious gems and pearls as gates as we are told in the Bible. Yes GOD'S foreknowledge shall not miss one person that He has called to salvation. There shall be no lost sheep. No more sin even the cerebral cortex shall be cleansed for good and the heart shall be different from one earth as well as the entire mind, because all shall be changed and the environment too. No conscience to sear which started in the Garden, or body to get old and age than too began in the Garden. Universal freedom for all the Saints. A Perfect Environment with no theatrical reality called time to enclose us, or divide us anymore. Perfect bodies with no more glasses, hearing aids, wheelchairs, pacemakers, medicines, canes, doctors, hospitals, dentists, cars, planes, trains, ships. There shall not be any more history to try and write, or permature futures or closed time. What else would, or could have GOD wanted for us, but a perfect environment like Adam and Eve first had? No more "isms", or religiosity, nationalities, "races", but the one human and Holy race. Ideologies and avarice shall not be for no sin shall be allowed here.

I had recalled my wife's life story when she was a small girl.

"I awoke this morning to an awesome sight, beautiful white snow laying on the grass, trees, everywhere... Snowflakes landing ever so gently, quietly on the already white ground. What a wondrous feat of nature to witness the bleakness of winter's landscape turned into a crystal white covering... As I watched the snow fall memories of my childhood flooded in. I even experience the excitement now as I felt then. Snowfalls then, meant making snowballs and throwing them at each other snowmen, sledding down the hill near my home and maybe... No School... As a young girl, I couldn't wait to 'bundle up' and go out to play. Snow is fascinating. It changes people. Mom would clean the house the day before an impending snow and baked a cocoanut cake while the snowflakes fell the next day. Dad on the other hand liked snow but didn't care for the shoveling or the slippery drive to and from his job. He always worked when it snowed.

"I would play snow games and wanted our parents and aunt and uncle who lived next door to us to join in. My uncle and aunt were more willing than my parents. We had a ball. We would invent all kinds of games to play and we played until our gloves were soaked and our hands were beginning to freeze. After we did our snowballing we reluctantly entered our house and cleaned up. Rick and I were treated to hot cocoa and cocoanut cake. Then after supper and as night fell, we would put on our boots and gear and head next door to Anna and Barney's place to watch television and drink more cocoa. What a wonderful childhood I remember during the snows of my innocence. Times have changed a great deal, my parents are gone, my uncle is gone and my aunt is 91. She can barely walk. Our home is now for sale, or has been sold. My childhood where I grew up will become another's memory. Anna still lives in her house and we visit occasionally, now the care giver, instead of her. But the snow continues to fall like it did many years ago.

"Today my body won't allow it, so I just walk through it marveling as I did as a child. This afternoon as my husband and I walked to the car, I couldn't resist to make a snowball and throw it at him."

I had prayed many years before I got married that I would be able to marry a Messianic Jewish woman and GOD answered my prayers.

A poem came to me that I wrote:

How blessed so have we've been
Jesus' shed blood for all our sin
Prepare your heart for GOD so calls
Salvation is open to His all
As day ends and night so comes
His gates of heaven are closing some
The calm before the storm
Safe is your heart in Jesus' form
Listen for the Gospel is being preached
By the blood of Jesus all sin is as snowy white bleached
White, or whiter than snow our raiments be
By Jesus' shed blood at Calvary
His death and resurrection can give you an eternal life
Before He returns for the church His Wife
The Bridegroom comes do not delay

Accept your Saviour on this very day
Ask Him to come and He shall not depart
Have a new mind and cleansed heart
Biblical salvation is only of one way
The blood of Jesus in faith please pray?
How long shall the gates to stay opened?
Believe and know in one's heart in Jesus do not just be hoping
For He is coming once again
Not for the removal of sin, but for His church at the end
Tribulation for this present earth
But for all His saints eternal safety and their birth
Wait no longer let Him in
Enter heaven for with Jesus there is no sin
He so waits now with open arms
With Christ as Saviour there is no eternal harm
Say "Lord Jesus, come into my heart
Cleanse me from all sin and let me have a new start
I repent of my sins and come to You
For with You each day is new
I believe you died for me and all sin
Come into my heart so deep within"
You are GOD who came in the flesh on this earth
Our way of salvation and rebirth
Like the egg which is one in three
Father, Son and Holy Spirit the Trinity
You are the Word that so became flesh in human form
To know of man's life and his mortal storm.
Lower than the angels You chose to come to earth
Born of the Virgin Mary in a mortal birth
Accept this GIFT for it is free
The price was paid at Calvary
GOD is LOVE so welcome Him in
With His shed blood there is no sin
Born in sin we are from Adam's fall
All have sinned and His children hear His call

GOD in the flesh, yes He came
Father, Son and Holy Spirit one in the same
In Chapter One in Genesis verse twenty six so reads
And GOD said, "Let US make man in our image and likeness so to be
No matter your age, no matter the sin
He loves you please let Him come in?
Yes, choice of salvation is a gift
But GOD does open the heart and does eternally lift
Jesus hears you wherever you are
The prayer of salvation is not far
Speak the words with your spiritual heart
Let Him be your Lord He shall never depart
He is the Truth and lift the veil and see
Be born again and be GODLY free
Confess with your mouth and believe in your heart
How great His love, how great Thou Art
He loves you very much
Please let Him into your heart to forever touch
Free from the bondage and free from the sin
He is waiting for you to let Him come in?
Come into His family the family of GOD for you
See Abraham, Isaac and Jacob in eternity too
"Isaiah 53" speaks of our Lord's prophetic crucifixion
It was written for it is fact and not fiction
He has come and will return
Salvation is free it cannot be earned
Can we not discern that the time might be near
Of Biblical prophecies that are rendering clear?
The Translation can come at anytime
Be with Jesus be left not behind
For His Bride the church He shall return
The end of this age can we not discern?

When Messiah returned for Doubting Thomas, He could walk through solid objects, such as doors and walls and could eat and

Thomas could still feel the nail prints in His hands and the spear hole in His side. His glorified body was already on earth. No more corrupt and immoral judges, no more mortal kings, lawyers to lie, but only the one true King, Messiah. The one GOD in 3 persons: Father, Elohim; Son, Messiah; and the Ruach Hakodesh, the Holy Spirit.

No more good vs evil, rich vs poor, black vs white vs yellow vs red, young vs old, believer vs believer, unbeliever vs believer. It shall be on earth as it is in heaven. Equal members in Messiah and not equality, for GOD does not make clones, or no two people alike have ever been procreated. Freewill shall not be needed, it shall always be His will. There shall be no more need or want, or desire to sin, or to procreate. GOD knew the exact number even before theatrical reality started. We shall be a people not peoples. Cleansed eternally by GOD'S shedded blood. Yes a New Earth in an unfallen state. No more death, nor more cemeteries and no more good-byes which means forever.

The earth is only about 10,000 years old, but shall be transformed and not destroyed. An infinity? Yes, since we were transformed into the eternal image of GOD completely. The present is in open time and is not complete with the future. Created for an eternity to worship and serve a loving GOD. To hold dearly Messiah in my arms, as HE embraces me. This is He. I too shall feel the nail prints and hole in his side not because I do not believe, but because I do believe and to know that the price for us He paid in full. We are saved by grace alone, undeserved merit for after all what was Calvary all about, if not His works and not ours?

Bodies that were tortured, crucified, sawed in half, such as Isaiah the Major Prophet and others burned at the stake, drowned at sea, shot with arrows, beheaded, buried alive shall all be whole and shall still be praising, singing, bowing down to glorify GOD. From about 4,000 BC till... In the Year of Our Lord, Anno Domino. All centers on Messiah. BC before Messiah (Christ) and again A.D. Anno Domino in the Year of Our Lord. No death for any created being angelic, or human, but an eternity in one of two places. We are either born twice and die once, or we are born once and die twice.

This Islam from Mohammed who in 622 at 40 years of age was a wealthy merchant from Mecca, but was forced to leave Medina in that same year with his Saracen system known as the Koran and when he died in 632 the caliphs followed and then came Umer. Christopher Columbus' first voyage on December 26, 1492 which was to establish trade routes to the Indies and all the educated men knew the world was round. Columbus wanted to rear flank the Moslems by sailing west to reach the east. He sailed not to discover a new world, but to find a way to recover the old one. He set sail for Jerusalem, but found America. Soon capitalism was given birth in the 15th Century and to Western Civilization. In the 7th and 8th Centuries Christianity disappeared from North Africa. Columbus hated blasphemy and profane swearing and would say "May GOD take you." He studied the TRADEWINDS when only the VARIABLES WINDS were known to the Christian world. The Variable Winds meant the Mediterranean and Europe Atlantic and the North Sea. The Trade Winds meant to blow in the same direction. In this era Oxford and Cambridge got their birth, Michalangelo, DeVinci and Gothic architecture, Gutenberg, Dante, Charlemagne, et cetera.

Bartolome de las Casas-Castellian friar who launched the first human rights effort on behalf of the American Indians. This was the first movement of it's kind known to the entire world. Bartolome was critical of Columbus, but said that Columbus was gentle, of worthy deeds, patient and a forgiver holding firm in Divine Providence. On his deathbed he said in 1506, "Into your hands O Lord I commend my spirit."

No more of a Narcissus' attitude which Lucifer had from the beginning and was thrown out of his heavenly high position as the highest position as the highest angel in the heavens and with about one third of the angelic hosts following their own freewill with GOD'S will knowing. Nothing impure shall enter heaven. Not an atom, molecule, chromosome, DNA, genetics, or spiritual code of any kind. The laws of physics shall change in relations to man's glorified body and even the animals shall transform along with the earth so that the lion and the lamb shall lie down together. Gravity tends or does pull downward, and no matter the weight of the object everything falls at the same rate of speed and hits the earth at the same time if dropped at the same height. Gravity, inertia, centrifugal force, lack of a water firmament, harmful sun rays and ultra-violet rays, et cetera shall change. Better than Adam who was innocent in a perfect environment. Messiah has protected eternity forever for man. "There are many rooms in my mansion." the angelic being has to stay in their proper position. GOD the Father can not come into contact with any sin, so He gave His only Son, Messiah who had no sin to die for us and Messiah chose this crucifixion which He already knew about and still kept to the Father's Word for He was the Word that became flesh. The theophany in Daniel and with Abraham and with Jacob was Y'eshua Messiah before His coming to earth for He had always been the second part of the Triune GOD HEAD. His appearance on earth did not mean He was just born, it meant His visitation to earth would interrupt history like no other event had, or ever would. It was Infinity come to earth and to time on this earth. He had chosen the Jews they did not choose Him, but yet they still did not believe and then showed who He was, because they saw power in a kingdom and not love and the personal GOD for them was missed and so was their kingdom for the time being. The "branches", the Gentiles were allowed to come in as they ate the crumbs off of the table as dogs, but now that would change to blessed sheep.

He destroyed the works of the devil and to provide the only way to GOD the Father. This is unconditional love. What justice could any sinful man ask for with GOD?

His eyes shall speak without talking as the eternal GOD and as I gaze as I had once before into them I shall see perfect love, compassion and the Fatherly loving discipline that says, "Welcome my child you are home with Me."

A fertilized ovum from the Ruach Hakodesh with the blood from the Father. If Adam was created and he was all other men had to be procreated. Messiah came by only His Father's blood without sin. This was the very precious and rare and eternal blood shed on Calvary's cross profusely. Mary and Joseph a Jewish couple who did not "know" each other before Messiah. The Ruach Hakodesh impregnated Mary who was with sin, but with GOD'S only Son, Messiah and Elizabeth's son jumped in her womb when Elizabeth heard the GOOD NEWS. This was John the Baptist in Elizabeth's womb. The forerunner of Messiah telling them and us to repent in a GODLY way and to be baptized which did not mean salvation, because there was no choice in this for the individual as a baby, but only by grace was accountable to GOD. He was later beheaded. "Begotten, not made or procreated, or created and one in being with the Father, Messiah."

In the hospital I could hear some ... conversations from my lonely environment, because rarely did I hear any human voices. My cerebral cortex was still operative.

My exact condition and how to communicate with me and that was by twitching my nose.

Hearing voices sometimes distant, but yet distinct. "The Antichrist was attacking from the North Alliance, but they had been defeated."

Why was I not euthanized? There was no voluntary mark of the beast on me, was there? I had not consented? Why this wait?

As time went by and not knowing, or being relative to it, I could only gauge it according to any conversation that I would hear.

Somehow this Wotan Cohen was to come to our building, but for what? The Great Tribulation was going on, I suppose, but I did not know where in this Tribulation it was.

I soon felt in my being the all consuming ...

This appeared in my spirit this huge majestic form above me as if to devour me, but was this, too, theatrical reality playing tricks with me and if not, then who and what? This was a fearful revelation to me instantly. Nothing verbally of this world was being said, although there was some kind of disturbance occurring. The Evilness was so great that it appeared to me in my spirit, or was I... "You can do anything to Job, but you cannot take his life." This was the Scripture that came to mind on it's own into my brain.

As I said before there was this one who could communicate with me, but why did he not tell? I am sure he knew this much? Could it be too that he was?

I knew if I was right the 144,000 Messianic Jews would escape probably to Petra in Edom which was originally Israel. Maybe this king thought I knew where they were? Why the visit if it was that at all and why was I not euthanized? What good, or use could I possibly be to them?

Then one day this came back and asked me plainly again, "If I could hear him?"

He had already known my condition, so why was he asking me again what he already knew, or did he? I twitched my nose to say I could understand him. He then left and that was that.

They were feeding me very little intravenously by computer, but my appetite was near zero. I was enclosed by a shell of a body, but with the only thing they could do would be either to euthanize or starve my food supply, but neither had occurred so far. At the time of the above experience when that all present Evil entered my room I now remember that I had an out of the body experience and could see crystal clear who it was before me and the sight was to scary to repeat in words.

It seemed endless in this state with ... My cerebral cortex still alive. How many days, weeks, months, or possibly year, or years had gone by I did not really know? I could vision being somewhere else.

I had lost all concept of time. When I would see Messiah then I would know I was home for good. There was no light as far as I knew in my room, unless I had been moved and it was again scary to think, IN A COFFIN? Whose will was it for me to live? Certainly not mine. Why did they not just get it over with, or did they? Would I be inside of something that I did not want to be in? I had been only a government employee, but I did help Messianic Jews who probably were part of the 144,000. Some probably had come to Israel with me and now were in Petra?

Suddenly one day I felt this searing pain in my arm. This was it for me... This was the lethal injection, I had waited for so to speak. Now it would probably only take seconds and all would be over with. Second by second went by, or was it minutes, but no asphyxiation, or suffocation, or gagging, or any other torturous feelings, but instead a deep sleep appeared with muddle voices all around. Sodium pentathal? But what for? I was a weak patient and could tell them nothing, besides I could not speak, but did they really believe that? They had to be sure that I was a zombie and not faking it? OH, how devious they were to do such a thing and why this now? What I had known was very little and what I could remember was little? Was I not in their care for so long? Maybe now they would see my condition as hopeless for them? They did not know my thoughts, but had me hooked up to a Doppler Brain Scanner probably to read my brain waves in the neo-cerebral cortex. Other times they just euthanized people quickly to get it over with. I thought again that too was a problem, about how they had to know that I had lived with Sal who earlier had died for his faith and was beheaded gruesomely as Rav Shaul had been in Rome. How had I remembered that far back?

They knew I was conscious of them from the Doppler Brain Scanner, or at least that my mind was still functioning? They could not read my mind, nor could the demons around my room, Total darkness and thought to myself it could not be? Had they buried me alive? But why was it that I could breathe? All I had to do was reach my hands, if I could lift them and then I would know the real truth. As if by no will of my own my arms moved ever so slightly and my hands went upward until they were straight, that is my arms. I would not have been able to do that in a coffin. Again almost spontaneously my body went forward as if I was doing a sit-up, but still it was pitch black. In fact it was very cold and I had something on me that felt like clothing. I next got off of what I was lying on, which felt like a litter of some sort. My feet then touched the ground and I stood up on both of my feet and realized that I no longer had any paralysis in my body. I started to walk in the darkness very slowly until I could find anything that my mind could recognize as a door handle, a light switch, or any other thing that could help me see, or get me out of where I was. There were no intravenous tubes or any other tubes of any kind attached to me. Finally, almost in despair I found a door handle and began slowly to turn the door knob to feel if it would open. As I turned the door knob and pulled then pushed very slowly the door gave movement and opened away from my body. In the far distance as I turned my head and stepped out past the door and looked to my right while with my left hand slid my hand on the door, I could see in the distance an infinitesimal tunnel like light that could barely be seen. I focused on that constant light as it grew bigger and bigger ever so slowly. It appeared I was in some kind of cave that appeared to extend for miles, but could not judge the real distance at all. I had been walking on my own without falling or losing my balance and all four extremities were working as if I had never been in a lost state. Was this more theatrical reality? Being oblivious to my surroundings because of the darkness and because of my miraculous ambulatory movement I continued forward, watching that light get bigger ever so slowly, and all I could hear was my breath and my feet shuffling on the ground below me. My feet had something on them to protect them and felt shoe like in their fit. Was this a dream in the subconscious or was I truly awake and if so, how was it I was totally moving on my own with no kind of external help but my motor functions from my brain? That only could mean that my middle and lower brain stem were functioning properly. The environment or atmosphere had an almost serenic feeling, but not perfect feeling, but a sense of a new revelation in my spirit. Somehow I could sense a total lack of fear on my part with no body aches or pains. What was this? Was this my glorified body? This omnipresence of good followed me wherever I went. Had I somehow passed through the Great Tribulation and if so, how? I had heard or seen nobody so far. As I got closer to the light it began to hurt my eyes somewhat so I started to squint. What was it that I was coming to? What generated this constant light? After walking slowly for what appeared so long, I then stopped to rest and started to move my head to the complete left and then to the complete right. Everything appeared normal as far as my mechanized movement. I then sat down and found the wall and went into a trance.

I got to see an elevator and finally got inside and it too had no numbers to tell one what floor one was on. How strange that was, I thought to myself. I got in the elevator and inside too there were no numbers either. This too was very strange. Only one button could one push, and there was no up or down button. I pushed the button and began to descend, it appeared, by the force that was released away from my body and downward with a slight ease on my entire body. Then the elevator stopped and the door opened and I got out and looked both left and right down the hallway. The elevator would not move any more so I looked for a stairwell and found one with an exit sign above it, and that only descended downward and with no floor marking. I began my downward flight on the stairs one step at a time until I came to a landing and again there was no marking, so I continued downward flight after flight until I could no longer go down any farther and so I opened the door and went out into another hallway. I all of a sudden saw what appeared to be in the far distance thousands upon thousands of children coming toward me very slowly. I began to sense this overwhelming fear of doom as these very small children if not even smaller, like infants, were coming towards me with their hands reaching straight forward as if to be begging. Endless and endless were these very small children that were crying out, it appeared, for help, but with no sound coming from their mouths. I closed the door and ran the only way I could back upstairs as fast as I possibly could. I then slipped and fell forward and then...

I got up from the floor where I had been in a trance and started again to walk towards that light that was now what appeared only about 2 blocks away. I could hear what appeared to be voices of some kind. The language I could not make out whether it was English or not because it appeared to be muffled. As I got closer the voices became clearer, but still I could not understand what was being said because it was in a different language. The language, though it was foreign, was yet so familiar. With more reasoning I deciphered that it was a Middle Eastern dialect or language. Was it Hebrew? Yes, Hebrew was what they were speaking since my family all spoke it fluently except me. There appeared before me people who appeared to be Israelis. They had a certain type of apparel on, but they did not at once notice me at all. It was as if I was invisible to them or in another dimension. Suddenly they looked directly at me and I stopped dead in my tracks and just stared back as if I had seen a ghost. They began to speak directly to me, but I could not respond.

The language barrier and because my mouth could not exit any words on my part. They spoke to me in what appeared to be Hebrew, but I, not being fluent in Hebrew, could not understand them. My mind had forgotten things.

One spoke in a strange language. I just kept staring at them. Now they too were perplexed as to what to do or say, or their faces made it appear that way. They must have gone through what seemed to be at least 10 or 15 languages. Finally the tallest one spoke what sounded like a language that I could translate in my brain or that part of the brain that deals with languages, but was talking too fast for me to understand. What was it? It was good old American English, but somehow hyphenated. They were asking me something about my name. I opened my mouth to speak and at first nothing came, but an inaudible sound and then finally one word at a time. I told them my first name, but was it right?

They then spoke again, but much slower and were asking WHO WAS I?

They had some kind of telepathy almost, once they knew I could speak English.

I said, "Me ...

They started to smile.

Then they asked me slowly, W-H-E-R-E- D-I-D-I-C-O-M-E F-R-O-M?"

I, without knowing how, heard a voice come out from inside of me explaining in slow speech, telling them my supposedly first name and that I was, or had been, a patient here and that I was an Israeli citizen. They looked at me, as if to say, "WHAT"?

As they later explained to me, there were no Gentiles in this part of the city, or at least they thought so. My attire, I suppose surprised them since I myself was all in white. Also being the fact that they had not run into anyone who could not speak Hebrew in this area for quite some time.

I then asked them, "What year are we in right now?"

They told me it was in the year 1 M, or 1 Millenium.

We had begun the 7th Day of GOD.

Then they blurted out, "The war is over but clean-up still is going on in Israel."

I thought to myself, "What war?"

Again they said, "The war is over, the war, the Battle of Armageddon. The one that started in Megiddo."

I then asked them who were they and where did they come from.

They said they came from Petra and were amongst the...

No it could not be. How could it?

They continued, "From the 144,000 from the 12 tribes of Israel."

Finally it dawned on me, about my past and why I was in the hospital. I must have somehow passed Daniel's 70th week unharmed and unknowingly. That is why I could walk and see and hear and now speak. It was all coming back to me bit by bit. I was in the OLAM HABA where Messiah would reign from Jerusalem and Satan would be put away for 1,000 years. Had I died and then been resurrected, or had I remained alive all along.?

I knew that they did not have glorified bodies, but did I?

I thought about Jerusalem and what it looked like now.

I was in the real Israel in a body, and Messiah would now or had now started to reign for the next 1,000 years. Israel would be a light to all the nations. Had America made it into these nations? As I was thinking the group of 12 men disappeared.

My thoughts were about the end of the OLAM HABA and then the Second Resurrection of all the unbelievers into the Great White Throne Judgment and then they would be thrown into the burning lake of fire. Hell had been done away with. It was originally for Satan and his cohorts, but first would come a rebellion called metaphorically "Gog and Magog" and then a New Heaven and a New Earth, which then immediately made me think of my family.

When would I see Marie, Rachel, Alex, Abraham and Jacob and all the other Old and New Testament Saints, such as Moses, Isaiah, Jeremiah, Daniel, Rev Shaul, Joseph, Mary, Matthew, John, Mark and all the other believers? I knew they would all be here with the Lord in glorified bodies, or in heaven. Yes, I wanted too to see Shimon HaShaliach and all the remaining Apostles ruling with Messiah. The "roots" would rule; I too would be a part of the Temple in Jerusalem to help Messiah. There were different levels of heaven for the ones with glorified bodies in the New Heaven.

The Old Testament Scriptures were written between 1450-400 B.C. starting with Moses and ending with Malachi. Where had that come from?

Yes then would come a New Heaven and glorified bodies and a New Earth, unglorified bodies and world without end. There would be no sun, for GOD would be the eternal light. Heaven would be so beautiful and was beautiful now with all the pure gold and precious gems and stones with a Tree of Life and fruits for every month.

GOD was never poor and did not need man's invention of avarice and power, but man's allowable free will chose the wrong path. Was 80 years of life on average worth an eternity in the burning lake of fire, just to fulfill one's fleshly desires that were corrupt and vile?

During the OLAM HABA, who could man blame if Satan would be put away? Procreation would continue in this OLAM HABA and would death?

The earth would not be destroyed but transformed, and the lion and the lamb would lie down with each other. Yes, even all creation and species would change in nature.

I would approach His throne with reverence and worship and would see literally Messiah and the nail prints and hole in his side and He would embrace me as a father embraces a son. He would reach out to me as He had done before; yes, me a Gentile believer. His eyes would tell me he knew of me before the foundation of the earth. "The Word that became flesh and dwells amongst us forever."

As an American Biblical I remember this important quotation, "The sacred rights of mankind are not to be rummaged from among old parchments or musty records. They are written as a sunbeam in the whole volume of human nature, by the hand of GOD Himself and can never be erased or obscured by mortal power," Alexander Hamilton. In other words, it was not the documents that would make America, but GOD Himself.

I would feel like the woman at the well. "I AM the One speaking to you."

This living water everlasting. If I would see Messiah, I would see the Father through the Son, for the Father literally can never be seen. He gave His life for us; a minute speck in the universe, but nonetheless a person made in His image and a child of His. He had taken good care of me all of my life, and the Tribulation He had carried me through. Ever vigilant and watchful to all brothers in Y'eshua Messiah. What a family of GOD this would be; in a mature world state.

Abraham/Jacob my twins, and no one would need glasses or medicine, or have a handicap, et cetera. Their glorified bodies would transport them by thought anywhere instantaneously. As Messiah had to ascend to the Father then and then return, he then could be touched, but also walk through solid objects and appear and reappear instantaneously for 40 days. He could eat and drink too. What a wonderful thought all this was for my Marie, Rachel, Alex, Abraham and Jacob. "I once was lost, but now I have found." Oh, how this applied to me for sure. This eternal security and not the world's theatrical reality anymore. No more being on the stage of life with sinful roles to play, either by free will or the old man Adam, or even by Satan's temptation. Free will would be in this OLAM HABA, but for the Translated they would not have to worry in their glorified bodies, or the unglorified bodies would be in the Temple with Messiah. "Blessed is He who comes in the name of the Lord." The Father of Abraham, Isaac and Jacob and of course my "Abraham and Jacob".

Suddenly I saw what I never really had thought about, and that was angels before my very eyes and my fascination with them continued for some time. The angels could speak, but were too busy going about their Father's work. They had a hierarchy set by GOD Himself. Who was my guardian angel, I thought? No sooner thought than there one appeared before me to assist me in my future endeavors. The next 1,000 years would be very different but quite busy and exciting. But what if all this was just some kind of illusion. Theatrical reality was never like this. Sin would still be around through procreation in the OLAM HABA, but I was a saint of GOD that had gone through the TRIBULATION? What was once yesterday was no longer so, but was completed in part until the New Heaven and a New Earth would eventually appear in the future. There would then no longer be any mortal man but only saints in glorified or unglorified bodies. Not one person would be destroyed, but would remain forever in the presence of GOD, or the total absence of GOD forever. I would not be able to have my marriage with Marie, but I could still marry in the OLAM HABA and start a new family since I would be bound on earth for the next 1,000 years? Somehow the mystery of being a saint while not being Translated or killed in the Tribulation stayed in my mind and my heart. As I was transformed, so would the earth be transformed.

As I looked in the horizon I could see all kinds of animals at peace with one another and at peace with man as well as man being at peace with them. This transformation was more than I had ever imagined. Sideshadowing the present. The unglorified people would all know each other, and the glorified bodies would know all who were for the next 1,000 years. Children would be 100 years old. The 1,000 years would in part be like a "century".

What would this life bring me, since I had been miraculously transformed into sainthood for an eternity? I then awoke in a cold sweat with Marie by my side...

Finally a black Moslem President from Harvard had made America turn its back on GOD and was trying to destroy Israel no matter what he professed, and his actions were as such that now the world was very very near to the Great ...